Prais

M000044115

"This is the perfect small-town romantic mystery." ★★★★★

- Mandy Baggot, International Bestselling Romance Author

"It was so, so clear that this is an ownvoices book in the best possible way. The disabled characters were written so well and I had to keep on reading because it's so rare to find such good representation. Especially in romance, where normally the disabled character is considered broken until they are cured."

- Holly, NetGalley Reviewer

"Wow Katie Mettner really delivered with this book. . . . I will definitely be looking for more books by this author."

- Rachel, NetGalley Reviewer

"Katie Mettner knows how to add the perfect mix of suspense, mystery, secrets and love to create the a heartfelt memorable story." ★★★★★

- Sheri, Amazon Reviewer

"I love a great, sexy romantic suspense and Katie Mettner is a master at writing them." ★★★★★

- I am, Amazon Reviewer

"It doesn't matter what the genre is, Katie Mettner delivers!" ★★★★★

- Debra, Amazon Reviewer

Butterflies
& Hazel Eyes

BUTTERFLY JUNCTION, BOOK 1

Katie Mettner

Breaking
Night
PRESS

Published by Breaking Night Press in 2021.

Breaking Night Press
52 W. 3rd Street, Box 26551
Collegeville, PA 19426

breakingnightpress.com

Paperback ISBN: 978-1-7357253-0-7
eBook ASIN: B08T7RTFLH

Cover Design by Carrie Butler

For Linda.

Chapter One

You often hear about places like this. Places where the clock ticks slower than anywhere else, and where the townspeople stay because they know deep in their soul there is no better place than where they are. Places where when the sun shines, be it summer or winter, the magic it reveals steals your breath and holds you captive. When I arrived at the only campground in Plentiful, Wisconsin, last night at nearly eleven, the deepest part of my soul told me it was one of those places. Even the sky told me so. The stars didn't twinkle. They sang to each other in a melody of light. The breeze didn't whiz past you in a hurry to reach its next destination. It caressed your face softly to welcome you to its home.

I travel this country for a living, and I know how rare it is to find a place that offers that kind of soul-deep peace. "What do you think of Plentiful, Mojo?" I asked my lumbering oaf of a dog as we hiked up the street. "It's a quintessential small town, that's for sure," I answered since he didn't. "What do you think? Should we stay here for a few weeks before we head to our next job?"

Honestly, Mojo couldn't care less. As long as he was fed,

had a place to sleep, and got an occasional hot dog, he was happy. Mojo is, well, a muttstiff. His mastiff lineage shows in his height and the shape of his back end, but it's the rest of his lineage that earns him the mutt moniker. Mojo has the face of a collie, the ears of a Doberman, the feet of a sheepdog, and the hair of a schnauzer. Some would say he's homelier than a mud fence, but I promise you, when he's at my side, no one bothers me. Presently, he was staring me down, his eyebrows furrowed as if to ask, *Are we there yet?*

I rubbed his big head and checked the address on the sticky note stuck to my computer bag. I was searching for 100 Industrial Road, which meant nothing to me since the town consisted of a marina, a campground, a bar, a diner, and a small grocery store. Come to think of it, maybe this wouldn't be such a great place to hang out for a few weeks. "Are we lost, Mojo?"

I spun in a circle, wondering how on earth I was supposed to find a place that didn't exist. I'd done my homework and had indeed verified that a company called Butterfly Junction existed and was run by a Mr. Gulliver Winsome before I took the job. What the heck they did at Butterfly Junction, I had no clue, nor did I care as long as I got paid. Get paid to do what exactly? Some people like to call it hacking. I prefer to call it being a server patch technician. Sometimes it's all about how you spin things.

While I did my homework on the man, I should have mapped the address on Google Maps before setting out. I grabbed my phone from my pocket while I searched the street signs for clues. I might have to ask Google about this one.

A woman was walking toward me and waved excitedly when she got closer. Mojo stood at attention in front of me, his protection mode activated.

"Hello!" she called from thirty feet away.

"Chill, Mojo," I said before she reached us. He huffed and plopped his butt onto the sidewalk, bummed that I wouldn't let him play guard dog.

"Hello," I said to the woman when she stopped in front of me.

"You must be new here," she said just as she noticed Mojo and took a step back. "Hello, doggy."

I chuckled and motioned at him. "This is Mojo. He looks scary, but really he just wants to know if you have any hot dogs."

The woman tossed her head back and laughed, the sound spreading out across the sky like a sparkle of happiness. "Not with me, but I do own the diner up the street. We have plenty of delicious treats there. Well, now I know the dog's name. What's yours?"

"Oh!" I said, laughing with her. "I'm Charity Puck," I said, thrusting my hand out to shake hers.

"Nice to meet you, Charity. I'm Lucy Havens. My husband, Kevin, and I own the diner in town. You should stop in for the breakfast buffet. It's to die for."

"Now that's something I can get behind," I said, a smile on my face. "First, I have a job to do, and I can't find the address. It's 100 Industrial Road."

Lucy's brows went up. "Oh, that's Butterfly Junction! It's right there," she said, her arm pointing out to her right. I followed her finger and spotted a brick building behind the marina that I hadn't noticed before.

I put my hand to my heart with relief. "Well, I'm glad I ran into you, Lucy. I would never have found that without help. I thought that was part of the marina."

She brushed her hand at me. "That's a common mistake. Butterfly Junction is a hidden gem in more ways than one. I better let you get to work, but it was nice to meet you, Charity. You, too, Mojo," she said, smiling at the dog. "Be sure to stop in for breakfast if you get a chance before you leave town."

I promised to do just that and waved as she departed. Mojo and I trucked toward ours and discovered a beautiful piece of shoreline that swept to the right of the Butterfly Junction building.

"Lucy was delightful," I said to Mojo as we trotted up to the door. "I bet she'd even give you a hot dog, big boy."

I chuckled to myself at the image of Mojo sitting next to me inside the diner chowing down hot dogs while everyone looked on. *Totally normal, folks. Carry on.*

I adjusted my computer bag on my shoulder when I paused in front of the double glass doors etched with the words *Butterfly Junction.* "Time to work, buddy," I said, patting his head.

I would do the job Mr. Winsome required of me and then stay in Plentiful for a few days to recharge. Maybe I'd take a boat ride on the lake, or a spin around town on one of the bikes I'd noticed at the campground today.

The job at Butterfly Junction might be my last as a freelance white hat hacker. Why? Well, two weeks ago my dream job landed unexpectedly in my lap. I was finishing a job in Florida when I got the call from the parent company of a hotel conglomerate. They were looking for a lead IT technician with white hat skills. I was more than curious. Since I'd already agreed to the job at Butterfly Junction, I stopped in Gary, Indiana, on my way here for an interview. What they were offering me was everything I'd been searching for over the last nine years. My home base would be in Gary, but I'd have the opportunity to travel around the country occasionally to do work on location at their hotels. I'd worked for myself for years because I could never find a position within a company that encompassed what I do, so this offer was intriguing.

What was holding me back? The part about my home base being in Gary, Indiana. Not because of the geographical location, but rather the home-base part. I wasn't sure if I could stay in one place like a normal person. I'd been roaming around this country for so long, I wasn't sure I could stop. I had three months before I was required to be there, but I didn't have any other jobs lined up after this one. I had plenty of offers, but I hadn't taken a break from the road in six years, and my body was tired.

When I woke up in Plentiful this morning and looked out my window to see the sun glinting off the waves of Lake Superior, I decided this was the place to stay for a few weeks while I considered the job offer. I wasn't good at making important decisions about my life without weighing every aspect of the change first. Since I loved finding out-of-the-way places I could explore, Plentiful was a good place to hang out while I made the most important decision of my life.

I took a deep breath and let it out at the thought. I have time for that later. First, work. As stressful as driving around the country is, the work I do is often more stressful. As a white hat working for big-name companies and smaller no-name businesses, my skills were a race against the clock. I was always called in *after* someone's business had been hacked or their data stolen, and it was my job to patch their security to keep it from happening again. As I said, stressful.

I checked out my reflection in the spotless glass doors to be sure I was presentable before I went inside. My curly, long blonde hair was covered with a child-sized straw fedora I'd picked up at a flea market in Nevada. It was probably worn once to church by a young boy before being discarded a year later as too small. It was perfect for me considering I would be small forever. This morning I'd dressed my four-foot frame in cargo shorts and a plain white tee complemented by a tie-dye scarf around my neck. I suppose most people would call the style *hippie*. I call it thrift-store chic. Considering I live in a motor home and love thrift stores, I guess I do have a little bit of hippie in me. I smoothed the shirt down and nodded at my reflection. *Charity Puck, white hat extraordinaire, at your service.*

I took a breath and tugged open the door, yanking Mojo in behind me. The front reception area of Butterfly Junction was open and airy when I stepped inside. It reminded me of the great room of someone's home rather than an office building. There was beautiful artwork of butterflies and other nature scenes adorning the walls, which fit the feel of the building well. The walls were done in a soft green while the floors were carpeted in a beige tweed that met vanilla-flecked tile near the reception area. The address may say industrial, but there was nothing industrial about it.

To the left of the reception desk was a closed mahogany door with a keypad on the wall, and to the right a hallway that had four identical wood doors, all closed. I stood in front of a desk that held a desktop computer, phone, and a nameplate that said, *HONEY*. Sitting in front of the computer was a large butterfly made of cloth. All the parts of the butterfly were labeled, which immediately drew me in for a closer look. I had to admit it was oddly fascinating. Unfortunately, the receptionist was missing from her desk. "Hello? Is anyone here?" I called out.

The closed door at the end of the hallway opened, and a woman scurried toward me. Her curly chestnut-brown hair flew around her with every step, and her giant brown eyes were the focal point of her face. She was gorgeous in a girl-next-door kind of way. Understated but stunning.

"Can I help you?" She pointed at Mojo as soon as she saw him. "Your dog can't be in here."

I glanced down at the beast and back to her. "I'm here to see Mr. Winsome," I said, ignoring her dig at Mojo.

Her eyes lit up in recognition. "Oh, you must be Charity Puck."

"I am," I agreed, a smile filling my face as the woman approached me and shook my hand. "I know you were expecting me two days ago, but the weather didn't cooperate most of the way here from Tampa."

She waved away the apology. "No worries. Mr. Winsome understood. I'm Honey, by the way."

"Nice to meet you, Honey. You have a beautiful building, even if it is hard to find."

Honey chuckled as if she'd heard that before. "That's true, but I'm glad you found us."

"I ran into Lucy on the sidewalk, and she pointed you out. I can't take credit for the discovery."

Honey put her hand to her chest. "I love Lucy. She and her husband own the diner, and they're also my landlords. I live above the diner."

"Wow," I said, a grin on my lips. "I bet it's a little like heaven and a little like hell living above a place like that."

Her laughter filled the space, and with the vaulted ceilings, it traveled far and wide before it died off. "You're not kidding, especially on broccoli day." She waved her arm in front of her nose dramatically.

We laughed together before she motioned at the group of chairs in the corner by the window. "Have a seat, and I'll see if Gulliver is finished with his conference call."

"Thank you," I said politely, leading Mojo to a small love seat in the corner. There were several long, rectangular windows facing the street that let in light. They were meticulously clean, as was the rest of the office, and the walls displayed framed photos of butterflies. There were butterflies of every shape and color that were taken by a talented, experienced photographer. Each butterfly had something about them that engaged you and drew you deeper into what the photographer was experiencing at the time of the shot. A blue butterfly caught in the middle of liftoff from a thistle. A monarch butterfly resting on the branch of a tree. A pink butterfly, its wings almost transparent, flitting amid a flower garden. I still didn't know exactly what they did here at Butterfly Junction, but it definitely had something to do with butterflies. I chuckled to myself. *You're a seasoned detective, Charity. Keep up the hard work.*

"Miss Puck, follow me," Honey said.

"Just call me Charity, Honey," I said, keeping Mojo tight to my leg. It was more like I held him tightly to my waist, considering our height discrepancies.

"Of course." She smiled. "If you need anything, just let me know."

Honey motioned me through the office door and silently closed it behind me. A man sat behind an executive's desk that was covered in papers, folders, and computers. He wore a button-down plaid shirt covered by a sweater sporting—what were those? Bees? Beetles? Dragonflies?

The man glanced down at his sweater and back to my face. "Grasshoppers."

Grasshoppers. Noted.

First impression of Gulliver Winsome? He was all about his business. If the sweater wasn't enough to tell me that, the collections of bugs, butterflies, and moths in display boxes scattered around the room were. The man himself? Gulliver Winsome was more than a little easy on the eyes. My gaze traveled across his broad chest and shoulders. Both made the sweater of grasshoppers stretch prominently with the strength and power of his physique. When his arm shot forward to shake my hand, his bicep flexed and I begged myself not to whimper. He might wear weird sweaters, but this man was built.

"You must be Charity." The awkward smile on his face was something I was used to. I was never what people expected when they pictured a white hat hacker.

I dropped Mojo's leash to the ground, and he lowered his butt to the floor as I shook the man's hand. "I am, and you must be

Gulliver Winsome."

He released my hand and motioned at himself dramatically. "Indeed I am. The lucky guy who was saddled with the worst name in the history of the world."

I laughed, his relaxed manner putting me at ease immediately. "Well, you know what they say. You win some. You lose some."

Gulliver's eyes smiled when he laughed. "Never was that joke delivered more perfectly. Have a seat," he said, indicating the chair in front of his desk. The chair was an awkward height for my short frame, and I had to half jump and half wiggle onto it. Gulliver pointed at my companion. "What's the dog's name?"

"Mojo," I answered immediately.

His eyebrow tugged up toward his hairline, and his delectable hazel eyes hit me like a shot to the solar plexus. I'd never seen eyes that color before, but they were a pair I could get lost in for hours. The color swirled from brown to gold and then settled on green for a hairbreadth before swirling into a green flecked with sparkles of gold. I'd traveled all fifty states and met people of all nationalities and never had a pair of eyes held me captive for so long. They were smoky while he assessed me assessing him. Oh, I could get lost in that pair of eyes for the rest of my life if I wasn't careful.

"You named a dog Mojo," Gulliver said, more a statement than a question.

"I did. I've always wanted to say to someone, 'I've lost my Mojo. Will you help me find him?'"

"I'm picturing it." He shook with laughter. "That would be epic."

I held out my hand as if to say, *I know, right?* "The problem is, he's never run away in the six years I've owned him, so he's kind of a disappointment."

Gulliver laughed again, this time a tinge of discomfort

creeping in at the end. "Honey said he's your service dog. Are you disabled?"

He leaned back in his chair and waited for my answer. Since he wasn't hiring me as an employee, he could ask me if I was disabled, but it was slightly rude all the same.

"I never said he was my service dog. Honey was mistaken. Mojo is more like my protection detail. He comes with me to every job, regardless of how many times people tell me he can't. I'm four-feet two-inches tall, a woman, live in a motor home, and work only at night. Mojo is all that stands between me and an early grave."

Gulliver's delectable eyes shuttered, but he nodded once. "I see. Well, you will be working here at night, but you won't be alone. I'll be here working with you. I don't leave the business unattended with an independent contractor inside."

"Perfectly acceptable. I never expect to be alone, but you wouldn't believe how often I am. Also, I don't have a car, so I hoof it in from Plentiful Campground, which means he's my only protection."

Gulliver tapped his pen on the desk as he eyed me longer than necessary. "I'm afraid I can't allow you to be walking around town in the dark alone, even if you have Mojo. There are too many wild animals, namely wolves, in this area. I'll pick you up tonight at eight and drive you back to the campground when you're finished."

"Okay," I answered agreeably. After all, it was his business. I didn't care what he did as long as at the end of the night, I got paid.

His eyes flashed with an emotion I couldn't decipher, and he sat forward again. "Okay? You mean you're not going to give me a hard time? Most women give me a hard time when I order them around."

"Gosh, I can't imagine why," I said, tongue in cheek. "If I wanted to, I could give you a hard time about my independence and not needing a man, blah, blah, but in this case, it took me thirty minutes to get here on foot. I'll gladly take a ride."

"Excellent. How about if I show you around Butterfly Junction? This is the first floor, and below us is the research department."

Ahh, one more clue to what Butterfly Junction does. "Sounds great, since I don't know what you do here other than it having something to do with butterflies. Mojo will stay here. His aura says big and bad, but mostly he's just lazy."

Gulliver chuckled and tipped his head to the left. "Not an untold story when it comes to dogs." His gaze settled on me, and it was warm but intense. The longer his eyes traveled up and down my body, the more I felt like he could see all the secrets in my soul. Finally, his gaze lifted to mine and held it before he spoke. "I'm sure you know why I called you in, Miss Puck."

"Charity," I said. "I prefer Charity."

"Okay, Charity it is," he said on a nod. "As I was saying, I'm concerned that my server has been hacked. I cannot afford to let someone get the research we're working on."

"As you mentioned," I agreed. "You're talking about the research you're doing downstairs?"

"Correct. I followed your suggestion from our first conversation and changed the password. Since I did that, it seems to have solved the problem."

"You didn't solve the problem. You patched a leak that won't hold for long."

"That's what I'm afraid of," he agreed. "I'm worried that eventually they'll get to the research we have stored there. I have to make sure the server is secure before we put any more information on it."

"Say no more. I'm your gal. This doesn't sound like it will take me too long. I should be able to knock it out in one night. Two at most."

I groaned internally. *Way to jinx yourself, Charity.* Whenever I got too cocky, it always backfired on me.

"That would be great," Gulliver said as he bent over. "We are at a point in our research that would spell disaster if the information fell into the wrong hands." He straightened again and had a pair of crutches on each forearm. He hoisted himself out of the chair and joined me at the end of the desk.

My mouth dropped open as I took in his six-foot frame before me. His left shoe had a black lift sole glued to it that was at least four inches thick. "Now I understand why you were upset about Mojo," I said with a grimace, and he chuckled, his head shaking.

"Don't worry about it. I'll admit it does irritate me when people pretend to have service dogs just to take them shopping or inside a restaurant."

I grasped my hands behind my back and bit my lip. "That's not something I would ever do. He's with me most of the time, but he waits in the motor home or outside if I go into a store. It must be hard for you when you run into those situations, though."

"Hey, you don't grow up the way I did without developing a thick skin, which is good since I have thin bones," he said, waiting to see if I would get the punch line. When I didn't, he motioned at his legs. "Rickets cause weak and thin bones," he explained. "But don't worry, everything else below the waist developed perfectly fine."

He crutched off toward the door and left me standing there with my jaw slightly ajar. Who was Gulliver Winsome, and was he for real? The bigger question was, why was I so interested in figuring out what made him tick? I shook off the questions and followed him out the door and into an elevator. The first question I needed an answer to was what this interesting guy did in this building. As we stepped onto the elevator car, something told me the answer wasn't going to be simple. When my gaze swept his frame again, his muscles flexed as he braced the crutches on the floor, I wasn't sure I cared if the answer was complicated. When those exquisite hazel eyes met mine with the same air of curiosity in them, I secretly hoped I'd jinxed myself after all.

Chapter Two

After Gulliver gave me the nickel tour of Butterfly Junction, he offered to take me to lunch at the local bar and pizzeria to discuss the finer points of the business. The finer points would be difficult for me since I was still having trouble grasping what their business was. I was never one to turn down a pizza, though, so I agreed.

"Do you always take your independent contractors out for pizza?" I asked, sipping from the glass of root beer I'd ordered when we arrived. It was spicy and frosty, just the way I liked it.

Gulliver set his mug down. "Small-town nice, you know?" he teased. "I'm kidding. You're the first, but I've never had a drop-dead gorgeous, bigger-than-life, brilliant independent contractor like you walk through my office door before."

I broke eye contact and took another sip of my root beer. "Thank you for the compliment. My pixie-sized frame always takes people by surprise, but I promise you, my skills are anything but small."

"Now that I believe," he said with light laughter as his head nodded vigorously. "You come highly recommended, and we'll need all your skills."

"Let me get this straight," I said, leaning on the table as I took notes on my notepad. I always keep a notebook with me when I'm working with a new client, so I don't forget important details. "Your business is research and development for eco-friendly pesticides."

Gulliver nodded once as he lowered his mug. "Correct. We are developing a pesticide formula now and the herbicide and fungicide will follow. Our goal is to kill pests without killing other non-crop-threatening insects."

I finished writing and glanced at him. "Non-crop-threatening insects. There's something you don't hear every day. How on earth did you get into this line of business?" I laid my pen down and checked under the table out of habit, only to remember Mojo was hanging out at the office with Honey.

"He's fine, you know. Honey will feed him things she shouldn't and make him a bed in the corner out of blankets."

I laughed and sighed at the same time. The laughter was at Gulliver's words, and the sigh was because he was right. "I feel naked without him since he's my constant companion on every job. I bet Mojo is thrilled to have Charity-free time, though. I'm always bossing him around."

Gulliver stared me down as he leaned back in the booth comfortably. "I doubt anyone would be thrilled to be away from you, but I definitely can picture your bossy side. Though I don't think being bossy is always a bad thing."

I lowered my pop glass slowly and thought about what he said. I wasn't sure if I should take it as a compliment or an offense. I had to chuckle because the more time I spent with him, the more I realized I might always feel that way with Gulliver Winsome. He'd say something off-color, but he did it in a way that you didn't care to call him on it. While slightly frustrating, it was also endearing. I suspected he played people in this way to keep them from delving into his personal life or asking too many questions about why he used crutches. Too bad I wasn't staying in Plentiful for very long. I wouldn't mind spending more time with Gulliver. "You didn't answer my question."

Rather than speak, he pointed at a pink-haired woman in a black apron carrying a giant round pie of cheesy delight. I grabbed a plate while Gulliver prepared the cheese and spices for the gooey goodness about to land on our table. The masterpiece was set down, and the waitress grinned, her head swiveling back and forth between us. "Who's your friend, Gulliver?" she asked with giddy curiosity.

"I'm Charity," I said, reaching out to shake her hand.

"You must be new here. When you work in the only bar in town, you know all the regulars."

"Charity is here doing some computer work at Butterfly Junction," Gulliver said to quell the awkwardness.

I motioned at the handsome man across from me whose cinnamon-flecked eyes kept distracting me with every blink of his ridiculously long lashes. The good Lord had blessed this man with lashes any woman would pay to have. Through the entire tour, every time he stopped to explain something to me, I'd lose focus because I couldn't stop staring into his eyes. Considering our height difference, it took a lot for his eyes to capture me the way they did. "I'm helping them set up a new website. I'm afraid I won't be in town long, but Gulliver insisted I had to try the pizza here."

Debbie, as her name tag read, bobbed her pink-haired head while she gripped Gulliver's shoulder. If she wasn't twice his age, I bet she'd be chasing him around town. "Mr. Winsome speaks the truth. Well, I'm sorry you won't be sticking around, but it was sure nice to meet you. Anything else for you two?"

I bit my lip to keep from laughing at the way she asked it. She made it sound like we were on our first date stumbling through our meet-cute. It was clear that as far as Debbie was concerned, when

Gulliver Winsome showed up with a woman, it was a big deal.

"We could use a refill on our drinks, Debbie. Thanks," he said, handing his mug over, so I did the same with mine. When she was gone, he loaded up my plate with the cracker-thin pizza crust covered in cheese, pepperoni, sausage, and black olives. "This is the only place in the state where you can get truly amazing pizza," he informed me. "When you pass it on the street, you think it's a dive, and let's face it, Plentiful isn't New York City, but the food is spectacular. Dig in," he said, motioning at the plate.

I guess we weren't going to discuss anything until we'd eaten, so I did as he instructed. Gulliver was right about one thing; the food was spectacular. "Mmmm," I moaned as I finished chewing. "I haven't had pizza like this since the last time I was in Jersey. I'm starting to like Plentiful more and more."

"Not much to like here," he said offhand, his smile of thanks bright when Debbie set down two more mugs and left again without a word.

"Not true," I said between bites. "There's the lake, the silence, the smell of fresh air and sunshine, the lack of traffic, and the brilliant stars in the sky. When I pulled into the campground last night around eleven, the stars were swirling like ballroom dancers. If you look around, you'll find plenty of reasons to like this town."

Gulliver motioned out the side door of the bar toward Butterfly Junction. "The lake is one of the reasons I stay. I love to kayak in the summer. I'm also a fan of the glass-bottomed boat tours to the Apostle Islands. You glide across the water and under your feet, the secrets of the Lady of the Lake are revealed. There are so many shipwrecks on the bottom of that lake. I've done it a dozen times but still see something new every time I go."

My head snapped up when he mentioned the islands. "I want in," I said immediately.

His laughter told me he was tickled by my enthusiasm. "You

are a most unusual woman, Charity Puck. Most people find Lake Superior relatively ho-hum after a few years of being around here."

I washed my pizza down with some root beer before I answered. "I'm from Michigan, but we didn't live by the lake. I moved to California when I was eighteen and lived on the water off and on for three years, which is probably why I love camping on the shores of Lake Superior now. I travel nonstop and see the ocean on both coasts, but there's nothing quite like the Midwest."

Gulliver lowered his fork and made eye contact. I could tell whatever he was going to say would make me uncomfortable. "You're right, and I love your enthusiasm for life. You might be bossy, but you're also positive and bright about everything. Positivity is rare these days."

Yup, uncomfortable. Why? Because no one understood what made me tick. I was never around long enough for someone to get to know me that well. When Gulliver looked me in the eye, though, I sensed he already knew who I was at my base. There was some kind of pull between us that I couldn't define, but I had never met anyone as unique as Gulliver Winsome, so maybe that was why. He stirred something inside me. A connection of commonality. A familiarity even when unfamiliar.

I gave him a flick of my shoulder. "I didn't grow up in an environment reeking of positivity or brightness, so I made a pact to always keep those as my top two motivators." Silence stretched between us at my awkward admittance. I needed to change the subject. "Where do you live, Gulliver?"

He tipped his head with indecision. "Why, Miss Puck, my place of residence is a private matter," he said in a terrible Scarlett O'Hara voice.

I took a drink just as he said it, and root beer went up my nose and back out it again. I coughed and choked, accepting the napkin Gulliver handed me to clean myself up. When I could speak again, I gave him a dirty look. "You're a real card, Mr. Winsome," I said, wiping my shirt of root beer splatter. "I get it. Keep your nose out of my business, Charity Puck. You're here to do a job and nothing else," I said on a laugh.

He grinned, his mug near his lips. "Nah, I was messing with you. Everyone in town knows where I live. It's not a secret. I have quarters off the reception area at Butterfly Junction."

The door to the left of Honey's desk ran through my mind. "I wouldn't have guessed. Not a bad idea, though. I suppose that makes the commute easy and relaxing."

He pointed at me with his fork. "You're not kidding, especially with those things," he said, hooking a thumb at the crutches. "I have a one-bedroom apartment, which is all I need. I'm in the research lab late most nights anyway, so it's handy to be able to fall into bed after a short trot up the stairs."

I tsked. "You know what they say," I said, drawing out the last word. When he didn't respond, I filled in the blank. "All work and no play makes Gulliver a very boring boy."

Charity! I scolded myself. *Stop flirting with him! You never mix business with pleasure, yet here you are, batting your eyelashes and making googly eyes at this guy. Next thing you know you'll be flipping your hair around like you are Marilyn Monroe.*

I had to bite back a chuckle. *Great comparison there. You're only a foot shorter and far less gorgeous than Marilyn but keep trying.*

"Trust me, if there were more people in this town like you, I wouldn't be bored, but when you live in a place where not a lot happens, you're bound to spend much of your time working."

I finished my pizza and leaned on the table. "Why do you live here then? Can't you do this kind of work anywhere?"

Gulliver shook his head as he swallowed. "Not anywhere, no. We need access to farm fields to test our products. Being so close to the lake means we have the added benefit of testing for runoff in the waterways."

"I would say that makes sense, but I'm still not clear on your background, Gulliver. How did you get into this line of work?"

"I'm an entomologist with a sub-degree as a lepidopterist." He squirmed slightly in his seat as though he had a hard time admitting the truth.

I raised my brows in tandem. "A what now?"

His laughter was rich and deep, and when it settled, you felt oddly comforted yet longed to hear it again. "Believe me when I say you aren't the first one to wonder what I'm talking about, which is why I don't mention it often. It applies to the job you're going to do, so I'll explain. An entomologist studies bugs, and a lepidopterist studies butterflies and moths, otherwise known as lepidopterans."

"Butterfly Junction," I said slowly, hitting my forehead lightly with the palm of my hand. "It all makes sense now." I paused with my hand on my head. "Wait, no, it doesn't, other than the name."

When Debbie returned to the table, Gulliver handed her some cash and asked her to box up the rest of the pizza. "There are several aspects to the business, but the most important is research and development. My business partner, Mathias Jørgensen, and I are working to develop pesticides to protect the lepidopterans while being effective against other pests that harm crops. If we don't find -cides—and 'cide' means 'to kill'—that are safe for bees and butterflies as well as other pollinating insects, our food supplies will dwindle until there's nothing."

"Because all the pollinating insects will be dead," I said in a low whisper.

He pointed at me with a grim smile on his lips. "Bingo. We're also trying to protect the waterways. Herbicides and fertilizers ruin many of our lakes in the farm belt. The runoff causes algae blooms and fish kills. It's a real problem we need to solve, or we won't have water to drink either. Without food and water—"

"We don't exist."

He threw his hands up in the air and did some hushed cheering. "And she wins the gold."

"I have to give you credit, Gulliver. I've learned more than one new thing today. Terrifying but new. I assume there are plenty of scientists like you out there trying to fix a problem most of us don't even know exists?"

He bowed slightly in acceptance of the compliment. "It's a burden to carry, but we do it for the greater good of keeping our food supply healthy and prevalent. There's also hope we can find a way for farmers in developing countries around the world to produce the product. If we can do that, they'll be able to protect their water supply at the same time."

"Wow," I said, my voice tinged with impressed surprise. "Right now, I'm thrilled I took this job. I'm completely taken aback by all of this, but I'm fascinated at the same time. Thank you for explaining it to me. I have to admit I'm feeling a bit intimidated, but I'm sure I'll get over it in time."

When he smiled, the gold flecks swirled through those bronzed globes of goodness like a kaleidoscope. They reminded me of the reflections off the lake at sunrise, and I forced myself not to sigh like a schoolgirl. Then I noticed the edges of his eyes crinkled in the most adorable way and the sigh escaped. The laugh lines gave him the look of a distinguished older gentleman while wearing that boy-next-door grin. Everything about Gulliver Winsome was open and inviting, and you wanted to make him laugh just to see that smile again.

"You're welcome," he said, which drew my wandering mind back to the conversation, "but don't feel intimidated, please. I'm not about my degree. I believe we all have important skills to offer the world. We're all here doing what we do for a reason. For instance, I'm so desperate to have my computer server checked for security leaks that I begged a woman to drive across the country to take this job. Maybe I can develop eco-friendly pesticides, but I can't write a line of code, much less hack a server."

I offered him a shy smile. "Thank you for saying so. You would think I'd be over the terrifying fear of inferiority after all these years, but the human psyche is an interesting thing."

Gulliver finished his pop and set it down on the table. "And you're an interesting woman," he said, tipping his head toward me in a bow. "I can't wait to get to know you better."

The look in his eye while his brow was crooked upward told me he was serious about that too. Too bad I wouldn't be staying in Plentiful long enough for that to happen. I could do much worse than hanging out with Gulliver Winsome on a summer evening around a campfire. Sure, he might be two feet taller than I am, but that's not unusual. As a little person, everyone is two feet taller than I am. It made me wonder, though. If I laid my head on his belly, would it be soft under my cheek or would there be a six-pack hiding under that sweater of grasshoppers. Not too many guys could pull off a sweater like that and not look ridiculous. Gulliver could. There was just something about the way he looked at me that drew a shiver of anticipation up my spine.

"I suppose we'd better head back," he finally said after we'd stared at each other in mutual curiosity for a few moments. "Honey and Mojo will be wondering where we are. Maybe they'll want to share the rest of the pizza."

I picked up the pizza box while he worked his way out of the booth and grabbed his crutches. "I know Mojo will without question," I said with laughter.

I waved at Debbie as I followed Gulliver to the door. "Nice to meet you, Debbie!" I called.

"You, too, Charity!" she called back. "Hope to see you again soon!"

I'd be back without question. If I was going to stay in Plentiful for a few weeks, I would definitely have to get another pizza. Maybe I'd be lucky enough to share it with Gulliver again.

I held the door open for him, and he crutched through, waiting for me to join him on the sidewalk before we started back toward Butterfly Junction. Since the bar was only a few blocks from the office, he'd insisted we go on foot. I wondered if it was painful for him to walk with his legs the way they were. His right one was bowed out at the knee in a truly unnatural angle, and the thick lift on the sole of the left shoe made every step with that foot more of a swing and a bounce than an actual step. I wondered if he was exhausted by the end of the day just from walking. I hadn't known him long, but something told me no. I had a feeling he was one of those people who just did their thing, regardless of the obstacles thrown in their path.

"We have a full-service grocery store and a meat market for anything you might need," he said as we strolled along. "They sell staples at the camp store too. I suppose you don't need much since it's just you and Mojo, though."

I chuckled and enjoyed the sun beating down on my back and the fresh air filling my lungs. I'd been in Tampa for ten days, and while the sun was hot there, fresh air was hard to come by. "It's true, we don't need much, but since I'll be in town for a bit after this job, I'll stock up on what I need at the grocery store."

"Oh," he said, surprised. "I didn't know you were staying in town."

I made the so-so hand. "I have another job lined up in a few months, but until then I'm taking a break. I spend a lot of time on the road, and sometimes you have to take a break for longer than a few days. The drive here from Tampa nearly killed me. I need to stay in one place and stretch out my legs again. Then I'll head on up the road to Indiana."

"That's down the road," Gulliver said on a chuckle and a wink.

Damn, that wink of his was going to be the death of me. Being so much shorter than him, whenever he winked at me, I got the full effect of his sexiness. He winked at me a lot, but it wasn't in a flirty or inappropriate way. It was in a Gulliver Winsome way, and I couldn't define it better than that. "You're right. Regardless, for now I'll concentrate on the job you need me to do."

We had reached Butterfly Junction, and I held the door for him and followed in behind him. I enjoyed Gulliver's company, so sticking around Plentiful to enjoy it was not a bad idea. When the travel bug hit again, I'd do what I always did: climb into Myrtle and see where the road takes me.

After Gulliver gave me a ride back to the campground, I decided to check in at the main office before returning to Myrtle for a nap. The office was closed when I arrived last night, but they were expecting me and had my campsite ready. I had checked out the shower house this morning and was pleasantly surprised to find a newer building that was clean and bright. The lack of spiders was a huge plus. Even Mojo was impressed. Every so often, I made him take a shower, too, and no self-respecting dog wanted to take a shower from a hose next to an old Dodge motor home. They wanted the lap of luxury with manly smelling shampoo in a nicely lit building and a curtain for their privacy. At least Mojo wanted the lap of luxury. Sometimes he got it. Sometimes he got the hose next to the Dodge. Considering I take him into the workplace with me, I was always cognizant of his odor, so I made sure he was bathed regularly.

The thought of taking Mojo to work led me back to Gulliver's creamy coffee-colored eyes. A dreamy sigh escaped my lips. "Why do I find this guy so fascinating?" I asked the dog as I shuffled my feet along the gravel-packed path. "He's a client. I shouldn't be looking at him like he's breakfast, lunch, *and* dinner, right?"

Mojo stared up at me and waited. I guess he wanted me to answer the question. I rubbed his head and rolled my eyes to the expansive blue sky. "I don't know, buddy," I said, shaking my head. "Gulliver is unusual. I like unusual because I'm an unusual kind of woman. He's interesting and engaging. He's smart but kind. None of that can be said about a lot of guys I meet on the road."

Considering I spent a lot of time with extremely weird people, unusual was a massive step in the right direction. It was easy to see that Gulliver's blustery in-your-face persona stemmed from his leg condition. I'd tried to engage him about his disability, but he changed the subject at every turn. The face he showed the world wasn't the real Gulliver Winsome. I conjured up a scenario in my mind where he closed the door to his apartment at night and removed the mask of over-the-top self-assuredness to let himself breathe for a little while.

My childhood had been all about masks of deception. I learned early on in life how to look behind the mask to see who someone really was. What I saw in Gulliver more than sparked my curiosity, both as someone who enjoys the study of human nature and as a woman. He was strong, smart, and kind to everyone we met while we were out, but most of all his aura was captivating. It was harder and harder to find someone who spent time with you without distractions, but Gulliver was a master at it. I was excited to spend the night with him tonight.

I rolled my eyes at myself. *You'll both be working, girl. Put a lid on your libido.*

"There's no law against looking at a fine man, right, Mojo?" I asked as we followed the paved road around and passed a fish house. Mojo didn't answer me, but the rank air did raise his interest a hair.

Another few minutes of strolling down the path and I found the main office. When the door swung open, the scent of nachos mixed with beer wafted toward me. If I weren't still stuffed from that fantastic pizza, I'd be taking some of those nachos back to Myrtle with me.

Basking in the cold air for a moment, I took in the cute, cozy, and well-stocked store before I strode to the counter with Mojo at my side. My eye caught movement from the corner, and I waved at a woman scooping up nachos into a bowl. "Good afternoon," I said, holding tight to Mojo's leash. "I'm Charity Puck. We spoke on the phone earlier this week."

"I remember," she answered as she held up a finger, carrying the nachos through the racks of food and out a door to a large wooden balcony. I stood on my tiptoes and noticed the balcony overlooked the lake. There were umbrellaed tables for those who wanted to relax with a beer while taking in a spectacular view of Mother Nature's glory.

"I'm going to have to check that balcony out, Mojo," I said as the woman strolled back through the door and approached the desk. It was a shame I couldn't remember her name for the life of me.

When she spied Mojo, her steps faltered, and she came to a halt. "Um, we allow dogs in the campground but not in the store," she stuttered.

I smiled the smile I always use when I'm trying to feather Mojo into staying with me somewhere. "I'm sorry, we just got back from town, and I wanted to stop in and pay my fees. We were at lunch with Gulliver Winsome. Do you know him?"

She gave Mojo a wide berth and scuttled back behind the counter. "Oh, ya," she said in the most Northern Wisconsin accent to ever hit my ears. "Everyone knows Gulliver. He's a great guy under all the . . ." She fluffed her hands around her chest while searching for the right words.

"Bluster?" I asked, and she grinned.

"Exactly. Gulliver does a lot for our little community. Anyway, you want to pay for your stay? You pay for six nights and get the seventh free," she explained, tapping a sign on the counter.

"Great," I said, happily handing her my card from my pocket. "I'll pay for the first week, but I plan to stay a couple weeks more, if not a month. It will depend on if I get called away for work. Would it be okay to keep paying by the week? If I have to take off, you can keep the money for whatever time I've paid for but don't use."

"Why sure, honey," she said sweetly. "You're welcome to stay as long as you'd like. What do you do for a living?"

Having done this song and dance many times, I had learned to sugarcoat the hell out of my profession. I'm a hacker, and I'm excellent at what I do, but I can't use that terminology. People instantly picture me in a hoodie, bent over my keyboard, and wreaking havoc on some unsuspecting business. "I'm a security patch technician," I explained. "I patch leaks in computer servers."

The woman rubbed her hands together, curiosity written across her sunbaked features. "Sounds exciting! I bet you have some great stories."

Oh boy, do I ever. "I have a few," I agreed. "How much is it for the week, then?"

"It's one seventy-five for the week, which includes your tank dumping fee. If you stay more than eight weeks, you'll have paid the seasonal rate, and I wouldn't charge you anything for the rest of the season."

"Really? Most campgrounds require you to pay up front if you want to stay for the season."

She slid my card through the machine. "I'm not most places. I don't take joy in screwing people out of hard-earned cash. Besides, you strike me as the kind of girl who could stand to be in one place for more than a day."

I laughed, but the sound was sad rather than amused. "You're not kidding. I haven't had a break in years. I could use a few weeks of not moving anywhere in a vehicle unless it's human powered."

"My name is Laverne, by the way. It's nice to meet you, Charity."

Ahh yes, Laverne. I should have remembered that since my dad's favorite show was *Laverne and Shirley* when I was a kid.

Laverne pointed to the balcony, which was half filled with campers doing nothing but gazing at the lake. "If you're going to take a break, this is the best place for it. We've got something for everyone. It's rarely too hot, the water is a great place to be on a summer day, and the sights are out of this world," she said, pointing at the ceiling. "I'm pointing up because there's a telescope on the roof that anyone can use."

"Wow, how awesome!" I exclaimed with my hand to my chest. "I was thinking last night when I arrived how beautiful the stars were. They didn't twinkle in the sky. They danced. They were three dimensional and shimmered. With so little light pollution here, stargazing must be a popular pastime."

Laverne leaned on the counter and nodded as she handed me my card. "They're beautiful, and the northern lights will leave you breathless."

I accepted my card and put it back in my pocket. "I'm dying to see the northern lights!" I said excitedly. "I travel all around this country but have yet to luck out."

"The good news is you don't need a telescope to see them here. If you stand on the dock by your campsite, the colors will encapsulate you. Soul changing is what it is, I'm telling you. I always keep my eye on the forecast for them. You'll be the first to know the next time the prediction for them is high."

I signed the paper receipt she'd handed me and tapped it with the pen. "I would appreciate it, Laverne. I think I'm going to like it here."

"I hope you do! If you need anything, we're open here at the store from six to nine every day but Sunday. We close at six p.m. on Sunday, but we have an emergency number to call." She bent down and searched for something under the counter before popping back up. She handed me a magnet. "Those numbers will be all you need for your stay. If you have any problems with your site, let me know, and I'll send our maintenance guy out to help."

I nodded once and stuck the magnet in my back pocket. "Thanks, Laverne. I think I'll go check out the lake and then shower before I head back to Butterfly Junction tonight."

Her eyebrows rose to her hairline as if she suddenly had a juicy tidbit of information no one else had. "You're working with Gulliver tonight?"

"I have to do my work at night when no one else is using the system. I suppose he will be there, but we won't be working together," I explained, and her brows fell in a disappointed plummet.

"I see—what a shame. Gulliver could stand to get out more. That boy spends too much time with butterflies."

"There certainly are a lot of butterflies around his office, but at least it's not bats or something equally creepy like spiders."

She laughed hysterically as she brushed her hand at me. "You're not kidding. Gulliver is a peculiar guy, but at least he's not into bats or spiders. Don't get me wrong, we love our Gulliver here. I just wish he'd stop working all the time and enjoy life a little bit."

I grasped Mojo's leash in my hand tightly as I started for the door. "You never know, Laverne. Stranger things have happened. Perhaps this will be the summer Gulliver decides to work less and enjoy the world around him just a little bit more."

Her sly smile told me she understood that I intended to be

the one to make that change in Gulliver. "You never know," she agreed, waving as I left the store.

When the door closed behind me, I let a smile slide across my face. I'd been in Plentiful for eighteen hours and already met five people who went out of their way to be kind and welcoming to me. Truth be told, Gulliver Winsome was the only one on my mind.

Chapter Three

Laverne had been right when she said Plentiful Campground was the best place to relax. Tonight, while I waited for Gulliver to pick me up, I had gazed at the beauty of the lake spread out before me like a smorgasbord to my senses. As a woman who had traveled from coast to coast, I can assure you, the Lady of the Lake held more beauty than the whole of the United States. I'd never seen Lake Superior before, much less camped out on her shores, but she drew me in with a siren's song the minute I laid eyes on her. While I ate dinner, I watched the eagles dance across the water in a modern-day ballet. The harmony of the waves lapping against the rocks reached my ears, and the scent of pine boughs tickled my nose. To say it was relaxing was an understatement. It was soul cleansing.

When Gulliver arrived to pick me up in his tricked-out cargo van complete with giant butterflies wrapped around the vehicle in bold colors of blue, gold, and orange, I couldn't help but smile. It should have been embarrassing to ride in that butterfly-mobile, as I had started calling it, but he was so comfortable in the van you couldn't help but ease back into the seat as well. He explained that he used it for his educational presentations he did for schools and nature reserves.

When we arrived at the building, he had Honey's desk cleared off and ready for me to use, so I'd been working for the last four hours while Mojo lay under my feet. Every time Gulliver came by to ask me if I needed anything, Mojo gave him the stink eye as if to say, *Watch it, pal.*

I leaned back in the desk chair and scratched my temple. What I was looking at didn't make sense. "Gulliver? Are you busy?" I called from where I sat at Honey's desk.

He arrived in a matter of seconds and grabbed the spare chair to sit next to me. "Nope. What's shakin', bacon?"

I stared at him for an extended period, but he didn't say anything. "You just called me a pig."

The expression on his face was questioning. "No, I said, 'What's shakin', bac—'" He dumped his head into his hands and groaned.

"Exactly," I said deadpan while trying not to laugh.

He peeked up at me, his cheeks ablaze with color under his tightly-trimmed beard. I was itching to smooth my palm across his cheek to see if it was as soft as it looked. "I'm sorry. I didn't mean to imply you're a pig. It rhymes, and I was trying to be cute, and—"

I held my hand up to halt his apology. "I was kidding, Gulliver. Man, I'm going to start calling you Gulliver the Gullible."

His shoulders slumped with relief but stiffened again instantly. "Hey! Did you just call me gullible?"

"If the shoe fits," I muttered, enjoying our camaraderie. I don't know why I felt comfortable joking back and forth with him the way I was. I'd only known him a day, but he spoke the same language of fun that I did. We were two souls connected by the commonality of a hard life that would be impossible to bear if you couldn't find things to laugh about. Usually, when I was on the job,

I was alone in a computer room with no one but Mojo to talk to for hours. Let's face it. He's not exactly the best conversationalist. Butterfly Junction was different. Gulliver Winsome was different. I was enjoying different.

"Did you call me out here because you needed something or to insult me?" he asked haughtily.

"Because I needed something," I said, laughing full out. "You distracted me, so it's your fault."

He rolled his eyes upward to gaze at the curly head of hair on his head. I had to admit it worked for him. His wavy chestnut locks were haphazardly tossed around his head, either accidentally or on purpose. If it was by accident, he was extremely good at wearing bedhead the right way. "Oh, sure, it's always the guy's fault," he said sarcastically.

I whistled long and low as a warning to him. "Sounds like someone has sour grapes going on here. Did the last girl blame you and then dump you?"

"Who has time to date?" he asked, sticking his tongue out.

The front door opened, and a man stumbled into the reception area. He wore a pin-striped suit with a white dress shirt and a blue tie with white anchors smattered across it. He was lean, fit, and wore a striking pair of blue eyes under a head of blond hair. His tie was hanging open, and I quickly realized his shirt was bloody and the suit was dirty.

"Gulliver," he said, grabbing for his shoulder before he tipped over.

"Mathias, you're back," Gulliver said, turning to the man. "What the hell?" He pulled a chair over, and Mathias sat down gingerly, holding his head in his hand.

"Do you need a doctor?" Gulliver asked, his gaze holding concern for his friend.

"I went to the hospital," he said, his fingers probing the back of his head. "I had the car drop me off here. Mine has to go into the shop."

"What car? Were you in an accident?" I asked, and Mathias looked up at me like he had just noticed me for the first time.

Gulliver motioned to me. "Mathias Jørgensen, meet Charity Puck."

I stuck my hand out just as Mojo stuck his head out. "Nice to meet you, Mathias. Jørgensen. That's . . ."

"Danish," he answered. "My parents are from Denmark." He glanced down at Mojo and tried to stand, but Gulliver grasped his shoulder to steady him.

"Relax, Mathias. That's Mojo. He's chill. Just don't get too close to Charity and he'll be your best friend."

"Especially if you have hot dogs," I said on a chuckle to ease the tension. "Mathias, I think you should have stayed at the hospital. You don't look well."

Mathias swung his head slightly. "No, they released me."

Gulliver sat next to his friend. "Tell us what happened."

"I was driving home from my parents' about midnight. I got caught up helping Far with something," he explained.

"Far?" I asked, glancing between them.

"'Far' means 'father' in Danish," Gulliver explained.

I made an O with my mouth and motioned for Mathias to continue.

"Some jerk came up on me in the left lane. I thought they were passing, but they forced me off the road. I was lucky I had the SUV and not the convertible or I'd be dead. I was able to slow down enough that when I hit the small trees, they didn't kill me. By the time I got my wits about me, the other car was long gone."

"It was probably someone on their phone," I said, my teeth clenched. "I can't tell you how many times someone almost killed me because they were on their phone instead of paying attention to the road."

Mathias went to swing his head no but seemed to think better of it. "No, this was very much on purpose."

"On purpose?" Gulliver asked.

"I have no doubt," he said, his hand going to the back of his head. "This wasn't a game of chicken or someone not paying attention. They purposely forced me off the road. I was too busy trying to stay alive to notice anything about the vehicle other than it was a black SUV of some kind."

"You have blood on your shirt," Gulliver said. "That means you were hurt."

I inspected Mathias's head and noticed his hair had been cut away and he had a row of stitches. "How did you crack your head open?" I asked, coming around the chair.

"When I hit the trees, everything flew around in the SUV. Something hit me. I think it was the snow scraper for the windows. I wasn't going to go to the hospital, but the EMTs didn't give me a choice. They said a head laceration like that will never heal without stitches. The doctors also said I have a concussion. I think they're wrong."

Gulliver's gaze met mine, and he lifted a brow before he spoke. "I don't think they're wrong. You have all the signs. You'll have to crash here in my apartment tonight so I can check on you."

Mathias waved his hand at his neck. "Honey is on her way down. She's going to drive me home in the Butterfly Junction van and stay with me."

"Good," Gulliver said on a nod. He worked a set of keys out of his pocket and handed them to Mathias. "Do you think this is because of the formula?"

"Oh yeah," Mathias agreed. "We have a problem on our hands, and it's getting worse if they're resorting to violence."

"I was just telling Gulliver that you definitely have a problem," I said.

Mathias glanced between me and Gulliver, then to the two computers I had open on the desk. "What kind of problem?"

I typed a bit on the keyboard before swinging the screen to face them. "I was able to get into the server in under thirty seconds."

Gulliver leaned in closer to see the screen better. "No, you can't be on the server. You mean you're just into the website where the store and information about the educational opportunities are, right? The research on our servers can't be accessed through the website."

I banged my head on the back of my chair in frustration. "Oh, dear, sweet, naive Gulliver. You have a website, and that makes you vulnerable. I can't see your research. Yet. If you give me another twenty minutes to dig for it, I could find it. I've been patching this for the last two hours, and when I'm done, the door will not only be closed but removed and drywalled over."

Gulliver's head shook immediately. "My web designer assured me no one could get into the whole system. He said he was making the encryption stronger." He waved his hand in the air. "Or something like that. I didn't understand it all."

Mathias whistled long and low. "I guess we weren't overreacting by calling you in," he said, his eyes glassy. "I was worried we were, but at the same time we couldn't chance waiting."

I motioned at the computer. "No, you made the right choice by calling me. You were days away from losing everything."

Both men sighed in response, but Mathias was the one to speak. "Are you done? Are we solid now?"

I nudged the computer out of my way and leaned on the desk.

"Sure, I can be done, if you don't care that your competition can steal every bit of information on your server without you knowing it. You're damn lucky that they haven't already. You have a security level on your server that I like to call, 'Come on in! Everyone's welcome!'" I said, throwing my hands around in excitement. "'Mi casa es sus casa. We have everything you could ever need to create eco-friendly pesticides. If you'd rather have fungicides, we have those too! Just ask!'" I finished with a gigantic clown grin on my face. I was relatively sure it was a little bit scary.

"Sarcasm, right?" Gulliver asked, nonplussed.

"Sarcasm with a serious undertone of absolutely accurate. I will say you're fortunate whoever is after your research wasn't successful before I got here. To be blunt, someone is trying to steal your information, and I don't know who it is. Yet." I quickly explained what I'd found once I was inside the server. "I do know they aren't an expert by any stretch of the imagination, or your data would already be gone."

"What do we do now then?" Gulliver asked.

"I've changed the passwords again. Honestly, your password wasn't strong enough to keep a four-year-old out of your phone, much less someone intent on stealing your information."

Gulliver grimaced on a nod. "I know, but the password had to be easy for everyone to remember."

"Not anymore," I said, my finger pointing at a sheet of paper on the desk. "From now on, only you two have them. I have generated passwords that are unhackable by anyone other than a black hat."

"Black hat?" Mathias asked, glancing between us.

"A black hat hacker is someone who will break into computer networks with malicious intent. I'm what you call a white hat hacker. I fix what the black hats destroy. You're lucky. We aren't dealing with a black hat here. If you were, they'd already have your research. Whoever is working your system is good but not that good. If you change the password every week and never use the same one twice, that's going to make it incredibly difficult for them to get in."

"Every week?" Gulliver asked with nervousness. "That's a lot to remember, Charity."

"It won't be forever," I promised. "We need to lock them out and buy time to find out who it is. Once this is cleared up, you'll only have to change the password once a month. Understood?"

Both men nodded.

"Good. If you don't do this, you're going to lose this precious research to someone trying to screw you over. Now you have someone hacking into your servers and someone running you off the road. That tells me the situation is escalating. Do either of you have any idea who this might be?"

"If I had to take a guess, I'd lean toward a competing company longing to be the first one to rush it to market," Mathias said.

Gulliver pointed at him in agreement. "That's the most likely scenario, though it could also be a conservation group that wants the formula to be public domain so no one makes money off the sale of it."

Mathias snorted with heavy sarcasm. "I don't know any conservation groups that are going to resort to this kind of violence to do that."

I waved my hand in the air. "Either way, the time is now to protect yourself before all of this implodes on you."

Gulliver kept constant eye contact with me while we talked, and his caramel globes sparked in the low light of the room every time his emotions flared. Most women would have gone gaga the moment Mathias walked into the room. He was handsome in a traditional blond, blue-eyed, sharp dresser, catch-every-woman's-attention kind of way, but Gulliver was handsome in the boy-next-door kind of way. His eyes were what drew you in, but his dark, curly hair made you sigh a little inside. He reminded me of Antonio Banderas if Antonio Banderas had short, curly hair. I'm a sucker for tall, dark, and handsome, but I'm also a sucker for depth of character. What I'd learned about Gulliver today was simple. Under his layer of overinflated fake ego, he was a sweet guy who believed in what he was doing, both with the pesticide and trying to protect the creatures he loved. I respected his devotion to both. I'd met so many guys who didn't care one way or the other about working for the greater good, especially at the expense of their personal lives. He could make fun of himself, and me, without sounding jerky or arrogant, but most importantly I'd learned that his ego was nothing more than a defense mechanism. Thus far tonight, I'd seen anger and fear in those globes of gold and copper.

"There is more work to do, though," I said, motioning at the computer. "I need to know how far you want me to go."

"All the way," they said in unison.

"How long can you stay and help us get this figured out?" Gulliver asked.

I let a smile work its way back to my lips. "I have until the end of July, but it won't take me that long. This is only the end of May. You're lucky, most businesses call me after it's too late, so you're ahead of the curve. What we need to do is shut this whole website down and rebuild a new one from scratch." I paused. "On second thought, I would suggest taking down everything but the front page. We can say something about the site undergoing maintenance and leave contact information to reach the business by phone or email. If we take the entire website down, we could tip whoever is behind this off that we're onto them. Before we rebuild it, I'll need to close all the holes in the security for your server."

"How long will that take?" Mathias asked, his eyes revealing a heavy dose of anger.

"I can get most of the security breaches done tonight, at least the most important ones. The rest I'll have to finish tomorrow night. Encoding all the research data to protect it will take much longer. Gulliver, you'll have to work closely with me on the website rebuild when we're ready. I can write code, but I don't know a thing about bugs."

"Done," Gulliver assured me.

I tapped the desk twice. "How long has Honey been here?"

Mathias shook his head before I finished the sentence. "No, she's beyond reproach," he said angrily and adamantly. "She's been my best friend for twenty years."

Gulliver grasped Mathias's shoulder to calm him. "She's been here about a year, but all she does is answer the phone and process orders, nothing more. She doesn't have access to the research lab either."

"Honey has nothing to do with this," Mathias said, a dangerous glint to his eye.

I held my hands up in defense. "I had to ask considering what we're dealing with. Is there any way she can work somewhere else for a week? I could sit at her desk during the day to work. I'll even answer the phone. By week's end, I'll have the research data encoded. When Honey returns the next week, Gulliver and I can work on putting the website back together again. That will take a bit of time as well. I'll want to make sure there are no vulnerabilities in the site before it goes live."

Mathias glanced at Gulliver and then back to me. "She can work from my condo. I have some other business she can attend to for the next week. I'll tell her, though. I don't want her to think we're accusing her of any—"

The front doors flew open, and Honey ran in. "Mattie!" she exclaimed, running over and nearly pushing Gulliver out of the way to get to him. "Oh my God, are you okay?" she asked, frantically checking him over. Her hands started to shake when she encountered the blood on his shirt, and several fingers on her right hand pointed straight up to the sky.

Mathias grasped her hand carefully and massaged the fingers while he spoke to her quietly. "I'm okay," he promised, running his fingers through her hair to straighten it out. He'd obviously rousted her from a deep sleep when he'd called her. "I have a few stitches in the back of my head and a concussion, the doctor said. He didn't want me to stay alone."

"Oh my God, a concussion?" she asked, her hand shaking again. "What happened?"

Mathias stood slowly, making sure his feet were under him before he spoke. "I'll tell you on the way to the condo. I need to put my head down for a little bit. It's starting to pound. I have the keys to the van in my pocket."

She hooked her arm through his and grasped his elbow to keep him steady. "I'll bring the van back when I come to work tomorrow," she said to Gulliver.

"About that," Mathias said, listing a bit until Honey pulled him tight to her side again. "I need you to work from the condo for the next week or so. I have some business I need you to look at that's not related to Butterfly Junction."

Her head twisted back and forth between the two men with a frown on her lips. "What about my job here? Who is going to answer the phone and take orders?" she asked logically.

"I am," I said, nodding at my computers. "I'm going to get a new website set up with better security, but I can answer the phone at the same time."

"No, Mattie," Honey insisted, her head swinging frantically. "I can look at your other business while I'm here. We can't ask Charity to do two jobs when she isn't even employed by the business!"

Gulliver held his hand out to her. "It's fine, Honey. Mathias needs your help, and we can spare you for a week while you do it. Besides, he's going to need someone to look after him for a few days after the knock to his head. I'd prefer if you were taking care of him. I don't want to worry about him and try to protect the company at the same time."

She bit her lip nervously as she eyed the man next to her and considered what Gulliver had said. "Okay, you're probably right. But if you need me…"

"I know where you are," Gulliver promised, hitting the button for the elevator. "Take him home. The van is in the garage next to the lab. Mathias has a card to get in."

Honey helped Mathias onto the elevator, and he put his head on her shoulder as the door closed. I noticed Gulliver chewing on his lip.

"He'll be okay. Honey will make sure of it," I assured him.

"I know," he said on a nod. "I was more worried about where I'd find time to help you with the new website. I have a lot of work to do during the day with the other scientists. Can we have Jim do the website instead?"

"Jim?" I asked, confused.

"Jim Parsons, my web designer."

I shook my head instantly. "Jim has to go, I'm sorry to say. We can't trust anyone who has ever worked inside this business besides your close investors. Anyone could be involved in this."

"Jim Parsons is a sixty-year-old grandpa, Charity," he said on such a disbelieving snort I thought he might swallow his tongue.

"Even grandpas need money, Gulliver," I answered pointedly.

While he thought it over, his eyes were squinted in the most adorable way. It was almost as if he was moving puzzle pieces around in his head until they all fit to form the real picture. I could tell by the look in his eyes when he opened them again that he was still missing a piece or two.

"Okay, fine. Jim goes. Can we work on the website in the evenings and on the weekends?"

"Not a problem. By then I'll be done working the reception desk during the day, so nights and weekends will be fine. We can do it at your place or mine, but I'll tell you this much: mine has a much better view."

His gaze roved over me in a blatant display of lusty interest. "Truer words were never spoken."

I carried Gulliver's plate back to the table and set it on his place mat while he settled his crutches against the wall. Once I slid into my seat, I rubbed my hands together when I faced my steaming plate of deliciousness. "Man, this is the best thing I've seen in days. Pancakes, eggs, bacon, biscuits, and whatever these things are," I said, poking at a ball of dough covered in sugar.

Gulliver snorted with laughter and had to cover his face with his napkin or risk spraying coffee across the table. "It's a doughnut hole, you nut," he finally answered when he finished coughing. "We're big fans of them here."

I picked it up and took a bite. "This is yum too. I like the cinnamon and sugar," I added, popping the last bite into my mouth.

He swung his fork around my face in a circle. "You need a napkin. You're drooling."

I gave him my har-har smile and grabbed my fork. "I'm in love with you already for suggesting we eat here," I said, shoveling eggs into my mouth. When I glanced up to get my juice, he was staring at me slack-jawed. "Figure of speech," I stuttered, but inside I was cringing. *What the heck, Charity? You're ridiculously bad at small talk, so just stop.*

"Of course," he replied and immediately changed the subject. "They have a breakfast buffet every morning, but Saturday and Sunday are the best days. They add extra items for the campers as they stumble into town to oust their hangovers. We got here early enough that the tourists won't overtake us, but most weekends there's a line out the door of this place."

I took a drink of coffee to wash down my eggs. "I can understand why, honestly. I've never seen a spread as copious as theirs," I said, jabbing toward the buffet with my fork. "Even in Vegas, and those casinos know how to do buffets."

"Well, if it isn't Gulliver Winsome," a short, portly man said as he approached our table. "And this must be Charity."

Gulliver winked at me before he motioned to the man in front of us. "Charity, this is Kevin Havens. He owns the diner with his wife, Lucy."

I wiped my hand on my napkin and stuck it out for him to shake. His large paw engulfed my hand as he shook it up and down so hard my shoulder got involved in the equation. "Nice to meet you, Kevin. I met Lucy the other day. I suppose she told you all about the new girl in town."

Kevin released my hand and rocked up on the balls of his feet. "She sure did. She mentioned a giant dog that liked hot dogs as well."

I chuckled and leaned back in my chair. "Mojo. We left him at Butterfly Junction. I didn't think you'd want a giant mutt hanging out in your diner trying to steal everyone's breakfast."

"You're probably right," he said, his eyes crinkling when he smiled. "I'm not sure the health department would look too kindly on that. Well, I just wanted to stop by and introduce myself. Have a great weekend."

"Thanks, Kevin," Gulliver said, and I waved as he sauntered

off toward another table.

"Nice guy," I said, going back to my plate. "Everyone here is super nice."

Gulliver nodded and lowered his coffee cup. "We're a small town, but we're also a tourist town. Being nice keeps your business alive."

I tipped my head with a chuckle of agreement and leaned back to give my stomach a little more room to stretch. "I need to ask you a question," I said, and he motioned for me to go ahead while he chewed. "Why is someone so interested in this formula you're trying to make? Aren't there other eco-friendly pesticides out there? There can't be a massive amount of money at play in eco-friendly pesticides, right?"

I turned my attention back on my breakfast while I waited for him to answer. I stabbed a sausage and took a bite. The casing snapped under the pressure of my teeth, and the juice poured into my mouth, spicy and sweet. When I glanced up, Gulliver was staring at me with his fork dangling in the air. "What?" I asked after I swallowed. "Can't a girl eat?"

He fidgeted with his juice glass. "I'm staring because I just realized you're equally as naive as I am, only this time about how competitive the eco-friendly pesticide industry is."

A variety of emotions flew across his face in quick succession as I lowered my fork to the plate.

"You're saying there's a lot of money in this business?"

He nodded his head up and down like a puppet on a string. "Billions of dollars are at play. Current pesticide companies don't have an eco-friendly pesticide for large-scale farming applications. It's a potential market disrupter, so everyone is going to want the patent. Charity, we're talking billions here, not millions."

I raised a brow. "Let me get this straight. We're talking billions of dollars to the company with the first large-scale eco-friendly pesticide."

He tipped his head as if to say, *Yep.*

"What do you plan to do with it once you have the formula?"

He lowered his coffee cup and glanced around at the other tables. He leaned in over his plate and lowered his voice as though everyone was paying attention to us when no one was. "We think we're nearing the completion of our pesticide, which means fungicide and herbicide will follow quickly. Our choices are to sell it to the highest bidder or produce it ourselves."

I leaned closer to him, and my gaze dropped to his plump lips. It was becoming harder and harder not to let my hand slip up his cheek and let his lips taste mine. I wanted his hands in my hair and the intensity of his gaze focused on nothing but me. Would his eyes swirl the shade of gingerbread while they swept my petite body with desire? Would his lips drop to mine for a tentative taste test of my lips under the moonlight? I shook my head. *Oh my God, Charity, stop! This is business! You're not staying in Plentiful. Get a grip! Better yet, get your head in the game.*

"I'm protecting it because it isn't finished yet," he was saying when I stopped lusting after him long enough to focus. "If someone were to get half the information and rushed the rest of the equation, then took something to market that was destructive, they could do great damage to the fields and the butterflies. That's why I'm protecting the research. It has nothing to do with the financial side of it. Maybe it does for Mathias, but not for me."

I set my coffee cup on the table and nodded thoughtfully. "My brain is spinning trying to take it all in. If I ask too many stupid questions, forgive me, and if you get tired of answering, just say so."

A smile crept across his face, and for the first time since early this morning, he relaxed a bit in his seat. I noticed the gold flecks in his eyes were vibrant, and the dots of green shone like the morning sun on the lake. I rested my cheek on my hand and smiled back at him like a dopey schoolgirl with a crush on her teacher.

"You can ask as many questions as you'd like, and I'll answer them all," he assured me. "There aren't a lot of people, especially women, interested in what I do. Most see my manly butterfly van and steer clear."

I pictured the butterflies in all their glory stretched across his van and couldn't stop the smile from lifting my lips. "I wasn't embarrassed riding in it. The more I get to know you, the more I know it's perfect for what you do and who you are." I yawned unexpectedly and covered my mouth with my hand. "My goodness. How rude. I'm sorry. I guess the night is catching up to me."

He grabbed his crutches from where they leaned against the wall. "If you're full, we'll grab Mojo from the office, and I'll drive you home."

I stretched and over the din of the restaurant I swear I heard him moan. I thought I was wrong until he coughed to cover it up. When I glanced up, his gaze held that intensity again while it swept over my body with appreciation. I stood and smoothed down my shirt. "I'm stuffed, but I'm coming back tomorrow morning again. I need more of this place."

"I'd love to join you." Gulliver stuck out his fist, and I bumped it. "I mean, if you want company, that is," he said, blushing.

My heart pounded for a moment at the idea of spending more private time with Gulliver Winsome. We'd already spent as much time outside of our professional capacities as we had in them. That was new, odd, and yet exciting for me to think about. It had been a long time since I'd slowed down long enough to enjoy someone's company in a personal way. Sure, I was working a job for him, but I wasn't his employee, so there was no reason we couldn't share a meal together here and there. After all, I'd be here longer than expected to help them finish the website. There was no harm in a little summer fling. And by fling, I meant nothing more than enjoying his enthusiasm for life. What you see is what you get with Gulliver Winsome, and for some reason that made me feel safe to be myself around him.

"I'd love some," I said, offering him a smile as we walked out the door.

Chapter Four

After breakfast, Gulliver intended to drop Mojo and me off at the campground and head home to bed, but Laverne noticed me struggling to get Mojo out of the cargo van and excitedly waved us into the office. She had insisted we share a drink on the empty balcony before he headed home. We were both tired, but we didn't want to hurt her feelings, so we accepted her invitation and settled at a table in the shade.

We gazed out across the lake, the slight breeze tippling the blue-green water into frothy peaks of white. When the sun reflected off the waves, the image left little doubt there indeed was a Lady of the Lake, and she was as alive as any woman you had ever met.

Gulliver's finger pointed out in front of me, and I naturally followed its arc. "Do you see those dots of land in the water?" he asked, and I stood, focusing on the area he was pointing to.

"Are those the Apostle Islands?" I asked.

"They are, and they are so worth seeing in person," he said. "There are twenty-one islands, many with old-world lighthouses. The lighthouses are automated now, but they still shine over the lake like sentries to protect the sailors. Lake Superior is more treacherous than the ocean. The waves can swamp a boat the size of a cruise ship without a second thought, and the cold water means it doesn't take long for sailors in the water to die of hypothermia."

I raised a brow. "My, someone is Mr. Doom and Gloom this morning. 'Hey, Charity,'" I said, lowering my voice, "'check out this beautiful view while I tell you all about how you can die out there.'"

His laughter this time was more of a giggle when he held up his hand. "Okay, you're right. My point was, the islands are beautiful and even though the lighthouses are automated, they're worth seeing."

"Okay, so how do you get out there?" I asked. "Ferry?"

"Ferries run to some of them, but you also have leisure cruises, private boat rentals, and kayaks."

I gave him a side-eye stare of disbelief. "I've never kayaked, and I don't think the first place I want to do it is Lake Superior."

He leaned back in his chair to relax. "Oh dear, sweet, naive Charity, how wrong you are. Lake Superior is the only place you should do it."

I smiled against my will at the man next to me. He had such energy for life and was determined to share his knowledge and excitement with everyone around him. I wasn't used to that. I was used to doing my thing and everyone else doing theirs. The contact I had with people was minimal, both when I was working and when I wasn't. I didn't think giving my order to a waitress at a diner on the side of the road counted as contact with people either. In two days, I'd spent more time with the people in this town than I had spent with anyone over the last year. That was depressing to admit but still the truth. I lacked a personal connection with anyone, and nothing made that more obvious than the town of Plentiful.

I shook off those thoughts and glanced up at him. "Would you teach me how?" I asked. "I don't think I'd be great at kayaking.

I'm ridiculously short, and my arms are shorter."

He eyed me up and down for longer than necessary, but I didn't mind. His perusal wasn't creepy or sneering, but rather caring and interested. "You are ridiculously short," he said, his voice filled with laughter.

I punched him lightly in the arm, laughing with him. "Watch it, buster. I work hard on this figure," I said, running my hands down my body seductively. "Not everyone can pull off being a little person."

His eyes widened in embarrassment immediately, and his fingers tenderly grasped my wrist. "I'm sorry, I didn't know you were an actual little person."

"An actual little person? Versus a fictitious little person?" I asked, amused by his wording.

When he grimaced, even that was adorable. He was adorable in general, but his facial expressions offered me insight into his inner emotions every time. "No, I meant, you know, the word you aren't supposed to use for little people because it's not politically correct."

"Oh," I said, suddenly understanding why he was uncomfortable. "Do you mean dwarf?"

His gaze darted around the balcony, for what reason I didn't know since we were alone. "Um, yeah."

He said nothing more, so I decided he was just waiting for me to answer. "I guess it comes down to each individual person and what they prefer to be called," I explained. "Dwarfism is the medical term for short stature, but movies and TV gave it such a negative connotation that people tend to avoid it. It's technically correct in a medical sense, but we prefer to use little person or person of short stature."

His fingers rubbed at his forehead for a few minutes while he held my gaze. "Right. I get it, I do. It's not as if my legs are exactly easy for people to pin a name on either."

My heart ached for him. His words held great sadness and pain, which told me more than anything else he could ever tell me about those legs. Tiny as my hand was, I gripped his shoulder for a moment to show him someone understood. He needed to know someone cared, even if that someone didn't plan to stick around to be part of his life for more than a few weeks. When I got to know someone, I wanted to get to know who they were under the surface. I wanted to know the things they didn't show everyone else. I wanted to see their vulnerabilities as well as their strengths. If you didn't take the time to do that, you couldn't say you really knew a person. I moved my hand over to rub his neck for a moment. It was all I could do not to smooth my palm over his cheek. "In my opinion, we're more than the attributes of our physical bodies, right?"

His shoulder tipped up, but it took a long time to go down again. "Supposedly, but in this day and age, our bodies carry a lot of weight when people form opinions about us."

I blew out a breath of acknowledgment and understanding. "You're absolutely right. I would imagine it's even harder for you. By all the medical definitions, I'm a little person, but my dwarfism is proportionate, which makes it easier for me to get through life. I don't suffer from any of the disabling conditions that some others with short stature do. I can't relate, nor would I ever claim to relate to those who truly suffer from the conditions that go along with dwarfism. I'm the size of a nine-year-old, and while that's often an inconvenience, as of right now, that's all it is."

"What about your arm?" he asked, his warm hand cradling my deformed right elbow. His thumb stroked the skin over the bones, and a shiver ran through me. No one had ever touched me the way he touched me, and I didn't want him to stop. "I know little people have problems with their arms, but this one looks far worse than your left one," he observed.

I glanced down, and the difference was obvious. The right elbow was large and bulbous while the forearm was deformed with a hump in the middle, making my hand hang at a funny angle at rest. I had far less range of motion at the elbow in the right than I did in the left one as well. "I broke it when I was seven. It was a messy compound fracture and they did surgery, but my dad wasn't great about getting me to the doctor appointments, much less therapy. Eventually it healed, but it was never right again. For that reason, I had to learn how to do everything left-handed. Fortunately, I was young when it happened, so that made it easier."

"Have you seen a doctor for it now that you're an adult?" he asked, caressing the elbow while we talked.

"I did and they talked about doing surgery, but it would have been extensive, and they couldn't say for sure that it would help. In fact, they were afraid because of my dwarfism, that they'd make it worse. Since I was functional with the arm and wasn't in pain, we decided it was better to leave it alone than make it worse. Sometimes you have to make those decisions."

His sarcastic laughter wasn't aimed at me, I could tell. It was aimed at himself. "Do I ever know that one," he said, his eyes rolling to the sky while his head shook. He recovered and when his eyes met mine again, he pointed out to the campground. "I have to ask then. How do you drive a gigantic motor home? How do you turn the steering wheel with your arms the size they are? I know you certainly can't reach those pedals either."

I chuckled, and my whole body shook. Gulliver often said things to tickle me all the way to my toes, and it had been years since anyone was able to do that as naturally as he did. "I have pedal extensions. Myrtle isn't gigantic at only twenty feet long, so the cab is just like driving a truck. I also have a spinner knob on the wheel, which makes it easier for my little arms. You're right, though. Anything bigger and I'd have serious issues. I think a Smart Car would be more up my alley, but what's the fun in that?"

Deep, rich laughter filled the balcony then, and he patted my back, his hand covering my entire shoulder. My skin tingled under his touch again, reminding me it had been too long since I'd been touched by a man.

"Now all I can picture is you zipping around in a little car with Mojo stuffed in the passenger seat and hanging his head out the window."

"I don't think the big man would enjoy a Smart Car as much as Myrtle. I better stick with her," I said, my laughter floating out across the lake.

"I feel guilty for hiring you for a one-night job, and now you're tied up for a couple of weeks," he said, his gaze holding mine. "I'll understand if you can't stay."

Before I thought about it, I brought my hand up to pat his face. I stroked his soft beard for a moment too long, and another shiver went through me. Oh God. It was even softer than I'd thought it would be. *What was going on with me?* There was an undeniable chemistry between us that I couldn't explain. I'd never been overly interested in dating, considering the life I led, but something about this man drew me right in. His gaze when I met it told me he was thinking the same thing. The way he tipped his cheek into my hand told me he needed the touch of a woman as much as I needed the touch of a man. "Don't feel guilty, Gulliver," I whispered. "I'm enjoying my time here in Plentiful. Mojo and I have been seriously lacking in relaxation lately. While I like to relax, I also like to work or I get bored, so this situation is the perfect mix for me. I can keep my skills sharp and still have plenty of time to enjoy the lake."

A smile worked its way across his face to replace the frown. "If you're sure, but if you need to leave before we finish with the website, just say the word."

My brows knitted in anger and frustration. "I'm not the kind of girl who leaves her friends in a lurch, Gulliver. I said I'd help you get this issue straightened out, and I meant it."

He took my hand and squeezed it, but I noticed he didn't let go. "I'll take you at your word then, thank you. I'm glad I hired you because I like being your friend, a lot. It's been a long time since I've found someone I can let my guard down with and just be me. That said, I did hire you, and you're going to be working at the business, so we need to discuss your pay. Your initial fee was for one night of work. Where do we go from here?"

I bit my lower lip, worrying it around. I'd expected Gulliver to mention this, but I wasn't sure how to respond. I didn't want to offend him, but at the same time I didn't want to charge him either. Butterfly Junction needed help, and I had the skills to do the job quickly and effectively.

"Let me ask you a question," I said, and he nodded. "I read all the aspects of the business on the website, but what part of it provides your targeted income?"

"The business stays alive because we offer to restock butterfly populations, organize seminars for conservationists, and sell safe seeds to homeowners to plant butterfly gardens, to name a few things. The research stays alive because Mathias funds us along with a few grants here and there that I apply for."

"I see," I said before I took a drink from my glass. "What you're saying is the research-and-development portion is secondary to what you do? Or is it vice versa?"

He pointed at me, and I noticed the light dim in his eyes a bit. Research and development were not his true love. Butterflies were. I wondered if he did the research just to keep the rest of the business open. "The latter. As an entomologist, the most important thing we can do is develop safe pesticides. If we don't, all the bugs will be gone, and the waterways will be destroyed. If that happens, there's no need for the products I sell."

"I imagine that must be stressful. Especially when you want to go do other things, but you're tied to the office."

Gulliver tossed his head back in laughter. When he lowered

it again, his gaze held mine, and the honesty in his eyes made me want to caress the crinkles at the corners. I didn't, but I wanted to. I wanted to touch him so he knew someone cared. "Charity, breakfast out with you was the first thing I've done socially in over a year."

I hung my head in sadness. Sadness that I understood all the way to my soul. "I'm sorry, Gulliver. You must lead an incredibly solitary life. I'm lonely, but that's to be expected doing what I do." I cocked my head as I stared him down. "Do you hang out with Mathias? Do you have family?"

His gaze flitted back to the lake so that I couldn't read his face. "Mathias is a great guy, don't get me wrong, but we don't have a whole lot in common. I'm not the kind of guy who spends weekends on yachts and fancy parties. He is. He makes his money by hobnobbing with the rich and famous. As for my family, I see them occasionally. We don't go out of our way to get together except once a year for an extended family reunion. My brother and I get together quite a bit, since he only lives an hour away. Well, we used to, anyway," he paused, "before this formula took over my life. I've stayed away from him now with the understanding that I don't want to put him and his family in danger."

"I'm sure he understood," I said as I grasped his arm.

"He does. He will be here to celebrate with me when the formula is complete, because he's always here for the big things in my life. I guess it's a twin thing. My mom, not so much. She was a single woman raising twin boys and was overwhelmed. She has bipolar one disorder and often refuses to take her medication. It hasn't been easy, but I've had to cut ties with her just to find a little bit of peace in life."

"Hey, I can commiserate with you about family. Mine won't win any awards either."

"We still haven't discussed your wage," he said, flipping the conversation back to business.

I could tell talking about his family made him vulnerable and too open to someone he'd only met yesterday. I wasn't sorry for asking, though. I had so little time to get to know him that I couldn't wait forever to ask him the questions that might make him uncomfortable. I didn't know a lot about life, but I did know that waiting for the right time meant it would never come.

"I'm not charging you, Gulliver. You've already paid my fee. As far as I'm concerned, that covers the rest of the hours I'll put in to secure my future. If you find a way to save the bees and pollinators of the world, I'll be able to keep eating. If you provide a solution to the field runoff so I have safe drinking water, I'll be happy. As far as I'm concerned, that's payment enough."

He twisted toward me slowly as if what I'd said didn't compute. "Seriously?"

My nod was all he needed to see to know that I was dead serious.

"Most people don't understand the importance of what I do, nor do they care. I feel like you truly understand it," he whispered.

I grasped the hand that was resting on his lap. "I understand more than you might think, Gulliver. I understand how you feel alone and like no one cares, about the work that you do or you as a person. Here's the truth. What you do matters, but more than that, you matter. If I can use my skills to prove that to you, then that's all the payment I need."

When my last word died off, he twisted in his chair, encapsulated my pint-size frame against his, and rested his cheek on the top of my head. When he let out a breath, I felt it through my own chest. It was heavy. He'd been holding it for too many days, months, and years. That breath escaping into the morning air told me he'd found a soul who sang the same song as his, and he could finally exhale.

I inhaled the scent of the lake mixed with the vestiges of last night's campfires that filled the town. The scents, sounds, and sights were fresh and different in every tourist community. One thing Plentiful had going for it was the wonder of Mother Nature. She came alive every morning at five a.m., and I loved to catch a glimpse of her beauty before the day got too busy. I always took a few moments each morning to enjoy a bit of that beauty on my dock with a cup of coffee before I headed into town to write code and answer the phones at Butterfly Junction. I didn't see Gulliver much during the day, but I found myself waiting for those snippets of time when I did. He always said something to make me laugh or had a story to tell me about butterfly hunting in British Columbia. Sometimes we'd eat our lunch on the table behind the building and watch the lake in companionable silence.

Honey would be back tomorrow, but I wished I had another week alone. Once she returned, I'd have to find someplace else to work while we started the upgraded website. At least their server was no longer hackable. I knew this because I'd tried for three nights straight from three different computers, on four separate IP addresses, and hot spots to boot. No one was getting the secrets to the Butterfly Code, as I had taken to calling it now. A fortress protected it, and anyone who tried to get in would show me their hand in the process.

Gulliver was getting more worried with each passing day that the website stayed down. The uptick in phone calls had continued all week, which told me he had every right to be concerned. The breach was fixed now, and it was time to get the website going again. I would work on it diligently this week, but I'd also use my feminine wiles to convince Gulliver to come out to the campground and have a bit of fun. He was too focused on his work and tended to forget normal people didn't work sixteen hours a day. It was Sunday today, exactly a week since we'd sat on the balcony and shared a hug, and it should be a day of rest. The problem was, I couldn't rest. I couldn't stop thinking about him. His eyes were so open and honest. Every time I gazed into them, I saw the emotions he was feeling in the moment. When we were working, there was often frustration, anger, and something deeper. If I had to guess, I would say it was unhappiness.

When those expressive eyes were focused on me, the emotions were far easier to read. The gold glowed with curiosity while the hazel darkened with desire. Those colors melded into a dusty copper whenever he touched me, even just a simple brush of our hands. He thought he had an excellent poker face when it came to his emotions, but I was here to tell him he was wrong. I could plainly see that I wasn't alone in wondering if we could be more than friends.

I sighed and gazed up at the bright blue sky. Mojo and I had walked into town for breakfast, but I couldn't stop thinking about the man residing at 100 Industrial Road. I wanted to knock on his door and ask him to breakfast, but I was afraid he'd say he was too busy. "Lord, preserve me. I'm never this weird. I mean, I'm weird, but this place is making me downright strange."

"Oh, honey, downright strange is the best way to be," a voice said behind me.

I jumped and twirled while Mojo lumbered to his feet to bare his teeth at the woman. Lucy froze with her coffee cup in one hand and held her breath. "Mojo, chill," I scolded. He proceeded to flop back down on the sidewalk to lie in the sunshine. I pointed at him. "Sorry, you scared me, and he reacted."

She waved her hand, but her feet didn't budge from their spot on the sidewalk. "No, it was my fault. I should know better than to sneak up on people. I forgot all about Mojo being part of the picture. At least he does his job well."

I smiled and offered her a wink. "He sure does, but don't worry, he's all bark and no bite. Just don't tell the bad guys that."

"Wouldn't dream of it," she said on a chuckle. "I'm surprised to still see you in town. The last time we chatted you made it sound like you were just here for a few days."

Lucy started walking again up the sidewalk, and I followed, tugging Mojo along behind me.

"I was, but as often happens, I start doing the job they think they need, and it turns out they need help in other areas of their technology. That was the case with Butterfly Junction, so I agreed to stay on and finish the job for them."

"They're lucky you have the time," she said, following the sidewalk around the curve toward the diner. Come to think of it, I could go for some pancakes and sausage.

"It worked out since my next job doesn't start for a few months. I needed a break, so I welcome the time to stay in one place. It helps that Havens Diner has the best breakfast buffet around," I teased.

She chuckled and sipped from her to-go cup of coffee. "We have locally grown fresh strawberries for the pancakes this morning, if you're interested."

"Interested? I'm there," I said, rubbing my hands together until I glanced down at Mojo. "On second thought, that's not going to work. I was taking Mojo for a walk and didn't plan to stop anywhere. He can't come into the restaurant with me."

Lucy eyed Mojo's giant lumbering mass as he strode down the street. "Will he be okay away from you? We have an office in the back. We could sneak him in, and he could sleep. No one would be the wiser."

I glanced down at him and back to her. "If we throw a couple of sausage links in to sweeten the deal, he'll be all in."

Lucy grinned and motioned for me to walk around the back of the diner. "I can do better than that. I can make him a breakfast he'll never forget."

She held the door open for me, and I tugged Mojo through and right into the open door of the office at the end of the hallway. It was the perfect place for him. We got him settled, and then I followed her out into the busy diner. She promised to take him a plate of food while I loaded up mine. I glanced around for a place to sit, surprised when I noticed a lone figure at a table in the corner. Her head was down over her plate, but she wasn't eating. She was just staring at it.

"Honey?" I asked, stopping at the end of the table. "Is everything okay?"

She glanced up, and her face was swollen on the right side with a streak of tears running down each cheek. "Hi," she said, her voice monotone.

"Good morning. Mind if I sit?" I asked, motioning at an empty chair. She didn't react, so I slid my butt over the chair and set my plate down. "I haven't seen you in a few days. Are you ready to come back to work?"

"Sure, work, yeah." Her head nodded. "Mathias. Never answers. Didn't try Butterfly Junction."

Something was terribly wrong. She wasn't even making sense. "Are you sure you're okay?" I didn't want to make a scene until I knew what the problem was, so I'd give her a chance to answer.

"I'm not hungry," she said, her eyes focused on the plate. "My arm is sore. I can't cook."

"It can be overwhelming when you aren't feeling well or you're hurting. I understand. Why is your arm sore? What can I do to help?"

"I think I—I think I—" She swallowed and closed her eyes.

"Fell and it hurts."

"Honeybee?" a voice said, and we both looked up to see Mathias and Gulliver standing at the end of the table. It was Mathias who was speaking. He sat down and put his arm around her. "I was worried when I couldn't reach you. Where's your phone?"

Gulliver lowered himself to the chair next to me and laid his crutches down. He leaned over and whispered in my ear, "I was going to call and see if you wanted to get breakfast, but we've been searching for Honey for the last thirty minutes."

"My phone is upstairs," Honey answered.

"Something is wrong," I told Mathias when Honey laid her head on his shoulder. "I think her arm is broken. She said she fell."

Mathias shifted her so he could see her right arm. "Honey, what happened?" he asked, his eyes wide when he glanced up at me.

"I fell," she said, pushing her hair back to reveal a giant bruise on her right temple and down her cheek that she managed to keep hidden with her long hair. "I think I—I think I hurt it."

"Honeybee, why didn't you call me?" Mathias asked. The tone of his voice said he was scared as he pushed the hair back off her face and inspected the bruised, mottled skin.

"I didn't want to bother anyone. I think—I can see the bone. Should it be like that?"

I jumped up and ran to the kitchen, asking for a clean wet towel before I ran back to the table and went to Honey's right side. She had a towel wrapped around her arm that was full of blood. The blood had dripped down to her elbow and dried there, which meant this had happened at least an hour ago.

"Honey, we're going to remove the towel and take a look, okay?" I asked, but she didn't react. She kept her head on Mathias's shoulder like it was far too much effort to lift it up.

My gaze met his and he nodded, so I carefully removed the towel and bit back a gasp. Mathias wasn't as successful. A curse word fell from his lips that told me he knew how bad this was.

"Okay, Mathias, you need to get her to the emergency room. Can you do that safely or should I call an ambulance?"

I asked because all the blood had drained from his face as soon as he saw the jagged piece of bone that stuck out of her arm at a stomach-churning angle.

"First, I'm going to wrap her arm in this wet towel. That will protect the bone and the skin until you get her there."

I talked while I laid the towel over her arm, expecting her to react in agony, but she barely grimaced. She was in shock, and it was setting in hard. She needed medical attention.

"Mathias, we need to get her there now. Should I call an ambulance?"

He shook his head to clear it. "No, I'll take her. I can get her there faster than waiting for the ambulance."

Gulliver pointed at the door. "Go," he said. "I'll walk back to Butterfly Junction. Go."

"Call one of us if you need anything," I said, patting Honey's shoulder before he helped her up. "Don't worry about Butterfly Junction. I'll take care of the work at the reception desk tomorrow. Keep us posted."

Mathias mouthed *thank you* and then put his arm around Honey. He cradled her right arm and urged her toward the door.

Gulliver rubbed his forehead. "Holy crap, Charity. My heart won't stop pounding after seeing that bone sticking out. How is she even walking?"

"Shock," I said. "I hope it doesn't get infected. Compound fractures like that should be treated immediately."

"How do you know so much about compound fractures?"

he asked, his eyes still on the door to the diner.

"This," I said, holding my right elbow. "Remember?" I turned and grasped his wrist. "You know Honey is having surgery today, right?"

He nodded, his teeth grasping his lower lip. "Oh yeah, without a doubt. Mathias will take her to Duluth and make sure she gets the best care. I'm worried about her, but at the same time I'm not. Mathias has her under his wing. He'll call his parents, and they'll break every law necessary to get to the hospital."

"Why does Mathias call her 'honeybee'?" I asked curiously. "Like, I get that her name is Honey, so it's a cutesy thing, but it's the way he says it. Like how my dad used to call me 'Charity case' as a joke, but it wasn't a joke," I explained.

Gulliver's eyes widened. "You're kidding me, right?"

"Wish I was," I said, shaking my head. "He thought it was funny. Mathias doesn't call her 'honeybee' to be funny, though. When he says it, there's reverence in his tone."

Gulliver shook his head as he snatched a strawberry from my plate. "No, it's not a funny-joke type nickname. Apparently, that's what his family has called her since she was a child. Mathias started using it the last few months, and I had to ask him why because it was kind of out of left field. Anyway, how are you?" He looked around under the table. "Is Mojo with Laverne?"

"No, he's in Lucy's office chowing down on a plate of sausage and eggs. She ran into me on the sidewalk, and before I knew it, we were here and she was talking about fresh strawberry pancakes."

His laughter filled the diner with joy, even over the din of the other patrons. "Now that sounds like Lucy. Somehow I'm also not surprised Mojo wormed his way in the door and into a plate of eggs. Is that when you found Honey?"

I pointed at her empty seat. "She was just sitting there with her head hung over her plate. I knew something was wrong right away. She was saying odd things about not knowing where Mathias was all weekend." He grimaced and I cocked my head to the side. "What?"

"Mathias is known to disappear for days, not answer his phone, and leave her to deal with stuff. That wasn't the case this weekend, he was working with me at the business, but she was in a real state."

I nodded my agreement. "After seeing that bruise, she's probably got a concussion too. She's going to need a few more weeks off, is my guess. I'll keep working at the front desk until we know for sure. We'll just have to work on the website in the evenings." I wasn't sad about that. Working in the evenings meant I got to spend quiet time alone with him.

He grasped my hand and held it in his. "Thank you. Honey needs help, and Mathias will make sure she gets it."

I shook his hand in mine. "You're right, so there's no sense in worrying about it right now. Let's get you some breakfast. I hear the pancakes are to die for!"

"I like the way you think," he said, wearing a grin. "Then we can get the big dog from the office and head back to the campground. I could stand to relax for a few hours."

I rubbed my hands together and mirrored the smile on his face. I had other plans, but I'd tell him about those later. For now, he needed sustenance. "I like that idea. Let's get a plate of fresh food."

"It's a bit busy right now," he said after checking the line out. "I'll have to wait."

I knew how uncomfortable he was being in the mix with a lot of other people around him. He worried he would trip someone with his crutches, or someone would trip him. Not to mention, he couldn't carry a plate and use two crutches at the same time.

I jumped up and grasped his shoulder. "Trust me?"

"Of course," he said, and I held up my finger, trotting to the buffet with a smile on my lips and his laughter in my ears.

Chapter Five

"You're waddling," he teased as we left the diner and strolled down the street toward Butterfly Junction. Mojo waddled along next to me. I think we both ate too much. "You must be stuffed."

"Did you see how much I ate? I won't need lunch or supper. Man, I never want to leave this town. Everything is so plentiful," I joked.

Gulliver chuckled, but his eyes lit as if I had said the exact thing that he wanted to hear. "Do you think it's inappropriate for us to be hanging out when we aren't working?" he asked, his eyes focused straight ahead rather than on me.

"I don't see a problem with it. I'm not your employee and you're not my boss. I look at it as helping out a friend while taking some time to recharge. There's nothing wrong with that. What do you think? Did someone say something to you about us?"

"Mathias," he said on a sigh. "He said mixing business with pleasure is always a bad idea. I can see his point of view, but we're adults and can differentiate the two."

"Why am I not surprised? He comes off as incredibly standoffish with everyone but Honey."

"Honestly, that's just the Dane in him. Don't take it personally. He was raised by a father who was tough, and Mathias has had a lot to live up to. He's been spiraling out of control lately, though, and I'm worried that he's going to lose sight of what we're doing here. Honey has been his best friend for twenty years and even she can't rein him in. That's why I've been keeping him busy on the weekends. If he's with me, he's not out partying."

"It sounds to me like he shouldn't be judging anyone else then, Gulliver. You can't white glove someone else's house when your own is a pigsty."

Gulliver stared at me for the longest time and then finally bent over laughing, his shoulders shaking with complete and total amusement. When he stood back up, he was wiping tears from his eyes. "Now that's some solid life advice."

I punched him lightly in the arm, and considering my size, he probably didn't even feel it. "Come on, you've never heard that saying before?" I teased, throwing him a wink.

We started walking again while he shook his head. "Not once in my life, but I see your point. As for me, I don't think it's a problem for us to enjoy breakfast after working all night or a campfire under the stars after working all day. He's probably just jealous that the most beautiful woman in Plentiful wants to hang out with me and not him. He's always the one to get any girl he wants."

I got a warm sensation in my cheeks whenever he called me *beautiful*. I never considered myself beautiful in the traditional sense of the word. Not the way I grew up. I was always the little girl from next door who didn't wear any clothes and ate like a starving dog. Even later on, after my father died and I had people taking care of me, I didn't see myself as beautiful. To hear him use the word often in reference to me was new, but I also knew he wasn't using it flippantly. He really believed I was the most beautiful woman in Plentiful.

"Mathias might argue that Honey is the most beautiful woman," I said.

He waved his hand when we stopped at the door of the building. "They're just friends, Charity. Don't get the wrong idea."

My eyes rolled so far back in my head I was afraid they were going to get lost. "Sure, okay, whatever you say, but I have eyes. I know what I saw this morning. Are we going into the office?" I asked, pointing at the door to change the subject.

"Would you mind? I'll take you home after we're done."

"I don't mind at all. What do you need?" I asked as he unlocked the door. I realized it was only nine a.m., and I'd already done half a day's worth of activities. There was probably a nap in my future. Then again, maybe that was just the pancakes talking.

Once we were in the building, he locked the door again and motioned me toward his office. I pointed for Mojo to stay by Honey's desk, and he happily lowered his overstuffed body to the floor to sleep off his sausages and eggs.

Gulliver leaned on the edge of his desk. "A little breathing room from the big dog," he said on a sigh. "I'm always afraid of getting too close to you or startling you and having Mojo get excited and knock me over."

I stood just inside the doorway of his office rather than get too close to him. I was afraid I might do something I shouldn't, like throw my arms around his neck and kiss him. "He would never physically harm you unless you were hurting me. I see what you mean, though. He's big and could easily trip you up and knock you over. I didn't consider your needs when I insisted he come with me. If you'd rather, I can leave him with Laverne."

He shook his head with a smile on his face. I noticed every time he wore it, one grew on my face too. "No, I can't, and won't, ask you to ditch your protection detail. We'll make him a bed to hang out on, and he won't bother us."

"If you give him a bed, he won't bother anyone, like, all day."

Gulliver laughed, his tone rich and deep, unlike the way it was the first time we met. It was like he'd relaxed into the knowledge I wasn't going to judge him and he could just be himself. "I was wondering if you wanted to help me get the office set up for this week, but then I remembered that Honey isn't coming back now."

"She will be, though I could see her being out another week. Once they do the surgery and get it in a cast, she'll be fine to come back to work a little at a time," I said. "In the meantime, I'll just keep doing what I've been doing. We'll still need a desk in here for me to work at when we get going on the website regardless of whether Honey is here or not."

"Good point," he agreed, nodding. "Your desk will have to be close to me since you'll have constant questions about the website, I'm sure."

I raised one brow in indignation. "Are you questioning my ability to write sensical information about bugs?" He raised both brows in response, and I broke into a fit of giggles. "You're right. What I know about bugs involves how to get them off the bottom of my shoe." I gasped and slapped my hand over my mouth. "Sorry," I croaked from behind it.

He laughed and waved it away. "Don't worry. I'm not so naive that I think people rescue flies and put them outside to live another day. I do request you save the honeybees and the butterflies, though."

I made the cross-my-heart sign. "Done. Now, what do you want me to do?"

He pointed at a desk against the wall. "That desk will be yours until we're done with the site. When it's time to work, you can set up one of your fancy-dancy computers, and we can rock and roll."

"Fancy-dancy computers, you say?" I laughed because he wasn't wrong. My computers weren't something the average person was going to understand how to use. "I like the L-shape setup. Since you're going to have to show me things constantly, it keeps me from having to get up every time. As long as it won't cramp your style to have me so close."

"You don't cramp my style, Charity, not even a little bit. I like being with you," he promised as I approached his desk. His hand snaked toward me, but he stopped it at the last moment before he touched my hand.

I didn't let his fall back to the desk before I grabbed it and held on tight. "I like being with you too. You make me laugh, and I genuinely can't wait to spend time with you. I'd like to do more things outside the office together. I mean, if you'd like to," I lamely added when I realized I'd just asked him out on a date.

His free hand slipped up along the side of my face, and his thumb ran across my cheekbone. "I'd like to spend more time with you, but I don't want to hold you back."

I tipped my head into his hand, the warmth of his skin grounding me and exciting me at the same time. When he touched me, my skin came alive with little zaps of pleasure that traveled through every part of me. "Hold me back? What do you mean?"

"Physically," he answered. Anxiety, fear, sadness, and pain rolled across the movie screen of his eyes, but the only thing that stayed was pain. "I don't want you to hang out with me because you feel sorry for me."

I swung my head from side to side. "I have no reason to feel sorry for you, Gulliver. My God, you're far more successful than I could ever be, not to mention smart, funny, cute, and a great conversationalist. I want to spend more time with you for those reasons and nothing else."

He blinked several times, and finally a smile curved his lips.

"No one has ever said I'm cute before," he said on a breath. "I like being cute."

"Keep it up, and I'll rescind the cute part of the sentence," I said, poking him in the ribs.

He let out a bark of laughter and bent over to protect his side. When he ducked his head, our eyes met, and he leaned in, his lips seeking mine in a hesitant kiss. I relaxed into him slightly to tell him I wanted this as much as he did. He kept the kiss light, but the unexpected emotion that filled me was heavy. Headiness, anticipation, joy. All those emotions soared inside me to have his lips on mine. Warmth spread through me, and I wanted more. In that moment I wanted it all. His warm hands tenderly gripped my waist, and the warmth of his kiss spread lower now, pooling in places long forgotten after years alone on the road. God, how wonderful it felt to connect with someone like this again. His tongue traced the lines of my lips, and I moaned low in my throat.

Correction. The word I was looking for was *finally*. It felt wonderful to connect with someone like this finally.

The electricity that bounced between us was in shared commonality of our differences. I wanted him and he wanted me, which meant none of them mattered. The sound I made low in my throat then was plaintive, but it acknowledged the desire coursing through the both of us as though we were one.

He let the kiss end naturally, but never drew his gaze away. What reflected back at me was wonderment at such a beautiful moment shared between us. There was also a tinge of fear. Had he crossed a line he shouldn't have? Uncertainty about the way I was going to react. I squeezed his hand I was still holding and offered up a smile. "The kiss was unexpected and wonderful," I whispered.

The sigh he released had his chin lowering to his chest. "I was worried I shouldn't have done it about halfway through."

"I could tell," I said, tipping his chin up. "I wouldn't have allowed it if I didn't want you to kiss me. We've been building up to the kiss since we met, and I'm glad we shared it. It was short but sweet and told me I want to get to know you better."

"I'd like the same, Charity. Maybe we could start today? We could go for a drive or share a campfire by Myrtle?"

I tapped his chest with my finger. "I was thinking of something a lot more fun. I saw Laverne this morning, and she offered to let us borrow the campground's boat. She knows I've been dying to see the island!"

"The island? Which one? There are twenty-one of them," he said, his laughter teasing.

"Laverne said something about Oak Island?"

He nodded once and grasped my slight shoulder in his hand. "Oak Island is the perfect choice. There's a nice place to tie up the boat, and Mojo will love all the new smells. With any luck, we'll even see a butterfly or two."

I gave him a fist bump and a grin because I was all about new adventures, especially if he was part of them.

"Do you need a boost in?" Gulliver asked, motioning to his truck. It sat at about the same height as my motor home but didn't have a step to help me get in.

"Sure, if you could," I agreed. Gulliver's crutches fell to the ground, and I propped my left leg on the edge of the door. He boosted me in, leaving tingles of anticipation along my thigh, which made me look forward to the next time I'd need a boost up into this gorgeous truck by this gorgeous man. Once I was inside, he shut the door, grabbed his crutches, and cruised around to his side. I buckled in while little tingles of happiness zipped through my body to be spending the day with him. "You never said you drove a fully restored 1959 Dodge pickup truck," I said, rubbing the gleaming wood dash.

A smile tipped his lips as he buckled his seat belt. "You have to let a dude have a little bit of mystery about him, Miss Puck. Besides, most women aren't interested in old trucks."

"Most women don't drive around the country in a 1964 Dodge motor home," I volleyed.

"How did you come by old Myrtle?" he asked, his body twisted toward me.

I raised a brow, surprised by his question. "It's a funny story. It was a surfer dude's gnarly haven. He'd redone the interior in the nautical theme and used it to drive from beach to beach with his boards on the top."

"So how did you get it?"

I laughed and buried my hand in my hair. "Like, dude, he needed money for the dudette he knocked up while being a gnarly surfer dude. I was backpacking through California at the time and hated every minute of it. When I happened upon the motor home for sale, I counted out the cash into his hand and never looked back. That was six years ago now, and she just keeps humming along."

"You've certainly lived an interesting life to date, Charity," he said, laughter filling his voice. "As for this truck, it wasn't nearly as exciting. I picked it up at an auction shortly after I graduated college. It was being repossessed, so I got it for a song."

I ran my hand across the red and white leather bench seat. "You've taken good care of it. Sitting in it lets me create childhood memories in my mind."

"Come again?" he asked, his brows knitting in the most adorable way.

I stared out the window rather than make eye contact with him. The whole idea was a bit ridiculous, but now I had to answer him. "It's the kind of truck I picture my grandpa would have driven back in the day, if I had a grandpa. He would have picked me up and taken me for ice cream or down to the pond to fish. He'd throw his old dog, Barney, in the back, and we'd drive down to the five-and-dime or the feedstore."

He rubbed my arm for a moment before his hand fell to the seat. "I'm sorry you have to make up a wonderful childhood rather than have real memories of it. You can feature my truck in them as much as you'd like, as long as you share your creative stories with me."

I leaned against the door to take the pressure off my overfull tummy while he started the truck and headed toward the campground. Mojo sat on the floor of the truck and peered up at me with great confusion. I rubbed his big head to soothe myself as well as him.

"You've made a few references to your family. Was it really that bad?"

A sarcastic chuckle left my lips. "Well, let's see. My mother decided to *find herself* when she was twenty-five, which left five-year-old me with my dad, who was the ripe old age of fifty-five. I'm pretty sure when the newness of the older man–younger woman thing wore off, she changed her mind about the feasibility of a long-term relationship with him. Who wants to be tied down to a guy who had more hair on his legs than his head and wore his belt around his nipples? My dad subsisted on a military pension, which he drank away every month. We lived in an old run-down apartment building where we sometimes had hot water, but we always had mice and roaches. If it weren't for the neighbors, I probably wouldn't have survived my childhood. They fed me and gave me their kids' hand-me-down clothes and shoes. Obviously, my father never won Father of the Year."

"Wow," he said as he turned onto the road leading to the campground. "I didn't have a father and my childhood was kind of crappy, but you win the prize for the crappiest without contest." He pulled the truck into a spot in front of the motor home and killed the engine.

"Thanks, I think?" I asked on half a laugh. I unbuckled my seat belt, and Mojo whined low in his throat until I opened the door and he hopped down.

"Do I get to see the inside of the infamous Myrtle the Turtle?"

I peeked over at the motor home and bit my lip, worried he'd struggle to get up the steps. "You're welcome to come in and meet Myrtle. Just be careful."

I never should have doubted his abilities. He was up the two steps and into the motor home before I finished securing the door open. When I walked in, he was gazing around the space appreciatively. "This is cool. I don't even need the crutches. It's small enough I can hold on to the counters."

I grinned as I leaned on the wall in my bedroom. "I was living the tiny-home life long before it was cool."

He eyed the dorm fridge, three-burner stove, and bucket-sized stainless steel sink before he spoke. "Maybe, but I think it's perfect for you. Everything is Charity sized."

I chuckled as he lowered himself to the red Naugahyde couch. "You're not wrong there," I agreed as I ducked into my bedroom. He had informed me I needed my hat, hiking boots, sunscreen, and a rain parka because on Lake Superior it could decide to rain in the blink of an eye. He wasn't kidding either. I'd already experienced the change-on-a-dime weather in the short time I'd been here. Sunny one minute, raining the next, and then sunny again. It was like Mother Nature was suffering some severe mental distress.

"You should put her on the ferry over to Madeline Island. People take RVs over there all the time and camp out for a weekend. There are tons of little shops, great restaurants, and neat places to hike. If you haven't been there, you shouldn't leave the area until you go," he informed me from where he sat.

"I'll add it to my bucket list. I'm searching for more fun in my life, and that sounds like a blast. I'm glad you don't mind doing these things with me. I know you've probably done them one hundred times already. It's always nicer to have a buddy to share in the experience, though."

I stopped speaking long enough to yank my shirt over my head when he muttered something I couldn't quite make out. It sounded like, *Great, now I'm a buddy*, but I couldn't be sure.

Gulliver cleared his throat. "After we finish the website, we'll go over for a weekend. We'll make it our reward for a job well done."

I opened the accordion door from my bedroom and fastened it to the wall. "I think you need it as much as I do," I said, standing in front of him. Even sitting, he had to look down at me, which was something I was used to. "For the record, I don't think of you as a buddy. I think of you as a friend who could be more. Someone I enjoy spending time with and who I'm attracted to, both physically and intellectually. I can't define it more than that right now."

"Understood," he said, taking my hands. "And for the record, I feel the same. Also, for the record, you're awfully darn cute in your little outfit," he said, tugging on my khaki hiking shorts.

I did a curtsy at his compliment. "Thank you, thank you," I joked, grabbing a sun hat from the closet. "I'm packing a pair of pants in my sleeping bag in case it gets cool."

"Sleeping bag?" he asked, one brow up in the air.

I held up the blue bag rolled tightly and tied with a black string. "Mojo will want to sleep on something soft in the boat. He's not an adventurous kind of guy."

Gulliver threw his hand to his chest in mock surprise. "I'm shocked by this. We could leave him with Laverne. She never minds keeping him."

I gathered my raincoat and draped it over the sleeping bag on the small dinette. "She offered, but Mojo loves to explore new places, and he needs the exercise. He won't be any trouble."

Gulliver sat patiently while I jammed everything in a bag to take with us. "True, and he will keep the bears from getting too curious about us as well."

I spun on my heel with my heart pounding. "Bears? You're kidding me, right? It's an island."

"Fun fact. Bears love to swim because they love to fish. There are black bears all over the Apostle Islands."

I threw up my hands in frustration. "Forget it. I'm not going." I plunked down on the dinette while he laughed, falling to the side of the couch, his whole body shaking. As much as I wanted to be mad at him for laughing at me, he was too cute. When he sat up, there was a smile on his lips, and his eyes were shining bright, the green and brown vying for dominance in the sunshine reflected in them. "What's so funny?" I huffed.

"Dear, sweet—"

I waved my hand around. "Yeah, yeah, I know, dear, sweet, naive Charity."

Gulliver struggled to hold in his laughter again while he tried to compose himself. "All I'm saying is, if you think you're safe from bears in this campground, you're delusional. We're in the middle of Northern Wisconsin. There are bears everywhere."

"We shouldn't go, Gulliver," I said, gripping his shirt. "What if we run into a grizzly?"

He grasped my hand and removed it from his shirt, holding it lightly in his. "We don't have grizzly bears here. Only black bears live in Northern Wisconsin and Minnesota. Remember, they're more scared of us than we are of them. We'll be safe today. We aren't camping, and we'll leave the cooler on the boat. Also, Mojo will be with us, and bears are afraid of dogs. Not to mention it's a beautiful, warm summer day in June. There will be plenty of people on the islands, and bears won't come around."

"If you're sure. I'm a chicken, but I'm also the size of one and a bear could eat me for lunch in one bite."

He tickled my side gently. "Nah, you're far too grizzled for them to pick you for lunch."

I shoved him in the shoulder as he laughed until I couldn't help but join him. Finally, he held up his hands. "I'm kidding. If I were a black bear, I'd pick you to eat first."

The innuendo was there, and I could hear the heat in his voice. After our kiss at Butterfly Junction, he wanted more than a stolen kiss in his office from me. The question I asked myself as we walked down to the dock to load the boat was if it was fair to keep spending time with him when I knew I couldn't stay.

I excelled at two things in life: hacking and fearing commitment.

So far, I was two for two with Gulliver Winsome.

Chapter Six

Laverne's boat was bigger than I expected it to be, considering the way she described it. It was a twenty-foot Boston Whaler with a gigantic one-hundred-and-fifty horsepower motor on the back. The canopy over us blocked the sun, and the boat rode over the waves of Lake Superior with no problems. It was a beautiful day to be out boating, especially with someone who enjoyed nature the way Gulliver did.

"We better get back to the campground," Gulliver said, helping me over the side of the boat and to a chair. "It would be nice to get there before dark. I was hoping we could have a campfire by Myrtle."

"I even have hot dogs!" I exclaimed, and Mojo's ears perked up.

Gulliver chuckled as he untied the boat and started the motor. "I suggested it because I happened to hear from a little bird named Laverne that the aurora borealis are predicted to be visible tonight."

I spun toward him with my mouth open. "Seriously? The northern lights? Tonight?"

He nodded as he backed the boat away from the dock and headed for open water. "Laverne said they'd be a three tonight, which is bottom of the barrel in vibrancy for this area, but they'll still put on a show. If you haven't seen them, you don't want to miss the chance."

I clapped with my hands near my chin. "I haven't! It's the last item on my bucket list. I'm so in! I'll drink twenty cups of coffee to stay awake if I have to!"

Gulliver's laughter could be heard over the motor as he pushed the throttle forward. "Darling, I think twenty cups of coffee would fill you from head to toe."

The motor was too loud now for conversation, so I sat back against the seat and watched the scenery go by. We'd spent the afternoon on Oak Island hiking, staring out over the water, and talking. Gulliver's prediction that there would be a lot of visitors on the island was accurate, but I took notice of none of them. As we talked, laughed, searched for butterflies, and tossed sticks for Mojo, we were the only two who existed on the island as far as I was concerned. I was sad when it was time to leave, but it was smart to get back to shore before dark. Being on Lake Superior in a small boat in the dark was more than dangerous. It was suicide. If the waves picked up on the big lake, they'd sink this boat faster than they sank the *Edmund Fitzgerald*.

He slowed the boat down near the shore of a small island and pointed forward with his finger. "You see the rock there?" he asked. It was a little hard to miss the golden monolith off the shore. It was stacked on top of several other tall boulders. "They call it Lookout Point."

The sun was setting around it, making the rocks glow like a shiny gold coin. "It's beautiful. How would you get up there, though?"

His laughter floated across the water like a wave of sunshine even as the sun set. "It used to be connected to the island," he explained, motioning at the pile of rocks between the point and the other side of the island. "The lake wore a keyhole through it until it collapsed."

"I bet things change on this lake almost every ti—"

The engine made a hiss and a *pop*, and the boat jerked suddenly. When smoke billowed out from under the black motor cover, Gulliver flew into action, turned the key off, and grabbed a fire extinguisher. Before he could say anything, flames shot from the motor, and the smell of burning plastic filled our nostrils. He unloaded the fire extinguisher onto the motor, the stream of powder putting the flames out immediately, but he gave it a couple of extra shots while I steadied him with my hands on his waist.

"What happened?" I asked, my voice trembling and my heart pounding. "Why on earth did it just erupt into flames."

Gulliver set the fire extinguisher down and wiped his hand across his forehead. "Major motor failure, apparently. We're not going anywhere without a tow." He grabbed a towel from the chair and wiped off the top of the motor, then used the towel to work the motor cover off to the side. It didn't come off as much as it just melted off and onto the deck. "Hard to tell what's wrong with it now that it was on fire. Looks like all the electronics are fried for sure. Also, where is the oil cap?" he asked, pointing at the hole on the motor.

"I have no idea, but we have to make a decision here, Gulliver," I said, my head tipping toward the setting sun. The moon was rising already, and now we were stuck in the middle of the lake. "What are we going to do? It's not safe to be out here in the dark."

Gulliver spun around carefully and took my shoulders in his hands. "We're going to throw the trolling motor in the water and get ourselves to shore. We're not so far out from Hermit Island that we can't beach the boat there and wait for help. The area around this island is filled with brownstone from the quarry that used to be here, so we have to be careful. We can't risk putting a hole in the hull of the boat."

I lowered myself to the seat and grabbed hold of Mojo so he didn't make any sudden moves. "What do we do when we get to shore?"

After Gulliver hooked up the trolling motor and dropped it into the water to counteract the wind, he answered. "The first thing we do is see if we can get a signal out here and call Laverne."

"What if we can't get a signal?" I asked, working my phone from my pocket with one hand while my other held on to Mojo.

"We'll make a pan-pan call, but I'd rather get help from Laverne if we can," he said.

"What's a pan-pan call?" I asked with curiosity. "I've never been boating before."

"It's like a mayday call but less urgent," he explained while he patiently steered us toward shore. "It would alert anyone in the area that we're in trouble and need help. I don't want to do that unless we have to, and not until daylight. This area is too rocky to approach in the dark for a boat any bigger than the one we are in."

I checked my phone and frowned. "Nothing. No bars." I sighed, figuring it would be way too easy to have cell coverage in the middle of Lake Superior.

"We'll try again once we're safely on shore," he said tightly, his body rigid as he concentrated on the job at hand.

We'd be okay. It was summer, and with a good fire, Mojo by our sides, and a cooler full of food and water, we were doing nothing more than camping out under the stars. The getting-stranded part didn't bother me as much as the getting-stranded-with-him part did. I've never enjoyed spending time with someone the way I enjoyed it with Gulliver. Spending an entire night with him in such an intimate setting might cause feelings to lodge even deeper in places they shouldn't. He was ensconced in Plentiful with a business, friends, and a reason to stay.

I only had one certainty in life right now, and that was my dream job waiting for me a few states away. I wasn't ensconced in Plentiful and only had one reason to stay. Gulliver. He was uncharted waters. He was everything I'd avoided the last six years. Stability. Companionship. Roots.

No. This was never going to work.

"Grab the paddle. Another few hundred feet and I'll have to pull this motor up too. There are too many rocks. We'll use the paddle to get us up onto the sand. Beaching the boat onshore will give us shelter if it rains."

"Why can't we just leave it anchored in the water?" I asked, working at getting the paddle out of the holder on the side of the boat.

"If a strong gale comes up, the boat will bang against the rocks on the bottom until there's a hole," he explained patiently.

I sighed and held the paddle up. "I get it, but I'm not sure I can do anything with this. It's bigger than I am."

Gulliver snorted with laughter and locked the now dripping trolling motor up on the side of the boat. "I'm going to do it, and you're going to steady me," he explained. Once he was in position next to the driver's seat, I grasped his waist, and he paddled the huge boat closer to shore. He had a trajectory in mind, and I didn't say a word to keep from breaking his concentration. The water was clear as we neared the shore, and you could see several large rocks we would have to avoid or they would take out the entire bottom of the boat. He used the paddle to brace against the flat rocks on the bottom to avoid the sharp, jagged ones surrounding us. He managed to slip the boat between the dangerous rocks and shove the front half up on the shore.

"We're going to throw the anchor line into the brush," he

said, pointing straight ahead into the fading light. "Just an extra precaution in case the wind does pick up tonight."

"Let's check and make sure the motor isn't smoldering before we leave the boat," I suggested, pointing to the back.

Gulliver grabbed a flashlight, and we both walked to the back where he shone the light over the engine. "It's still odd that the oil cap is missing. I don't think Laverne would send us out here if the motor wasn't running properly. Besides, it ran fine all the way to the island." He dropped the flashlight to his side and turned to me. "There's nothing we can do to fix it now, I guess. We need to get set up for the night and try to reach someone to tow us out in the morning. Chances are, if we can't reach Laverne and she notices we aren't back, she'll send out a search party."

I nodded once and leaned over the edge of the boat to inspect the terrain. "This isn't good, Gulliver. Now I see why Laverne told me to avoid the smaller islands. She said it would be too difficult for you to navigate them without a dock. I'm not sure how I'm going to get onto the sand either," I fretted.

"I'm not incapable, Charity!" he exclaimed, throwing his hands up. "It might appear I am, but I can manage to get us in and out of a damn boat without dying. Laverne worries too much, and so do you," he said, slamming the bench down on the back of the boat. He'd yanked out a couple of bundles from inside it and rolled them toward the front of the boat. In his anger, he flipped on all the lights, then tossed everything onto the sand. After everything was safely on land but us, he stood up and brushed off his hands.

"Can Mojo swim?" Gulliver asked, his tone short and clipped. "I'm assuming you can't lift him."

I laughed sarcastically. "He weighs more than I do, Gulliver, but yes, he can swim."

He pointed to the back of the boat. "I'm going to put him in the water and get him to swim to shore once you're waiting on the beach. It's the only way."

I nodded my agreement, since I didn't want to say or do anything more to upset him. We were both stressed, but I was hurt that he thought I considered him unable to take care of us. I wasn't questioning his abilities. I was questioning the intelligence of getting off the boat.

After he dropped a rope ladder down the side of the boat, I climbed down, jumped onto the sand, and called up to him. "I'm good!"

He gave me a thumbs-up then lowered Mojo into the water. I whistled and called his name. He doggy paddled around the side until he got his feet on the rocks; then he ran through the water, and I took three steps back as soon as he hit the sand. If I didn't, I'd be the one wet when he finished shaking the water off. The water sprayed through the air the way a sprinkler does on a hot, sunny afternoon, and I couldn't stop laughing at him.

I glanced up, and Gulliver was leaning over the boat. "I'm going to hand you my crutches, toss my shoes over, and take the same route as Mojo did. I can't climb, but I can swim."

I didn't say anything even though I was scared to death. If he fell or got hurt, I was never going to forgive myself for coming up with the idea of visiting the islands.

In less than thirty seconds, he joined me onshore. "Wow, a swim in Lake Superior is always refreshing," he joked. He sat on the rocks in the shallow water and crab-walked with one leg to shore. "Grab me a towel and my shoes, or I can't get up. Towels are in the blue one," he said, pointing at a blue plastic tote.

I unsnapped the buckle and unrolled a beach towel, running back to him on the shore with the towel and shoes. Once he had zipped the bottom of his wet pants off, leaving him in shorts, he stood and took his crutches from me. "Thanks. Now, we only have a little time to make camp, and you're going to have to do most of it.

Are you up for it?" he asked, one brow lowered.

I nodded once. We were in this mess because of me, and I'd do anything to make sure Gulliver still liked me when this was all said and done.

Chapter Seven

Gulliver was able to get a signal on his phone, and he called Laverne, letting her know the motor was fried and that we needed a rescue. She wanted to send someone immediately, but Gulliver insisted we were fine and it could wait until morning.

We were fine, truthfully. It wasn't going to rain, the weather was warm, we had food and water, and a beautiful fire was blazing on the beach. I didn't wander too far into the woods to look for kindling and logs for the fire, though. The way our day was going, I would meet a bear.

I heard a snap behind us and I jumped, but Gulliver pulled me in close to him and rubbed my back. "You're okay. It was just Mojo."

I lingered in his arms because he always made me feel safe. That was a disturbing fact for someone like me. I was used to being alone, right? Maybe I was, but that didn't mean I didn't yearn for the touch of a man. I did, I just didn't realize how much until I met Gulliver.

I sat up and straightened my shirt, hating that I was so jumpy in such a beautiful location, but rarely did I camp out where wild animals could eat me in one bite. Namely bears.

"How did you know this little strip of sand was here?" I asked, relaxing against a long piece of driftwood I'd found on the edge of the beach. After dragging it over, we buried our butts in the warm sand and stretched our legs out toward the fire. It was spookily comfortable yet disturbingly creepy. It was nearly ten p.m., dark other than a slight sliver of the moon in the sky, and there wasn't another soul around.

"I've been to this island before with my kayak," he explained. "I paddled around the whole island and happened to stop in this very place a few years ago. I've been trying to do some recon work here, but the foliage is too thick to get through. The island hasn't seen life for a long time. At least not human life."

"I had no idea anyone once lived here. It's a beautiful place but ridiculously remote. What must it have been like to live here in the middle of a winter storm? The only word that comes to mind is 'brutal.'"

"I can't even imagine," he agreed. "I bet you never dreamed you'd end up on a deserted island your first trip out on the lake." He shook his head as he stared up at the stars.

"I'm not on a deserted island. You're with me," I said, bumping him in the shoulder.

Gulliver laughed at himself and gave me the palms up. "No one can say I don't know how to show a woman a good time."

We sat in companionable silence again, listening to the water lap on the shore and the owls hoot while hidden off somewhere in a tree. "Why do you have Laverne's number?"

Gulliver laughed and threw the last of the stick he was fiddling with into the fire. "Everyone has Laverne's cell number. She's the clerk of courts and the treasurer. In small towns like Plentiful, everyone does more than one job."

"Ahhh." I laughed, mostly at myself. "It never crossed my mind that Laverne did anything else in the community. That leads me to my next question," I said, pausing.

"What other things do I do?" he asked, and I nodded. "I'm the science curriculum director for the school district."

My mouth hung open until he closed it with his finger.

"Sounds strange, I know. You could probably say I'm more of a collaborator. I work with them on what the students should be learning, and they take that information and write or buy the curriculum. It's fun, and something different than what I do on a day-to-day basis. I always enjoy being part of what the next generation is taught."

"In my world of big cities, that doesn't happen."

"What big city are you from?" he asked, his eyebrow raised. "You said you were from Michigan."

I drew a heart in the sand but immediately ran my hand through it to erase it. "I'm from outside of Flint. I lived there until I was fourteen."

"What happened at fourteen?"

"My dad, who was sixty-four, died of liver failure. They shipped me off to live with my mom. The problem was, I hadn't seen her since she left when I was five. She was even less interested in being my mom at fourteen."

"Damn, what did you do?" he asked. The way his gaze held mine told me he was genuinely interested in my story.

I laughed sardonically. "I did what every bitter, self-educated, angry teenager does."

"Run away? Get in trouble?"

"Get even," I answered immediately. "Sometimes the truth hurts when you have to say it out loud." I wiggled my shoulders uncomfortably while I worked out what else I wanted to say.

Gulliver sat patiently waiting, as if he understood this was difficult at best. "I wanted to be an emancipated minor, but I had no way to support myself and no education. My dad claimed I was being homeschooled, but he did absolutely nothing to teach me anything other than how to lift a bottle to your lips. When I arrived at my mom's house, she had a new husband, and he wanted nothing to do with me either. There was no way I was living with her."

Gulliver rubbed my arm rhythmically for comfort, but when he touched me, he raised goose bumps of desire on my skin. "I'm sorry, Charity. My family is messed up, but at least my brother and I are still close."

I stared into the fire, remembering back to those days when everything in my life was so uncertain. I had lived my childhood hidden away in an apartment with little outside contact other than the neighbors, so every new experience was terrifying. "There was no love in my family. I was an inconvenience from the day I was born, and I had to figure out on my own how to make it in a world with the deck stacked against me in multiple different ways."

"So you got a degree and took off for parts unknown?" he asked, trying to fill in the blanks.

I giggled and leaned back against the log again. "No, I hacked into my stepdaddy's bank account and stole a couple thousand dollars. I did the same thing to my mom's account and several other people she worked with at her business. I took six thousand in total." I held up my hand before he could say anything. "In my defense, I put it in a new account so they could have it back. I didn't do it for the money."

"What did you want then? And how did you learn how to hack?"

"One question at a time," I teased.

Gulliver opened the cooler and grabbed a beer, handing me one. "We might as well enjoy these. We aren't going anywhere tonight."

I cracked mine open and took a long swallow. Considering I was about to purge all my demons to someone for the first time since I'd left therapy a decade ago, and allow him to judge me for them, the alcohol would be a welcome addition to the mix. I buried the bottle in the sand so it didn't tip and let the warm granules run through my fingers. I wanted to tell the story in a way that helped him understand the circumstances behind the desperate plan I'd hatched. If he could understand why I did what I did, he might not judge me as harshly. I had no idea why it mattered so much to me that he didn't judge me, but it did. A lot.

"I wanted out of her house but running away didn't work. They just dragged me back each time. Getting in trouble with the courts meant I got a new home."

Gulliver lowered his bottle from his lips. "Yeah, a new home in juvie."

"Ding-ding." I sipped the beer again for liquid courage. "At least in juvie, I got three squares, a bed, and a chance at an education."

Those amber orbs revealed the exact second when the lightbulb lit. His lips formed an O before he spoke. "Your basic living needs were finally met. That never crossed my mind."

"Why would it? It doesn't make sense unless you were in the same situation. I'd never had three meals a day and a bed of my own. I'd never been to school or even had decent clothes to wear. I was in heaven, even if I was technically incarcerated. My first day of juvie was on my fifteenth birthday, and by the time I was released at eighteen, I had my GED and was old enough to be on my own. I had productively honed my hacking skills, as my instructor put it. Which meant I learned the difference between a black hat and a white hat and why it was important not to cross the line between them. I planned to set out and find a job working for a company, and I tried, but it never worked out. I was never the right fit, or the job was only temporary. I moved around a lot in the first three years after juvie to find work. Then I bought Myrtle, and I built the business from just enough jobs to keep gas in the tank to more jobs than I can accept."

"I'm impressed, Charity," he whispered. "Not many people would take what you started with and make it work for them."

I leaned back against the log and stretched my legs out. "I never wanted to use my hacking skills for evil, Gulliver. I'm not an evil kind of person. I was a desperate kid in a desperate situation."

He grasped my right arm and cradled my elbow in one hand while he rubbed my forearm up and down, as if he were trying to comfort both of us. "I still don't know how you learned to hack if you never went to school or used a computer."

"Dad was passed out drunk half the time, so once I was old enough, I went to the library and studied videos on YouTube. Tutorials, actually, on how to hack other people's computers. I had dreams of becoming a professional, but first I had to learn how to read better. My next-door neighbor had taught me the basics of how to read and write, but Dad wouldn't allow her to send me to school with her kids. He was afraid social services would take me away, and he would lose my benefits."

"He wasn't a father," Gulliver said. "He wasn't even a caretaker."

"How right you are. As I said, I lucked out with my neighbor. I spent a lot of time there learning how to be a normal kid. She taught me proper hygiene, how to eat without acting like a starved animal, and how to socialize properly. Since I spent so much time in the library, the librarian started recommending reading material for me. If I wasn't on the computer, I was reading a book about coding. After a year, I had absorbed so much information I wanted to put it to work, but I didn't have a computer. The librarian took pity on me and offered me one they were replacing for the price of organizing old books and preparing them for sale, washing bookshelves, and other odd little jobs. I was happy to do them, considering it kept me out of the apartment and earned me a computer to boot. The first thing I learned how to do was hack into someone else's internet so I could use it at home. Looking back, I can see that if I'd been left with no one but my father, I wouldn't be here. If it weren't for all the people on the periphery of my life, I'd be dead somewhere or wishing I were."

He put his arm around me in silent comfort. "I'm sorry. It's not right for people to have kids and not take care of them. It aggravates me to no end."

I eyed his legs, noticing they both bowed out since he didn't have his heavy shoe on the left one or the brace on the right. I had never seen his bare legs, but he had zipped off the pants portion after they got wet. He had his legs stretched out and relaxed, and you noticed the issues immediately.

Gulliver sighed as his gaze followed mine to his battered legs. "My mom took care of us the best she could. She tried, but she didn't have a lot of resources. My health condition is a direct result of poverty," he explained. "I was a normal kid growing up until I was seven and busted my left femur trying to jump over a log. Don't ask me how it happened, I don't remember the incident, but I broke the growth plate."

"Oh boy," I said as I tossed another log on the fire to keep it going and to ward off visitors from the woods. Sparks flew up into the night, and it reminded me of the Fourth of July when fireworks light up the sky. "Now I understand why your left leg is shorter than your right."

"It is. It never grew again, and while they tried several surgeries to lengthen it," he explained, holding up his shorts to show me pinhole scars covering the leg, "nothing worked. I got infections, and the infections caused even more damage to the bones. We didn't have indoor plumbing or much hygiene in our home then, if you could even call it a home. My healthcare was free, but after the second infection, the doctors deemed it time to stop before I lost the leg or my life. I was fitted with a shoe lift, and they just kept increasing the height of the lift as the other leg grew."

"I hate to say I'm sorry, so I won't. I will say I wish like hell you didn't have to go through it then, and now," I whispered, slipping my hand into his.

"You know, as a kid it didn't cross my mind that I was different except for when they were doing surgeries and attempting to lengthen the bone. I was in constant pain then, so it was a relief once it healed from the final surgery and infection. It didn't hurt anymore, and for a few years all was well, even wearing the lift. I could run, chase my brother, ride a bike, and just be a kid."

"If it's okay to ask, what happened to the right leg then? You mentioned rickets to me initially."

He patted the knee on the right and gave me a grim smile. "Rickets is an easy explanation, but not the truth. Have you ever heard of Blount's disease?"

I shook my head but held tight to his hand. "Never. Another childhood thing?"

"It can be," he agreed, finishing his beer and putting the bottle back in the cooler. "In my case, I didn't get it in infancy, but rather the adolescent form. I was thirteen when the bowing started. It's always unilateral, so of course, it would be the only good, strong leg I had. Even though we were in better living conditions by then, with my history of infections, the doctors decided against surgery for it. They made a special brace to apply pressure at the femur, knee, and ankle in alternating directions. The point was to realign the knee and keep it stable."

I grimaced as I stared at his leg. "It didn't work."

"It did, actually, at least a little bit," he said, as he righted himself against the log. "It used to be more severe than it is now, if you can believe that. The brace was never going to correct the issue; that ship sailed." He laughed and the sound was sardonic to my ears. It was several minutes before he spoke again. "No pun intended."

I leaned over and wrapped my short, thin arms around his chest, offering an impromptu hug. "I like your sense of humor, Gulliver. You make me laugh just by being you. That's not something just anyone can do."

"You're saying you're a tough nut to crack up?" With his arms wrapped around me, his laughter flowed through me and out my lips. I chuckled but didn't end the hug, and neither did he. Being in his arms calmed me and offered comfort in a world where I had none. The way he rested his cheek on the top of my head was tender and gentle, as though I was going to break if he didn't treat me with the utmost care. That did something to the inside of my chest when I thought about how such a simple action, one he probably didn't even think about doing, could be a piece of tape to my shattered crystal heart. Every shard was an experience in my past that chipped away at the crystal until it crumbled from the force of life.

"You make me forget for a few minutes that my life consists of jacked-up legs that fill me with complicated situations and feelings no one else understands or wants to deal with."

"I don't imagine that's easy, but you're doing something right, Gulliver. You're successful, smart, and have a good life. Not everyone can say the same."

"I suppose not," he agreed. "I would probably give it all up for what my brother has, though."

"I always wanted a sibling. It would be nice to have someone to talk to sometimes. What's his name?" I asked, stroking his arm as we sat in the night air. "You said you'd give it all up for what he has. What does he have that you don't?"

"His name is Jonathan. He lucked out in the name department too," he said sarcastically, rolling his eyes. "He's married to a beautiful woman named Petra, and his little boy, Levi, adores him. He goes home every night to people who love him. I work until I'm too tired to do anything but go home and sleep. Then I get up and do it all over again the next day because I have nothing else in my life."

"Your work matters to all of us, Gulliver," I assured him, squeezing his hand.

He leaned back against the log and sighed. "I know, but I should be able to do my work and still have a personal life, right?"

"Absolutely," I agreed. "What's stopping you?"

He immediately flopped his legs on the sand. "These."

It was as if the one word encompassed everything he had to say about the subject, but one word wasn't going to do it for me. "I'm not sure I understand. Why do your legs stop you from dating women?"

"It's hard to start a date off on the right foot when you have to pick her up on crutches, Charity. You're instantly friend-zoned. They go through with a date or two out of pity, and then they just stop answering your calls. I don't even bother anymore. It's not worth the heartache."

I ran my hand down his shoulder, grasping his tight bicep and squeezing. "Do you know the first thing I noticed about you when we met?" He shook his head. "How strong your arms were. Your biceps bulged to the point I noticed them under that grasshopper sweater covering them."

This time he laughed full on, and it filled my heart with joy to have broken through his darkness to help him find light again. "You're just saying that. I don't even work out."

"But you do," I shared honestly. "Every time you get up and strap on those crutches, you're working out. Every step you take is a workout for your arms. You just don't think about it because the crutches have been part of your life for so long. I guess what I'm saying is, they don't matter to every woman. They won't matter to the right woman. I want you to understand they don't matter to me. I didn't even notice them when we first met."

"You sorely lack observational skills then."

I waited for him to say more, but he didn't, so I did. "No, I'm incredibly observant. My job is to be observant. I notice everything. The difference is, I can easily pick out what should concern me and what shouldn't. I should have said I noticed the crutches, but they weren't a concern for me because your legs were never a concern to me. I don't mean that in the way it sounds," I said, pausing. "I mean that I would never consider your legs to be a reason not to hang out with you. Look at me. I don't roll that way with anyone, Gulliver."

He rubbed his right knee again, and what I had thought was a nervous habit, I realized was because of pain. "I would guess that you're probably used to dealing with discrimination too."

I shook my head. "I'm underestimated a lot because of my size, but I see that as a challenge rather than an insult. I have enough experience with being the underdog to realize the sum of you doesn't culminate in your legs. There's far more to who you are than your mobility aids. It wouldn't be any different if you were sitting in a wheelchair."

"And I might be someday," he admitted. "There's a real possibility my legs will give out."

"None of the above factors mean you aren't worthy of finding someone to be with, Gulliver. I understand there's a self-esteem issue there, and you've come by it rightly so, but not everyone sees your legs and automatically thinks you're incapable. I never did. When you stood up that day from behind your desk, I just saw Gulliver Winsome. The most interesting man I'd ever met dressed in a goofy grasshopper sweater and wearing the most engaging pair of honest hazel eyes I'd ever had the pleasure to gaze upon."

He lowered one brow toward his nose. "Sure, whatever you say, *Miss Laverne Says to Stay Away from the Island.*"

I laughed softly and held up my hands. "I'm guilty there, but I was worried about your safety and nothing else. I don't want you to get hurt, which I think means nothing more than I care about you."

"I care about you too. I wish there weren't such an age gap between us."

"There's an age gap?" I asked, surprised. "How old are you?"

"Thirty-four." His resulting sigh was heavy and deep. I felt all thirty-four years in that sigh. The weight of who Gulliver Winsome was sat on my shoulders like the weight of one thousand men. The pain of his childhood surgeries. The pain of growing up next to a brother who was his mirror image but could do everything he couldn't. The pain of rejection over and over again for years until finally his psyche couldn't take it anymore and shut down. I wanted to open him up again. I wanted to show him how one person, the right person, could start to change his life, regardless of his age.

I made the mind-blown motion near my head. "Wow, seven whole years. That's almost unheard of in this day and age. Scandalous even. What will my father think if I date a man with so much more worldly knowledge than me?" I asked in a fake Southern-belle accent.

Gulliver grasped my shoulders and hauled me into his chest. My eyes fluttered closed, giving him permission to kiss me, and he took it. He laid his lips on mine tenderly, sliding his hands into my hair and tipping my head to the left. I wrapped my arms around his neck and kissed him back, parting my lips when his tongue skimmed across the top of them. He didn't take the kiss any farther, though, and when I gave a low whimper, he pulled back and leaned his forehead against mine.

Our eyes locked together in wonderment and awe of the moment we'd just shared. I could read his intentions in those eyes of caramel, and I understood that he wasn't going to take advantage of the situation we were in. He wanted to explore the feelings growing between us but wouldn't ruin it by moving too fast.

"Your father's dead," he whispered, running his thumb along the ridge of my upper lip, still dewy from the kiss. "And just so you know, I wanted that kiss to be so much more, but I don't want to scare you and risk pushing you away."

"Since my father is dead, that gives me permission to do whatever the hell I want to," I said emphatically. "If I want to hang out with a guy who's seven years older than me, I will. If I want to kiss you until my lips are singed off and my tongue is raw, I will. If I want to date a guy who uses crutches or sits in a wheelchair, I will. I don't give a damn what other people think. I'm a minuscule woman who drives an old motor home around the country with nothing but a mashed-up mutt for company. That lifestyle alone should tell you I don't care what anyone thinks about my life choices. They're my choices, no one else's." I caressed his face while I spoke, his beard soft against my palm. "I love your beard, Gulliver. It's so soft, and I love the way it tickles my palm. I'm sorry if I touch it too much, but I can't help myself."

He captured my hand to his cheek and held it there. "You never have to apologize for touching me. I yearn for the moments that your sweet, tiny hand caresses my face. You always make me feel like I'm the only person in your world when you do it. You're an unusual woman, Charity Puck," he whispered, "in an excellent way. I've smiled, laughed, and felt more in the last week than I have in the last decade."

I frowned at the idea he was so alone in the world. "It saddens me to think you've spent years being lonely, but I'm content to know you've found a little happiness with me. Well, other than this," I said, motioning around the darkened beach.

He wrapped me in his arms, resting my head on his shoulder. "I don't know. This isn't so bad. If we'd gone back to shore, I would have told you good night and gone home to an empty apartment. Here, I have a fire, a beautiful woman in my arms, and the stars to watch."

I patted his chest absently. "I didn't think of it that way, but since you mentioned it, I'm all about this."

He chuckled, and the sound made his chest rattle under my cheek. It was comforting, and the heat of his chest made me sleepy. I yawned and he rubbed my arm in a way that said he knew I was tired. "It's late. Why don't you sleep for a bit? I have to stay awake and watch the boat."

I gazed up at him. "Where is it going to go?"

One of those bright hazel eyes winked at me. "Nowhere, hopefully. But I have to be sure it doesn't float out into open water while we sleep."

I sat up and forced my backbone straight. "I'll stay awake too. You'll need the company."

He pointed up at the sky. "I have the stars to count, a fire to stoke, and a book to read. I'll be fine."

I yawned again, covering my mouth with my hand. "My goodness, you're right, the long day is catching up to me. You carry a book around with you?"

Gulliver grabbed my sleeping bag from the sand and spread it out in front of the fire. "No, I found it on the boat while I was grabbing the supplies out of the back. It was once waterlogged, but it dried out, and I think it's still readable."

He motioned me into the sleeping bag, and I reluctantly climbed inside it as Mojo lumbered over to get closer to me like he always does. "What book is it?"

"*Gulliver's Travels.*"

"Seriously?" I asked, unable to control the giggle that escaped. He held it up, and indeed it was *Gulliver's Travels*. "And here we are, stranded on a deserted island. Wait," I said, my head tipped to the side. "Didn't Jonathan Swift write *Gulliver's Travels*?"

Gulliver threw his head back and laughed with abandon, the sound traveling all the way to the stars to dance with them there. "Now you see why I said he lucked out in the name department." His lid came down over one sexy orb and left me more than a little hot and bothered.

"That's hilarious," I said, shaking my head. "I've never read *Gulliver's Travels*. Would you read it to me? No one has ever read to me before." I snuggled deeper into the bag, surprised by how chilled I had become in the night air.

"No one? Ever?" he asked, a brow dipped down in question.

"Not unless it was when I was a baby. My parents weren't exactly about the bedtime stories."

He zipped the bag a little bit more and patted my hip. "Okay, but only if you stay in the bag and snooze," he ordered. I promised with a head nod and a yawn, so he cracked the book open and aimed a penlight at the page. "'Part one, a voyage to Lilliput,'" he began.

His voice filled the night with an air of comfort and normalcy. Listening to him read helped me relax, but it also made me wonder if this was how a child felt when snuggled warmly in bed with someone who loved them reading aloud. I mean, not that he loved me, but it was the idea of being cared about by another human in this world. I had to admit to myself as he turned the page that if there was one man in the world I'd want to care about me, it would be Gulliver Winsome. When he kissed me, little shards of my crystal heart found their way back together. No one had ever done that for me before. Gulliver was different. He was exciting in the simplicity of who he was. He didn't pretend to be someone he wasn't. He wore his heart on his sleeve, even if he didn't know it. He showed the people he cared about that they were important to him, and he did it in a way that came across as genuine. He was sincere in everything he did, and that was how I knew he wasn't forcing anything between us.

What was going on with me? Why was I feeling this way about someone I'd just met? What was this feeling? My brain was too tired to puzzle it out tonight. I would have to be content to know that something inside me was changing because Gulliver had come into my life.

My eyes grew heavier with every flip of the page, and I forced my ears to listen for several more paragraphs, but I never did find out if Gulliver got free of his bindings before I dropped off to sleep.

Chapter Eight

"Charity," Gulliver whispered as he shook my hip. "Wake up." I opened my eyes to his smoky ones gazing straight into mine. He pointed up, and I flipped to my back to stare into the night sky. I gasped when my brain registered the green light undulating across the stars, illuminating the sky. The pink and white layers merged with the green, leaving the blackness of the night above it to appear wholly lost in space. The stars were brilliant pinpricks of light, and I was confident I could touch them if I reached my hand out toward the dancing lights. The streaks were vivid but fleeting, while the aurora bounced around us. The lights were quickly chased away by one color, only to return in a breath with a new one.

"This is unlike anything I ever expected." I sighed with my gaze transfixed on the sky. "I'll never be the same."

We sat for the next half an hour in silence, save for an occasional gasp or *look at that* breaking the silence of the night. We stared into the sky until the lights started to fade and the stars and night stole back their canvas. While the green remained a light hue in the sky, the vividness slowly dissipated. Gulliver was holding my hand as I lie in the sleeping bag and he rested next to me, wrapped up in the spare blanket Laverne kept on the boat. The fire had died down, and now that I wasn't so distracted, I noticed he had put sand on it to lessen the light on the beach. He let go of my hand and got up to throw fresh wood on the coals until it flared to life again and offered much-needed heat for our chilled bodies. It might be June, but on Lake Superior, summer was elusive.

He sat next to me again and yawned. "What time is it?" I asked, rubbing my eyes.

"It's a little before three a.m.," he answered. "I was watching for the aurora, hoping it would pop up so I could wake you."

"I'd forgotten about it in the insanity of the last few hours, but the northern lights were the last thing on my bucket list," I said, taking his hand in mine.

He cocked his head at me. "You have a bucket list at twenty-six?"

"Well, yeah," I said. "Everyone should have a bucket list, regardless of their age."

Gulliver considered that thought for a moment before answering. "I guess you never know how long you have on earth, so starting a bucket list early isn't a bad idea. How many things did you have on it?"

"Fifty, one for each state. It's taken me six years, but now—" I held my arms out as if to say there was nothing left. "I'll have to do some serious thinking when we get back to shore."

"Why? Unless there's a hole in the bucket, you can always keep filling it."

I chuckled into the night air. "You're right. Leave it to you to point out the obvious. I added things as I completed others, but I was down to the one last original entry. To see the aurora borealis over the Great Lakes. I avoided taking jobs around this area, so I never thought I'd cross it off."

"Why did you avoid this?" he asked, stymied. "The Great Lakes are the very definition of Mother Nature. You can visit the Great Lakes once a year for the rest of your life and never learn everything there is to know about them."

"You're right, again," I said, tongue in cheek. "I guess the answer is, as long as the aurora borealis were elusive, then I didn't have to change anything about my life. See, I made a promise to myself that when I finished the items on my original bucket list, I'd think about changing my lifestyle. Try to make it more permanent. Hunt down that dream job and go for it."

"Jeez. If I had known how much turmoil they'd leave you in, I would have let you sleep. I had no idea the northern lights held such deep meaning for you."

I nudged him with my shoulder while I rested my head on his arm to stare up into the night sky. "No, I'm glad you woke me up. It was one of those love-hate things. They were breathtaking. I wasn't disappointed."

Gulliver scooted closer to me and wrapped his arm around my waist, tugging me onto his lap. "I was supposed to be reading, but I was watching you sleep for the better part of the last three hours. Mojo was giving me the stink eye the whole time."

I laughed softly because the dog was giving him the stink eye right now. "Regardless of what happens in the future, no one will take the memory of tonight away from us."

A smile of agreement and happiness spread across his face. "I'll remember this night forever. I'm glad we spent it together."

"Me too," I said, running my fingers through the hair at his temple.

Gulliver sighed and the sound was weighty and filled with uncertainty. "I know there's so much more to learn about you. You live to experience life at full speed. Maybe you'll drive out of my life as quickly as you drove in, but the ride so far has been breathtaking."

A smile tugged at my lips as I stared into his bronzed eyes. The fire drew out the gold in them, and while the green was still abundant, the gold got to dance for all it was worth. "You're a beautiful person, Gulliver, and you understand what's important in life."

I pulled his lips to mine and kissed him, tentatively at first, until he gave in to my lips and melted against me. God, I loved kissing this man. He gave himself over to me and let me control and deepen the kiss. I let my tongue rove over his lips until he parted them, and I got my first taste. I was addicted in an instant. I had never kissed him with as much hunger and desire as I was tonight, but I couldn't hold the dam back any longer. Not after the things we'd shared with each other. The moan that ripped from my throat was proof that I'd never found this same level of desire with anyone else before. *No commitments, Charity,* my inner voice reminded me, but he silenced that voice with a quiet moan and a velvety-soft stroke of his tongue against mine.

Exhaustion had kicked in, and I still had many more hours to go for the night. Once I finished the next order, I promised myself I'd get up and grab another cup of coffee. It was nearly ten p.m., but considering we didn't get back to the mainland until noon, I was still working in Gulliver's office. I hadn't seen him since the moment we got back to the dock. His disappearance was making it difficult to get much done on the website, so I was trying to catch up on all the orders that had come in over the last few days.

A cup of coffee was set down on the desk, and I glanced up, my heart thudding from the intrusion. Gulliver stood in front of me, dressed in a pair of jeans and a polo shirt, his hair still damp. "Hi," he said. "Figured you might need a pick-me-up."

"Hi," I greeted him in return, before sipping the hot brew.

"You're a lifesaver. I was just finishing this order, and I was going to find some coffee. You've been busy today," I said, setting the mug down.

His lips tugged into a grim line, and he motioned at the mess on the desk. "It's been a long day for both of us, it looks like. I need some food, and I would guess you do too?"

I could tell by the change in his demeanor that whatever had kept him busy for the day wasn't a good thing. "Sure, I'm starving," I said, following him down the hall to his apartment door.

When the sun had risen this morning, our fire was out, we were both passed out on the sand sound asleep, and the boat was still anchored to the beach. The churning of a motor woke us, and we both scrambled to our feet when a towboat chartered by Laverne honked from a safe distance away. We packed our boat, hooked it up to their towline, climbed aboard their craft, and motored home. When we arrived back at the dock, Gulliver's phone started going off at the speed of sound. He pretended it was no big deal, but I could tell that it was. I made him head out while I talked to Laverne, showered, changed, and then walked into town with Mojo. I wasn't worried since I knew Gulliver would give me a ride back tonight.

"Is there anywhere open this late?" I asked, trying to keep up with his hurried pace down the hallway.

"There are several bars open, but I want to talk in private. I thought I'd grill some steaks on the patio. I don't want to leave the building empty tonight."

"Sounds perfect," I agreed. "The only thing to make it better would be to have a bottle of prosecco involved." When we walked out the door to the back patio, he already had the grill going and the cooler waiting. "You're prepared." I laughed as I stared out over the lake. Whenever I was within sight of the water, my gaze was immediately drawn to it. There was some truth to the legend of the Lady of the Lake. The locals claimed she was a siren who never released your heart once she held it.

The sizzle of the meat as it landed on a hot rack hit my ears until he closed the lid of the grill. "I showered and hoped you'd want to share dinner with me, so I got it ready. The steaks won't take long. I also have potato salad and beans, but they're cold. I only eat cold beans. I think it's a Wisconsin thing, so it's perfectly fine if you don't want them."

I spun on my heel to where he stood by the grill. "I love cold beans. I never eat them any other way. Please don't give any to Mojo, though," I said, waving my hand in front of my nose.

My silliness spurred laughter from deep within him, and I sensed it was the first thing he'd had to laugh about today. He grabbed me and hugged me tightly, burying his lips in my neck when his laughter faded. "I needed some levity in the day. You always know how to do that. Thank you," he whispered.

He released me so he could flip the steaks, and I lowered myself to a chair at the round, two-person patio table. The top was glass and pinged when he set a chilled bottle of wine on it. In seconds, there were two filled glasses, and I was guiding one to my lips before sighing with satisfaction. "And you always know what I need. Steak and wine might earn me a one-way ticket to falling asleep on your couch, though."

"Which is why I have a couch. You're more than welcome to it, but Mojo has to sleep on the floor," he said, winking conspiratorially.

I swear the dog huffed at him from under the table. A smile tipped my lips while I grabbed the silverware and napkins from the basket on the table and spread them out so we could eat. He set the beans and potato salad down, then grabbed the steaks off the grill. The scent of nicely charred meat met my nostrils, and I moaned with happiness. "I know this is going to taste like heaven," I sighed as the steam rose from the sirloin. When I sliced into the meat, the juices poured onto my plate, making my mouth water with anticipation, until a paw patted my leg.

I stared into Mojo's eyes and sighed. "You already ate your dinner, big guy," I said firmly, snapping and pointing for him to get down.

Mojo gave me a whine followed by a grunt, and I worried Gulliver was going to choke on his steak. I sliced a small piece off the edge of mine and held it in the palm of my hand. "Fine, I'll share, but you can't bug me the whole meal," I scolded while he chomped down the steak.

Gulliver was laughing behind his hand. "Oh, he can, and he probably will."

I rolled my eyes to the stars and shook my head. "Mojo's a steak lover. Always has been. He doesn't beg at the table, but when a steak is involved, everything is fair game for Mojo."

"I don't mind if you share to keep him happy. He's been working hard. He kept us safe from the bears last night, so he deserves an extra treat."

I chuckled and waved my fork at him sarcastically. "Sure, there were so many bears last night."

Gulliver's knife stopped sawing through the meat. "There were, while you were sleeping. Several curious black bears decided to visit. Mojo stood up, bared his teeth at them, and they took off like a shot."

My fork clattered to the plate. "I had no idea. Why didn't you tell me? Good heavens, we could have died!"

He pointed at me with his knife while he chewed. "That's why I didn't tell you. You have a thing about bears."

"No, I have a thing about being eaten by bears," I corrected him.

I rubbed Mojo's head and gave him another piece of steak, cooing at him for being a good boy.

"Tell me how you adopted Mojo," he encouraged.

"Ah, the story of Mojo," I teased. "It's a short one. I hadn't had Myrtle a week when I pulled over at a rest stop in California. I could hear something thwacking under the hood and decided I better check it out."

"Thwacking," he repeated, "doesn't sound good."

I leaned forward and punched his arm lightly. "Don't make fun of me. I'm not a mechanic. I got out of the motor home and left the side door open. With my head under the hood, I didn't see a wee pup jump inside. It turned out the handle on the battery had come loose and was thwacking around," I said pointedly. "It was a simple fix, and when I climbed back into the motor home to clean up, a little Mojo sat in the middle of the floor, gazing up at me with his sad puppy eyes."

"Oh, the poor guy." He frowned at the idea of baby Mojo all alone. "How did you know he was a stray?"

I gave the dog another piece of steak while I chewed a bit of it myself. When I finished, I answered. "He was skinny and scraggly. There was no doubt he didn't have owners. I know you won't believe me, but when I first got him, he fit in the kitchen sink in the motor home."

"No way!" he said, his voice filled with laughter. I was thrilled that talking about Mojo was taking his mind off whatever had happened today, but still planned to grill him about it later.

"It's true," I promised, holding up three fingers like the Girl Scout pledge. "I bathed him right there in the sink and fed him milk and toast since I had no dog food. He fell asleep all wrapped up in an old blanket on the passenger seat. He hasn't left my side since. I took him to the vet, and he told me Mojo was probably abandoned with the rest of his litter but somehow escaped. He wasn't even old enough to be away from his mom. Apparently, with the right food and a little love, my Mojo forgot to stop growing."

Gulliver lowered his knife to the plate and picked up his last piece of steak, holding it out on his palm to the dog, and since he was an equal opportunity steak eater, Mojo quickly snapped it up. "He's a good boy. I bet he sensed if he jumped into your motor home, you'd take care of him forever."

"We were destined to be together. We're more alike than different, to be honest. His family abandoned him, and so did mine. All he needed was someone to love him, and I needed the same. When he kept growing and I realized he was going to be a gigantic dog, I knew he'd protect me no matter what, so I do the same for him. As you can see, he never leaves my side. I'm surprised he has stayed with Laverne and here at the business as much as he has without me, to be honest."

Gulliver finished his potato salad and leaned back in the uncomfortable wrought iron seat. "I suppose it just means he's comfortable here. Laverne probably treats him like a king. I know Honey is always cooing about him every time she's around."

I laughed happily and nodded after finishing the last of my wine. "Laverne was scared of Mojo when we first got there, and now she's making him a bed in the corner and letting him sleep on the dock in the sunshine. He has a way of sensing those who are scared of him and ingratiating himself into their lives."

"He's no dummy. He knows what he wants. It's not much different from what I want, actually," he said pensively. "The difference is, he's already got the girl."

I slid my hand across the table and took his. "He'll share, I promise." I winked, and his seriousness fell away when he grasped my hand.

"I hope so because after last night, I find it hard to think about anything but you."

"It doesn't make sense to me, but I understand the way you're feeling, Gulliver. I feel the same way. It's confusing and scary."

"Is it a little bit exciting too?" he asked. "Because I know it is for me."

I squeezed his hand in solidarity of our mutual feelings, even if neither of us understood them right now. "It's more than a little bit exciting," I promised.

I stood, nudging myself between his legs so I could slide my hand up his face and caress his cheek. His eyes bored into mine, and he lowered his head, waiting for me to close the distance. I did, hungrily attacking his lips to tell him what my words couldn't. I might be confused and scared, but I was also excited by my desire for him. He slid his hands into my hair and grasped my face, tipping my head to change the angle, allowing his tongue to sneak between my lips and tease me into a heightened sense of awareness. The night sounds were amplified as his soft, warm tongue danced with mine in the moonlight.

Mojo barked sharply, and we broke apart, our chests heaving but our eyes scanning the darkness just beyond the patio.

"Let's go inside," he said, his voice urgent. "We're too exposed out here."

His words were ominous and rang in my ears as we made quick work of packing the cooler, making sure the grill was cool, and cleaning up the dirty dishes. I followed him through the door toward his apartment and wondered if what he was going to tell me, coupled with what I had to tell him, would mean I was going to have to leave this wonderful place just to stay alive.

Chapter Nine

Gulliver motioned me through his front door, and I pulled the cooler in behind me, stopping to take in the apartment. It was spectacular, and completely Gulliver.

"What?" he asked, closing the door behind him. "Too many bugs?"

"Give me a chance to absorb it," I whispered on a giggle. The kitchen was galley style, with room for a small table against the opposite wall. A half wall divided the kitchen from the living room, which held a well-loved sofa, recliner, and TV. The walls were the feature of the room, though, since they were covered in small memory boxes, each one filled with a butterfly or moth of a different color or size. They were breathtaking as groupings above the television and couch. "Where on earth did you get all these butterflies? Are they models?"

Gulliver shook his head and followed me into the living room. "No, they're all butterflies I've found dead during my travels to other parts of the country and world. Some people think they're too macabre to use for decorating, but it's me, so they shouldn't."

My eyes were glued to the groupings on the wall as I nodded. "They're fascinating. I never get to really look at a butterfly up close. Unless you count when I find them smashed against the grill of my motor home." I groaned and hit myself in the forehead. "Not again," I moaned. "Ignore me."

Gulliver laughed and rubbed my arms as a silent assurance. "It's the circle of life," he sang, his tone gone way off the rails. "You make me laugh, so don't worry about it. Bugs aren't supposed to live for years and years. They're important to our ecosystem, but there will always be another one."

"Until there isn't," I said grimly.

He pointed at me while wearing a grimace. "Until there isn't."

"Mind if I use a bowl to give Mojo some water?" I asked.

"Absolutely. There are plastic ones under the sink. I'll be right back," he said, walking through a door that had to be his bedroom.

I hurried back to the kitchen and found the perfect bowl, filling it with water and setting it on a towel for Mojo to slurp up. When I got back to the couch, Gulliver was sitting in his recliner, his brace and shoe off and his chair reclined. He smiled sheepishly. "I hope you don't mind if I relax. After last night and today, my knee is killing me," he explained.

I scooted off the couch again. "Do you have an ice pack? That might help."

"Good idea," he said, reaching for the handle of the chair, but I held my hand out to him.

"Stay put. I'll get it." I rifled through the freezer and came up with a gel pack that I rested across his knee. "And don't apologize. I'm just glad you're comfortable enough with me to relax without being self-conscious."

He held the pack to his knee and avoided eye contact. "Oh,

I'm self-conscious," he said, his voice barely audible. "But you didn't appear overly bothered by my legs last night, so . . ."

"I'm not bothered by your legs, Gulliver, unless they hurt; then I'm bothered. I don't want you to be in pain when we're spending time together." I sat on the couch and tucked my legs under me. "Now, tell me what happened this morning. You took off, and I haven't seen you in hours. Laverne called me several hours ago to tell me the marina guys had a chance to look at the motor. It turns out someone tampered with it. The wires were cut halfway through and the motor was drained of most of its oil. The people behind the vandalism knew either the lack of oil or the wires were going to strand us out there. I asked her if she told anyone where we were going and she said no. It seems strange that someone would mess with it there."

"Taking into consideration what happened here while we were gone, it might not be as strange as you think," he said grimly. "Last night the silent alarm was tripped. Mathias ran over to see what was going on since he was staying with Honey to keep an eye on her. When he got here, someone had broken in and was trying to get into the research lab. They escaped, and he never caught a glimpse of them, but he also doesn't know if they found any information before he interrupted them. He turned the information and the tapes over to the cops when they arrived, but there wasn't much to go on."

"They broke in because they knew we were stranded out on the island."

"Most likely," he agreed.

"Did you find anything missing this morning?"

"No. An iPad was out, but it was locked from too many attempts at the password. And there were no fingerprints, which means they wore gloves."

"The iPads concern me. I didn't know there were iPads in

the mix. How many and are there any other phones or tablets tied to the account?"

"We have four iPads, and we use them to document our research with pictures and video. Once the work is complete, we upload them to our computer server and wipe them. We don't use a cloud."

I shook my head in exasperation and sighed. "You think that means they're safe, but they aren't. I can promise you, the information is on a cloud somewhere, Gulliver. I need to check the iPads. I'm going to have to change passwords and encrypt the email. Unless you're using the same email as the one for your website; then it's already encrypted."

He grimaced and shook his head. "It doesn't matter because there is no cloud. I know you think there is, but there isn't. I'm telling you, we erase the data once we upload it to the safe server, or what we thought was the safe server."

"Nothing is safe. Even when we encrypt and protect, nothing is completely safe. The fewer places you have the data, the fewer issues you'll have with it going rogue."

"The good news is," he said, winking, "there are only the four iPads. There are no other devices connected to it. I have one here in case you wanted to go over it. It's on my bed. Would you grab it?"

"Sure." I wandered behind his chair to the bedroom door, and I had to take a steeling breath before I stepped into the room.

Faced with his most personal space, I wanted to get in and out as quickly as possible, but the second I stood in the room, I realized that was never going to happen. In a daze, I stared at the mural before me. It encompassed the wall to the left of the bed, and I couldn't draw my gaze away from the wonderment of it. The mural enveloped my senses with a field of clover and monarch butterflies that flitted from clover to clover. The room was small, but the mural put you in the middle of an endless garden of butterflies. I stared at it in fascination and wonder, waiting for one of the butterflies to fly over and land on my nose. I picked up the iPad, but I still couldn't take my gaze off the mural.

That wall told me more about him than anything had thus far. I turned and left the room, stopping next to his chair with the iPad under my arm. "The mural is breathtaking," I whispered. "Absolutely riveting, Gulliver."

A slow smile lifted his lips. "Thank you. It took me a year to finish, but I'm happy with it. I discovered you could paint by number on your walls, too."

"You painted that mural?" I asked in shock and surprise.

"I don't have a lot of spare time, but I have nothing to do with what spare time I do have," he explained with a shrug. "Someone had done something similar at a convention once, and I wanted to recreate it. It's funny because I spent a year working on it, but no one gets to see it. I probably should have painted it on the wall in the front office."

I sat on the couch and made myself comfortable again. "No, it's perfect where it is. No one else would appreciate the scene the way you do, I'm sure."

I scratched my temple to try and shift my head back into the cat-and-mouse game we were unwilling participants in. "Do you think the break-in is the reason we were stranded? That doesn't make sense, though. They could have just done it when we were on the island."

"The flaw in your logic is, we might appear remote out here, but we're not. There are enough people around during the day that they'd report someone sneaking around the building. If the people behind this wanted in, they had to do it at night, and they planned it that way. They also know I live here, which means they had to be certain I was gone for the night."

I sighed in irritation. "By stranding us in the middle of the lake, they had enough time to get the job done."

He nodded once. "I suspect the person did just enough damage to get us off the island and halfway across the lake. They had to hope we couldn't find a ride back, or it would be after dark before we did."

"Man," I said, my voice holding a tinge of fear, "someone is devoted to the cause to go to all the trouble of stranding us. They had to travel eight miles across the lake in a boat and mess with the motor without getting caught."

"No one would think twice about it, honestly. The island docks are always full of boats in the summer, so they'd get lost in the fray easily. As long as we didn't catch them in the act, they could do whatever they wanted to the boat, and no one would ask questions. If anyone noticed them by the motor, they would just think they were fixing it. Not a soul would know it wasn't their motor."

"They post a lookout to make sure we stay on the other side of the island, snip a few wires, drain out some oil, and they're gone," I finished.

"What I don't know is how they figured out we'd be on the island. We didn't talk about it in public, and I didn't tell anyone I was going," he pondered.

"We only told Laverne and she didn't tell anyone," I pointed out. "That means someone is constantly aware of what you're doing, and they saw us leave on the boat and followed." I groaned in a low, unhappy tone.

His face was pinched now. "It appears so. I'll have to make things right with Laverne for the cost of the motor and tow. I had no idea someone would go to these extremes to get this information."

"People will do anything if they think it will somehow improve their bottom line. Never underestimate the power of money, Gulliver."

"And whoever develops this kind of technology stands to make a lot of it," he added. "There will be payouts for this formula forever. If Butterfly Junction is the first one out with it, we are leaning toward producing it ourselves so we can control it. It was developed for the greater good, and that is what we want to do with it."

"You're in the minority," I assured him.

"We're close, Charity. It's more important than ever that we protect the formula."

"How close?" I asked, my head cocked to the side.

"Imminently. The last round of testing was so promising that Thomas, our head scientist, thinks we're within striking distance."

"That's great!" I exclaimed, sitting forward a bit on the couch. "What happens then?"

"Then we have to start the next round of trials on bigger fields and bodies of water. By then, the formula will be patented, though. If someone stole it, we would have proof it was ours."

I held up the iPad. "I need to do a quick reconnaissance of this immediately then. What's the passcode?"

"It's 1961."

I typed it in and was rewarded with the home screen. After some clicking about, I was in the system and finding run-of-the-mill emails without much information tied to them. I glanced up. "Your emails are innocuous. I'm going to check the cloud," I explained, clicking the Drive symbol.

"You won't find anything," he insisted.

When the app loaded, I was not disappointed. I scrolled through it before I turned it around to show him. "Are you sure? This one says, 'June second data.'"

His face paled under the light of the lamp. "What the hell?" he asked, his voice filled with shock as he leaned forward. "We purposely avoid uploading to clouds."

"Well, you consciously avoid it, but the accounts are linked, and you have sync on," I explained as I punched buttons on the screen. "Let's sign into iCloud now," I suggested, afraid of what I'd find. Sure enough, another copy of the data was there. I showed him everything, and the expression he wore reminded me of someone with bad heartburn.

"No, this isn't right. Someone did this thinking I wouldn't find out," Gulliver insisted. "I should have checked more often."

"It's easy to assume once we set up devices, the settings will never change, but that's not always the case. Sometimes a simple update to the device OS can change settings without us realizing it. Regardless, for now, we have to fix this. We're going to wipe these clouds and add some security. Is all this information backed up on the server?"

"Yes, we didn't do any work today because we were tied up with the burglary attempt. There's nothing new on there."

"Perfect," I said as I tapped and typed. "You have four iPads only, right?"

"Yes, only four."

I showed him the iCloud information. "This tells us there are three other iPads synced, so we have to delete backups on each one," I explained as I worked. "Once the backups are deleted, we have to delete all the files."

"Can't we just delete iCloud in general?"

I paused in my tapping. "We can, but deleting it doesn't get rid of your information. It's still floating in cyberspace. Even after you delete your files, it can take thirty days to disappear completely from the cloud. I'll need to check and make sure the files stay gone. I have a tool I'll use to wipe the iPads back to factory settings without losing your apps. Once I finish clearing your Google Drive, I'll disconnect it from your account. It will still be there, but it will be dormant and empty," I explained as I worked. "Do you have old useless data we can upload to the iCloud once it's cleared?"

"I mean, sure, but to what end?" he asked, his head cocked to the side.

"If we have something in iCloud, it makes it appear we have no idea someone is after the information. We just want to be sure whatever is in there isn't tied to your research. Once we've planted the information, I'll keep checking to see if anyone can breach the cloud and get the data. If they can, that might give me a trail to follow."

"But you just yelled at me about security."

I shook my head and held in the sigh of fatigue and impatience waiting to come out. "I'm talking about a formula as basic as something a home gardener might make and use, Gulliver. If they take the information via the cloud, then you'll have to reconsider what technology equipment you're using."

"Maybe we should just stop using the iPads. It would be inconvenient, but far less so than losing all our research."

I kept tapping and shook my head. "No, this serves several purposes. I could always encrypt the data in the cloud, but since you really shouldn't be using it for information storage anyway, I'm not going to bother. Uploading fake information to the cloud assures me they won't go digging for anything else they can't see on the surface. They'll be too busy frothing at the mouth over what they can see. We will need a new password and passcode. Something like butterflyjunction is so easy a third-grader could get it in two tries."

The sheepish expression on his face was enough to tell me he was the culprit responsible for that atrocity. "Guess I failed there."

"Major fail," I joked, "but we can fix it. Only two people will know the password though, you and Mathias. There's no reason they need to know the password to work the device. Pictures and videos can be uploaded to the server by you only."

"What about a passcode into the device?"

"We'll change that too. Only the people using them will know it. If it gets out to anyone else, you have an extremely narrow group of people to accuse. Make sense?"

"It does," he agreed. "What are you going to use?"

"The unlock password is a four-number key. I'll use 1862."

He laughed in a surprised and oddly tickled way. "How random."

"No, it's pointed," I explained. "The famous lepidopterist Margaret Fountaine was born in 1862."

"Whoa." He paused. "How do you know about Margaret Fountaine?"

"I've been doing some research to learn more about lepidopterists. Did you know she had a diary of more than a million words? A million handwritten words," I said in shock.

He gave me a palms up. "I did know that, but I am a lepidopterist. I think it's the perfect date to use."

Once I had the new passcode set, I moved on to the password. "You'll use the same list I gave you for the website, but again on rotation every month. Never use the same one more than once a year and never the same one you're using for the server that month."

He leaned over and took my hand off the iPad. "I know I'm fortunate to have hired Charity Puck. Not only is she brilliant at her job, but she's beautiful. Thank you for spending so much time protecting my business. Saying thank you doesn't seem like enough."

I squeezed his hand and met his gaze. "It's simple. Find a solution to this pesticide problem so I can eat, and we'll call it even."

I winked as I started my work again, but the truth was,

what he wasn't paying me in monetary rewards was made up for in emotional rewards. If I could just stop running from everything and everyone, I might be able to have a normal life. At least as normal as possible for someone who grew up shut away from the world. The last eleven years have been about therapy for me. When I went to juvie, they offered me counselors, love, and answers to my questions about why I'd had to grow up in the kind of environment my dad created. They offered me a place to be angry without hurting anyone, and they offered me a second chance I may not have had if I'd run away or become emancipated. Juvie was usually portrayed as the worst place to be, but for me, it was a saving grace of stability, discipline, and love I'd never had before.

The last six years had been about answering three questions. Who am I? What do I want out of life? And how am I going to get those things? Every mile driven was a minute of my childhood forgotten. Every bucket list entry was an experience I missed in childhood. For the last two thousand and one hundred days, I'd been running from my past. I hadn't figured out how to stop yet.

"Tell me some of your bucket list items," he encouraged.

I let out a relaxed chuckle to keep him from worrying. "You noticed I was lost in thought," I said without glancing up.

"Your face is uniquely expressive when you're working, but those expressions are rarely about your work. I have a feeling your brain runs away with the past when you're concentrating on those lines of code. It's time to express those thoughts so you can deal with what needs dealing with and let it go."

I glanced up from the iPad. "I've let go of what needs to go, Gulliver. Most of it, anyway. The things I hang on to are kept for a specific reason."

"Which is?"

I held the power button down on the iPad, restarted it, and waited. "A reminder there is always a way out of any situation.

My parents never believed that, and I refuse to be another statistic. I'll do what I have to do to survive, but I'll never compromise my morals to do it. Sticking to such a simple idea has taken me down a road that has never asked me to compromise to get to the next day. The situations I'm faced with are sometimes difficult, but there has always been a way to keep my moral compass intact. I can say it's not easy, especially when you have the skills to make a lot of money quickly."

He nodded pensively, his fingers fidgeting with the ice pack on his knee. "I'm sure your hacking skills are highly sought after by the people trolling the darker side of the Web than the light."

Another mirthless chuckle left my lips. "The pay is four times what I'm making now, but there is no reward in that kind of work. I'll stay aboveground in the light, make enough money to live and be happy, and maintain my ability to sleep at night."

"You have the right idea about life, Charity," Gulliver said, his smile turning bright as he gazed at me. "It's what I love about you. You don't mince words, but you're open, honest, and caring."

I swallowed hard, and the words stuck in my throat. *It's what he loves about me? How do I respond to such a statement? Do I gloss over it? Do I say something? Do I ask questions?* Maybe it was nothing more than him using a common phrase without thinking about it.

"Now, the bucket list," he said instantaneously. "I know about the northern lights. What are some of the others?"

He leaned back as if he wanted to motor past his unexpected drop of the L-word, so I did too. "Let's see, one of the first was to drive the Pacific Coast Highway from start to finish," I said as the iPad lit up again with life. "It was breathtaking. I camped in Limekiln State Park and visited the waterfalls. The beauty there wasn't unlike what you'll find here. I made sure to see the Bixby Bridge and the Golden Gate Bridge. I visited Hearst Castle, which was massive and took me nearly an entire day to get through. The indoor pool was breathtaking, and I wanted to take a swim more than anything."

He raised a brow in question. "I assume taking a swim is a no-no?"

"A big no-no. You can't even dip your foot in the pool."

"What else did you do?" he asked, prodding me along.

I typed while I talked so I didn't waste time in clearing the pad of its data. "While I was in California, I had to visit Disneyland, of course. Ever since I was a little girl, I desperately wanted to ride the Teacups, so I made sure to get to Disneyland as quickly as possible. I'd like to go back someday with my child. It was fun, but I think experiencing it with a child would make it even better."

He nodded, and I noticed his eyes dimmed at the mention of kids. "I suppose you're probably right. I've never been there."

I leaned back on the couch to relax. "You'd have a ball, Gulliver. There are butterflies everywhere. They flit and float in and among the people as if we're in their way. Oh, speaking of butterflies, Busch Gardens," I said, my hand over my heart. "Gorgeous."

He shifted in the chair to make better eye contact with me. "I haven't been there either, but I have been to the Victoria Butterfly Garden in British Columbia. It's where I fell in love with butterflies and their flirty ways. I was a third-year college student, and it cemented my decision to go on to be a lepidopterist. It's funny how life works."

I rested my head on the couch, exhaustion setting in after a long couple of days. "I agree, there's something out there for everyone. I've stood on top of the Space Needle, flown in a bush plane over Alaska, gazed upon the Grand Canyon, holed up in the Alamo, dodged gators in Florida, and visited the birthplace of Baron von Steuben."

"Baron von who?" he asked, leaning forward.

"You don't know who Baron von Steuben is?" My mouth

fell agape in shock and horror. "The guy responsible for training the troops at Valley Forge?" His gaze was vacant, and I did a facepalm. I waved my hand in the air. "Okay, never mind. I visited the capitol, of course, but was only impressed with the Tomb of the Unknowns and Arlington Cemetery."

"I agree. The White House was cool, but they were cooler. Oh, and the National Archives Museum. Let me tell you, the Constitution sat before me, and I couldn't believe I was that close to it."

I pointed at him in excitement for a shared experience. "Yes! I marveled at how it was bigger than I am," I joked, laughing with him. "It's interesting how you can find so many things to do when you open your eyes to what's out there in this big, big world. I found the little things equally as exciting as the big things that I did."

"What little things?" he asked curiously. I could tell he was genuinely interested in my life experiences and not just making small talk. I wanted to sit and talk to him forever. He was always eager to hear what I had to say, and the way his eyes gazed at me with curiosity and lust made me eager to spend time with him too.

"Things like stopping at a roadside diner and discovering the best chili ever made, or noticing a roadside fruit stand with a grizzled old man tending to his wares. You stop for an orange, but he tells you about how he immigrated here from Poland during World War II and how he's made his living by selling fruit. You park your motor home in a state park for the night, planning to leave in the morning, but when the sun comes up, you see waterfalls, lush green paths, and quiet reflection pools, so you stay and explore. North Dakota is pretty remote in some areas, so you'd find a town and stop, only to discover the best biscuits and gravy, or a classic drive-in movie theater showing films from the good old days."

I went quiet and considered my past travels for a moment before continuing. "Mostly it's about not always taking the blacktopped path. Veering off to find the things no one talked about was an actual bucket list entry of mine. I veered off the path in every state at least once, sometimes more. Like the time Myrtle broke down in Nevada, and I had to stick around for a few days while they fixed her. I rented a car and drove around the area. The best part was sitting among the Joshua trees. Mind-blowing silence is the only way I can describe it. I'll never forget them."

"I would say you're well-traveled, at least within the fifty states, but I think it would be more accurate to say you've figured out what's important when you travel."

"When you put it that way, I suppose so. I visited Canada for a few days, but that's the only place I've been that's out of the country. I want to go back there and see Thunder Bay and the amethyst mine." I paused. "Oh, can I add the amethyst mine to the bucket list?"

He held his hand out for a high five. "You can. It appears the bucket list is still going strong."

I pondered his words for a few minutes while I finished up what I could on the iPad without my computer. I glanced up at him when it was complete. "I think it's important to have dreams, Gulliver, even if they're small ones. That's what the bucket list was for me. The lifestyle I live isn't all fun and games, but I've learned sometimes you take the good with the bad in life. I enjoyed having the freedom to be my own boss and chase my dreams even if that meant I never put down roots anywhere. I guess that's why the opportunity waiting up the road in Indiana is the best of both worlds."

"What does it offer you that being your own boss doesn't?" he asked, his fingers tapping nervously on the armchair.

"That job would give me flexibility but also a place to call home. It would give me the opportunity to travel around to their different properties, with a home base where I can live the way normal people live. An apartment. A car. A sense of belonging.

Those things are hard for me, though."

"Why? They're basic adult situations, Charity."

I stared him down for a breath, trying to decide if being honest with him about my inability to commit was the smart thing to do. Maybe it wasn't, but it was the right thing to do. Gulliver should know the truth about who I am at my core, so he didn't get ideas about things I will never be able to give him.

"I know they are, Gulliver. I'm just not good at commitments that last longer than one job. I'm always wondering what I'm missing if I pass on the next job or the next job. I think that stems from the fact that my entire childhood was about missing out on life. I don't want to waste more time missing out on new life experiences."

"An argument could be made that you're missing out on new life experiences by not committing, Charity," he said quietly. "A lot of them, actually. You've been here a little over two weeks. Do you feel like you're missing out on the next job by staying here? Because if you do, I don't want to hold you back."

His words were tight and pained. I had hurt him by telling him the truth. I could read that loud and clear on his face. Gulliver never could hide his emotions, which was what I liked about him, but when I was the one to put the pain in those beautiful eyes, I didn't like it so much. It made me feel like the worst person in the world. He was an open book, and I was a locked tome. There was little chance we'd ever last even if we tried.

I reached for his hand, but he pulled it back before I could grasp it. "No, I don't feel like I'm missing out on the next big thing, Gulliver. We aren't done here. We still have to get your business tight."

The light in his eyes had gone out, and all I saw was exhaustion there now. *Damn it, Charity,* I scolded myself, *way to ruin a great night.* I knew it had to be done though. I couldn't lead him on forever.

I held up the iPad. "We'll get there. I've cleaned out the cloud, and tomorrow I'll use the tool I have to reset all four of them. That way the documents won't hang around for thirty days. Then we'll upload some relatively benign files and set up alerts for them. I would highly suggest you use these as little as possible. If you have to scan something in, use the scanner on the pad and not an outside app. Once you've got it uploaded, delete it immediately. Don't save passwords either. Hopefully you won't have to do this forever, but for the next few months—or until you catch whoever is behind the attempt to steal your data—it's important to stay vigilant."

He gave me a jaunty salute of *yes, ma'am*. "I agree, and we're going to change the way we do things to keep better control of our information. You've opened my eyes to a lot of things in both my personal and private life. I owe you more than I can ever afford to pay you."

"You are paying me. Maybe not in monetary ways, but in more important ways. There is more to life than money. Money allows me to do what I want to do, but it doesn't control me. If I don't have money to do X experience, I find a free one to do instead."

"More people need to see the world the way you do. If they did, we'd all be a lot better off. If they did, I might not need to risk everything to make sure the human race can continue to eat." His folded hands were tapping his chin in frustration, and his face was pinched from fatigue, pain, and anger.

"I know you're caught up in the idea you have to save the world's food supply, but I sense you'd rather be concentrating on something else."

"I'd rather concentrate on butterfly and honeybee habitat,"— he waved his hand as if to flick the idea way—"but that would be a fool's errand until I solve the problem of the current pesticides killing all of them. If I don't solve the pesticide problem first, a habitat is pointless. The butterflies would just carry the pesticide to my habitat and kill it."

I wore a frustrated frown. Frustration for Gulliver and all of us as a global community. "I'll do what I can to help, but something tells me it will be years before it happens."

He did the so-so hand. "We need to concentrate on teaching farmers and others alike that the cheaper pesticides will be the end to our existence. That will be an even bigger hurdle to jump, and let me tell you, with my legs, I might never clear it."

"Gulliver, stop. You've come this far. Don't cheapen what you've done by using what you see as your weakness as an excuse to stop this fight. Your legs are the strongest damn pair in this entire business because they're the driving force behind making sure this gets done. Sure, Mathias can throw all the money he wants at the project, but we both know he doesn't understand the cause and effect of this the way you do. Thomas can work to perfect the formula, but it's not his reputation on the line if it fails. You are strong. If you take one step at a time, you'll get there. You just keep the goal in sight, and your goal is to build a habitat for butterflies."

Gulliver shook his head a fraction of an inch. "No, the goal is to one day build an entire reserve," he explained. "Maybe it's a pipe dream, but it drives me to do what I'm doing now. You're right, if I don't take this step, I can't take the next one or the next one."

I stood and leaned over both arms of his chair, my mouth inches from his. "You're a good man, Gulliver Winsome, and you'll accomplish every goal you set for yourself, but not if you don't get some sleep," I insisted.

I brought my lips to his gently, my only intention to offer him a little bit of support for his dreams. When he sighed low in the back of his throat, I couldn't pull away. He needed me tonight. He needed to feel wanted, the same way I did. I slipped my hand up his face to bury itself at the nape and tugged him closer. I was going to own this kiss with my tongue, my lips, and my whole being. Gulliver sighed again, and his lips parted, waiting for my tongue to waltz in and take what it wanted from him. It wanted all of him.

Every breath. Every fear. Every dream.

His hands grasped my face, and his long fingers massaged the back of my neck while his lips massaged mine. "God, Charity," he hissed when the kiss ended. "You have become my light in this dark world. I don't know how to even express how much I needed that."

I leaned my forehead against his and nodded. "You don't have to because I already understand," I promised, brushing some curls off his forehead. His eyes told me he was tired, and it was time for him to get some rest. "Do you want me to crash here tonight so you don't have to drive me back to the campground? I'm sure tongues won't wag in this small town when I'm not at the campground tomorrow morning."

"Let them wag," he whispered, and then his lips found mine again with precise agility. He tugged me over his lap and slid his hands up my shoulders to grasp my neck. His long, warm, slender fingers tipped my head to the right while his lips massaged mine until I released a moan that parted my lips. His tongue used it to its advantage, and with one swipe of the roof of my mouth, he took what he'd wanted since the day I walked into his office.

All of me.

Chapter Ten

The sun streamed brightly through the window of my bedroom, and I moaned when the beam landed directly in my eyes. I grabbed my blanket and yanked it over my head, unsure if I was ready to get up and face the day. It was Saturday, and I wasn't surprised I'd missed the sunrise this morning, considering I'd been up late every night this week. With the threat of theft looming over them, Gulliver and the team were working hard to finish their research, which meant there was no way for me to work on the website with him until the evening. Once he went off to bed, I would write code for several more hours when it was quiet. Since Honey wasn't coming back until Monday, I spent the majority of the day answering phones and organizing orders. That meant if I wasn't sleeping, I was working, but sometimes that's what had to be done.

Now I was nearly ready to launch the website. I had a few more hours of cleaning the site up and testing links, but I planned to finish it today. Once I was confident it was ready to go live, I'd go over it with Gulliver before we published it. Unfortunately, after I hit the publish button, my work at Butterfly Junction would be done. Honey would be back to work on Monday, which meant there was no longer any reason for me to be there.

I didn't know how to feel about not being there to spend part of each day with him. Sad. Upset. Jealous. All of those were ridiculous feelings to have after knowing someone less than a month, but I did and that was new for me. It was a foreign sensation to miss someone after being apart for only a few hours, but I did. We'd shared meals, secrets, and kisses, and I'd come to live for the time I shared with Gulliver.

I worried once I was no longer useful to him or when he no longer needed me for the business, that he'd stop coming around. It wouldn't surprise me, though. No one in my life had ever stuck around once they had gotten from me what they wanted. Hell, my parents hadn't wanted me. What made me think a man like Gulliver Winsome would? His kisses might be hot as hell, and his luscious hazel eyes might be filled with desire every time they met mine, but there was a difference between sexual desire and being in it for the long haul.

The next week without a job stretched before me, and I hummed low in my throat. I had months until I had to be in Indiana for the next job. Perhaps I needed to find more work to fill the time until then. After thinking about the heartache of staying in Plentiful but not seeing Gulliver every day, I couldn't do it. And I wouldn't. I would do what I always did, and that was leave.

Every time I got in Myrtle to drive to the next job, I was running. I was running from the memory of my mother walking out the door that warm August day even as I begged her with tears running down my face to stay. When she refused, I begged her to take me with her, promising her all the things a little girl of five would promise. *I'll be good, Momma! I won't be in the way! I'll be quiet! Take me with you!* She didn't. She got in the car, and she drove away. When I saw her nine years later in her new life, I could see it fit her better than the one she'd left behind, but it was still hard to understand why I couldn't have fit into that picture with her. There was no room for my tiny footprint in her life, though.

I groaned and threw the blanket back off my face to stare at the ceiling. "Damn it, Charity. Why did you have to go and think through all of that?"

Probably because running from it was getting too hard. I was tired. I was too old to carry her baggage when she wasn't even part of my life anymore. I was supposed to leave all that baggage on the side of the road somewhere, but I hadn't. It still sat on my shoulders and ruined everything else I'd tried to do to forget my past. I was never going to do that as long as I carried those little pieces of her around like an albatross around my neck.

I let out a heavy moan and rocked my head back and forth on the pillow. It was time to motor out of Plentiful and leave behind more innocent victims of my disastrous life. I paused when Mojo patted me with his paw. He always knew when I was getting ready to move on. He sensed the uncertainty in the space around us and wanted to offer me comfort. "What do you think, buddy?" I asked him, my voice breaking the silence of the morning while I rubbed his head. "Do we stay or do we go?"

He didn't answer other than to wiggle his eyebrows at me with concern. I sighed. Would staying help me fix some of the disastrous parts of my childhood? Whenever I rode the BMX bike Laverne loaned me, I felt like a normal kid on a normal summer afternoon. I'd pedal my heart out as the wind blew across my face, offering me abandon, joy, adventure, and unabashed happiness to be that free.

If I had to choose a word to use about where I was in life right now, it would be *torn*. Part of me wanted to stay in Plentiful and be a kid forever, part of me wanted to motor down to Indiana and set up shop with my dream job, and part of me wanted to fire up Myrtle from site forty-seven of Plentiful Campground and hit the open road. The open road was safe. Most people didn't understand that, but when you never had a home, the open road and endless miles *are* your home.

I climbed out of bed, surprised to see the clock read nearly one in the afternoon. No wonder Mojo was staring at me with disgust. I set his breakfast out for him by the picnic table and thought about walking down to the dock for a few minutes, but there was an urgency in my gut to get the website up and running again for Butterfly Junction. As much as I didn't want my time with Gulliver to end, the sooner the website was running, the sooner he could use it to educate people about the precarious situation we're in with the pollinators. Not to mention, if we didn't do something as a society, the Great Lakes would be too polluted to use as a source of drinking water. It was concerning how few people understood that our resources weren't limitless.

I climbed back into Myrtle and made a piece of toast, and while I sat there eating it, the peanut butter smeared with a sweet layer of honey, I couldn't help but ponder the truth that was staring me in the face. If I hadn't agreed to drive across the country to do this job, I wouldn't know that we had such a serious problem facing our society either. I'd still be out there innocently living my life, not knowing that our own behavior was destroying our future.

I shook my head of those thoughts and got to work on the website again, checking links, adjusting themes, and scanning for spelling errors. It was tedious work, but one of the most important jobs I had to do before I could call it a wrap. When I finished, I was confident it was ready to show Gulliver. I had plans to text him later and ask him to breakfast tomorrow with the excuse I had the site ready to go. I didn't know if I needed an excuse to have breakfast with him, but just in case I did, I'd use it.

I stood and stretched, poured a glass of iced tea from the pitcher, and sipped it leaning against the sink. With my work done for the day, I checked the clock. It was only three, which gave me plenty of time to either take the bike for a ride around the area or head into town and visit the little thrift shop I'd noticed the other day. They had vintage clothing that looked right up my alley, but I wasn't sure if they had kids' clothes as well. Since I wear the same size as a ten-year-old, that was a must. Tonight I'd make a campfire and share some hot dogs with Mojo. It wouldn't be as much fun as a campfire on the beach with Gulliver under the northern lights, but it would have to do.

A voice from outside the camper floated in and I paused. If I wasn't mistaken . . .

I peeked out the door silently, watching as the man I'd come to like a little bit too much stroked Mojo's head while he talked to him calmly. My big, bad guard dog was eating up the attention like he hadn't seen him in a week rather than a day. Mojo rolled over and whined every time Gulliver rubbed his belly.

"Hey there, stranger," I called.

His head snapped up, and he almost fell over on his crutches. "Hey, yourself," he answered, righting himself. "I was telling Mojo how I couldn't stay away even though I should be working."

I jumped down from Myrtle's door and ran to him, throwing my arms around his waist in a hug. "I missed you," I whispered while he gathered me into his arms. My head rested on his soft belly and I loved how it felt under my cheek. I might love it a little too much, especially when his cologne drifted into my atmosphere and parts of me came to life that had been dormant for years. Sad to say considering I'm only twenty-six, but life on the road doesn't offer too many chances for tangled sheets in the morning. Gulliver was different, though. His hugs were different.

The tingles of excitement. The joy of anticipation. The pounding of my heart. The settling of my heart. There was so much happening in a simple hug that I didn't know if I should weep or laugh.

"I want to feel your arms around my neck," he whispered from over my head. "Will I hurt you if I pick you up?"

I shook my head, and he lifted me so I could slide my arms around his neck. His arms were wrapped around my waist tightly, and he swung me gently side to side while he trailed kisses from my collarbone all the way to my ear. He bit down gently on the lobe, and a shudder ran through me.

"I love being able to hold you like this, Charity," he whispered into my ear. "Your doll-sized arms around my neck and your sweet, warm body against my chest settles my insecurities about who I am as a man every time."

I buried my nose in his neck to inhale the essence of him, and a shiver ran through me again.

He tightened his arms around me. "Is this scaring you? You're shivering."

"No," I whispered back. I teased his ear lobe with my tongue. "I never want you to put me down, Gulliver. Being in your arms just . . ." I paused, searching for the right words.

"Settles everything?" he asked. His warm lips kissed my neck tenderly, and goose bumps broke out across my skin. "That's what your arms do for me."

I nodded, my lips finding his in a shared understanding of what we were both feeling. His tongue had no patience and pushed its way in to tangle with mine, both of us humming with unchecked desire. Mojo barked and our lips fell apart with laughter on them.

"I guess he's had enough of his girl being in another man's arms," Gulliver said, lowering me to the ground.

I pointed at the dog, who wasn't even looking at us. "He probably saw a chipmunk. He's never met one yet that he likes," I teased, putting my arms around Gulliver's waist again. I gazed up at him and smiled, loving the relaxed look on his face after our kiss. "I was going to text you a bit later. I finished the website a few minutes ago. I thought we could share breakfast tomorrow morning and go over it. I know you want it live as soon as possible."

His gaze held mine, and he lowered himself to the picnic table bench after he dropped his crutches. "I'm all in for breakfast tomorrow morning," he promised while his hand slipped up my face to hold my cheek. "You might as well know I'm going to kiss you again," he said before his lips came down on mine. His tongue meandered across the roof of my mouth while his hands stroked my shoulders and slipped into my hair, tugging me even closer to him. I grasped his trim waist, partly to steady myself, but mostly to have my hands on him. Whenever we were together, I wanted his lips on mine, his hands in my hair, and my hands all over him. It was heady and exciting, but it was also a physical need I yearned for when we were apart.

Gulliver slowed the kiss and stroked my tongue languidly one more time before the kiss ended and we both inhaled deeply. Our hands stayed wrapped up in each other, but his eyelid came down in a wink that left me more hot than bothered. "I have other plans for today," he said, his voice breathy. "Plans that don't involve kissing you all day, though I could without complaint."

"What kind of plans?" I asked, my heart still pounding from the kiss. Why did he have to be so good with that tongue of his? The thought of what that tongue could do to other parts of me racked my body with a shiver of anticipation.

"It's a surprise."

"I don't like surprises, Gulliver," I said, one brow lowered toward my nose in a scolding librarian pose.

"You'll like this one. It involves the Lady of the Lake."

"Tempting, very tempting. I would consider it as long as it doesn't involve bears or boat motors exploding."

He let out a laugh loud enough to scare Mojo; then he grabbed me around the waist and dragged me into him. His gaze was filled with lusty desire that left my knees weak and my heart pounding. "You make me happier than I've ever been, Charity. It's like I get up in the morning now with a purpose instead of as a requirement. I work with a deadline for the day in mind instead of assuming I'll work until I drop. You've filled my days with excitement again, and the laughter and kisses are a bonus in my life. I don't want to think about what my life will be like when you leave."

His lips found my still plump, dewy ones again, but this kiss was different. It was filled with promise. He poured himself into me with his tongue. When he moaned, I trapped it inside my soul to harbor forever. He gave to me what no one else ever had before. Desire. Need. Anticipation. Contentment. As though finding that other person who fit into all your empty spaces just perfectly was enough to get you to the next breath. The next hour. The next day.

When the kiss ended, I smoothed my palm over his cheek to feel the warmth of his skin through his downy beard. "You make me just as happy, Gulliver, but I'm afraid our work together is drawing to a close. I didn't want to finish the website today because I knew once I did, our time together at Butterfly Junction ends."

He hugged me to him and rocked me back and forth. "Let's not think about it today," he said, holding me out by my shoulders. "Grab a bag with a towel and your water shoes." He paused. "I should have asked if you had plans for today first."

I shook my head and planted my hands on my hips. "Nothing other than sharing a pack of hot dogs over a campfire with Mojo tonight. I wanted to call you, but I figured you'd be working."

He chuckled and bent over, planting a kiss on the tip of my nose. "Normally I would be working, but you've changed that about me in the last three weeks. I love spending time with you, and I'm all for a campfire and hot dogs when we get back. Do you think Mojo will share?"

I grinned at the dog sitting at attention by my side. "I'm sure he will. Oh, wait. What am I going to do with Mojo? Can he come with us?"

He put his arm at the small of my back and propelled me toward Myrtle's door. "Laverne is going to keep him. I already talked to her."

"I sure am," Laverne said, walking toward us through the grass. "I hear my buddy needs some time alone with his Aunt Laverne."

I couldn't hold in my laughter when Mojo stood up, his back end wagging so hard I thought it might wiggle right off. He lowered his front paws to the ground and whined until Laverne lavished him with much love and attention about what a good boy he was.

"I guess he does," I said, shaking my head. "He's such a ship jumper. One minute he won't leave my side, and the next he's pretending I don't exist."

Laverne was laughing right along with me when Mojo rolled over to present his belly for a rub. "Nah, he's secure knowing you're safe with Gulliver, so he can take a break," she said, standing and clapping her thigh. "Come on, Mojo. There's sun on the dock that's lonely."

I handed her his leash, and she hooked it to his collar. "We'll stop down and get him when we're back from whatever it is Mr. Winsome has planned," I promised.

"No rush," she sang as though she knew something she didn't. "I might even have a hot dog or two that needs a home in a big dog's belly. Have fun, you two," she called. Laverne trundled my dog away as quickly as she'd come, and all I could do was shake my head.

"She's something else. Wonderful, but something else," I said on a laugh.

Gulliver took a step closer and leaned down, balancing his forehead on mine. "I know someone else who is just as wonderful. I can't wait to see her face when she sees the surprise I have in store. If I'm lucky, it just might sell her on staying in this small town forever."

Before I had a chance to respond, or maybe so I couldn't, his lips found mine. There was no holding back this time, and he deepened the kiss instantly, teasing my lips with his warm tongue until they parted. He slipped his tongue inside where it glided alongside mine in velvet harmony. He nipped and tugged on my bottom lip, pulling it through his teeth gently until the kiss ended. His chest was heaving against mine, and I had his shirt wrapped up in both of my fists.

"Oh, Gulliver, keep kissing me like that and you just might tempt me to stay," I murmured before his lips found mine again.

I went down the steps backward with his crutches and hoped he didn't fall as we made our way to the beach. I couldn't stop him if he did fall, and I would go rolling right down with him.

His laughter filled my ears when we were halfway down. "You're petrified. Relax, I'm not going to fall and take you with me," he promised, holding on to the railing tightly with each step.

"How did you know my exact thoughts?" I asked, laughing with him but grateful we were nearing the bottom.

"It's written all over your face. You're cute when you're worried."

I scrunched up my nose. "I still don't know if this is safe," I said, glancing down to the beach. "How do you walk on the sand with these things?" I asked, holding the crutches up.

We took the last two steps to the sand before he answered. "Maybe you've noticed I only use them for balance. I don't use them as traditional crutches, I just use them to take the pressure off my knee and hip. If I don't, I'll end up with everything hurting at the end of the day."

I handed him the crutches, and he tucked his arms into them, then walked through the sand carefully. "There's our ride," he said, stopping and pointing.

I followed his finger to the orange sea kayak parked on the sand. "A kayak? And only one?"

He kept crutching toward the boat, his head nodding. "We only need one."

In another couple of feet, I discovered why. "A tandem kayak?" I asked, surprised.

"The best kind," he said, laughing. "It's Mathias's. He's letting us borrow it for the afternoon. He knows I can't haul the kayaks around down here with the steps, so he always drops it off for me."

"Hey, did Mathias say how Honey is doing?" I asked. I saw an opportunity to see if they still needed me at Butterfly Junction. I was going to take it.

"He said she's doing a little bit better but still in pain. He can't convince her not to come back to work on Monday, though. We will have to see what happens."

My heart jumped at his words. Not because Honey was still in pain, but that they might still need me at the business. "I'm always available, Gulliver. It's probably better if she starts slow and works her way up to the whole day. I can be there to help."

"Charity?" he asked, and I glanced up at him, afraid of what I'd see in his eyes. "You don't need an excuse to see me, okay? I'm not going to disappear from your life just because your work at Butterfly Junction is done. The only way that will happen is if you leave. You don't have to make yourself useful in order for me to want to spend time with you. Do you understand me?"

I nodded, swallowing around the lump in my throat. "How do you always know the things I'm not saying?" I asked, grasping his shirt in my fist. "No one has ever stuck around in my life, Gulliver. Ever."

"Yet," he answered. When he kissed me, it was so tender I wanted to cry. "'Yet' is the word you're looking for, my sweet Charity."

"Yet," I whispered. "I suppose the last six years it was my fault that no one stuck around considering that I didn't."

His head bobbed as his fingers grasped my fist still holding his shirt. "That does make it a bit harder for someone to stick around, sweetheart. It doesn't make it impossible, though. Fair warning."

I nodded once. "Warning heard."

He handed me a life jacket, which I noticed was perfectly sized just for me. "Good, now it's time for some fun."

Before I strapped it on, I looked up at him. "Um, Gulliver. I don't know how to kayak, and my arm isn't . . ."

He put his finger to my lips. "That's why it's a tandem kayak. I'll sit in the back and do the paddling. You get to enjoy the scenery."

"Won't that be a lot of work for you?" I asked while he checked the hatch.

"No, you weigh nothing. It's not going to be a problem," he assured me.

I strapped on the vest, excitement building in my belly to take a ride on the big lake while sitting so close to the water. "Mathias thought of everything. There's even a cooler."

"It's got water, protein bars, fire starter, and a first-aid kit. If we were to get stranded, at least we could survive the night," he explained.

I groaned but it immediately switched to laughter. "Could we not get stranded again? Please?"

Gulliver laughed with me and folded his crutches down into a one-foot-long piece, wrapping a tie around them and fastening it. "I promise we aren't going far enough out to have to worry about it, but we'll take it along to be on the safe side." He tugged the soft-sided cooler out and set it on the sand so he could tuck his crutches into the center hatch and lock it. "Now, you'll sit in the front with the cooler between your legs. I'll take the back."

He continued to instruct me on what to do and how to help him launch the kayak from the sand until we were both inside the boat, the spray skirts around our middles, and his paddle making quick work of the water to propel us along the shoreline.

"Where are we going?" I asked, taking in the beauty before me. "It's getting late in the afternoon."

"You'll see in a few minutes," he promised. "It's late in the afternoon on purpose."

Rather than answer, I leaned back and watched the eagles swoop over the water, their sharp talons snatching fish from the waves before they flew off toward a nest or the shore to feast.

"It's beyond beautiful out here," I sighed, the water glistening around us. "I don't even have a word for it."

"Just wait," he said, his voice low and steady behind me. "You haven't seen anything yet."

Before I could figure out what he was talking about, we rounded a curve on the shoreline. I gasped from the sheer beauty of what sat before me. My mouth hung open, my head swiveling to check out the rock formations from all angles. The way the afternoon sun glinted off the rocks gave them the impression of pure gold.

"This is incredible." I was breathless as I focused on the rock formations created by Mother Nature. "The Lady of the Lake is an amazing artist."

Gulliver paddled slower now, his voice behind me secondary to the vision before me. "These are called the mainland sea caves," he explained. "They're a favorite hangout of kayakers."

I turned slightly to see him. "We can go inside them?" I asked in total awe.

"Of course," he said, chuckling. "That's why I didn't bring you here when we went to Oak Island. I wanted you to have the whole experience. The caves are created by the lapping of Lake Superior. People often question the power of this lake; then they see the caves and they no longer do."

The smile on my face was reflected on his. "Thank you, Gulliver. Seriously, if I had known these existed, they would have been on my bucket list."

"You're welcome, sweet Charity. Sometimes the best part of the bucket list is not having one, right?"

I thought about what he'd said for a moment and nodded. "I guess you're right. The surprise of discovering something I didn't even know existed was far more satisfying than checking something off a piece of paper. I'm still stunned by their beauty."

"There are more out by Devil's Island, but you'd need a much bigger boat to get to them. The caves here will ice over in the winter, and if the lake freezes hard enough, you can come out and walk through them. The wonder of Mother Nature never ceases here."

"Wow," I said, my head turned back to the giant monoliths before me. "I would love to see that."

"Well, if you're ready, I'm about to give you the tour of a lifetime," he promised as his paddle dipped into the water.

"I'm ready," I agreed, clapping excitedly as he glided us through the first keyhole in the shimmering golden rock.

"They're so beautiful. I'm so in love right now."

"They are, and I am," he whispered.

His words reached my ears and rang there before lodging in places I hadn't known were empty.

Chapter Eleven

The fire had burned down, and we held our hot dog sticks over the low flame in anticipation. The hot dogs warmed, crinkled, and charred almost instantly, testing our reflexes to pluck them from the fire before ignition. Mojo sat whining by my chair, waiting for the first dogs to land in his bowl. I blew on them, knowing he'd burn his mouth in his haste to enjoy the strange delicacy that dogs and humans alike loved to snarf down if I didn't.

"He's hilarious." Gulliver laughed at Mojo as he pranced from foot to foot as if the ground were hot lava.

"He knows what's coming. I got his favorite ones too. He loves the snap when he bites into them."

"I'm personally rather excited about the snap myself," Gulliver agreed, carefully transferring the hot dogs into buns and snapping into the first one. My dog glared at him as if to say he should have had the first one of the night.

I laughed and tossed one into his bowl while I blew on the other one. Mojo inhaled the first one and licked his chops until I put the second one down. He ate that one slower while I loaded up the stick again.

Gulliver handed me his second dog. "Relax. Enjoy this one before you make more. You must be starving. Not only are you a kayaking rock star, but you made this most epic fire in a matter of minutes."

I smiled as I chewed, the hot, juicy meat making my eyes roll around in my head. "I don't know about a kayaking rock star. You did all the paddling while I gazed slack-jawed at the caves."

He winked and held more dogs out over the fire. "Maybe, but you didn't tip the boat, so that makes you a rock star."

"I was too frozen in place by the sight before me, Gulliver. I'd never done anything as exciting as kayaking through caves before. It was beyond cool. Sliding through some crevices barely big enough for us was scary for someone my size. The reward of a new, bigger cave to explore was a blast, though. It was an afternoon to remember for the rest of my life. Thank you for doing it in a way I could get the most enjoyment from it."

He squeezed my shoulder in encouragement. "I didn't want to wait too long to show them to you. I was afraid you might decide to take off, and we'd never get to experience the caves together."

I grasped his hand on my shoulder and held it tightly. "To be honest, this morning I was thinking since the website was done it might be time to head out, but I don't know if I'm ready yet. I'm torn."

"I guess I can understand that," he said with a nod of his head. "I'm just worried you're going to leave without any warning, and I won't be ready for it. I don't want to go back to the life I had before you arrived, Charity."

"I can't make any promises, Gulliver, but I would never leave without saying goodbye. I promise you that right now, okay?" He didn't respond and kept his gaze focused on the flames, so I decided a subject change was in order. "Do you have any idea who's behind the break-in? There has to be someone who has shown enough interest in what you're doing to heighten your suspicions." I lowered the hot dog fork to the ground and leaned back in my chair.

"The list is endless, Charity," he said on a sardonic laugh. "There are several different groups that want a successful pesticide for large operations for different reasons, but for those watching my research closely, it's for one reason."

"Money," I answered immediately.

"Everything in life is controlled by money. Mathias is doing some digging, and he might hire a private investigator if he can find a promising avenue to direct them down. I don't have time to deal with it, nor do I have the means or ability. Mathias does."

"Is it safe for you to be living at Butterfly Junction in the meantime, though?" I asked. "I don't want you to get hurt."

"I'm safe. No one can pick the lock on my door or unlock a window from the outside. They would have to break one, which would set off the alarm. Sure, they could try to smoke me out, but I have an emergency exit to the outside, and the fire system immediately calls the police and fire station if it goes off."

"You're telling me to stop worrying?" I asked, half-joking.

Our chairs were next to each other, and he slipped his hand into mine. "I like how you worry about me, but I don't want it to consume you. I'm safe, I promise." He patted my hand between his. "I hope you don't think I hold your hand too much," he whispered. "I always want to hold your hand when we're walking, but I can't, so I have to take the opportunity where I can."

I let him twine his fingers in mine the way two couples do when walking together without a care in the world. "I'm glad you do, Gulliver. My heart aches that you feel like you have to explain yourself. You don't. There is nothing typical about the two of us, both together and apart. All I know is the lack of human companionship over the last six years has been hard on me. I didn't realize how much until you started holding my hand."

"You didn't date at all?" he asked, his voice incredulous.

"How could I? I was rarely in one place for longer than a week. Occasionally, I would go out with a group of people from one of the places I was working, but never anything serious. In hindsight, I realize I was too busy creating the childhood I'd never had, so being an adult fell by the wayside. It sounds weird, but I think you understand."

He brushed his lips across my knuckles in affirmation of my words. "I do. You didn't have time to date because you were busy living. I understand how important living and exploring is, but like you, I miss the companionship. I understood I'd always go it alone in this world, considering everything I went through as a kid. Then you appeared and showed me maybe I'm not as alone as I had always believed."

I was moving before I made the mental decision to do so. I straddled his thighs and cupped his face. "Listen to me right now, Gulliver Winsome, you are not alone. Do you hear me?" I asked, my tiny fingers squeezing his cheeks until he grimaced.

He grasped my hands and held them loosely to his cheeks. "I hear you," he promised. "But I also see you."

I tipped my head, puzzled by his words. "You see me?"

His hands trailed down my waist to my thighs, leaving pinpricks of electricity on my skin. "You don't just talk the talk, but you keep showing up and engaging with me in a genuine, caring way. Other women have claimed not to care about my leg issues, but in the end, they never lasted more than a couple of nice dinners out. They worried too much about the things I couldn't do. You don't believe there's anything I can't do."

I rubbed at the frown lines between his eyes. "Because there's nothing you can't do!" I exclaimed in a hushed tone. I was never more grateful my campsite was at the back of the campground, away from prying eyes.

"There's plenty I can't do, Charity, at least not the same way most guys do them. I can't take a shower without a bench to sit on. I can't ride a bike, run, or do most physical things other guys strut around bragging about."

"Those are little things, Gulliver. And you can ride a bike—they make handcycles—running is overrated, and I hate macho guys who strut around like they're the best thing since sliced bread. Spoiler alert, they never are. They're usually shallow jerks who forget that beauty doesn't last, but brains do. I guess what I'm saying is, I prefer to focus on things we can do together rather than what we can't. It's ridiculous to think we have to be exactly alike to enjoy spending time with each other. You can't type the beginning of a line of code, and I can't pick out a dung beetle from any other beetle. Life isn't a competition. It's a journey."

He smiled, his hands back to caressing my waist. "I'm smiling because you're right, but also because most people don't use logic to realize we're not in a competition. Humans write people off and never give it a second thought, when the reality is, they might have just written off the one person they were meant to be with."

I rubbed my hands on his chest to relax against him. "I think about all the people who have written me off in my life, and all the people who haven't, and I can see the difference with clear delineations. Those who wrote me off did so because of their own insecurities. Those who stayed did so because they understood my insecurities. Which camp do you fall into?" I asked seriously. "If it's the former, I'd like to know now. If it's the latter, then kiss me and know I'll never write you off because I understand your insecurities too."

His hand cupped my neck and hauled me toward him, and I fell against his chest, both our hearts finally beating together in the same place. It was simple, but oh so beautiful when his lips teased mine into complacency. He worked them over, his tongue stroking them with adoration, but never pushing past them to take the kiss to a higher level. Instead, he let me rest against his chest with his lips on my forehead. We shared warmth, but more than that, we shared a bond in commonality of our pain and disappointments.

"You're more than I could ever hope to find, Charity." His gaze locked with mine, and when I didn't glance away, he kissed me again, this time with the pent-up passion of a man determined to show me with his lips and tongue how important this moment was. We had cemented a feeling, an indescribable emotion, one we both shared but couldn't name.

I wrapped my arms around his neck, holding my chest to his while he rocketed the kiss all the way to the moon. He rocked me into orbit with his tongue, and it took some doing but I eventually stole a taste of him too. His chest hummed with the desire of a man losing control. He wanted so much more than stolen kisses by the campfire. The part of him that he couldn't control, the virile man reacting to a woman on his lap and in his arms, was growing harder with every soft brush of my belly against him.

Gulliver grasped my shoulders and pulled me away from him, the gold flecks in his eyes spinning like a kaleidoscope in the light from the fire. "Charity, I didn't know these feelings could exist within me," he sighed. "I didn't know. God, please tell me I'm not the only one feeling this."

I climbed off his lap and stood next to him, resting my bottom on the arm of the chair. "Definitely not," I promised. "I'm feeling the same passion and need for you, but mine is just less obvious." I winked, and in the light from the fire, I noticed him blush as he adjusted himself discreetly.

"I understand that we're in a weird place with your lifestyle compared to mine," he said with honesty. "I'm tied here, and you aren't. If you can't find what you need in Plentiful, I would never ask you to stunt whatever your soul needs just to stay with me."

I caressed his face, my finger trailing across his beard while I gazed into his mesmerizing eyes. "I don't know everything my soul needs, but I do know it needed to meet you. My life is shifting, and it's scaring me. If I had a crystal ball, I'd use it right now, just to sort out what I'm supposed to do. I don't have the answer, but I know I'm not good at staying in one place."

"I might have something to help," he said, kissing me on the cheek. "Sit, I'll grab it from my truck."

I stood and handed him his crutches, then poked at the fire. I should have been tired after all the cave exploring today, but I wasn't. I was wired more than anything and didn't know how to settle down. He was right when he said his life was here, and mine, well, wasn't. Admitting I was scared wasn't easy, but at the same time I wanted him to know it wasn't him making me indecisive, but my own insecurities and questions about life. In six years, I'd never stayed in one place longer than a month, and every time I tried, it had been a dismal failure. Maybe it was because I'm a Gemini, and I'm destined to roam the world forever. More likely it was because that scared, unloved little girl who used to survive off the kindness of others still hadn't learned how to trust anyone.

As he closed the truck door, his phone rang, taking us both by surprise. Gulliver held up his finger. "It's Mathias," he said, answering the call.

The short conversation was concerning, and I stood, waiting for him to finish. He ended the call and stuck his phone in his pocket, crutching back to me. I noticed the fatigue immediately. It was easy to see when he needed to rest his body just by watching him walk. "What was that about?" I asked when he reached me by the fire.

He lowered himself back to the chair and tossed his sticks to the ground. "Honey's mom had a massive heart attack tonight."

I gasped with surprise. "Oh my. Is she alive?"

He nodded and my shoulders sank in relief. "She is, but if

they don't do a triple bypass, she won't stay that way. He has to take Honey to Superior tonight to be with her parents. That means she won't be able to work this week."

I waved my hand in the air. "Not a problem. I'll do it. She should be with her family right now. Besides, it will give her arm extra time to heal."

He lowered his brow at me. "Charity, we can hire a temp. You're in no way bound to do this."

"I know," I assured him, nodding when he took my hand. "I don't want you to hire a temp, though. I already know what's going on at Butterfly Junction and am already part of the team," I said, making air quotes with my free hand. "Adding someone new is a risk, and it could put them in danger too. I know you don't want to do that."

His shoulders slumped with the weight of the world on them. "I didn't think of that. You're right, though. If I bring someone new in, I'd have to vet them and somehow protect them from what's going on there."

"That's why I'm the perfect solution," I said again, rubbing my hand on my leg. I was nervous he'd say no, and I was desperate for him to say yes.

"You have to let me pay you," he said, his brow going down.

I rested my hand on his shirt, secretly thrilled he was agreeing to this. "I would rather you pay Honey. She can't work, but she still needs to pay her rent. I know Mathias would take care of her, but it's the right thing to do."

"I will, but you need to live too. You've been working for free for weeks now. It can't continue."

I clapped my hands once with an idea. "Fine, you feed me lunch and dinner and throw in a bag of Mojo's dog food, and we've got a deal." I held my hand out for him to shake, but he didn't.

"Charity, that's hardly fair. You don't eat that much. Besides, I want to eat lunch and dinner with you all the time anyway. That isn't exactly a hardship."

I tipped my head back and forth a couple of times as if weighing what he'd said. "True, but food for us is the only thing we really need right now. As long as that's covered, I need no other payment. It's not forever, Gulliver. I'll be fine."

He let out the breath he'd been holding and nodded. "Okay, but only until we know more about what's happening with Honey's mom. You have to promise to tell me if you have to leave or you get tired of working all day."

I crossed my heart and planted a kiss on his lips. "I promise. You don't know how relieved I am to know I have something to go back to on Monday."

He pulled a box out of his pocket and held it up. "I was going to give this to you tomorrow to thank you for all the work you've done to protect the business. Instead, I'll give it to you tonight as a way to say thank you, both for your hard work in the business and for all the time you've spent with me. You've reminded me there is more to life than work and bugs. Well, actually, this gift . . ." He waved his hand around. "Never mind."

He thrust the box toward me, and I accepted it, one brow in the air. "Are you slightly indecisive about giving me this?"

He shook his head and chuckled at himself. "No, not at all. I realized I couldn't say this has nothing to do with bugs because it does."

I eyed the box. "Nothing alive is going to pop out of here, is it?"

He burst into laughter, his body shaking as tears ran from his eyes. I wondered if he was losing it, tired, nervous, or all three. Finally, he held up his hand and wiped his eyes. "Sorry. I admit my explanation sounded weird. There's nothing alive in there. You'll see. Just open it."

I tugged on the ribbon until it fell away and cracked the box open, lifting it closer to my face to make it out in the low light of the fire. He toggled open his phone's flashlight and held it over the necklace. "Oh, Gulliver. It's beautiful," I gasped. The pink, oval necklace was gorgeous in its simplicity. "I'm having a hard time seeing what it is. Is it a leaf? Wait, leaves aren't pink." The pattern on the necklace was pink, with thin black lines running through it.

"It's a butterfly wing," he explained, pointing at the black lines. "Don't worry. It was already dead by the time I found it. I often find just a wing of a butterfly when I'm out hiking. I gather them and make necklaces or earrings. Maybe it's morbid, but the butterfly is meant for beauty, and that should be enjoyed long after they're gone."

I stared at it as he spoke, finally lifting my gaze to his. "I love it. I don't think it's morbid at all. Especially not in this setting. I love that they can continue to share their beauty with us, just in a different way."

"I'm glad you understand," he said, smiling. "These butterflies only live a week, sometimes two before they become part of the earth again. They're small and often don't live even that long in the wild, considering they have multiple predators." He rolled his eyes to his hairline. "Sorry, you don't need a lesson in butterflies."

"But I do because I know next to nothing about them. I didn't know there were pink butterflies, but this is gorgeous. I'll treasure it, especially since I know you made it."

His smile was tired but bright. There was a touch of relief there, too, that his gift had been well received. "Whenever I think of you, I think of the tiniest butterfly flitting through a field of clover. I just want to protect you and keep you safe so you can share your beauty with the rest of the world for a long time to come."

I ran my fingers over his beard to pull him down for a kiss.

It turned hot and hungry immediately, his tongue reminding mine that it was the boss. Oh God, I loved the way this man kissed me. Hot, languid, but filled with an underlying sense of urgency for the next moment of our lives together.

I broke the kiss and rested my forehead on his. "Thank you. This means the world to me."

Gulliver took it off the display board and held it up. "Should I put it on?"

"Please," I agreed and let him fasten it behind my neck. It rested perfectly on my chest, and I patted it with my hand. "I like how it has a short enough chain that it doesn't go all the way to my navel."

His lid lowered in a wink to cover his beautiful eye for a moment. "I figured you were going to need a shorter one. The necklace is even more gorgeous on you than I pictured it being. A pink butterfly symbolizes happiness. If there's one thing I wish for you always, it's happiness. Whether you find it here or out roaming the country, I hope you find it every single day you live. I also hope you found a little bit of happiness here with me in the last few weeks."

I cupped his cheek in my hand and guided him to me until we were nose to nose. "I found more than a little bit. I found a happiness here that I never experienced anywhere else in this country."

"Well, score one for Plentiful," he whispered. He never said another thing, at least not with his words. His lips, on the other hand, told me a different story. His lips capturing mine in a kiss of gentleness was that first chapter. The meet-cute. The tentative dance of getting to know you. Chapter two opened with his warm, velvety tongue trailing along my lips. Chapter three was the music soft, low, and romantic as we danced tangled together as one. Each new chapter opened up before me as he slipped his tongue between my parted lips to taste, tease, and taunt me. He was mine in the darkness with no one else around to witness everything I took from him as he poured it into me. If a kiss was just a kiss, then this wasn't a kiss. This wasn't the end either. His low moan and hardness pressed against me was just the start of a new chapter.

Chapter Twelve

I stood from the uncomfortable desk chair and stretched my back out. It was nearly nine p.m., and I hadn't seen Gulliver since lunch. He was working closely with Thomas as they dissected all the information they'd gotten from their last application of the pesticide to a farmer's field. I didn't understand it all, but I did understand that they were getting close, and that was exciting.

I grabbed Mojo's ball and called for him to follow me outside. The day had been warm, but as the sun was sinking lower toward the horizon of Lake Superior, the air was cooling off considerably. "Come on, big dog, let's go have a little playtime. We've worked long enough today."

Mojo barked once, with little enthusiasm, but followed me through the door and around the back of the building to the small strip of sand near the marina. He loved playing ball there so he could romp in the waves lapping against the shore.

I threw his ball, watching it arc through the air and land in the sand where Mojo pounced on it, scooped it up, sand flying everywhere and his ears flopping as he ran through the water's edge back to me. The ball fell from his lips, and he sat, his gaze bouncing between me and the ball.

I laughed, scooping up the slobbery yellow toy and tossing it again. Mojo's tongue lolled as he chased it back down the beach. I shucked my shoes and waded into the water while I waited for Mojo to bring the ball back. I didn't walk too far in, just stayed on the edge where the water was frothy and the bubbles tickled my toes. Lake Superior was still cold, even in the middle of June, but it was nice to relax after a long day of work.

Mojo bounded back to me, and I picked up his ball, lobbing it into the grass so he had to run farther to get it. I swished my toe through the water as I thought about tomorrow's date. June seventeenth. The day Charity Puck had come wailing into the world at a minuscule three and a half pounds and sixteen inches long. That date changed my parents' lives, and not in a good way, so I never made a big deal about my birthday. This year, I was in an awkward position. I wanted to ask Gulliver to do something fun with me, but I didn't want to make my birthday the reason he felt obligated to do so. I wanted to see him regardless of the date, but I also didn't want to spend the day alone. It was a real conundrum I hadn't worked out yet.

Usually, my birthday involved a bottle of wine and a cupcake out on the open road somewhere. Occasionally, if I was in the right town, I might stop into a local pub or diner for a meal and a drink, but I never mentioned that it was a celebration dinner. Probably because it never was. It was just another lonely day in the life of Charity Puck. It was too much to ponder the idea that no one had ever really loved me unconditionally, especially not the two people who'd creat—

What was that sound? I rolled to my side and slapped the space around me, the noise making my head pound. Barking. Mojo.

"Mojo," I moaned, "hush your face. You're hurting my head."

"Charity!" Gulliver's voice was frantic and far away when he yelled. "Charity, tell Mojo to stand down so we can come help you!"

Help me? Why did he need to help me? Why was I wet? Why was Mojo barking and growling like a crazy fool?

"Mojo!" I exclaimed. "It's okay, boy," I soothed, reaching my hand out to encounter his lumbering body next to mine. He was pushing his bottom against my hip, and I realized we were both wet. "Let Gulliver come over, boy. You know he's a friend."

Mojo stopped barking and lowered himself down, a soft whine the only thing left in his throat as footsteps moved toward me. I struggled to sit up but collapsed back to the sand when it felt like my head was going to explode.

"Charity!" Gulliver said when he reached me. "What hurts?"

"My head," I said instantly.

I opened my eyes to gaze into two concerned pairs, a deep hazel and a bright blue. The guy with the blue pair spoke. "We need to get you out of the surf before you get too cold. Mojo has been bracing against you to keep you from floating out," Mathias explained. "I'm sure he's getting tired too. Does your neck hurt?"

I shook my head but stopped, grimacing when my temple throbbed with pain. "No, just the right side of my head. Help me sit up."

Mathias braced a hand under my armpit and one behind my back, raising me to a sitting position. I moaned, but together we managed to scoot back out of the surf, and Mojo followed.

"What happened?" Gulliver asked, dropping his crutches and himself to the sand. "We came up from the basement to see if you wanted to grab some dinner when we heard Mojo carrying on out here. He wouldn't let us get close enough to check on you."

I started to shiver, the cold seeping into my clothes now that they were wet and the sun was almost set. "I—I was throwing his ball for exercise," I explained, holding my head. "I was trying to decide if I should ask you to do something for my birthday tomorrow, and that's the last thing I remember."

Gulliver cocked his head at me. "Wait, it's your birthday tomorrow? Why didn't you tell me?"

Mathias put his hand on Gulliver's shoulder. "We can talk about this later. She needs a doctor."

I brushed Mathias away and got to my knees, the world tilting for a moment before it righted itself again. "Oaf," I said, rubbing my temple while I sat on my knees. "I'm going to feel that in the morning."

"You need to see a doctor, Charity," Gulliver insisted. "You probably have a concussion. You could have a skull fracture for all we know!"

"Gulliver, relax," Mathias said calmly, grasping his shoulder with one hand and steadying me with the other. "Tell us what happened."

I pointed up the beach toward the grass behind the marina. "I had lobbed Mojo's ball up there, and it got stuck under a boat. I saw him digging it out, so I left him to it. I was wading in the water and thinking, and that's the last thing I remember until I heard him barking."

Mathias's lips thinned. "Which means someone purposely did this."

I held my hand to my temple and grimaced. "I didn't do it to myself."

"We need to get her inside," Gulliver said, his voice thick. "She's going to get cold out here."

Mathias nodded. "I'll help her. You get your crutches and Mojo."

I pushed myself to my feet, and Mathias steadied my shoulders until I could walk without stumbling. Gulliver set me down in his office while Mathias went in search of ice. I lowered my head to my hand to quell the pounding.

"Charity," Gulliver said, falling to the floor to brush the hair off my face and inspect the spot on my head. "I want you to go to the ER. Butterfly Junction will pay for it. Let's just get you checked out and make sure you're okay."

I brushed some sand off his beard, my gaze holding his deeply concerned one. "I'm okay. I promise. My head hurts, but a little bit of ice and ibuprofen will take care of that. I'm going to need a ride home, though. I can—"

"Gulliver!" Mathias yelled from the outer office, and we both looked up. "Come here, now!"

We both moved at the same time, me slower than Gulliver, but we both worked our way out to the reception area where Mathias stood with a bag of ice in one hand and his other hand pointing at something on Honey's desk.

Gulliver moved toward the desk, but Mathias grabbed his sleeve. "Don't touch it. We need to call the police."

Gulliver leaned over and read the note aloud. "'We know your people. No one is safe.'"

Gulliver turned back to us with fire filling those copper eyes. He was angry, and he wasn't going to let anyone get away with taking something that wasn't theirs. "Call Chief Flats. I don't want anyone but him here dealing with this."

"How did that note get there?" I asked, glancing between the two men.

"Did you lock the front doors before you went outside?" Mathias asked, jogging toward them to check.

"I don't remember," I said, rubbing my temple.

He peered through the glass door and shook his head. "The lock isn't engaged."

I walked back to Gulliver's office and lowered myself to a chair. "I'm so sorry," I moaned, my head resting on the arm of the chair again. "I totally forgot to lock the doors because I was working in the office all night and not at the reception desk."

Gulliver rested his hand on my shoulder. "Sweetheart, any other day or week it wouldn't matter if the doors were unlocked. Plentiful is the kind of town you don't need to lock your doors at night. At least it used to be."

Mathias had his hand on his hip and a frown on his lips. "I'm going to pull the security footage after I call Chief Flats. We have to contain this. We don't want word getting out that someone is breaking into businesses and knocking people unconscious. That will hurt other people's businesses during prime tourist season. We know these are isolated incidents aimed at us, and we know why. Agreed?"

Gulliver nodded, and so did I. "Someone wants to benefit off our hard work. I'm not going to let that happen," Gulliver said through clenched teeth.

Mathias squeezed his shoulder once. "Neither am I. We both have deep stakes in this game, and we're too close to the finish line to let this stop us." He glanced at me. "Charity, Chief Flats will want your statement once we take care of the note situation."

I waved my hand at him. "No problem, I'll be at Myrtle. He can come around once this headache goes away."

Gulliver looked up at Mathias. "She'll be in my apartment. She can't be alone after being unconscious. I'll stay with her, and if you guys need to talk to me, come to my apartment."

"Agreed," Mathias said on a nod. He handed me the bag of ice. "I'll be down to check on you once the chief leaves. If you get double vision or pass out again, you're going to the ER. Right?"

I gave him a jaunty salute. "Yes, Dr. Mathias," I promised, earning me a one-sided grin. "I know you just went through this after your accident, but I assure you, I'm fine other than a headache."

He pointed to the door, and Gulliver punched in his code and helped me down the hallway, Mojo's nails clicking on the tile from behind me. Gulliver was punching in the code for his apartment when a thought struck me.

I turned and ran back down the hallway, nearly falling twice before I burst through the door again. "Mathias!"

He spun around with the phone to his ear. "What's the matter?" he asked, striding toward me instantly.

"Honey! The note says they know your people and no one is safe. You have to get to Honey!"

He put his hand on my shoulder to calm me. "I just sent a car to pick her up. She will be back here in a few hours."

"She can't stay at her apartment, though," I said, shaking my head. I would have tipped over if Gulliver's strong hands hadn't caught me. "They could get to her there."

This time Mathias rested his hand on the top of my head. "She'll stay with me at the condo. I have a security system. Okay?" He nodded and I nodded along with him. "Good, now go lie down and put that ice on your head before it melts completely. I'll keep you updated."

This time when Gulliver ushered me down the hallway, he walked behind me, herding me along like a small, scared child who was ready for bed. Truth be told, I was small and I was scared and I wouldn't mind closing my eyes for a few minutes. Whatever had happened out there told me that safety was nothing more than an illusion.

If I wasn't safe in a Mayberry-type town like Plentiful, Wisconsin, I wasn't safe anywhere.

"Thanks for coming, Chief," Gulliver said, shaking his hand again as the man, who was much younger than I'd expected, nodded.

"I wish we had better footage from the camera," he said, planting his hands on his hips. "The person came prepared with that mask and bulky coat. We don't know anything about them other than their height, and that's not going to help us. With any luck, we'll get prints off the note or the door." He turned to point at me. "Make sure you take care of yourself, little lady. I'm sorry this happened to you in a place like Plentiful. We have the lowest crime rate in the state, for obvious reasons. This is out of character for our area."

I held the ice pack to my head and smiled. "I understand, Chief. I know this is an isolated incident because of the things going on here at Butterfly Junction. There's no reason to worry about me running through the streets crying fire. As far as anyone else needs to know, I fell and hit my head."

He nodded once with a smile back on his face. "Very much appreciated. If you think of anything else, you call the station and we'll get together to talk about it. In the meantime, I'll be working on trying to get a line on who these idiots are."

Gulliver walked with the chief to the back door where his squad car was parked. It had been hours since we came back inside, and while my clothes had dried, I was covered in sand and needed a shower. It was also way after eleven and my head was telling me it was time for sleep.

Gulliver came back into the apartment and closed the door, locking it with the code on the pad beside it. He crutched toward me and lowered himself to the couch, using great gentleness when he gathered me into his arms and held me to him. "I was so scared when we found you. I couldn't get to you, and I was terrified. Mojo is a good boy, but he doesn't seem to know when someone is there to help and not hurt."

I buried my nose in his shirt and inhaled deeply. His cologne always comforted me and settled the churning in my brain. Then again, maybe it wasn't the cologne as much as it was the man wearing it. "Honestly, it was strange that he didn't let you help me. If he knows someone, he would never keep them from helping me. I think he sensed the danger that was still around us and wasn't backing down until I told him to, or he knew the threat was gone."

"You think they were still there watching?" he asked, carefully stroking my hair, sand falling to the floor from the strands.

"If I had to guess, my answer would be yes. I know Mojo and he wouldn't back down as long as he thought the threat remained. It sounds like they didn't find much on the video, though?"

"If by not much you mean Bill Clinton in a winter parka three times too big and not a smidgen of skin showing, then yeah, we didn't find much."

"They just walked into Butterfly Junction at nine at night wearing a Bill Clinton mask and they didn't think someone might notice?"

"At that time of night, they had a pretty good chance that no one would," he assured me. "Especially as far down the block as we are. Once the marina closes at night, there isn't much traffic unless someone is going to the campground."

I sat up and rubbed the bump on my temple. It was much smaller now that I'd taken some ibuprofen and kept ice on it. "This is what I can't figure out," I said, setting the melting ice bag onto the side table. "What were they going to do if the door was locked? Where would they have put the note? Also, why me? Why not you or Mathias?"

"I can answer the one question. There was a pin on the paper.

We didn't notice it until the chief lifted it up. I think the plan was to just pin it to the victim, but since the doors were open, they decided putting it on the reception desk proved they can get to us and we, and our research, aren't safe from them."

"Whoever 'them' are," I said sarcastically. "That also means there were at least two of them. One to hit me over the head and one to drop the note."

"Or one guy did both," Gulliver said logically.

"Could be, but I doubt it. A team of two makes more sense in this situation. They'd want to watch each other's backs."

Gulliver's head bobbed. "That's true. I hope the police can find them, but I highly doubt it. The guy delivering the note was wearing gloves, so I'm sure that note will be clean of prints. I think I can answer the why-you part too," he said, patting his knee. "I think they've been watching us. They knew the right person to attack if they wanted to scare me into making a mistake."

"I don't understand," I said, my head cocked to the side. "I do have a head injury, though."

His hands held mine, and he brushed sand off my elbow gently. He was always gentle when he touched me and it did things to my heart I couldn't explain. "They know the person I care about, Charity. We gave them the opportunity to hurt that person, and they took it."

"Do you mean we have to stop spending time together?" I asked, the words choppy and soft. "Do you think I need to leave town?"

He rubbed my arms as if he understood what was running through my head right now. "I want to say you should leave town, but Chief Flats told me you might be in even more danger out on the roads. He suggests you stay here until this is resolved. I know you have the other job waiting, but it shouldn't take that long to figure out who's behind this and then you —"

I put my finger to his lips. "I have time before I have to head to Indiana, okay?" I asked, and his head nodded. "I'll keep working at Butterfly Junction with Honey, which means two of us in the reception area at all times. We will have Mojo by us as well, and if someone gets aggressive, he will take care of the problem. He would have tonight, but whoever hit me waited for him to be distracted. That won't happen again. We will start keeping the front door locked, and people will have to buzz to come through. If we're nervous about a situation, we don't buzz the person in. We don't get that much foot traffic anyway. It's mostly delivery guys."

"No, I don't want you anywhere near this business, Charity. It's not safe here, not after what happened tonight!"

I threw my arms up in the air, and Mojo sat up on alert, a growl low in his throat. I held my hand out to him, and he lowered himself again with a huff. "If I'm not safe here, then I'm certainly not safe at the campground. Think about where Myrtle is parked, Gulliver," I said, pausing for a minute while he thought about it. "My site butts up to the woods on one side and lake access on the other. Sure, there's a shortcut to the main office, but that shortcut still takes five minutes. If someone did hear me screaming for help, they'd never get to me in time. I weigh less than ninety pounds, and anyone can pick me up, dump me in a boat, and be gone before anyone is the wiser. At least here there's a security system and other people around."

He tapped his chin while he considered the options. "You know you've won this one, don't you?"

I ran my hand lightly up and down his forearm to calm him. "I'm not trying to win anything, Gulliver. I'm not making this up just to win an argument. If the people behind this have been paying attention like you said they are, then I'm a sitting duck out there."

He bit his lip out of nervousness and some other emotion I couldn't pin down. "It didn't cross my mind, but you're right. One well-placed bullet and Mojo is a goner, immediately followed by you. I don't think we're anywhere near the danger level of death yet, but there's no way to guess where the line will be crossed."

"I agree. At least at the office Mojo has a purpose, and he will do his job. He's my protection detail, and he will protect anyone in this building the same way. Someone might get a bullet in him, but not before he gets his teeth into them." I swallowed hard and rubbed my forehead. "Man, I hate talking about the big guy this way."

Gulliver put his arm around my back and held me, his lips finding their way to my temple. "I do too. I have to admit that I'm glad you're here with me tonight. I have to make sure you're safe, and the only way to do that is to have you next to me."

His fingers stroked my cheek lightly while he inspected the knot on my head. "I'll be fine on the couch, Gulliver. Don't worry about me."

"I do worry about you because I care about you, Charity. My heart still isn't beating right, and it's been hours since we found you out there. I couldn't figure out why Mojo was being so loud and why you weren't hushing him. When we hit those doors running and saw you there on the sand . . ." He paused and shook his head. "I don't know. I just know that tonight, you're going to sleep in my bed where you're comfortable. You're going to shower and put on one of my clean T-shirts, then get some sleep. I have to wake you up every two hours, so don't get mad at me."

My laughter filled the room, and I captured his hand to my face. "I understand, and I won't get mad at you. I promise, I'm fine, though. I will take you up on the offer of a shower. I have sand everywhere. Once that's done, I need some sleep."

"I know you do. Tomorrow is your birthday, and you only turn twenty-seven once." I grimaced at his words and dropped my gaze rather than hold his. "Why didn't you tell me it was your birthday, Charity? I thought we had a connection here. I know it's not serious for you, but I'm hurt that you didn't want me to know."

I glanced up and saw the deep hurt undulating in his eyes. I braced my hand against his chest and shook my head. "You're not the reason I didn't mention it," I promised. "I'm the reason."

"I don't understand," he said, confusion on his face while he checked my temple again. "Are you sure you're okay?"

I took his hand down and held it, so he didn't distract me from what I was trying to say. Every time he touched me, the heat and electricity that flowed through his fingers and across my skin made me want to throw myself into his arms and kiss him senseless.

"I don't celebrate my birthday because I have no one to celebrate with. It's not like there's anyone out there who cares that I was born. This year I had hoped to celebrate it with someone who does, but at the same time I didn't want to tell you and make it awkward."

He grasped my shoulder, his other hand holding my waist as he stared me down. The intensity flashing in his juniper eyes gave me the answers to my questions without him saying a word. "Why would telling me it was your birthday make things awkward? And for the record, I care about you and your birthday."

I flipped my hand around until he grabbed it and held it still. "I think what I meant was I didn't want you to feel obligated to have to spend it with me?"

"Are you asking a question or making a statement, because it sounded like a question."

"I suppose a little of both," I admitted. "You're a busy guy, but at the same time I want to spend it with you, even if we're just working."

He lifted my hand to his lips and kissed it. "I'm busy, but not too busy to celebrate with you. For the record, I don't feel obligated to spend time with you, Charity. If anything, I worry I'm coming on too strong. The problem is, I can't stay away from you. When I'm not with you, I'm thinking about you."

"You're saying I'm like an earwig?" I asked, joking around. He cocked his head in question. "Don't they say earwigs burrow into things and just stick around to bug you?"

He shook his head at me as if I were a first-grader with a lot to learn. "We're going to have to have a lesson or two on bugs, Miss Puck. What was I saying? Oh yeah, I have a giant crush on you, and I want to spend as much time with you as I can before you leave." His eyes bugged out, no pun intended, and he swallowed. "I said that crush part out loud, didn't I?" he asked, his voice barely audible. "I wasn't planning on saying it out loud."

I trailed a finger down his cheek. "I'm glad you did. It helps me to know the way I'm feeling is normal."

His lips crushed mine in a frantic, heated show of passion and desperation. I slid my hands into his hair and moaned when his tongue knocked on my lips for entrance. I willingly opened them, and it strode in filled with heat and wetness that drove a moan from my chest. His lips left mine, and he kissed his way down my neck, nipping and kissing the sting away each time. His sharp intake of breath immediately turned to a soft moan when he sucked my earlobe between his teeth and tugged. When he released it, he whispered in my ear, "Everyone should get to share their birthday with someone they care about, Charity, and I don't just mean at work. We'll see how your head is tomorrow and decide what you'd like to do, okay?"

I cleared my throat, wondering if I would be able to speak without the words shaking from desire. "I like that idea."

Gulliver's shoulders relaxed, and he lost some of his intensity when he started stroking my cheek, a smile of pure happiness on his face.

"When's your birthday?" I asked, suddenly aware that I didn't know.

"You missed it. We were born on January thirteenth," he said, resting his head against mine again.

"Maybe I missed it this year, but you'll have another one in six months."

"Are you going to be here in six months, Charity Puck?" His voice held a twinge of disbelief in the question. I made him worry, which made my heart ache, but I was secretly thrilled he wanted me to stay.

My heart pounded in my chest with unanswered questions. Had I found a home? Was this the place where I could put down roots and make a life? That was never going to be easy for me, but this man had shown me more about life in a few short weeks than all my years of wandering had.

Would I be here in six months when his birthday came around? Probably not. My track record was zero when it came to commitment. I didn't want to hurt him. It wasn't him. If I were a normal woman, I'd settle right into this town and let it grow it's love up around me, but I wasn't normal. I never have been, and that meant one thing. I was more likely to break Gulliver's heart than fix it.

Chapter Thirteen

I flipped through the butterfly book in my hand, studying each one's markings and the vital information about their habitat and life cycle. I paged through the book until I found the butterfly I was looking for. The wing I wore around my neck belonged to a pink glasswing butterfly common in Central America. It was one of the fastest butterflies, able to fly up to eight miles an hour. I turned the page and kept reading, enjoying the fun facts and beautiful photos in the book. It was written for children, but it had kept me interested for over an hour. I flipped it closed again and stared at the cover. Yup, I'd read it right. I knew the author.

"Whatcha doing?" Gulliver asked, coming up to the desk.

My head snapped up, and my gaze locked on to his, loving when he pinned those sexy bronzed globes on me. "Why didn't you tell me you wrote a book?" I held it up instead of answering his question.

He eyed the book and sighed. "It's a children's book, Charity. No big deal."

I opened it again and pointed to the image of a butterfly on a flower. "You're wrong. It is a big deal. I've been reading it for an hour. The pictures are beautiful, and the facts are just enough for those of us who know nothing about butterflies to build confidence in our knowledge."

He brushed his hand at me. "Thanks, but I know you're just trying to make me feel good."

I stood, shaking my head. "No, I'm not. I'm serious. You could sell this book as a field guide for the beginning butterfly enthusiast. You've taken a ton of technical information and funneled it down into usable information, and not just for kids. If you aren't selling this, you should be."

He stuck his hands in his back pockets, his crutches crossing behind him in an odd dance of symmetry. "I use the book when I go to schools and nature preserves. They're easy for kids to read, and they always enjoy the pictures. I also sell them in a few gift shops, but I never considered it a field guide. You actually believe they'd sell?"

I clapped excitedly at his question. Maybe he was going to get on board with my idea without a lot of convincing. "I do. Would it be okay if I did some research on how to publish and promote them on the internet? Why aren't they on your website?"

Gulliver held his hands out to calm my enthusiasm before I got carried away. "Again, I used them for my nature presentations. I have a classroom set only. Of course, I have the files to order more if I need them."

I patted the book with my hand. "Let me research this when I have downtime the rest of the week. I'll see what I can come up with, and we'll talk about it together, okay?"

"Sure, I mean, if you want to. Don't think you have to, though."

I chuckled with a tinge of frustration. The man always downplayed everything he did. He was humble, but sometimes he needed to take the credit he was due. "I truly believe people would benefit from a book like this. Think about how many people might decide to stop using pesticides in their gardens if they read this book. Or how many people might order seeds from Butterfly Junction and plant a butterfly garden? The ways a book like this could change the minds of everyday people are limitless. Do you think Honey would mind if I hold on to this copy? I found it in her desk drawer. I'll return it when I finish with it."

Gulliver held up his finger and crutched past my desk and down to his office. When he returned a few minutes later, he held out a book to me. "Happy birthday. Don't worry, it's not all I got you, but since you're so taken with it, you should have your own copy."

I held it against my chest. "Thank you, Gulliver. I'm happy to have it. Now I can go butterfly hunting and know what I'm searching for." I flipped the book open and noticed the handwritten message. It read, *To Charity. You're more beautiful than any painted lady in this book. I hope you remember me with fondness on your birthday and always. Gulliver.* I put my hand to my heart. "What sweet words, thank you. And I know the painted lady is orange and yellow, has four eyes on their wings, and are sometimes called the thistle butterfly."

His brows spiked upward with surprise and possibly a touch of admiration. "Wow, you did learn a lot over the last hour."

I held up the book and shook it. "Like I said, useful information you made easy to understand. I hope the part about remembering you with fondness isn't a bad omen for the future, though." I tapped the edge of the book on the desk until he took it from my hand and laid it down again.

"No, but I'm bad at knowing what to say and how to say it sometimes. I meant I hope I'll always remain in your favor." He sighed. "See, dumb."

I slipped my arms around his waist and hugged him carefully

so I didn't knock him off balance. "It didn't sound dumb. It sounded honest, and I like honesty." I ended the hug and looked up into his handsome face. "Are you done for the day? It's barely eight."

He leaned on the edge of the desk and swung his heavy boot against the back of it. "Charity, if we're going to celebrate your birthday, I have to stop working."

"If you have work to do, I'll understand," I promised, planting my hand on his chest firmly. "It's just another day."

"If you believe this is just another day, then we're definitely going out tonight. It matters to me that you were born, Miss Puck, and we're going to celebrate June seventeenth as the day a beautiful soul arrived in this world. You might think no one cares, but I do, which means now you can't claim no one does. Besides, if Mojo could talk, I know he would care too."

I chuckled and hugged him again, resting my head on his belly. "Only if my birthday meant he got extra hot dogs or steak."

Gulliver rubbed my back and feathered kisses along the bruise on the side of my head. "I think I can arrange some steak for the big dog if he stays with Thomas long enough for me to take you to dinner. Do you feel up to it or should we order dinner in and eat it here?"

I glanced over to see what Mojo was doing, and it involved having his eyes closed and snoring. "He can hardly contain his excitement. As for me, I would love to go to dinner! I've been resting off and on all day, and my head doesn't hurt unless you push on the bruise. Did Mathias tell you that Honey won't be working here?"

His finger traced an imaginary line down my cheek until it landed on my lips. I kissed it, and he bent down, adding his lips to mine for barely a breath before he answered. "Yes, he wants to keep her at his condo. I agree with him. She's already injured, and I don't want her here right now. Hell, I don't want you here right now, but you're—"

"An earwig you can't get rid of," I teased, pressing my

forehead into his belly while I laughed.

His long, slender fingers tickled my side. "No, I was going to say you're safer here than in Myrtle."

He lifted my chin and stared into my soul long and hard. The heat of it filled my chest with an indescribable sensation. It was a fullness that had never been there before. There was also so damn much desire for this man who was supposed to be in my life for one night. There was a quickening in my chest to know I was still here twenty-one nights later and still gazing into the most inviting pair of eyes I'd ever known.

Tonight, his eyes were melted caramel, smoldering, and glowed with desire for a woman he didn't want to let go. Those eyes told me being loved by Gulliver Winsome would be an experience better than all fifty on my bucket list. That idea grabbed on to something deep in my chest and wouldn't let go.

"If I knew no one was watching right now, I'd give you a birthday kiss to remember, Miss Puck, but I don't want to be interrupted, so it's going to wait." He winked that long-lashed left eye at me and stepped back. "Get your things. We're going to dinner."

The spell broken, I nodded and bounced up on my toes. "I can't wait. And to thank Thomas, we'll buy him a steak too."

Gulliver laughed while I grabbed my bag and encouraged Mojo to get up and follow us down the hallway. "Suddenly I have to buy four steaks instead of two?"

"What can I say? I'm an expensive date," I said, pausing on the word.

He stopped instantly, his crutches squeaking on the floor like brakes of a car. "Can we call this a date?" he asked, his hand coming up to trail a finger down my cheek.

"I think it's probably time, don't you?" I whisper asked.

"It's past time, beautiful," he agreed. "Long past time for me to put my fears and apprehension aside and show the world I'm proud to have you on my arm."

I grasped his hand, and he almost hummed with nervousness and excitement. "What fear and apprehension? You have nothing to fear from me."

His eyes swirled to a shade of ginger as he spoke. "Oh, but I do, beautiful Charity. I have everything to fear, including a broken heart when you drive away."

My heart twisted in my chest so hard I wanted to gasp for air. I stepped closer to him and grasped his wrist. "I don't want to break your heart, Gulliver, but I don't know what my life will look like a month from now. I don't want to get my heart broken either, but at the same time, I can't stay away from you."

Gulliver leaned down, his lips barely brushing mine. He always left me wanting so much more. I was constantly aware of him now that I was living in his apartment and sleeping in his bed. While he was the perfect gentleman, and indeed slept in his recliner last night, I still wanted him more than I'd wanted any man before. No, more than I wanted any soul before, I realized.

His head hanging down over me like a hawk, and his lips near mine, he whispered the words that would stay with me for the rest of my life. "Imagine what we could be together if we both let our fear go. I'm willing to try. Are you?"

He turned and nudged Mojo down the stairs toward Thomas while I stood frozen in place. We could be everything together if fear wasn't in the way. That answer was simple. Was I willing to try? That was the million-dollar question.

"It's nice to be out enjoying the evening with you instead of locked up inside Butterfly Junction. Are we sure it's safe?" I asked as we drove toward our destination.

"Mathias hired a team to watch us, Charity. Whether we're in the building or out, someone is close at hand. Not so close that we can see them, but they're there. I didn't want to tell you, but I knew I had to," he said, his gaze pointed out the window. "There's a car behind us with two guys, and when we get to the restaurant, they will take up their post there."

"Bodyguards?" I asked, my voice low. "Isn't that a bit excessive? Is Thomas safe at the building with Mojo?" I asked, spinning in the seat to face him. "We shouldn't have left him alone!"

He nodded since he couldn't take his hands off the hand controls on the truck. "He's fine. There's a team there now too. No one is going to get to him. As for being excessive? No, it's not. We are within a month of completing the project, which makes it money well spent. After what happened to you last night, the motor sabotage, Mathias being run off the road, and the break-in, we aren't taking any chances."

My brow went up when he lined it up like that. "Do you think Honey was hurt by one of these goons and she just doesn't want to say?" I asked, my voice low inside the truck. It was almost too horrifying to say aloud.

He shook his head. "No, she would have told Mathias instantly. They are tight, Charity. I mean tighter than tight."

I held up my hands in defense. "Okay, I was just checking. I was worried it was more than coincidence that she broke her arm at the same time Mathias got hurt and when all of this is going on."

He swung into a gravel parking lot, and I was surprised by the number of cars in the lot. "Good thought, but I know Honey and she would never not tell Mathias something like that. I swear to God, she tells him when she gets a hangnail, and then he kisses it and makes it all better." He rolled his eyes and pretended to gag.

I couldn't hold in my laughter and let the giggle out into the truck. "Duh, they're in love with each other. Too bad they can't figure that much out for themselves." Gulliver parked the truck in a spot, and I faced the building head-on. "You're taking me to a barn for my birthday?"

"It's a barn, but it's also a restaurant. The Apple Orchard's the place to be here in Plentiful. They grill the most fantastic steak, which makes sense. It is a barn, after all." He winked and climbed out of the truck while I gathered my purse and slipped it over my shoulder. His strong hands grasped my waist, and he gently lifted me down to the ground, holding me until I got my feet under me. "Are you steady enough after riding?" he asked, running a finger down my cheek until he got to my shoulder, where he flipped my hair back over it.

"I'm fine, but I should probably think before I drink too much tonight."

Gulliver bopped my nose. "You deserve a birthday drink, but just one."

I paused for a moment. "Do I hear music too?"

He grinned, his eyes crinkling in the corners when he did. "That's the house band. They play all kinds of music from the '50s and '60s to country and pop. We're late enough that people are already dancing, I'm sure. There are several tables on the patio on the other side of the barn to get away and enjoy some quiet, though."

"Sounds like a fun place," I agreed, meeting him at the door. "Let's do this."

He tugged the door open and motioned me in, but I held it for him to go through with his crutches. I didn't want the heavy door to hit him and knock him down. When the door swung shut, I noticed the room had gone silent. When I spun around, there was a huge banner hanging from a rafter that said *HAPPY BIRTHDAY* splashed in red across white paper. The whole room broke into applause, and everyone yelled, "Happy birthday!"

I took a step back and ran into Gulliver's hip. The band was playing the happy birthday song while the crowd sang and clapped. I recognized so many of the people who were clapping along, giant smiles on their faces as they sang. Lucy and Kevin, Honey and Mathias, and before I could say anything, another familiar figure ran through the crowd with her arms open wide.

"Happy birthday, Charity!" Laverne said as she hugged me tightly. "You didn't think Plentiful was going to let your special day go by without a celebration, did you?"

"Uh, yeah?" I asked while she squeezed the breath out of me.

Laverne released me and checked me over the way a mother would, frowning when she found the goose egg on my temple. She glanced up at Gulliver. "You weren't kidding. She did a number on herself. I'm glad you're okay, darling. As for Plentiful ignoring your birthday, not a chance! We're always happy to have a reason to party here. Don't think you're exempt just because you're new. We have good food and sweet cake waiting. Are you hungry? Do you need a drink?" Laverne asked one question after the next until Gulliver's hands wrapped around my shoulders.

"Why don't you show us to our table, Laverne? We'll let her catch her breath and gather herself before we order drinks and work the room."

Laverne made finger guns and wiggled them at us. "You got it. Follow me," she said, forcing the crowd to part as she led us to the back of the barn. It took three times longer than necessary since everyone stopped to wish me a happy birthday. By the time we made it to the patio, my head was spinning. "Take your time and come back in when you're ready for a drink and some food," she said, patted my shoulder, and disappeared through the door.

There was a table set for two with a vase of red roses in the middle. I caressed one of the petals and then inhaled the scent from the fragrant buds. "There must be two dozen here," I whispered.

He wrapped his arms around my waist, his crutches leaning against the chair. "There are twenty-one," he whispered in my ear. "One for every day you've been in my life."

I twisted in his arms and laid my head against his belly. "Thank you. No one has ever given me flowers before. I'm overwhelmed. I apologize if I cry."

He rubbed my back patiently while I kept my face buried in his shirt. His silky polo was cool and smooth against my face. His cologne was heady, though, and made me want to inhale deeply every time I was near him. "It's okay to cry if you want to. I hope they're happy tears, though, and not from the head injury," he teased. "In my defense, I told Laverne we were coming in for your birthday dinner. I didn't know she'd invite half the town."

I laughed, deeply tickled by the whole idea. "It's Laverne, Gulliver. Of course she invited half the town."

He squeezed me tightly to ground me in the space with him. To remind me that no one else in the room mattered but us. "Laverne has a tendency to do things up right, but we can stay out here and avoid the crowd if you'd be more comfortable."

"Happy birthday, Charity," a voice said from the doorway, and we both turned. It was Lucy who was waiting with open arms for a hug. I willingly ran to her and held her tightly.

"Thank you," I whispered. "It was so nice of you to come."

Honey hugged me next. "We want to celebrate with you, but we also don't want to overwhelm you because of your head injury. We know what that's like. Enjoy a quiet dinner out here with Gulliver and then come inside for cake, okay? Everyone is already out dancing, so you can take your time. No pressure."

I smiled up at her and Kevin, Lucy, and Mathias, who were all nodding. "I'm willing to do a little bit of mingling on the way to the buffet I see over there, but after that I'm stuffing my face before

I do anything else!"

Honey, Lucy, and I broke into a fit of giggles while the three men herded us back inside the noisy restaurant toward the bar and buffet. Never in my entire life had I been hugged so many times in a row with so much love surrounding me. The hugs, smiles, and birthday wishes I got from everyone on the way to the buffet were real. The people here cared. Sure, there was someone out there who didn't, I thought, rubbing my temple, but most of the people in Plentiful cared about me. Tonight, they were all here to celebrate with me on the one day a year I thought no one cared that I was in this world. Did that make them my tribe? Was that an actual thing in a community like this? A place where people cared about each other and took care of each other not because they had to but because they wanted to?

Honey grabbed a plate for me, and Mathias held Gulliver's while we pointed out what we wanted to eat. Gulliver, unable to carry his plate, and me, unable to reach the buffet because of my height, were being helped along by two people who didn't expect anything in return other than us to enjoy our night. Honey smiled at me, pointing out her favorites and encouraging me to try the chicken, steak, and burgers because you only have a birthday once a year.

You sure do, and in Plentiful, they never let you down.

Chapter Fourteen

I leaned back in my chair and rubbed my belly. I was stuffed, but it was the best feeling in the world. "You weren't kidding. The food here is delicious."

Gulliver ran a hand-cut steak fry through a dredge of ketchup, popped it into his mouth, and chewed. After he washed it down, he leaned back to give his belly some extra room too. "You see why Laverne calls it the Cattle Hand and Ranchers Extravaganza. I want you to know, not just anyone gets this kind of spread for their birthday," he said, winking.

"I had no idea Laverne worked at a second business. Is she the manager here or what?" I asked, sipping my drink.

He picked up his glass and took a drink too. "Remember when we talked about people having multiple jobs here in Plentiful?"

I nodded my answer as I was swallowing.

"Well, if they're in hospitality, they often have multiple businesses."

"Laverne owns the campground and the Apple Orchard?" I

asked incredulously. "How does she do it all?"

"She's Wonder Woman?" he asked with one brow in the air.

I almost choked on my drink. I swiped at the liquid that escaped my lips with a napkin. "Thanks," I said, laughing at myself. "I wouldn't have come up with Wonder Woman on my own." I winked to show him I was kidding.

He tipped his glass toward me. "The truth is, Laverne has a big family, and together they run both businesses successfully. Her daughter, Ava-Grace, manages the restaurant, but Laverne's here often."

I smiled lazily from the food and drink. "This has been the best birthday ever."

"You haven't even had the cake yet. Just wait, it'll get better. I haven't given you my gift either. I want to wait until we're alone before I do that."

I tipped my head, and I patted my chest, searching for the necklace. "You already gave me this beautiful necklace and flowers. Not to mention this party," I said. "I know you're behind it, even if you're blaming Laverne."

Gulliver smiled that naughty smile of his and blew me a kiss. "You deserve so much more than this, but I didn't have much time to plan something. We have twenty-six years of birthdays to make up for tonight."

I took his hand in mine and squeezed it. "Tonight is better than if I'd had twenty-six birthday parties as a kid. Tonight means the world to me. I never had anything in my childhood, and I'm not talking about gifts, food, or clothes. I'm talking about people who cared about me and did things to help not because they felt obligated but because they wanted to. Growing up, no one spent time with me because they wanted to. They spent time with me because they knew my father was going to kill me if they didn't. There's a difference. The people here have invested a part of themselves in me tonight.

Whether they just wished me a happy birthday or when they spent all night cooking a spread like that buffet. I'll never forget tonight because I shared it with you, but also because of all those other people out there."

He kept hold of my hand, and his lips brushed across my knuckles. "My evil plan is in full swing," he said, winking once. "I've been working hard to make sure you struggle with leaving our little town, and me."

This felt like dangerous territory, and I knew I'd better change the subject fast. I couldn't stay in Plentiful, even if the romanticized idea of it on a warm summer night was leading me down that path. In the end, I'd still break his heart when I left, whether it was next month or next year. Eventually I'd leave. I always leave.

"Hey, I have a question about this necklace," I said, holding it up off my neck.

He brushed his lips across my knuckles again and set my hand back on the table. "I probably have the answer, so ask away."

"I was reading in your book that glasswing butterflies are from Central America. How did you get it if they're not in the US?"

His lips flipped up into a cagey smile, and he shook his finger at me. "I picked up that little butterfly when I visited Costa Rica in my final year of college. It was even better than British Columbia, Charity. I can't begin to describe to you how beautiful the butterflies are down there. I would love to write a book about butterflies from South America, but I'd have to go back and do more research first."

I let the necklace fall to my chest. "Really? How do you keep a butterfly wing for years?" I asked, surprised. "Wouldn't it just rot away?"

"It would, yeah," he agreed, biting his lip uncomfortably at my question. "But I made the necklace as soon as I got back from Costa Rica. I tucked it away and planned to give it to a woman when the time came."

"A woman?" The way he worded the sentence gave me pause.

He twirled his glass on the table without making eye contact. "A woman I cared about," he finished.

"Which means you've held on to this necklace for a decade," I whispered.

"Twelve years," he corrected. "Up until last week, it hadn't seen the light of day in twelve years. I never found a woman who deserved it or would do the beauty of the butterfly justice. That day we shared breakfast at the diner, the necklace floated through my mind. A glasswing butterfly is tiny, fragile, and oh, so stunning. That's exactly what I think of when I think of you. You're my beautiful glasswing butterfly. That morning when I went back to the office, I dug the necklace out of the safe knowing it had finally found a home."

I curled my hand around it while an unexpected feeling of joy and happiness heated my body. "It has," I whispered, twining my fingers with his. "Knowing the story behind it now makes it that much more special to me. You always surprise me, Gulliver. The first day I met you, I wasn't so sure about you. You had more defense mechanisms than anyone I'd ever met, and I worried you would never let your guard down. You have, though, and I feel like I'm getting to know the real you. It's incredibly special to know what this necklace means to you. Thank you for sharing the story with me."

He hauled me up into his arms and laid his lips on mine. The kiss deepened, and neither of us cared that we were standing on a patio in a place filled with people. No one existed but us. The sounds around us faded away when his tongue convinced mine to hear nothing but what it was telling me. He could give me the moon and the stars. I wanted, more than anything tonight, to live in the moment. His groans of pleasure were enough to tell me that making love to him would fill me with a completely different emotion.

Pleasure. Desire. Validation. Happiness welled up inside me and slid down my cheeks as he made love to my tongue.

Gulliver broke the kiss and held my cheek, wiping away the tears from my eyes. "I didn't want to tell you the truth about how long I've had it. I'm not used to being this honest with someone about my struggles in life. You're so different, though, Charity. You understand my struggles before I even explain them." He wiped a bit of moisture from my temple. "This is how I know. Sometimes, your understanding spills down your cheeks."

I gazed into his eyes, the green and gold flecks beautiful in the bright light of the moon. "Kiss me again, Mr. Winsome," I whispered.

He obliged my request, his lips teasing mine until they opened, and his tongue danced in for a gentle caress. It was heady, sexy, and he made my heart pound and my stomach swoop when he caressed the roof of my mouth slowly and with precision. Someone cleared their throat, and he ended the kiss abruptly. We sheepishly swiveled toward the sound, and I was sure he was blushing.

Laverne stood in the doorway. "Sorry to interrupt," she said, but I could tell by the slight grin on her face that she wasn't sorry at all. "I was hoping the birthday girl was done eating and ready for cake and a little dancing?"

"We're done," I agreed, "but you don't have to make a big deal about the cake."

"We do things right here at the Apple Orchard. Come on," she said, waving us in.

Gulliver grabbed his crutches and gave me a smile and wink, motioning for me to go first. I followed Laverne into the barn, but my feet skittered to a halt when I saw the cake. It sat in the middle of a table and read, *Happy 27th Birthday, Charity!* Around it sat sheet cakes for the crowd to share with us.

I put my hand to my chest, tears on my face. "I've never had a birthday cake, much less one with my name on it," I whispered while Laverne tugged me up to the table by my elbow.

She put her arm around my shoulder and squeezed it. "It's past time then, sweetie. Ready to blow out your candles?"

Laverne passed me to Gulliver, and he rested his hand on my waist and waited while she lit the two and seven sitting on the top of the cake. The crowd sang and clapped along while the band played *Happy Birthday*. Honey, Mathias, Lucy, and Kevin stood behind us singing while Gulliver sang into my ear, so I could hear him wishing me the happiest of birthdays. When the music ended, I took a deep breath and blew out the candles on the first try. Everyone cheered and clapped, while I hugged Gulliver and then Laverne, thanking her profusely. I held up my finger and jogged to the stage, asking the lead singer for the microphone. He gladly handed it over, and I tapped the top until the crowd quieted down.

"Hi, everyone," I said nervously into the microphone. "I want to thank you all for coming tonight, but I think it would take me until midnight if I thanked everyone individually, plus I know you all want to get some dancing in." There was more clapping and hooting until I held up my hand. "I won't make you wait any longer. I want to say thank you for making my birthday so incredible, from the food and drink to the company and the cake. I'll never forget tonight, and I have all of you to thank for it. Plentiful has welcomed me in a way no other town has in my life. You're all incredibly special people, and you deserve all the happiness in the world. Thank you again!" I waved and handed the microphone back to the lead singer before Gulliver took my hand so I could jump down.

He hugged me, right there in front of everyone, and whispered in my ear, "In Plentiful, you can have your cake and eat it too."

As I cut into the sweet treat, I had no doubt that he was right. I'd seen it with my own eyes. Unfortunately for me, my eyes were still too clouded with the past to see any kind of future with Gulliver

Winsome in a town the size of Plentiful, Wisconsin.

Gulliver tossed his crutches into the bed of the truck after he helped me in and then climbed in himself, firing up the engine. "Are you tired or are you up for a little adventure?" he asked, glancing at me before backing the truck out.

"I'm fine, and you know how I love a new adventure."

"It won't take us long to get there," he promised, aiming the truck back down the old country road we'd taken on the way to the restaurant. "I want to show you something on the lake."

"If you're tired or would rather not . . ." I said, but he shook his head.

"I don't want the night to end yet. I know it's getting late and we have to work tomorrow, but I don't want to go home. I want to watch the stars with you for a little bit and give you my gift."

I rubbed his shoulder since I couldn't hold his hand. "I wish you hadn't gone out of your way for all of this, but I truly enjoyed myself tonight. I'm glad Mathias and Honey are both doing better."

He took a sharp right onto a dark path and the tall grass tickled the underside of the truck. When he spoke, his tone was filled with concern. "He's doing okay, but he's worried about Honey. She's had a lot thrown at her lately, and she's not reacting well to it. That's the other reason he's keeping her at the condo. He doesn't want her to be alone."

"They have a weird vibe for best friends," I said, and he lowered a brow at me. I held up my hands in my defense. "I'm just saying. Where are we going?"

He pointed ahead at a grass berm while he slowed the truck to a stop. "We'll park here and walk down the berm to the beach. Then again, I might slide down," he joked, climbing out and grabbing his crutches from the back. He picked his way around the truck to my door and opened it. "If I help you down, can you carry the bag? It's behind the seat."

I nodded and jumped out of the truck before flipping the lever to lean the seat forward. There was a shopping bag almost the size of me in the back, the weight of which surprised me when I hefted it up from the floor. "Where are we and is it safe to be here when people are out to hurt us?"

"Our detail is watching. Unless someone comes at us from the lake, we're fine, but I doubt they'd know I'd planned to take you to this little beach before I did. Forget about it. We're safe."

He waited for my eyes to adjust to the moonlight and started hiking, pointing out what path to take to get down to the beach. It wasn't easy for him, but the view was worth it.

"Wow," I whispered. The stars stretched down to touch the water, and it was the most spectacular thing I'd seen since the northern lights. "This is incredible."

"This is a little-known beach a friend of mine and I usually use to launch our kayaks. It's perfect for paddling around the shoreline." He took the bag and motioned for me to sit on a piece of driftwood. Once we were comfortable, he opened the bag and hauled out a soft-sided cooler. "How about a toast?" he asked, opening the cooler and lifting out a bottle of champagne.

"You have champagne?" I asked, surprised. "That's so, so wonderful," I finally said over the lump in my throat. "I've never shared a champagne toast with anyone before. Let's do it," I said excitedly, rubbing my hands together.

Gulliver plucked two plastic wineglasses from the bag, and I held them while he worked the wire cage off the cork. He wrapped a rag over the top and raised a brow. "Ready?"

I scrunched up my shoulders around my ears. "Ready!"

He worked the cork until it popped off with a resounding *thud*. We laughed while I chased the bubbly liquid around with the glasses. He rested the bottle in the sand, and I handed him a glass that he raised.

"To Charity on her birthday. May she always remember the joy of turning twenty-seven, even when she's turning seventy-seven."

I held my glass up and clicked his, though it sounded more like a knock, and we each took a sip. "Thank you for taking the time to bring me here. You're incredibly special to me, Gulliver. So is this lake, and you know that."

He stretched his legs out into the sand to relax. "You're incredibly special to me too. I just wanted you to have a birthday to remember. It's okay to live on the one day every year that reminds you you're here on this earth for a reason. It's why I wanted you to see this beach."

I tipped my head to get a better view of him. "This specific beach?"

"This specific beach. I wanted you to see the lake from a different shore. You've seen it from the campground, the two islands, the sea caves, and now from this beach. When you compare the different views, what's the same?" He sucked down his glass of champagne like a dying man.

I let my gaze drift back to the cold, black water and starry sky. "I see the ripples on the water when they catch the moonlight. The sparkles bounce around like fireworks on the Fourth of July. The moon is as big as it is at the campground, and the stars are equally as copious."

"Good observations," he agreed. "What's different?"

I focused on the water, but the champagne hit my bloodstream, and I was starting to feel tipsy. "The way it makes me feel," I whispered. "The campground makes me feel like a kid without a care in the world. I don't have the same feeling here." I swallowed more champagne and kept my gaze trained on the water.

"How do you feel out here, Charity?" he asked, putting his arm around me and holding me to his warm chest.

"Diminutive yet bigger than life. Out here, I see how vulnerable I am, but also how much I'm in control of my destiny. There's a shaky fear here," I said, holding my hand to my belly, "of making the wrong decisions. But on the other hand, there's a settling in here," I said, tapping my chest, "of peace. Out here, it doesn't matter what I do for a living. Out here, the only thing that matters is sitting on the shore and staring out over this magnificent creation. I realize now I need to sit out here and experience the fear and the peace at the same time because in life you can't have one without a little bit of the other."

"Wow," he sighed, his breath warm on my neck as he leaned in close and kissed my collarbone, nuzzling his nose in for a moment longer before he spoke. "You're incredible. You always blow me away with the way you see the world."

I remained silent while a bird drifted in the air off in the distance, its wings defying gravity in a way we take for granted. "More than anything," I said slowly, "is realizing how vast this lake is. It doesn't matter what side of it I stand on, I know I'll never see the opposite shore. There's an air of mystery about the lake, and it keeps my imagination alive in ways other places around the country don't. Considering I've seen just about all the wonders this country has to offer, it's a huge thing for me to be this enamored."

He leaned forward and tossed back the rest of his champagne. "I should never have doubted you," he said with laughter on his lips. I liked how the alcohol freed his tongue and relaxed his shoulders. "I wondered if you'd understand why I brought you here. Now I know that you do."

I finished the last of the liquid in my glass and set it in

the sand. "You're trying to show me how hard it's going to be to leave Plentiful and the lake," I said. His head bobbed to the left in acknowledgment, but I put my hand on his chest. "But what you're really doing is trying to show me how hard it's going to be to leave you." His head bobbed again. "Every moment we spend together is another reminder to my heart of how hard it will be to leave you. The thing is, I've left places as beautiful as this before because, in the end, there wasn't enough to hold me there. Plentiful is different. This lake is different. You are different," I whispered.

His eyes closed, and he swallowed. "If I kiss you right now, I might never stop."

"Then I'll be the one to kiss you," I whispered, tugging his head down to my lips. When they connected, everything between us changed. The wind no longer blew against my face because his lips blocked it to keep me warm. I no longer heard the sound of the lake or the seagulls because his moans filled my head with unexpected bubbles of emotion.

When the kiss ended, he wrapped his long arms around me and held me to him, his lips still close to mine. "Happy birthday, Charity," he whispered, kissing my lips with the tenderness of a man as enamored as the woman he was holding. "I never want this night to end."

I rubbed his back in the moonlight while we sat on a piece of driftwood, our hearts beating together in harmony. "I don't either," I whispered. "Out here, we're truly alone with no interruptions and nothing pressing down on us. It's just us and nature. When I'm staring out over the lake, I can let all the stuff I've gone through in my life go and enjoy what I'm experiencing in the moment. I love the spontaneous moments in life as much as I rely on the dependability, I guess."

"I think you're going to love what I got you for your birthday after hearing you say that," he said, his finger up in the air.

"I said you didn't have t—"

The words weren't even out of my mouth before he had me in his arms, his lips on mine. He curled his fingers into my hair, and I wrapped my arms around his neck to hang on tight. I whimpered under his lips, but instead of ending the kiss, he trailed his tongue across my lips until they opened. He traced the ridges of my tongue with his in a seductive dance that told me exactly what he'd do if we were alone in his apartment. A sound of desire ripped from my throat, my wants no longer hidden by the dark. He knew the truth now. I was drunk on Gulliver Winsome.

He tried to end the kiss, but his lips went back to mine for three more short kisses before he could. "I know I didn't have to get you anything, but I wanted to. I hope you see in it exactly what you just said, spontaneity and living in the moment, but also the reliability of life. It's in the bag," he said, motioning at the paper bag lying forgotten on the sand.

I tore the paper off, and he helped me open the tape on the box. When I lifted the lid, I froze in place, lowering the top again and staring at him. "What?" I whispered, the box lid shaking as I held it down over the picture inside.

"Do you hate it?" he asked nervously as he lifted the picture from the box. "It's okay if you do."

My hands shook when I took it from him and rested it on my lap. He bent down, touched something on the back, and it lit up. I almost dropped the wooden frame as my breath hitched. "No one has ever given me anything so perfect," I whispered. I ran my hand over the image of me lying on the sand with the northern lights swimming above me in green, yellow, and pink.

"Do you remember that little bluff on the island?" he asked, and I nodded. "Well, when the lights started rolling, before I woke you, I sneaked away to the top of it. It was the perfect place to take a picture of you sleeping under your final bucket list item. I don't know what possessed me to take it other than the idea that I'd have something to remember you by when you left town. Last night when I was racking my brain for something to give you, I remembered I had it. I use these boxes for my butterfly displays, so I thought I'd see how it looked with a little bit of light behind it. When I flipped the light on, it just took me right back to our night on the sandy beach doing nothing but experiencing the lights together."

I nodded, my hand continually brushing across the glass on the frame. It was surreal, and joyful tears ran down my face. "It's gorgeous," I said, my voice cracking. "This is the first birthday gift I've ever gotten, and it's the perfect fit."

"You see it, too, don't you?" he asked while his thumb wiped a tear from my cheek.

I gazed at the image for a long time before I answered. "How I'm supposed to be living under that little part of the sky for the rest of my life?" I asked, noticing his head bob out of the corner of my eye. "I see nothing else. Unfortunately, seeing isn't always believing, Gulliver. This is the perfect picture, but my life is anything but perfect."

His head shook slightly, but he never tore his focus from me. "No one's life is perfect, Charity. Life will never be a picture. We use pictures to remember our life. Isn't it better when other people are in them?"

It was, but I couldn't force those words from my lips. "We burn hot together, Gulliver. I can't deny that. Apart, we're underestimated because of our physical differences, but when we're together, we're sympatico just like the stars that make up the constellations."

His finger trailed down my cheek and ended at my lips, where I kissed it. "What scares you about that?"

"Stars burn out, Gulliver. Stars fall from the sky and land back on earth cold and useless. I don't want to stay long enough for us to burn out. I want to remember this night forever as the night we danced as the brightest stars over Lake Superior."

I leaned my head on his shoulder and gazed up at him until his eyes met mine. I read everything he didn't want to say in those cinnamon eyes before mine closed and his lips took over. His kiss silenced all the thoughts in my head about staying or leaving, and believing or not believing, and quietly reminded me that living in the moment is sometimes the only choice we have.

Chapter Fifteen

"What a beautiful day," I said, tossing some of Mojo's favorite sweet potato snacks on the ground for him.

"You couldn't ask for a better Fourth of July," Honey said next to me. "If only we didn't have a detail in order to be able to enjoy it."

"I agree," I said, biting my lip. "It feels like a waste of money now. There haven't been any issues at the business in two weeks."

Honey laughed, but the sound wasn't amused as much as it was sarcastic. "That's because we have a detail, Charity. Trust me, Mathias is in this for the long haul," she said, rubbing her arm absently. "He knew the risk when he invested in the project, and he doesn't care about the money he's putting out to keep us safe. It's a drop in the bucket in comparison to what they'll have when the formula is finished. Letting the bodyguards go now gives them an opening to come in and hurt someone again. I can assure you, Mathias won't let that happen."

"You make a good point," I said, feeling silly. "I didn't think of it that way. Of course there wouldn't be attempts to break in or hurt us when they know we have security now." I pointed at the removable cast on her arm. "How is your arm now that the stitches are out?"

Honey glanced down at it and grimaced for half a second before she brought her lips back up into a smile. "Much better. I have another three weeks in the brace and then a lot of physical therapy to do, but by the end of summer, it should be nothing but a memory."

"I'm glad. That must have been some fall," I said casually, still wondering if she was lying about how it had happened.

"It was the strangest thing," she said, her head shaking. "The doctor said I must have hit it just right on the step for it to fracture that way, but apparently, it happens quite often."

Apparently, she was going to stick to her falling-on-the-steps story. I still wasn't convinced, but I had no way to prove my suspicions, so I had to let it go.

"Have you seen Gulliver or Mathias?" I asked, glancing around when I realized they had disappeared. They were nowhere in sight as I gazed out over the town of Plentiful, surprised by the number of people who had come into town to celebrate before the fireworks. Gulliver told me about the fair food, games for the kids, and music, but I didn't believe him until I was in the thick of it.

When he suggested we spend our Sunday here, I was a bit skeptical. After all, there were larger celebrations for the Fourth of July in towns like Bayfield and Duluth. He assured me I wouldn't mind once I was in the thick of the festival, and he was right. As a bonus, there were far fewer people here than in the bigger cities, which meant you could enjoy your day without worrying about large crowds. That was important when one of you used crutches and the other was a little person.

"I think they went off to find some food," she answered. "Mathias and I are going to his parents' house to watch the Duluth fireworks over the lake. Do you and Gulliver want to come? I'm sure Mojo doesn't want to," Honey said, shaking her head at the dog.

I chuckled and rubbed the big dog's head. "No, he's going to stay in the basement of Butterfly Junction. He won't hear much booming down there. He's not a fan. As for us, Gulliver talked about a super-secret beach where we could see Bayfield's fireworks, so I guess we are going there."

My heart was pounding with excitement for what was to come tonight. I loved fireworks, and I waited all year for the Fourth of July. I was proud to say I'd never seen the same display twice. This year would be another one I could add to the logbook, but something told me fireworks over Lake Superior would likely top any I'd seen so far.

I couldn't help but wonder where I would be a year from now, what fireworks display I'd be watching, and who I'd be watching them with. Would it be just Mojo and me in a town far away from Plentiful, watching the fireworks from the side of the road with no one but each other? I didn't know, but the ache in my heart at the idea was more than I wanted to let settle in on a day like today.

Since my birthday, Gulliver and I had found a schedule that worked for us. We stayed in the office from eight in the morning until seven at night and then shared dinner together in his apartment, where we found joy playing games and watching movies. We always shared his bed at night, simply because it was the only bed he had and neither one of us could work eleven hours a day if we didn't get good sleep. I still didn't get a lot of sleep, not that we'd shared anything more than some kisses, but because his mural came alive at night. The first night I was in his bed, the room spinning slightly from the head injury, I noticed the butterflies had a secret you couldn't see during the day. He had used glow-in-the-dark paint, so when the lights went out, the butterflies glowed with their natural colors.

As promised, I was working on his books. Yes, books. I learned he'd written three, but only one was ever printed. The other two were manuscripts he'd had ready for a few years but hadn't had time to put pictures in or find a publisher. After much research, I decided self-publishing the books was the way to go. Considering there were few books of this type available, he could clean up when people ordered his books from online booksellers. If he also made them available on his website and in gift shops, he'd do an excellent little side business from what I could see.

Plentiful continued to welcome me as if I'd been part of the town all my life. More so, they welcomed me as if I'd continue to be part of the town forever. It was enough to feel like I belonged somewhere, and that was new for me. I had never belonged anywhere. When I was a kid, people felt sorry for me and provided for me, but it was out of pity rather than acceptance. Here, they nurtured more than they provided, and they loved me because they wanted to, not because they had to. If you studied the way they lived in Plentiful, and I mean really took the time to witness what they did with their hearts here, you'd understand how the name truly fit the people.

Honey's arm shot out, and I followed her finger automatically. "There they are."

I watched Gulliver walk toward us, and I couldn't help but notice the change in him. He made eye contact with people now instead of staring over their shoulder. The fake bluster and bravado I noticed the first day was gone. The real Gulliver Winsome had been hiding behind the boastfulness to protect his heart. He felt like he could be himself now, and I was glad I could be part of that change in his life. He let me rub his bowed knee when it was sore, and he didn't get self-conscious about me seeing his bare legs. When I first met him, he walked with his head down, staring at the street. Now he walked with his shoulders back and his chin up, meeting life head-on. I was proud that if I had accomplished nothing else here in Plentiful, I had given him a little bit of self-confidence back.

When they neared, I noticed Mathias was carrying a box in his arms and they were both grinning from ear to ear.

"Hi," Honey and I said in unison.

Gulliver smiled and kissed my cheek, sitting next to me while Mathias sat next to Honey. "We got dinner."

I leaned over and indeed, inside the box was a whole carton of food and four bottles of IPA.

Mathias passed out the food, and we bit into our turkey legs, grilled to perfection, with juice running down our lips. Mojo peered at me longingly until I gave him a few pieces on the ground to keep him from shifting over to the guilt stare. When those pieces were gone, he moved on to the next person until they tossed him some turkey too.

"Wow," Honey said, laughing as she wiped her face. "He knows how to work a room."

"That's because he usually doesn't have a room to work!" I said, laughing. "It's usually one and done, so he's in heaven here. Mmm, this is wonderful," I said, taking a swig of the beer. "You know how to treat a girl right," I said, giving Gulliver a shoulder bump. With our height difference, it was always more like an upper arm bump, though.

Gulliver grinned and wiped his face with a napkin from the box. "I figured this might be right up your alley. The corn, you have to try," he insisted, pointing at the ears in the box, still wrapped in their husks, crispy from the grill.

"I don't know what to do," I said, motioning at it. "Won't all the silk get stuck in my teeth?"

All three of them laughed in unison. "They remove the silk," Honey explained.

"You always know how to make me laugh," he whispered in my ear as he helped me pull the husk down.

"Be careful, it's going to be hard to hold in that miniature hand of yours," Honey said, stripping the husk off her own piece. "You don't want to drop it and have Mojo steal it."

I glanced down at the dog, who was sitting impatiently, bouncing between his front paws with a whine in his throat. "I think Mojo wants me to drop it." While everyone else laughed, I held the corn in both hands and bit into the juicy sweetness, butter spraying everywhere as I reveled in the summertime treat. "Holy man, this is eye-opening. I didn't know corn could taste like this," I said after I swallowed. "Cajun seasoning?"

Gulliver smiled with corn up both sides of his face. I used a napkin to wipe it away and gave him a wink. "I think she mixes her own spices, but it does have a Cajun taste to it," he agreed, taking another bite.

"Honey knows exactly what's in the mix," Mathias said, wiping his hands. "She ran the booth last year."

"Really?" I asked. "Is it run by different groups each year?"

Honey shook her head as I gave Mojo my corncob to gnaw on. His eyes lit up in delight, and he carried it away so I couldn't grab it back. "No, Suzi runs it every year," Honey explained, setting her garbage in the box. "She broke her arm last year right before the Fourth and couldn't do all the work with a cast on." She held up her arm. "Irony, right?"

We all chuckled and nodded at the irony of it indeed.

"This is one of her biggest festivals, so I didn't want her to lose out on all the cash. I just did what she told me to do, and we made it through. In the process, I had to mix the spices for the seasonings, but I was sworn to secrecy," she said, crossing her heart and zipping her lips.

"I won't grill you for it then." I winked. "See what I did there?"

"You got me," she said, taking Mathias's garbage and dumping that in the box too. "I suppose we better get going if we're going to make Superior by dark."

Mathias sighed, his gaze assessing the festival area with precision. "I'm still not comfortable having both of us out of the business tonight. I know my team is around the perimeter, but I'm still nervous."

I glanced at Gulliver and back to Mathias. "He's probably right, as much as I hate to admit it."

Honey turned to Mathias. "Charity is a guest in the town. We'll stay back. Everyone should get to witness the fireworks over the lake once in their life, and we've had the privilege of so many."

Gulliver jumped in before he could say anything. "Go, Mathias. I know you need to check on both sets of parents. Charity and I will watch the fireworks from the beach behind Butterfly Junction."

I nodded, jumping down off the bench. "He's right. It doesn't matter where we watch them from. You guys have plans, so we'll stick close to the building tonight. Go, have fun. You don't want to disappoint your parents. I know if I had a pair, I'd want to celebrate the big holidays with them too."

Honey grabbed my hands and squeezed them. "Are you sure? We don't want to ruin your night."

I smiled brightly and then hugged her for good measure. "My night isn't going to be ruined. I'm going to spend it with someone I care about while watching the fireworks over Lake Superior. It doesn't matter to me if it's behind the business or off on some super-secret shore. The place isn't why I want to be there." I winked, knowing she'd understand, and a smile did tip her lips up.

"Okay, if you're sure."

"Positive," Gulliver assured them, leaving his left hand on my shoulder while he shook Mathias's hand. "Have fun and say high to your mom and dad."

Honey hugged me one last time. "It was great spending time with you again, Charity. I feel bad about tonight, but I'll make it up to you."

I waved her words away. "Don't even worry about it. I'd rather be sure this formula doesn't end up in the wrong hands too." I rubbed my temple absently. "I'm invested now."

Mathias nodded grimly, his hand going to the back of his head. "I agree."

They grabbed the box of food and took off for the car while I tugged Mojo away from the now completely clean corncob. "Man, you must have enjoyed it, big dog," I teased, tossing it in the garbage before I caught up to Gulliver.

"What a beautiful summer evening," I sighed, strolling down the sidewalk. "I had a ton of fun today. Are you upset about the fireworks?"

He gave me a lip tilt. "Not even a little bit. Mathias is right, and I just didn't think about it. I'm happy being wherever you are, so I don't care where we watch them from. I usually don't come down to the festival on the Fourth, but I'm glad we came today."

I tipped my head in question. "Why don't you go to the festival?"

He shrugged, which wasn't easy when he was using crutches. "I guess because I didn't like going alone. There's nothing worse than tagging along with another couple or walking through town alone while watching all the families having fun. I stopped being able to handle it by the time I was thirty." He was about to say more when his phone rang. He stopped and answered it, listening for a moment before assuring them he'd be there in three minutes.

His fast crutch up the street made it hard for me to keep pace with my little legs, so I jogged alongside him, Mojo at my side. "What's the matter?"

"I don't know. All I know is, they need me back at the

building."

Butterfly Junction came into view, and a fire truck, ambulance, and police car were waiting in the parking lot, their lights flashing.

This didn't look good.

The cold water lapped against my knees, and the pebbles were rough under my feet. Lake Superior was calmer than I'd ever seen her, and I was standing on her shore, wrapped in the arms of a man who would do anything for me. He had me snuggled up against his chest, his arms around my waist to steady me, and his chin resting on the top of my head. We might only be a few steps from the business, but we still stood on the shores of the most beautiful lady in the world. As far as I was concerned, that was all that mattered. We arrived at the beach as dusk drifted to night and the fireworks were ready to fly into the sky. He had rolled my shorts up my thighs, took my hand, and pulled me into the shallows of the water. He insisted standing in the water was the only way to watch the fireworks.

I wasn't sure we'd be watching them once we'd arrived back at the building earlier this evening. We'd feared the worst, and it turned out we had every right to feel that way. While we were out, someone tried to start a fire. That someone wore a Bill Clinton mask according to Simon, the one security team member who got a look at him. *Bill* had timed it out perfectly, waiting for the team to be at the front of the building before he darted in, poured gasoline along the garage, and lit it up. Simon came around the back to do his rounds and found the fire blazing dangerously close to the garage bay. Mathias had noticed the situation on his way out of town and stopped immediately, but once they talked to Chief Flats, we insisted he follow through with his plans for the night. These guys weren't coming back around tonight, and we'd be here with the security team anyway. Somehow, after all of that, we still made it to the lake for the big show.

The Lady of the Lake was calm, but I wasn't. Neither was he. I could sense it. We both had questions we didn't have answers to and desires we couldn't put into words. For now, I tried to put my questions from my mind. My face was aimed at the summer sky where rockets of red, blue, white, green, and gold were forming starbursts, smiley faces, and tendrils of fire. As soon as the sun had disappeared, he'd pointed up above the small ridge on the shoreline. Sure enough, within seconds the bursts of color began, and they were breathtaking. I'd seen fireworks dozens of times, but this was a glorious display of man-made beauty reflected in Mother Nature's beauty. It was stunning the way the colors reflected in the lake, offering you a second show if you opened your eyes to the hidden images.

We'd been standing there long enough I was starting to shiver in the cold water. Gulliver's lips connected with my ear, and he kissed it before he spoke. "Grand finale is coming up. Do you want to get out of the water?"

I shook my head in a daze. "When it's over, I'll build a fire to warm us." While this wasn't a super-secret beach, it also wasn't for public use, so we were alone other than our security team at the back of the building.

When the show ended, the smell of the powder filled the air, and the haze of the explosions were momentarily burned into the night sky, the same way the memory of tonight was burned into my mind. "All I can think about is the simplicity of the complicated," I whispered.

"Simplicity of the complicated?" Gulliver asked, his lips tucked into my chilled neck.

I motioned out to the view before us and the waves shimmering in the moonlight. "A fireworks show is complicated to execute, but to those of us watching, the simplicity is all we see. The massive formation of this lake and everything working in harmony to create its ecosystem is complicated, but all we see is the simple beauty it offers every day."

He grasped my shoulders and turned me, then lowered his lips close to mine. "The power and depth of my feelings for you are complicated, but all I see is the beauty you offer me every day, and the simplicity of kissing you on a summer night," he whispered, his lips closing the distance to mine. He was warm, heating me from the outside in as his tongue teased and taunted me. I leaned into him, my moan bouncing off the water in an echo of need. This man had me, and he understood how completely.

The kiss slowed, and I whimpered when he lifted his lips from mine. "You're shivering. We need to warm you up. Let's start a fire," he encouraged, helping me out of the water. He grabbed his crutches that were lying in the sand and followed me to a small spot that offered us privacy from the security team.

I arranged the kindling quickly and lit it, waiting for a moment until it caught. I fanned it, encouraging the flames until I could rest bigger logs in a tepee fashion. Once it was blazing high into the sky, we sat on an old piece of driftwood up against the sand berm. Gulliver handed me a wine cooler, and we tapped bottles, both taking a long swallow of the cold liquid.

"I feel like I should be drinking coffee instead. I'm cold." I chuckled, stretching my feet out to the fire.

"You're the fire goddess, and you'll be warm right quick," he promised even as he wrapped a sweatshirt around my shoulders to ward off the chill. He rubbed my back up and down while he stretched his legs out toward the fire to dry.

I held the sweatshirt around me and leaned into him. "Fire goddess, huh? I don't think so, but I pride myself in knowing the basic skills of survival. You never know what situation you might find yourself in when driving around the country in a motor home that's twice as old as you are. It's good to know how to get yourself out of any situation safely."

"You're right, but I still think you're better than most at it. Did you have fun today?" he asked, kissing my forehead when I leaned into him.

I gazed up at him, noticing the gold flecks in his eyes dancing in the firelight. "Today has been the best Fourth of July in the twenty-seven years I've been alive. The festival, the fireworks, the fire, and you. It's been surreal and yet . . ." I paused, searching for the word I couldn't find.

"Complicated but simplistic?" he asked.

"Apparently," I joked, but the rush of emotion clogged up my throat and made a tear leak from my eye. Gulliver wiped it away and tightened his hold on me.

"It's okay to feel overwhelmed by it all, Charity. You're experiencing a paradigm shift in how you approach life. That can't happen without strong emotions of fear and excitement."

"A paradigm shift, huh? Maybe that's what it is. I know my approach to life is shifting, and I don't feel like an active participant in that shift, if that makes sense. I need to sort out what my life is shifting into."

I poked the fire to give myself time to think while Gulliver's warm hand massaged my neck. I finished my wine cooler and grabbed a bottle of hard lemonade from the cooler. If I had enough to drink, all the complicated parts would fall away until morning and I wouldn't have to think about them. Not exactly a healthy way to deal with life, but for tonight I would allow it.

"You need to stop working at Butterfly Junction so you have some time to yourself," he said pointedly.

I drank half the bottle of lemonade and shrugged. "I have plenty of time to think. You'll be done with the formula soon enough, and then I'll have even more time on my hands."

"As long as you aren't using my business as a way to run from your life," he said, finishing his bottle and setting it back in the cooler. I noticed he didn't take a second one.

Hmm, so he wanted to play that game? I would volley, but I'd do it with far more tact.

"I was finishing up the formatting on the last book you gave me," I started, waiting for a reaction that didn't come, so I plowed on. "I was wondering if I should upload the two manuscripts we have ready and order proofs? Then we can go over them, and you can tell me what needs to be changed or what you don't like. After the changes are made, we can decide what to do for the printing options of the field guides."

"If you think they're ready. What did you decide to do for covers? We hadn't discussed possible cover designs."

I held up my finger while I dug around for my phone. "I found a few samples from premade companies and made three new ones. I chose a design we could use across all three so people would recognize them as being from the same author, yet they're graphically pleasing and eye-catching."

I handed him my phone, and he flipped back and forth between the three pictures several times. "I like them. They're what I would have done the last time if I'd had a choice—*A Butterfly Lover's Guide to the Americas, Central Americas, and Asia.* You did good, young grasshopper," he said, winking.

I took my phone back from him with a grin on my lips. "Good, then I'll get it all set up and order the proofs to be delivered. I think the faster we do it the better since summer is half over. We'll want to get a classroom set of them as well."

Gulliver's shoulders hunched, and he leaned toward the fire. "There's not much time for classroom work right now, so no hurry, but I am anxious to see the final product. I spent so much time gathering those images and the information and paring it down into quick, bite-size pieces. It was a ton of work that has sat useless for years. Then you show up and suddenly the books are almost a reality. I can't thank you enough, Charity."

"It was my pleasure, Gulliver. I've learned so much about butterflies since I drove into this little town, which is honestly the strangest but coolest side adventure I've ever experienced in the years I've been on the road." I copied his posture and twisted my almost empty bottle of lemonade in my hand. He had started the game, and now I would change the rules. "I'm confused about something, though," I said and waited for him to respond.

His head swiveled in my direction, and he wore a curious expression. "About the books?"

"No, about your life. What did you originally start Butterfly Junction for?" I asked, finishing the last few drops of liquid in my bottle.

"You know this," he said, his words short and pointed. "I originally started Butterfly Junction as an educational company. I added the research side to protect butterfly and bee habitat."

"How many years ago?"

His gaze pivoted back to the sky for a moment while he did the math in his head. "I guess about a decade now."

"And during those ten years, how many of them did you spend being an educational company working to protect butterfly and bee habitats?"

"I don't know, maybe five. Why? Does it matter?" he asked, his hands out in front of him in question.

"I think it does. Somewhere in there you had a paradigm shift to this obsession with finding a safe pesticide."

"It goes along with protecting butterfly and bee habitat, Charity. You know this."

I did the so-so hand in the dark, the sharp inflection of his words a loud and clear sign that I'd hit the nerve I was looking for right on the head. "It depends on how you approach it. You can protect butterfly and bee habitats without being knee-deep in the production of eco-friendly pesticide."

"No, you can't!" Gulliver exclaimed with his hands thrown up in the air in frustration. "You can have the best habitat in the world, but if a bee or butterfly carries a pesticide with them from another part of the country—and they will—your habitat is gone. It will be completely wiped out, and all your work goes down the drain."

"Why can't you let Mathias and Thomas do the pesticide research, and you continue to do the educational and habitat research? Why do you, as a lepidopterist, have to be involved in something outside of your field? You aren't a chemist or a biochemical engineer. You can offer insight to the creatures they're trying to save, but why does the research side of the business have to wholly consume everything you do while squeezing out the one thing you love the most?"

"I'm not going to discuss my business with you like this, Charity," he said, his words seething and his teeth mashed together. He wouldn't make eye contact, and his side profile told me I had pushed him too far. "Butterfly Junction is my business, not yours. I'll do what I want, when I want, and how I want. You have no right to tell me otherwise, suggest I'm doing it wrong, or meddle in the way I do business."

I jumped up from the log, a fire of anger and hurt roaring through my veins. "You know what? Fine. You're right. Butterfly Junction is yours. You can do what you want, when you want, and how you want, but so can I. I may not have a right to suggest you're doing it wrong, but I'm going to say you're doing it wrong. I watch it every damn day I'm here. The only time I ever see you happy and content is when you're working on the books with me. You can keep burying your head in this damn sand as much as you'd like, but I'm out," I said, grabbing my sweatshirt from the log and running up the beach and through the marina yard.

With each step, my heart broke a little bit more. Every time Gulliver called my name, desperation in his voice, my heart cracked open further. When I stumbled and my hands dug into the gravel, tears welled in my eyes. A few more steps and the tears stopped welling and started to fall, so I swiped angrily at them, determined not to be a girl about this. I would go back to the campground, load up Myrtle, and motor on down the road. Gulliver was just another person in my life who couldn't stick around when the going got tough. He couldn't share his darkest fears and dreams with me because he didn't trust me. I guess that told me more than his words ever could.

My heart broken, I dodged to the left and stumbled onto the road that led to the campground. A sob tore from my lips as I trudged up the dark road, the lights of a few campers glowing in the distance. The corn rustled in the fields on each side of me, and the sound made me whimper. I was leaving Plentiful. I was leaving Laverne, Lucy, Kevin, Honey . . . Another sob tore from my lips, and I fell to my knee, using my shoulder to wipe the tears off my face.

"It's okay, Charity," I said aloud to myself when I stood up and started walking again. "You and Mojo have been alone for six years. You can be alone for another six years. You won't even be alone. You'll have new coworkers and people you can hang out with on a Saturday night when your pathetic butt doesn't have anyone else in her life. Maybe, eventually, perhaps after a few years, you might even consider them a friend." Sarcastic laughter escaped. "That will never happen. I'm going to blow right past Gary, Indiana, and keep running," I sobbed, swiping at my nose again. "Come on, Mojo."

I froze before I could take the next step. Mojo! I left him in the basement at Butterfly Junction. I jumped up and down angrily, throwing gravel and dust around when I kicked the pebbles at my feet. "Damn it, Charity!"

I took a deep breath and let it back out. "He's safe there. I'll get Myrtle loaded, have one of the security team members let me in to get him, and be gone without Gulliver even knowing I was there."

A broad figure stepped into my path when I looked up, and I froze. "Miss Puck. You'll need to come with me now."

Chapter Sixteen

Simon helped me out of the SUV and to the back door of Butterfly Junction. The door flew open, and Gulliver stood there, his chest heaving. His face wore a mask of fear, pain, and something likened to shame. He kept his gaze on the floor rather than look at me or Simon. Mojo was at his side and pushed past him to get to me. He would have bowled me over if Simon hadn't grabbed me at the last minute. I grabbed the dog and hugged his neck tightly, glad to be reunited with him.

"I assume she will be safe here for the night now?" Simon asked, herding all of us to Gulliver's apartment.

Gulliver assured him I would be and closed the door. "I just want to talk, Charity," he said when I wouldn't turn around. "I don't want to leave it like this."

"Fine, but then I'm going back to Myrtle," I said, my voice nasally.

I couldn't shut off my feelings for him just because I was mad at him. I would let him talk, but then I would take some time to sort out my feelings.

"Sit down and hear me out?" he asked. "I know you're upset and hurt, but I hope you'll give me a chance to apologize. We're mature adults, and we can talk about this without storming off like children and never speaking again. I don't want that to happen between us, Charity."

My shoulders slumped, and I sighed, climbing up to sit at the far end of the couch. "You don't have to apologize if what you said is true, Gulliver. I can be hurt, but it can also be the truth. It is what it is." Mojo pressed himself against me, sensing I was upset. I rubbed his head, his giant chin covering my entire knee when it rested there.

"To a degree, it is true," he admitted. "The only way to save a butterfly habitat is to avoid poisoning the butterflies. When you started talking about the educational side of the business, you hit a nerve. A nerve that's been raw for some time now."

I held up my hands and waved them so he didn't think I wanted to hash this out all over again. "I wasn't trying to. I was wondering, nothing more."

"And a normal person wouldn't have been defensive about it. I apologize for not considering your feelings when I answered. The truth is, I know how everything I set out to do fell by the wayside the deeper we got into the research. Would I love to be out educating people about how to avoid harming the bees and pollinators we rely on to keep us alive? You bet I would, but it feels counterintuitive until we have a way for them to do it without spreading more pesticide around the community."

I held up my finger to pause his thought. "But if you go out and educate people about the issue, wouldn't that be a start in cutting down on the amount of -cides farmers are using on their fields? They're trying to feed us, but they don't realize they're killing the very things they need to pollinate their crops. It's a giant never-ending circle until they shine the spotlight on your research and more people join your cause. If you start educating people about the

-cides that are harming the pollinators, you might find a new army of investors, land suppliers, and farmers with crops you can use to test your product. Farmers are some of the best allies in your field, but not if they're unaware of the problem or the solution. They're out there on the frontline using products they know are causing bees to die, not to mention ruining our water. What they don't know is how close you are," I said, holding my fingers an inch apart, "to solving the problem. Do you see what I'm saying?"

"You're saying the farmers will help us finish our research so the product will get out faster. If we do it right, our first line of defense is already in place."

I motioned at him as if to say *exactly*. "I understand it's important to keep the research under wraps for now, but you don't have to keep the information about how bad the current pesticides are to yourself. If you're out teaching the farmers and conservation groups about the cause and effect now, they'll be more likely to switch to the safe pesticide when it becomes available."

He rubbed his temple while he considered what I said. "I didn't think of it that way, but you're right. The product does no good if it sits on the shelves because no one understands the importance of using it. We had blinders on while we worked to protect the information without thinking about what to do with said information once we had it. I need to talk to Mathias about this tomorrow. I may need to get back out on the street and start giving talks again, going to farmers' meetings, and visiting large operations."

I grasped the couch cushion to keep from going to him. I just wanted to touch him and remind myself I wasn't alone. "I could help you put together some information about the research, as well as the what and why of what you're trying to achieve, in flyer form. It's important to have the correct information for each group of people you're addressing. We'd have one for the small gardeners, the farmers, the beekeepers, and the conservationists."

"We could work together to make sure it was easy to understand and concise," he agreed, a smile tipping his lips again. He scooted forward and took my hands, holding them tightly. "I'm sorry for upsetting you. I truly am. I hate my work life right now, Charity. I'm not a chemist or a bioengineer, just like you said. I'm just a guy who loves chasing butterflies. I couldn't see a path or a way to change that until you showed me one. Your tiny footsteps were the ones that made it. I owe you so much, including half of my business for what you've done to save it."

"You don't owe me anything. I wasn't trying to upset you," I promised, shaking my head. "What you said about a paradigm shift got me thinking. Every day we're together, I watch you fighting against that shift. Sometimes you just have to let it happen and follow it."

He nodded, tracing a finger down my cheek. "I agree, and I think the same advice applies to you, right?" I nodded. "Good, then right now I want to stop fighting the way I feel about you and consciously allow the shift to happen."

"I don't understand, Gulliver," I whispered, but the words sounded desperate to my ears. I was desperate. Desperate to understand what he was trying to say.

His eyes closed, and his hands slipped up my face, where he stroked my temples with his thumbs. When his eyes opened again, the hazel was fathomless, but the gold was vibrant. I didn't know which one to get lost in first.

"Understand this, Miss Puck," he whispered. "I'm in love with you. I'm in love with every fiber of your being from the way you type code at ninety miles a minute to the way you stubbornly stomp down a gravel road on teeny feet, and everything in between. The day you walked through my door, the sun started to shine again." He let out a nervous breath and rubbed at his chest like he was in pain.

I gasped, my heart pounding in my chest and tears welling in my eyes. "Gulliver," I said, but he shook his head and laid his finger to my lips.

"Let me finish, please," he begged, so I nodded against his finger. "See, I believe that we only get one true meant-to-be. Everyone before and everyone after can be your love, your friend, and your partner, but they will never be your true one. When you walked through the door of Butterfly Junction and stood before me, it was a good thing I was sitting down. You were a knock-me-off-my-feet kind of beauty that I knew came along once in a lifetime. It only took one look in your eyes for me to know the truth. You were my true one. Whether you believe I'm yours or not is up to you to decide, but I know you're mine. Whether we keep feeling this way or not doesn't change what the universe has put into play here. The night we were stranded on the beach together, I spent hours memorizing your face while you slept, just in case you left the next day and I never got to spend another minute with you. When I kiss you, my heart pounds in the rhythm of love. When we're together, my whole soul screams out in need. I need to hold and protect you forever. Your lifestyle scares me, and I know I have to trust you, but it's not always easy. Opening my heart to you means it could get broken. I've accepted the possibility, but I won't let it control me any longer. I love you, Charity."

He paused and my heart soared with joy to hear those words. No one had ever said them to me before and I wasn't expecting so much emotion to burst forth from my chest. A smile stole across my face when he brushed a tender kiss across my knuckles.

"I never believed I would experience this kind of love in my life," Gulliver whispered. "I want you to know how much you've opened my eyes to the beauty of the world around me just by being you."

"Can you fall in love in such a short time?" I asked, my hand stroking his silky beard. "I've never been in love before, Gulliver, but if wanting to see you every second of the day, longing to spend time with you, losing myself in your eyes all day and your lips all night is love, then I love you too."

"It's undeniable between us, Charity," he whispered.

"I've never spent so much time dreaming about a life with someone before, Gulliver," I said with tears in my eyes. "When we first met, you were a nut to crack for me. I wanted to know what made you tick and why. I enjoyed spending time with you because you always had something truly thought-provoking to say. I know from experience how uncommon that is these days. Every time you put aside your plans to take me someplace special or to do something I've never done before, those three words bounced around in my head, and I prayed you'd hear them. Now I know that you did. It's why I got upset when you told me to mind my own business. Normally, it wouldn't bother me in the least, but when you care about someone, you want them to be happy. You want them to find the place in their soul that sings because they're doing what they love. For you, it's not research, it's butterflies. I want you to be happy, Gulliver. That's all I want for you."

His eyes glowed with that very emotion as he gazed at me. "You're right, you're brilliant, and I hope you're mine. At least for a little while. Until the travel bug bites again, and you have to climb into Myrtle and find greener pastures."

I desperately grasped his cheeks in my hands to hold us nose to nose. "I don't know how to give up that lifestyle, Gulliver. I'm so torn about leaving Plentiful, but at the same time, I'm equally torn about staying. Not because of you, but because of me. I'm not good at staying, and no one is good at staying for me."

He brought me in against his chest in a hug of fierce love and protection. "I understand that, Charity. I don't expect you to have everything figured out. All I ask is that you think about staying. Think about finding a permanent place where you can make a life. You deserve that. Whether that's in Indiana, on the open road, or here with me, all I want is for you to be where your soul tells you it needs to be. I want it to be here with me, but I also know you have a lot of soul-searching to do. I'm not pressuring you to make decisions that you can't make right now."

We sat and held each other with no words, just our hearts beating in rhythm as one. Gulliver's hands caressed my back and drew shivers of happiness and anticipation up and down them.

"Why do you think it's this difficult for us to know what the right thing to do is?" I whisper asked.

He chuckled, and his chest rumbled against my cheek. "If I were a psychiatrist, I would probably say because we never witnessed love and stability growing up. My mom was a single mom, and your dad was, well, your dad. We didn't learn the little cues of love and honor the way most kids did. It might be easier to talk about our feelings if we had grown up differently, but I don't believe we would have an easier time forging a relationship. I think that comes with time, determination, love, and forgiveness."

I nodded in agreement against his chest. "You'd make a good psychiatrist. I always feared falling in love because of what happened with my mom and dad. They were together until I was five, and then everything changed. Once I was an adult, I realized the honeymoon had been over before it started, but my mom stuck around because of me. Eventually, even I wasn't enough for her."

"You had nothing to do with it, Charity," he said, resting his forehead on mine. "She married someone thirty years her senior. She had some serious issues long before you arrived. The thing is, if we let what happened in the past define our future, we're never going to live up to our full potential."

"You're right. I learned my lesson during juvie. If I left there still carrying the same chip on my shoulder and the same opinion about life, I would be right back in the judicial system. I had to forget the past as much as possible, or I would never be successful.

I applied it professionally, but the same stands true in my personal life. At some point we have to say we've seen enough, experienced enough, touched enough, and lost enough to understand the only way forward is to make each day better than the last. Even in the darkest hours, the beauty of living is what we have to focus on."

Gulliver's hand rubbed my thigh in a way that made me forget where this conversation was going. The warmth of his skin against mine sent tingles of excitement through my body, and the only place I wanted to go was to his bed.

"You have a way with words, Miss Puck. Right now, the most beautiful sight in the world is right before me."

"Kiss me then, Gulliver," I begged.

The kiss heated to overdrive almost instantly when our lips touched. There was an electricity between us now that could no longer be contained. Saying *I love you* put the energy out into the atmosphere instead of holding it inside. The words were the spark to a powder keg, and there was no taking them back. I didn't want to. I wanted to celebrate the love we shared and let it fill me with joy and a sense of wonder for the rest of my life.

"Stop thinking," he whispered, his lips still against mine. "Stop thinking about where we go from here and what you're going to do in the future. Let yourself go and feel my love wrapped around you tonight, Charity. I'm not going anywhere, even if you do."

When he picked up the kiss where he'd left off, I fell into it, grasping the hair at his temples while I forced his tongue out of the way to make room for mine. "You're mine, Gulliver," I mewled before I straddled him to get closer. "I love you."

I stared at the bright orange and yellow painted lady and the brilliant cobalt morpho butterflies on his mural. My right hand was captured in his while he slept, but my mind wouldn't let my eyes stay closed.

"What are you thinking about?" he asked, rolling to his side.

My head drifted toward him, and I smiled. "I guess you aren't sleeping," I teased.

"I was, but I woke up and decided I'd rather talk to you than sleep."

His lips found mine in the darkness, and his tongue brushed mine in long, languid strokes. I finally broke the kiss to suck air into my burning lungs. "I don't think kissing can be considered talking."

"When you're in love, it can be," he assured me, his hands locked in my hair.

"Are you happy, Gulliver?" I asked, my hand braced on his chest. "Like, happier than you were before I came here?"

He sat up and tugged me over his lap so he could wrap his arms around my waist. "For the first time in my life I'm content, baby. I never let myself believe I'd experience this kind of settling in my soul, but being here with you tonight has quieted all my fears."

His lips took mine hostage, and I wrapped my arms around his neck to anchor myself and let him lead the kiss in whichever direction he needed it to go. It burned hot and intense immediately, his lips trailing their way from mine down to my chest and across my collarbone, where he nipped and licked the skin until I shivered in his arms.

He buried his nose in my neck, and a shiver ran through him as his need grew harder against my leg. "You're so beautiful, Charity Puck," he whispered. "I can't keep my hands and lips off you."

It was now or never. I grasped the bottom of my nightshirt and tugged it over my head, my hair falling down my back as it landed on the bed. I registered his sharp intake of breath when my perky white globes were revealed, but he said nothing.

"I know they're small," I whispered, crossing my arms over my chest, but he caught them and lowered them back to my side.

"You're perfect," he said, his voice low and husky. "I'm sorry I can't stop staring, but I'm savoring the moment. Once I touch you, I'll never be able to stop."

I took his hand and held it to my rib cage. "We don't have to wait, Gulliver."

His warm hand wrapped around my ribs, and his thumb stroked the side of my breast. "Yes, we do. Making love to you wasn't on my radar, and I don't have protection."

"Gulliver, I've had an implant for years. We don't have to worry about it. Unless there's something you're not telling me."

He shook his head, but his gaze never left my chest. "I'm clean if you're asking about diseases. I've only been with two women, and I've used protection each time." He ran his thumb down my shoulder and across the ridge of my breast, making me suck in air.

"Stop holding back and be with me then," I begged, pressing myself into his chest. His eyes closed, and he swallowed, his ragged breath bouncing off the walls of the room.

In a bold move, he cupped my breast, his thumb flicking lazily across my nipple. "Are you sure? I won't be able to stop once I start." His loud moan filled the night when I rubbed his belly just above the waistband of his boxers. "I mean, I would if you asked me to, but it's going to be hard."

"It's already hard," I teased, caressing the front of his boxers. He moaned and it filled my head and heart to overflowing.

"You're so tiny but so perfect," he whispered right before he ducked his head and captured my nipple between his lips. My ragged breath filled the room, and I squirmed against him, burying my hand in his curly locks.

He made love to my breasts with his lips and tongue while his fingers played with the waistband of my boy shorts, one finger sliding underneath and rubbing the tender skin on my abdomen. I shivered in anticipation and fear. The fear was there, but it wasn't about making love to him. It was about making love to him and then losing him.

"Gulliver," I cried, arching under his talented hands. "I need you to touch me," I called out, desperate for him to remove the remaining barriers between us.

Before my words faded away, he shifted me to the bed and made my panties disappear. He trailed his finger down my body and through my curls, where his hand cupped my triangle with reverence. "You're incredible, Charity. Just so perfectly you," he whispered. "You're everything I've ever wanted in this life. Your innocent beauty takes my breath away," he moaned again, his gaze sweeping me up and down. It was filled with lusty desire and so damn much love I wanted to weep. When I first arrived in Plentiful, I'd wondered what it would feel like to have all the intensity in his eyes focused solely on me. Now I knew. It felt like love.

"You have too many clothes on, Mr. Winsome," I whispered, reaching for the bottom of his shirt. He was on his hip, and I struggled to get him undressed. It only took one glance, and I noticed the desire I'd seen a moment ago in his caramel-colored eyes had been replaced with frustration and a tinge of fear. "What's the matter?" I asked, releasing his shirt and scooting closer to him. "Tell me. I can see there's something wrong. You can never hide anything from me, Gulliver. Your eyes give you away every time."

His Adam's apple bobbed, and he closed his eyes for a moment. "I can't use my knees. Like, I can't hold myself up on my knees. There are a lot of things I can't do in bed because of that, Charity."

"Gulliver," I whispered, caressing his face to calm him. "I understand everything you're saying and everything you're not saying, okay?" I asked, nodding my head until he did too. "We aren't the same as some other couples when it comes to our bodies, and you know what?" I asked, but he shook his head rather than answer. "That's what I love about us. We are special. We are unique. Do you trust me?"

This time his head nodded without pause. "I wouldn't be here unless I did."

I went up on my knees and plastered my lips to his, waiting for him to let my tongue in to dance with his. I mewled low in my throat, and he bucked against me, his head back in the game as he pushed my tongue out of the way to take control again.

"Mr. Winsome, it's time for you to make love to me," I said, ripping my lips from his to dart behind him and stack up a pile of pillows against the headboard. "You, there," I said, pointing.

His brow went up to his hairline. "You were right when you said you're bossy."

"Do you have a problem with my bossiness?" I asked, kneeling so I was the same height as he was sitting down.

"Not even a little bit," he said, sexy laughter filling his voice as he scooted back against the pillows.

I grasped each one of his legs with loving tenderness and settled them in the position I knew was comfortable when he was sitting down. My gaze never left his while I did it. I expected to see embarrassment or fear, but instead all I saw was love. So much love for me and for how I loved him. I stripped his shirt off, this time easily removing it from his lithe frame. I ran my hands through the soft hair on his chest, and it tickled my skin and teased my sense of touch. I leaned forward and placed kisses down his chest. His sharp intake of breath when my lips connected with his skin reminded me that I was about to make love to the man I'd just met but had been looking for since the day I was born. The thought was like a bolt of electricity to my heart, and I gasped. I wanted to hold him close to me forever.

His warm hands grasped mine, and his head dipped down to hold my gaze. "Are you okay?"

"I'm so much better than okay, Gulliver," I whispered. "I want all of you, the good, the bad, the painful. All of it, do you understand me?" I begged, holding his cheeks in my hands and kissing his lips hungrily. He rocketed his tongue through my mouth, his moans filling my head with a level of heat that made me instantly wet. I rocked on his thigh, and when he lifted it to offer me pressure, he dragged a moan from my lips that tore mine away from his.

I scooted off his legs and hooked my thumbs in his waistband. He lifted his butt, and I lowered them slowly, never breaking eye contact with him. There we both were, naked to each other with every single one of our imperfections front and center. "You are perfect for me, Gulliver," I whispered. My attention traveled lower, and there was no question he was ready for me. "You're, um . . ." I didn't finish the sentence because I didn't have the words.

"I'm normal size, Charity," Gulliver whispered, lifting my hand and settling it around him. "I know you're a porcelain doll, and I will treat you like one. I won't hurt you. Trust me?"

I didn't answer him with words. Instead, I explored him, reveling in the sharp intake of breath each time I neared his tip. When he thrust against my hand, a thrill shot through me at how much I turned him on.

"I trust you," I whispered, still holding him. I leaned forward, and his lips landed on mine — hungry, driven, and ready to show me he was worthy of my trust. We lost all semblance of time or place as we touched, tasted, kissed, and stroked each other to a frenzied pitch.

He grasped my waist and lifted me over him, settling me on his thighs, his need pressing against my belly. "You control everything," he whispered before he sucked a nipple between his teeth and suckled lightly. "Whenever you're ready," he hissed, my nipple still in his mouth. His instinctive thrust against my belly told me he was struggling to give me the control.

Be bold, Charity.

"You should know that once we're joined together, nothing can tear us apart," he whispered. "Not time. Not place. Not anything."

I had the fleeting thought that it wasn't true but refused to let it linger and ruin the moment. I lowered myself over him, and he shook with the restraint it took to not overpower me and take everything he wanted in one thrust. He didn't. He gave me all the power just like he'd promised. He was big, and I was little, but somehow we fit together perfectly. Lost in the sensation of true love, his voice filled my head with lyrics to a song I didn't know until we found each other.

I sat up half an inch and stilled, my head tossed back until I could see nothing but blackness and the stars that crept in around the edges of it. "No one has ever made me feel this much," I cried, unsure what was happening to me. "I'm scared," I whimpered when waves of pure, unadulterated pleasure rocketed through me.

Gulliver held my waist and thrust upward, raising us off the bed as one. "You're safe," he promised, his whole body shaking. "Don't be scared. Let it roll over you like the waves on the shore," he whispered.

When our gazes locked together, I instantly forgot about the fear and gave in to the power of our love. He grasped my face, moaning my name as he thrust into me, his hips shaking with desire and the need to find that release in the tumultuous waves. My eyes drifted closed as those sensations pulled me underwater into warmth and love.

"Open your eyes, Charity," he demanded.

I obeyed him, my eyes meeting his and leaving me breathless at what the universe had in store for me there. Our gazes locked together, he thrust one last time, and we both succumbed to the ripples of pleasure pulling us under the waves. When they ebbed, I collapsed on top of him, my chest heaving from exhaustion. He captured me against him and kissed my neck tenderly. "That was the most beautiful thing I've ever experienced, Charity. My heart is so full of love for you I can't contain it," he ground out before his teeth teased my earlobe.

"I've never experienced anything like that until tonight," I whispered. I was sure he could feel my tears on his chest as they fell from my eyes.

He tipped my chin up and smiled at me the way he had ever since I walked into Butterfly Junction the first day. It was the smile that had drawn me to discover who Gulliver Winsome was. Now I knew. He was mine for as long as I'd have him. He wiped my tears and laid a kiss of satisfaction on my lips. Still buried inside me, his need twitched from the vestiges of our love. "That's because before, you weren't with your meant-to-be," he promised, brushing the hair out of my eyes. "Tonight, you were."

I caressed his face in a rhythm of satisfaction and love. "Tonight, I found home. All my life I thought home was a place, a town, or a city. Somewhere that you put your things every night. Home is none of those things."

"What is home then, sweet Charity?" he asked, his fingers trailing up and down my rib cage, leaving goose bumps in their wake.

"Home is you, Gulliver."

"God, more than anything in this world, I hope you're right," he whispered as his arms came around me, and he captured my lips again. His kiss was hot, needy, and I could feel his desire growing inside me again.

I gave myself over to him and refused to concentrate on anything but how wonderful it felt to have a home. I'd figure everything else out down the road.

Chapter Seventeen

Last night had been wonderful. We'd made love two more times before the sun came up. We touched, tasted, loved, and trusted each other through the night and into the morning light. It was when we had to leave his apartment that the reality of our lives set in again. We were under lock and key because someone wanted to hurt us. Someone wanted something that wasn't theirs, and they weren't going to give up. If that wasn't enough to worry about, all I could think about was whether I should stay or go.

Normally, the thought of Myrtle brought a smile to my face every time. Now, when I thought about her, I saw a rusting behemoth that was way past her expiration date. The appeal of what she used to be to me had fallen along the roadside somewhere, much like a rusty tailpipe. While living the nomad life had gotten old long before I met Gulliver, I still wasn't sure how to stop. I had a job waiting for me down south, and if I drove her there, I'd still have the same decision to make. When was it time to let her go? Because letting her go was also committing to staying in one place and forcing myself to make it work. I wasn't sure I could do that. I also wasn't sure I could live without Gulliver now, and that scared the crap out of me. People have long-distance relationships all the time, right?

I had hundreds of questions running through my mind, and I couldn't answer any of them. What if, what if, what if. Those words played like a litany in my head hour after hour with no answers. Life had always been easy for me. Make money, play, go to bed. Rinse, repeat. My time in Plentiful taught me that wasn't life. That was running. Life was stopping long enough to find what makes you happy. Gulliver made me happy. Butterfly Junction made me happy.

Gulliver had talked with Mathias in-depth today about their current plan and how it wasn't working. Mathias agreed that I had an excellent point about a product with no home. If they took the time to talk about it now, let the farmers know it would soon be available, and teach them the importance of using it, they'd be further ahead.

I yanked Honey's middle desk drawer open to search for a paper clip for the order I was working on. Something pinged on the metal insert, and I tugged on my earlobe, realizing my earring had fallen out. I frowned as I pawed through the pens and pencils at the front of the tray, but it wasn't there. I searched the floor under the desk and found nothing but two breath mints and a paper clip. I sat back down in the chair, my frown deepening. It had to be somewhere in the desk. Carefully, I opened the drawer again, unsure where it could go since the organizer in the drawer was built in. There was nowhere else it could be, though.

I loosened the tabs and lifted the drawer out of the desk, determined to dump it out on the carpet in Gulliver's office. However, once it was on the floor, I noticed a crack between the drawer and organizer insert. "Maybe it slid down the front," I said to the empty air as I worked at the insert. But it wouldn't budge, so I unloaded the drawer and grabbed a screwdriver from the utility closet to pry the insert out. Sure enough, once it was removed, my earring rested at the bottom. I grabbed it and tucked it into my pocket, but something was off about the drawer. I ran my hand over it and realized there was something weird about the bottom. A piece of silver cardboard was made to match the metal, but it clearly wasn't metal. I knocked on it, and there was a dull thud, which meant it wasn't empty under there either.

I bit my lip. *Do I open it?* Honey was trying to hide something, which meant it was likely personal. I tapped my fingers on my knee while I stared at the drawer. What on earth could she be hiding, and why go to this extreme? Why not get a safety deposit box or install a safe at her house?

"Charity? Where are you?" Gulliver called from the reception area.

"In your office," I yelled back, not making a move to get up or put the stuff back into the drawer.

His crutches thumped on the floor, and in seconds he was standing in the doorway, leaning on the doorjamb. "Are you okay? Did you fall?" he asked, staring at the mess on the floor.

I motioned him in. "Close the door for a second," I said, my voice low and nervous.

His brows knitted, but he did what I said. "What's going on?"

I pointed at the mess. "My earring fell off and landed in Honey's desk drawer. At first glance, it appears the organizer tray is built into the bottom, but it's not. I took it out and found this," I explained, knocking on the top of the cardboard. "There's something else hidden under here. I can't decide if I should open it or not. Maybe she hides personal stuff there?"

He leaned forward and grasped his chin. "It would be a weird place to hide something personal. Why not just get a safety deposit box? Anyone can go through the drawers in a desk."

I held my hand out to say, *exactly*. "Honey clearly altered it since the drawer didn't come this way. She wants whatever is under there to blend in and appear to be the bottom of the drawer, and the steps she took to hide whatever this is tells me she has a good reason to keep it hidden. I don't know what it could be, but I fear it's treading into her personal life to open it. You would think if it were super important, she wouldn't have left it here, though."

He stood over me, studying the drawer. "Technically, it's my desk. She just uses it. Let's open it. Best-case scenario, it's nothing. If that's the case, we'll close it up and put it all back."

I didn't want to ask him what the worst case was, so I braced my fingers on the cardboard and wiggled it. "I have to open this in a way she can't tell we tampered with it. If she notices we did, we'd have to explain." I shook my fingers lightly on the top, and the cardboard slid into a notch. Once the opening in the back appeared, I could slide the cardboard out. Underneath were manila envelopes and flash drives, to the tune of half a dozen. I glanced up at Gulliver as I lifted the drawer and put it on top of the desk. "What the hell is all this?"

He lifted an envelope from the bottom and slid some papers out. When he turned them over and I noticed the printing, I inhaled sharply. "What?" he asked, flipping through them. "It's nothing more than rows and rows of zeros and ones."

I opened another envelope, only to find the same thing. "It's binary code, Gulliver," I explained, my voice shaking. "This is all encoded for some reason."

"Is she learning to code on the side?" he asked, perplexed.

I shook my head. "No, you don't code in binary. Binary code is what a computer does to process all the information coming at it. Everything breaks down to zeros and ones." I lifted a flash drive into the air. "I would guess these are filled with it too."

He scratched his temple. "But why? What does it mean?"

"I don't know, but my what-the-hell meter is screaming at

me."

"Can you decode these?" he asked, shaking the papers in his hands.

"I can, but it's going to take some time. I'll have to type it all into a decoding program. There are six envelopes, and I would guess each flash drive is full too. If the data on the flash drives is in binary, that's easier. I can copy and paste instead of typing it in."

I sighed and started straightening the papers. "She's not coming in today, right?" I asked, and he shook his head. "I'll take pictures of the papers, make copies of the flash drives, and return them all tonight. She'll never know."

He pointed at the copy machine in the corner. "You can make copies here."

I waved my hand at the machine. "I'd rather not. I'm not saying someone is keeping track of what we copy, but I also don't know for sure that they aren't. Pictures can be erased, and the burner phone I use for them can go in the garbage if what we find is bad. Leaving any kind of trace that we're on to her is a horrible idea."

"You're convinced whatever we're about to discover is bad news."

I dropped the papers into the drawer and rubbed my temples. "As much as I hate to say it, Gulliver, it probably is. No one does this. There's no other reason to use binary code except to hide something. We already know someone is trying to get your research, and now we come across this."

He tilted his head slowly. "You think Honey is part of the conspiracy to get the research?" He held up his hand as if to say *wait*. "I don't think so. She has no access to the research area. Not to mention, she wouldn't understand it if she did."

"Or so she lets on. The truth is, she might be smarter and more technologically advanced than you think. These papers are a case in point. She has to know something about technology to convert written word to binary code. I'm not sure I like where this is going, to be honest. She is best friends with Mathias."

He shook his head with determination when he caught my drift. "No, Mathias is aboveboard. He's the one who put his money into this research. There's no reason for him to sabotage it. He knows his payday goes bye-bye if this information lands in someone else's hands before we're finished. He also knows he will see the biggest payday because he's put the most money into the project."

"When you put it that way, you're right, but it's still very odd." I held up an envelope and shook it. "Maybe it's nothing. Let's stick with the plan. I'll decode this information before we do anything, including telling Mathias about it. Agreed?"

He leaned on his crutches and sighed. "Agreed, but we're nearing the end of the formula, so we need to make this our top priority, Charity."

"I'll take this to the apartment and start now," I promised. "I will have to hide what I'm doing. No one can know we found this until we know what it is."

"We've entered the land of the surreal, sweetheart. If you can find anything in those papers to help us figure this out, we'll owe you big-time."

I grasped his chin and pulled his head down so I could kiss his lips. "No, your success is as important to me as my own. No one is going to mess with you if I have the power to stop it. It's going to be time intensive, but I will find something to help you. I promise."

His eyes crinkled in a smile, but his gaze stayed laser focused on my lips. "You're the best ever," he whispered.

Then he kissed me with enough tongue to remind me he was the best ever too.

It was late and I was working in the apartment again, decoding and deciphering the paperwork I'd taken from Honey's desk. I had spent the better part of the last week painstakingly decoding the information, and whatever she was involved in, I couldn't necessarily link it to Butterfly Junction, but I also couldn't completely rule it out. The coded information was from a chat room or forum, and I sensed that the chats were in code. Without a sheet of code words, though, it didn't mean much to me.

My phone rang, and I answered when I saw it was the campground's number. "Hey, cutie, what's happening?" I asked Laverne.

"You haven't heard? They're calling for possible tornadoes tonight. I'm worried about Myrtle. I don't know what you want me to do about her," she explained. "I'm preparing the basement as we speak for the rest of our guests to ride it out."

I sat forward in surprise. "I didn't know this was tornado country."

"They don't happen often, but when they do, you don't want to be in the path of one."

I chewed on my lip for a moment. What do I do now? If I left Myrtle there, she could get flattened by a tree. If I tried to get out there and get back here, I could get flattened by a tree.

"The motor home is still locked up tight?" I asked, a tremor of fear in my voice.

"Yes, I've been checking on it every day. Lot of trees out at the site though."

A piercing sound came over the line, and I held the phone away from my ear. "What is that, Laverne?"

"Storm sirens," she yelled. "We're out of time."

"Be safe and don't worry about me or Myrtle. If you need help, call me, and I'll get help there immediately."

The line went dead at the same time the door to Gulliver's apartment slammed open. Simon, one of the security guys, blocked the doorway. He was easily six-two and two hundred pounds of muscle you didn't want to mess with. He could lift me one-handed without straining. "We've got to go, now," he called, catching the leash when I tossed it to him. He snapped it onto Mojo while I collected the three most important things in my life and ran for the basement as fast as my little legs would carry me.

When we got to the basement, I took Mojo's leash from Simon. "Thanks for your help, Simon."

"No problem. Just stay in the lab where it's safe."

Gulliver stood holding the door open for me and addressed Simon. "If it gets much worse, you get inside the doors," he ordered, pointing to the ones at the end of the hallway. "You can't be out there unprotected."

Simon gave him a salute. "Will do. I've got my guys upstairs watching the doors and windows there. They know their escape route to the basement."

Gulliver gave a nod and closed the lab door, the latch locking automatically once Mojo and I were safely inside. He kissed my cheek and took my computers from me. "I would have come and got you, but Simon can move three times as fast as I can, so I radioed up to him."

"It never crossed my mind that you weren't thinking about me, Gulliver." I set the other bag on the table and sighed. "I was talking to Laverne when he burst in. Everyone there was gathering in the storm shelter for the night. She was asking me what to do about Myrtle when the sirens went off and the line went dead. I hope they're okay out there."

"They'll be okay in the basement," he promised, putting his arms around me. "I can't promise Myrtle gets away unscathed, but at least you aren't in her." He kissed the top of my head for comfort then, and I sighed, leaning my head into his belly.

"If Myrtle goes down, she goes down. I can't control Mother Nature."

"What are you going to do if Myrtle bites it?" Gulliver asked, his head tipped to the side.

"I have no idea," I admitted, "but I know that would force me to answer the question that I still don't know the answer to." I glanced around the room, desperately searching for a way to change the subject. "This is set up as a living space," I said. "I haven't seen this part of the lab before."

There was a table sitting next to an efficiency kitchen with a fridge, microwave, and coffeepot. Along the other wall sat cots with pillows and blankets and several packs of water and pop.

"This is our break room for the researchers," he explained. "It keeps them from having to leave the area if they need to take a break but are working on something timed. They can grab something to eat and go back to work. If they're tired, they can lie down for a bit. The cots don't get used much, but I'm glad we have them tonight."

I lowered myself to one and bounced a little bit. "Comfy. Are we safe down here? Are the security guys safe?" I asked just as a crack of thunder raged overhead. Mojo whimpered and crawled under the cot in protest.

Gulliver sat and rubbed my back to soothe me. "We're all safe. They have access to get down here if a tornado comes in. Otherwise, they'll stand their posts and make sure if any windows are broken, they get boarded over quickly. I doubt anyone is going to try anything in this kind of weather, but better safe than sorry." I nodded, swallowing hard. He noticed and grabbed a water bottle, handing it to me after uncapping it. "You're okay. I'll keep you safe."

I drank from the bottle of water and slowly lowered it to my lap. "I know you will. I'm just exhausted from worrying about all of that . . ." I tipped my head at my computers rather than say more.

"Now the storm is stressing me out because I can't finish my work. We need to talk about it, but I'm not sure we should do that here."

"Why not?"

"Bugs," I said simply, "and not the six-legged kind."

"Nope," he answered, swinging his head back and forth. "This research area is swept regularly for them. We're clear down here. Upstairs, I can't say for sure, but here we can talk about anything."

I blew out a breath of relief and nervousness. It was time to let Gulliver see the documents. "I should show you what I found then. I can't make sense of any of it."

I unloaded my bags down to the last item, my birthday gift, and held it close to my chest to protect it. Gulliver's arm encapsulated my shoulders, and he held me to him. "I'm glad you didn't risk leaving it upstairs," he whispered before kissing the top of my head. He flipped the battery-operated light on and set it on the counter. The image of the northern lights lit up, and I let out a breath of relief.

"I know the chances it would get damaged were slim, but I had to bring it, just in case," I explained lamely.

"I understand," he promised, trailing a finger down my cheek. "You don't have to explain. I know you don't have a lot of personal possessions that are important to you."

He held out a chair for me, and I sat, opening the computer while he grabbed the other chair. After we were settled, I fired up the laptop, refusing to plug it in due to the lightning outside. I typed in the password and waited. "I've saved it all externally on a drive because I'm afraid someone will know I have the information. I'm aware that I'm paranoid but, as you said, better safe than sorry," I explained as I plugged in the flash drive and clicked on a document I'd made.

He read several of the entries and spun toward me in slow motion, as if his brain hadn't caught up to what his eyes told him was on the screen. "What the heck does this mean?"

I held up both hands. "I was hoping you would know. It's strange, to say the least."

Gulliver scratched his temple and read aloud. "'I've seen the weather, and I doubt we'll be able to do anything for the next few days. I don't think we'll get to load the fridge or see the Packers.'" He read a few more to himself and pointed at several of them. "They all say the same thing in one way or the other."

I tapped the screen with my pen. "Exactly what I thought, which is odd. At first I thought it might be a dating forum, but the communication is just too weird."

"I'm getting a sick feeling in my gut," he said, his frown deepening. "What if Honey is saying she's not going to be able to get in and load something on a computer or see the research?"

I dropped my hand from the keyboard in resignation. "That's my fear too. There's probably a sheet of code words somewhere, but so far I haven't come across it."

"These can't be all the messages, right?"

"No, but every one of them reads like this, which is what makes me think everything is in code. I have one envelope left to finish." I rolled my shoulders to stretch them out. The long hours of decoding this information were catching up to me. Everything felt bruised and battered, and I was thrilled to be almost done with it.

"This is a massive amount of work. You've gone above and beyond, Charity," Gulliver said, leaning back in the chair.

I was about to speak when a clap of thunder startled us, and the room was bathed in blackness. The only light remaining was the computer screen, and my eyes widened.

"Give it a second. The generator will kick in," Gulliver said calmly.

I held my breath, and in less than thirty seconds, the whir

of the generator filled the room, and the emergency lights lit up. There was enough light in the room to see comfortably, and I stood, meeting him at the table. "We should shut this down before the battery dies. We might need it." I signed out and turned it off before sliding it back into the case. "I hope the last envelope holds the key to the code or something to give us a clearer idea of who she's corresponding with."

"Do you think these are from her email? If you hack in, could you see who it is?"

I did the so-so hand. "I mean, I could try, but chances are Honey's not communicating over email. If I were involved in something shady, I'd use a chat board or some other type of anonymous forum. Using email is asking for trouble when you're on someone else's computer every day."

He rested his chin in his hand while his mind sorted out all the information he'd just read. "Hmmm, you're probably right. She's not the brains of the operation, whatever the operation is. You can sense she's their flunky from the messages being passed back and forth. The response to her messages is always standoffish and demanding. If she's in on it, then she gets what she deserves. If she's being coerced, which is what it sounds like in the last few messages, then I'm a little bit worried for her, to be honest. If she doesn't come up with the information and we take the pesticide to production, she'll be in danger."

"I keep seeing Honey's broken arm. Is she sticking with the story that she fell on the stairs?" I asked him. "I know I asked this before, but seeing this," I said, motioning at the computers, "I have to ask again."

"That's the story she told everyone, but only she knows for certain how it happened. The doctor told Mathias the injury was hours old by the time he got her to the emergency room, so that means it had to have happened in the early morning hours."

"And why was she on the stairs in the dark?" I asked. "That doesn't make sense. She sat there with a bone sticking out of her arm for hours and then decided to go to the diner instead of call for help? Very odd, Gulliver. I understand she was in shock, but once she got to the diner, one word to Lucy and she'd be in an ambulance. When I found her, she was in pain, but she was also terrified." I rubbed my forehead and motioned at the computers again. "I think we need to talk to Mathias about all of this."

Gulliver waved his hand near his throat. "Not yet. If it comes to it, I'll let Honey go and explain to him why I had to do it."

I grabbed his arm frantically, my fingers digging into the tissue firmly. "No, don't. If you fire Honey, the people behind this will know we're on to them, and they might hurt her."

He grimaced, and his lips thinned in anger and frustration. "If Honey's not the mastermind behind this, you might be right."

"She's not, the messages tell me that much," I said and laughed sardonically. "I pray she's playing her own game with them, because if not, she's in serious danger. Is there a way to get Mathias's private investigator to take a cursory glance at her life?"

He leaned forward and rested his elbows on the table. "I suppose I could ask, but then Mathias would find out for sure."

I stared at him steely-eyed. "It's probably time he knows, Gulliver. If my whole financial life were at stake, I wouldn't want to be blindsided by it."

He blew out a breath that was long and sad. "Okay, you're right. I'll talk to him on Monday. He's not in town this weekend, and Honey is with him, so at least she's safe for the next couple of days."

I glanced up at the ceiling just as the floor shook under our feet like an earthquake. The resulting clap of thunder had me throwing my hands over my ears. "I wonder what's going on out there."

Gulliver stood and, holding on to the table and counter, he made his way to the walkie-talkie by the fridge. "Simon, what's the report?" he asked, releasing the button and waiting as static filled the room.

"Trees down," Simon returned, his breath coming quickly. "I'm checking on my guys," he yelled into the receiver.

"Ten-four, keep me posted."

I jumped up, giving him my shoulder to lead him to the cot. He sat and tapped the walkie-talkie in his hand. "God, I don't need this," he said, lowering his head. "I hope they're okay."

I rubbed his back to comfort him the best I could. "They're professionals. I'm sure they're fine."

The radio crackled, and Simon's voice was choppy among the static. "Everyone is okay. The trees missed the business but took out all the power lines. One of the lines is lying across the garage area. I hope your friend has nowhere to go."

Gulliver depressed the button again as he spoke. "No, she's here to stay," he said, his head hanging a bit when he realized what he'd said, "for the night. We're going to turn in, but if you need me, call me over the radio. I'll keep it close."

"Ten-four. It appears the worst is over. I'll report the downed lines, but I doubt we'll get anyone out here before morning to take care of it."

"Thanks, Simon," Gulliver responded, releasing the button and setting the walkie-talkie on the bed. "We could go upstairs," he explained to me, "but we don't have any power up there or air-conditioning."

I tenderly rubbed at the back of his neck to relax him. "I'm okay down here. If there's a bathroom close by, I could use one."

He pointed at a door across the room from us. "Go ahead and get cleaned up. There are some clean shirts in there, too, if you want to put on something to sleep in."

I kissed his cheek and stood. "Hold my spot. I'll be right back," I promised.

I held the door long enough to see his head in his hands before I closed it. It was easy to see he was starting to crack under the pressure of the business coupled with my indecision about what I wanted out of life. I locked the door and leaned against it. I had to make a decision and it had to be the right one, but what that was, I didn't have a clue.

Chapter Eighteen

I woke slowly to Gulliver's hand stroking a pattern from my cheek up and over my ear. "What time is it?" I asked sleepily.

"It's only midnight," he answered softly. "I can't sleep. I'm sorry if I woke you."

"You're okay," I whispered, flipping over to face him. "Why can't you sleep? Worried?" I asked, rubbing at the frown lines near his eyes. "Are the guys okay upstairs?"

He grasped my hand and lifted it to his lips to kiss. "They're fine. No damage to the building, just trees in the parking lot and leaves and branches everywhere. They're standing guard since the security system might be sketchy with the power outage."

"I'm glad they're here, even though I feel guilty for being safe down here while they aren't."

Gulliver chuckled lazily. "They have guns, so don't feel too guilty. They're professionals. Now get some sleep."

I rolled my head back and forth on the pillow. "I can't. Not if you aren't. Tell me what's wrong."

"I'd rather kiss you," he whispered, his lips landing on mine before I could blink or even take a breath. He held me close on the narrow cot, and his tongue teased its way past my open lips. The velvety kiss cleared my mind of everything but how wonderful he made me feel. The stroking of his tongue against mine drove me to thrust against the hardness hiding under his thin cotton shorts.

"How alone are we?" My voice was breathy when I broke the kiss to speak.

"We're locked in and completely alone," he said, diving back to my lips in a frenzy of tongues, hands, and moans of pleasure.

Caught up in his fever pitch, I added my heat until we nearly combusted from just the kiss. Gulliver tugged my T-shirt up as he grasped my earlobe in his teeth. "Stay still," he ordered, and I did the best I could as his hands roamed my breasts and down to my triangle. "God, Charity," he moaned in my ear when his fingers parted me, and he discovered how ready I was for him. "Tell me you want this," he ground out as he thrust against me, his need powerful against my belly.

"With everything in me," I promised.

His lips feathered kisses along my neck and collarbone while he worked his shorts off.

"Gulliver," I moaned, pressing myself into him, "I want to feel you."

His strong arms lowered me over him, and he slid inside on a moan.

"Oh God, yeah," I cried. "How do we fit together so perfectly every time, Gulliver?"

"Because we're made for each other," he whispered, his breath raising goose bumps across my skin. "Don't move," he ground out, and his tone told me I shouldn't argue. It took everything I had to not squirm against his hand holding my back tautly. "Give me the control, baby," he hissed into my ear.

"I'm trying," I whimpered. "I can't help how good you make me feel. Your love fills me to overflowing every time, Gulliver. I love you."

Those three words were a bolt of lightning to his hips, and he thrust upward, making me cry out with pleasure. "More," I whispered, trying not to cry at how incredible it was to be so loved by this man. He held me to him and made love to me slowly and with perfectly timed strokes that had us both falling over the edge of pleasure and into love together. I was grateful we were alone since his name fell loudly from my lips when I landed back in his arms.

He stroked my face, his need still buried in me. "You're incredible," he whispered, his lips finding the tender spot in my neck. "I could make love to you every night and never get enough."

"I feel the same way. Sometimes it scares me to the point I'm paralyzed," I admitted into the silence of the room.

He moved his hand to my waist while he feathered kisses along my shoulder. "You don't have to be scared. I'm not going to hurt you."

"I know. I'm worried I'm going to hurt you."

He buried his nose back in my neck. "I'm worried about the same thing. Especially when you change the subject and don't answer my questions when I ask them."

I lay in his arms in the dark and didn't say a word. I wanted to stay in the darkness forever and never face the daylight, but life didn't work that way. "I don't answer them because I don't know how," I finally said. "I'm sorry if that hurts, but it's all I can say right now."

He brushed my hair off my neck and suckled the skin at the base until I couldn't hold in my sharp intake of breath. He paused and gave the skin a gentle lick. "Let me ask you this then. What would you do if Myrtle were damaged in the storm?"

I tossed my hand up into the air and let it fall back to my hip.

"I don't know. Myrtle has always been my way to get from one job to the next. Driving her was an excuse to keep taking the next job and the next job. While it wasn't always ideal, it was predictable. I have a job waiting for me. My dream job and now—"

"And now nothing is predictable?" he asked, his hands holding me to him with my chin over his shoulder.

"No, your love is predictable, but the rest, I don't know," I said, a tear in my voice. I swallowed it back, but one leaked out regardless.

He wiped it away with his thumb tenderly, a frown on his lips. "I didn't mean to make you cry."

I sighed and it was long and frustrated. "You didn't. I've been close to tears every day for weeks. Even if I wanted to stay in Plentiful, I wouldn't know where to start. I don't know how to live a normal life, Gulliver. I've never rented an apartment, paid rent, or worked a nine-to-five job. And before you say it, paying for a night or two at a campground doesn't count. I'm essentially like an eighteen-year-old who stepped out the door of their parents' house for the first time with no guidance."

"Shh," he whispered, kissing my cheek. "That's not true. You started a successful business by yourself and have made thousands of decisions for it over the years. Maybe you didn't do it traditionally, but that doesn't mean you can't do it. We can figure it all out together if you're willing to try. And you're wrong, by the way—you've been working a nine-to-five job here, and you're fantastic at it too."

I snickered, and he wiped away another tear. "Great. Well, one down, a dozen more to go."

His thumb ran across my forehead in a calming rhythm. "I'm not going to leave you alone to sort everything out, Charity. I love you, and I know you have to be the one to make the decision whether you stay or go, but if you choose to stay, I'll be here to help you," he promised, leaning down for another gentle, unassuming kiss.

I grasped his hand and held it to my chest desperately. "I love you, too, but I'm still unsure what I'm supposed to do. If Myrtle becomes a pancake, how do I get to Indiana? Or do I not go to Indiana at all and stay here with you instead? I don't know, I don't know, I don't know!"

"Shhh," he said, kissing my lips as he ran his fingers through my hair to calm me. "If Myrtle gets flattened and you decide to take the job in Indiana, you can take my truck."

I lowered a brow to my nose. "Your truck? Gulliver, you love that truck. Besides, what would you drive if I take the Dodge?"

"I do love the truck, but I love you more. I can drive the butterfly-mobile. If you have my truck, I know you'll come back to me someday, if for no other reason than to return the truck."

His words shattered my heart again with one fell swoop. He thought if I left, I'd never return unless I had a reason other than him. That was my fault. I never gave him a reason to believe otherwise. "Gulliver, I don't need your truck to come back to you. I need no other reason to return to Plentiful than you. People have long-distance relationships all the time."

"That's true," he agreed on a head nod. "My question is, what's the difference between Indiana and Plentiful? Either place you have to rent an apartment and start a new life."

"I know and that's why I'm scared!" I exclaimed. "My parents didn't want me. Do you understand that? They literally didn't want me, and my mother proved it a second time around! What makes me think you're any different? You say you love me, but so did they until I was five and demanded too much of their time! I was too much work and too much expense! I don't know if I can stay in one place now. Putting down roots has always been impossible for me to do!"

He lay behind me again and held me to his chest with his arms wrapped tightly around me. "God, Charity, you just broke my heart. Listen to me," he whispered before his lips kissed the tender skin behind my ear. "And I mean really listen to me, okay?" I nodded, glad I didn't have to look into that pair of eyes right now. "You were a casualty of your parents' immaturity. There's no question about that, but here is what you don't understand. There was something broken inside of them, not you. They were incapable of loving themselves or anyone else. You are not. You love with your whole little soul when you invest yourself in a situation for longer than eight hours. You can believe that I'm different for the sole reason that you're different, Charity. You aren't a scared kid anymore. You're a grown woman. I love you regardless of your past pain, current indecision, or future decisions. I love all of you not because of what you do for me, but because of who you are in here," he said, tapping my heart. "That's not going to change just because you get scared and run away. The question I have to ask is, wouldn't it be nice to have a few roots to anchor you to the ground in a storm?"

"Yes," I agreed quietly. "But when you grew up the way I did, you know roots don't always take. Sometimes they are choked off by matters beyond our control. I know you have roots here, but what if I'm terrible at staying in one place? After juvie, and before I bought Myrtle, I never stayed in one place longer than six months, Gulliver. The idea of passing on my dream job only to find out I can't stay here terrifies me."

He whispered his next words into my ear. "But the idea of taking your dream job only to find out you can't stay there either doesn't?"

"Exactly my point. Attempting to put down roots anywhere could lead to failure."

"And you're missing my point, Charity," he said, his hand grasping my hip possessively. "You're overthinking all of this.

You've already put down roots here. Your tiny roots have spread through the town and taken hold in the soil of Plentiful. You're the only one who doesn't realize it."

I stilled and took several long minutes to ponder what he said. "Do you think so?" The room was silent except for the sound of our breathing and Mojo's soft snoring.

"I know so. All I have to do is remember the scene at the Apple Orchard the night of your birthday. Every single person there wanted to spend time with you, talk to you, and wish you a happy day. Nights like that aren't a regular occurrence for tourists in Plentiful. A welcome like the one you received happens when someone is an important part of the community. You managed to worm your way into everyone's hearts here in Plentiful the moment you stepped out of that old motor home. Let me ask you a question. In the middle of a crisis, what did Laverne do tonight?"

"She called me, worried about my motor home," I said.

He kissed my palm tenderly before he answered. "She did because she is concerned for your future. She knows you rely on Myrtle to get from one place to the next. How many times have you shared a cup of coffee on the dock with her? How many times has she taken care of Mojo so you could have a little fun while you were here?"

"At least a dozen," I said, laughter in my voice as I remembered how the big dog had managed to win her over.

"At least, and do we even need to talk about Lucy and Kevin? They're like your adoptive parents, always bringing you extra dessert and making sure Mojo gets fed too."

I chuckled and nodded, tears in my eyes.

"If you notice, they don't bring me extra pie," he said, tickling my side until I let out a bark of laughter. "If those aren't roots, I don't know what are. Here is the most important part; are you listening?"

I nodded, my gaze searching his. They'd never lie to me, even if his lips would. "You wrapped your roots so deeply around my heart and soul that we became one root, and I have no intention of letting go. Do you understand that? When I said I love you, it wasn't for any other reason than it being the truth."

I smiled even though I was crying. "It helped to hear you say that. I'm bad at life, Gulliver," I said, trying to keep the tears from becoming major sobs. "I try, but I don't always feel like I succeed."

"You're not bad at life," he promised me, wiping my eyes and nose with the sheet. "You do more than succeed at it; you rock it. You're a force to be reckoned with, Charity. I wish you could see how successful you've been. You save businesses single-handedly and you don't seem to recognize how important that is. That brings me back to the idea of growing roots. Do you get the same kind of welcome in every town you go to?"

I shook my head immediately. "No, I'm rarely in any town longer than a few days, and I usually keep to myself if I'm at a campground."

"What made Plentiful different then?"

"The people. This job. You," I answered immediately. "No one let me be a stranger, if that makes sense. From the first day when I met Lucy, I was a friend. That's the difference more than anything. People here do things for you because they want to, not because they have to. I know the clock is ticking down, though, and I only have a limited amount of time before I have to decide if I stay or if I go," I whispered, my voice breaking. "I love you, but I already committed to the other job too. I'm scared of making the wrong decision."

He tucked me into his shoulder and held me close. "I love you more. We'll figure this out together."

I nodded against his chest as I lay there, exhausted and scared. "No one loves me for very long, Gulliver. That's why I'm so torn. You love me tonight and maybe tomorrow, but there's a long time until forever."

His hazel eyes grew dark in the low light of the room. "I'm going to say this in a way you can understand. I'm under no obligation to love you. I fell in love with you for who you are and how you make me feel inside, not because someone told me I had to. If you climb into Myrtle and head for Indiana, or anywhere else on this green earth, I'm still going to love you. I'm still going to want you. I'm still going to come find you. I'm going to do anything I have to, including sell my business and join the nomad lifestyle, if that's what it takes to be with you."

"No!" I exclaimed. "Gulliver, you can't sell Butterfly Junction!"

His lips kissed mine until I was quiet, and when he broke the kiss, he smiled, rubbing his thumb over my lips. "I'm not selling Butterfly Junction right now. What I'm saying is, I'm willing to. I'm willing to follow you to the ends of the earth if that's what it takes to keep you happy. All I want is for you to find joy in life, Charity. If you find joy out on the open road, then I'm more than ready to follow you there."

I wrapped my arms around him and buried my face in his neck without another word. I didn't think more words were needed. All that was left was for me to sit with the ones I already had and decide which ones I believed.

Chapter Nineteen

I glanced at the clock just as it flipped to four a.m. I'd fallen asleep in Gulliver's arms after we'd made love, but Mojo had startled me awake. Once I was up, I couldn't fall back to sleep, so I left Gulliver to sleep while I finished decoding the final few sheets of paper from Honey's desk. The words started to swim in front of my eyes, but I was determined to find something in them that would tell me how and why Honey was caught up in this.

After an hour of reading, I stretched my back out and debated going back to bed. I was going to regret it if I didn't, but I didn't have much left to finish. I clicked open the last file, and my heart stopped beating instantly. I gasped quietly at the first two words, 'Dear Mathias,' it read, and I held my breath. 'If you've found this, then I'm dead. I know that sounds dumb, because it's what everyone says, but in this case it will be true. I want you to know I didn't want to help them. I would never do anything to hurt you. You probably already know this, but I've been in love with you since I was eight. The thing is, I'm smart enough to know we can never be together for so many, many reasons, the least of which is my childhood. Unfortunately, it's common knowledge that I'm your friend; therefore, they used the weakest link to get to you. I'm sorry. I wish with all my heart I could have found another way out of this, but I couldn't. If I didn't do what they demanded, you'd die. If I didn't come up with the information they wanted, the information you're working so hard for, they'd kill you, my family, and then me. They made it clear exactly what they'd do if I told you or the police. Trust me when I say the carnage wasn't worth my life. I was dragging my feet, trying to give you time to get your research done, but if you're reading this, I ran out of time. I want you to know I didn't do this to hurt you. I did this to save you. I did this to protect you because between the two of us, you have the most potential to go on and save the world. I love you, Mathias. Always have and always will. Since I know my resting place is the cold-water castle of Lady Superior, whenever you stand on her shores, know I'm loving you from there. No matter where I am, in my eyes, you'll always walk on water, the same way you have for the last twenty years. I'm sorry, Mathias. All my misguided love. Honey.'

"Oh, my gosh. Oh, my gosh," I chanted, scanning it again. "This isn't good. Oh, this so isn't good. What the hell?"

Gulliver's hand came down on my shoulder before I realized I had said it aloud. "Charity, what is it, sweetheart?"

I glanced up, my whole body shaking, and took him in. He was dressed in his shorts with his Croc shoe on his left leg to even him out. "I found something," I stuttered. "I'm sorry, but I found something."

Gulliver sat at the table, his gaze going to the screen. He read the words, but I wasn't sure if it registered. His hand was in his hair, and his breathing was shallow. "What the hell is going on?" he asked, his voice high pitched. "We have to get to Mathias," he said, his tone telling me how scared he was. "He's in danger."

I grasped his arm, holding him to the table. "Wait. What does she mean by the cold-water castle of Lady Superior?"

He dropped his hands from his hair before he made eye contact with me. "The water in Lake Superior is so cold it inhibits bacterial growth year-round, which means bodies tend to sink rather than float. The locals say Lady Superior never gives up her dead, and they remain in her cold-water castle forever. Honey is telling Mathias not to look for her because she already knows that's where she'll be."

I inhaled sharply. "Okay, we have to bring this to Mathias carefully. We can't tip off whoever is behind it, because if they think Honey told someone, well" — I motioned at the computer — "carnage."

He grasped his hair in both hands. "We don't want carnage, but we also need to talk to Honey and Mathias. Once we have the full story, we'll be better able to protect them. Do we know who's behind it? Do we know who *they* are?"

I shook my head. "No, she's careful not to mention names. I read all the translations, and I found some inconsistencies, at least as far as I can tell. I was hoping you'd be able to tell me if I'm crazy or if what I'm reading doesn't jive."

He cocked his head, seeming perplexed. "What do you mean?"

I took the mouse back and clicked into the other document. "I think she's feeding them false information, but I don't know for sure because I don't know the information as intricately as you do. It's like she gave up on all the code and just started talking to them by the time I got to the last envelope. She's telling them things about the formula and the production schedule that aren't accurate, at least to my knowledge."

I twisted the computer back to him, and he read the entries. He pointed at one of them. "This is wrong. None of these are accurate percentages for our formula," he said, stunned. "She's feeding them bad information."

I scrolled down with the mouse. "Except here, Honey says she isn't sure if it's outdated because you're still working. We have to assume she means on the formula. The person behind the screen tells her to keep sending the information each week."

He laughed and I was surprised at how amused he was by this. "What she's sending them isn't a formula for our pesticide at all."

"What is it then?"

Gulliver kept chuckling the longer he read through the information on the screen. "From what I can see, Honey's giving them the formulas from the bottles of eco-friendly garden pesticides. It's what we used as a base to start ours, but now ours is nothing like it. This is actually kind of funny in a scary way. She's giving them what they want, but they're too stupid to realize it's not our formula."

"And what does that tell you?"

"This person has no idea what they're doing," he said without even pausing. "They're not from a big pesticide company, or they would know the formulas weren't for commercial operations and would have called her on it. If they are from a big company, they have to be stupid not to know the difference. Though, in this line of work, I've learned that's not uncommon."

"It also tells me she's playing with fire because if they figure it out—"

"She and Mathias are dead."

"What do we do?" I asked, shutting the computer down and placing it back in its case.

"We're going to have the team protecting Mathias and Honey get them back here safely. From there, we make a plan together, but this ends now."

"I'm nervous because if we tip our hand, they might be in

even more danger," I said, biting my lip. "The chats tell us Honey has been involved with them for at least nine months."

He paused as he folded the blanket on the cot. "I hired her in June of last year, so they had to have gotten to her immediately. I'm surprised she's held them off this long. She must be an amazing actress."

My heart stuttered in my chest, and my shoulders hunched unconsciously. "More like she's a woman in love, and she's determined to protect Mathias at the cost of her own life." My stomach churned, and I pressed my hand to it. "I just pray we aren't too late."

"Are you sure everything is okay, Charity?" Honey asked me from where we sat in Gulliver's office.

The sun was shining, and the damage to the town was stark in the light of day. There were so many trees down, Mathias and Honey had to come in by pontoon boat from a dock near his condo. At least it was something they commonly did, so Mathias had a spot at the marina to dock the boat while we talked.

"Everything is fine," I lied. "Gulliver was just concerned about some stuff he found in the research lab during the storm, so he wanted Mathias to look it over."

Technically not a lie. My phone beeped, and I glanced at the text. All it said was: *Ready.*

I motioned to the door. "They want us to run down there," I explained, following her down the stairs and waiting while she swiped her key card through the reader. Once the door clicked, she held it for me, and we stopped in the doorway.

Mathias paced with his back to us. "I don't understand any of this," he said. "Who are they, and why are they dabbling in this if they don't know the first thing about it. What in the hell is Honey thinking not coming to me about it?"

Honey gasped and Mathias whipped around, his hand falling to his side as he faced off with his best friend. I took her waist and urged her into the room gently, while Gulliver stood up from the table. I lowered her to a chair at the same time her face crumbled into tears. I eyed both men while I rubbed her back. They were going to have to be careful about how they questioned her, or they'd do more damage to her already stressed psyche.

Mathias sat and picked up Honey's hand off the table. "It's okay, sweetheart. We know you didn't want to do it."

Her head swung back and forth, and she tried to speak but no words would come out.

"You're scared they're going to hurt me, you, or both of us, right?"

She nodded, sucking up air as she worked to form a sentence. I handed her a tissue, and she wiped her eyes before she released a shuddering breath. "I'm afraid of them," she finally whispered.

Mathias trailed his thumb below her eye to wipe away a tear and waited for her to get herself under control.

"How did you find out?" she finally asked on a whisper.

I squeezed her shoulder and jumped up on the chair next to her. "I accidentally found the hidden documents in your desk drawer."

"But—but they were encoded," she huffed. "I wasn't supposed to make copies of anything, but I had to protect myself somehow. I found a program to encode them before I printed them off."

I clasped my hands together before I spoke. "As a hacker, I can decode binary code quickly. The massive amount of communication required some intensive work, but early this morning I finally got to the bottom of it. I found your letter to Mathias."

Honey lowered her head to the table and shivered uncontrollably. "The letter was only supposed to be read in the event of my death."

"We understand, Honey," I promised, "but we're here to make sure that doesn't happen. The letter is what finally put the situation together for us."

Mathias held her hand to his chest. "Honeybee, you know I always have your back in everything, from getting you this job to making sure you're safe and happy."

She lifted her gaze to his. "Did you read the letter?" He nodded, not breaking eye contact with her. "Great, just great," she sighed and lowered her head back to the table.

"We can worry about what was in the letter after we make sure you and Mathias are safe," Gulliver said, trying to keep the focus on the men behind this scheme. "We can't keep you safe until we know who they are and why they're threatening you. Can you help us fill in the blanks?"

"I can try," Honey said, finally lifting her head, "but I don't know where they are. I've met them in person under unfortunate circumstances," she said, holding up her arm.

Mathias slammed his fist down on the table. "They were the ones who broke your arm?"

Honey lowered it to her lap and hung her head. "They wanted more information than I could give them."

Mathias let out a curse word, and Gulliver grasped his shoulder. "Relax, Mathias," he said, giving him a don't-ruin-this stare. Mathias swallowed hard and took a deep breath. "Sweetheart, did they come to your apartment?" Her nod was immediate. "And you went to the diner with a compound fracture of your arm instead of calling me for help?"

"I wasn't thinking clearly," she whispered. "I just knew I needed help. I wanted to tell you, but they said they'd kill you. I couldn't risk it. I couldn't, Mattie," she said, her face crumbling into tears again. "I didn't care about myself, but I couldn't let them hurt you!"

Mathias gathered her close and held her, rocking her slowly back and forth while she shuddered in his arms. "You're okay now. No one is going to hurt you again," he whispered against her ear.

Once she was calm, Gulliver addressed her. "Do you have a way of contacting them outside the chat room? Like a number to text or an email?"

Honey shook her head, but her hand rubbed at the scar on her arm absently. "No. Occasionally, they show up at my apartment to shake me down for information. I have no way of knowing when they'll show up, though. All I knew for sure was I had to be in the chat room every Monday night at eleven."

Mathias cleared his throat, his body language calmer. "Do they know you're feeding them false formula equations?"

Her chin hit her chest before she answered. "How did you know?"

Gulliver chuckled, obviously amused. "I read the chats where you sent them the information. I know the ingredients and percentages you were feeding them were straight from the bottle at the store."

"I won't sabotage the research," she vowed with her chin held level to stare down both men, "even if they kill me. I don't care who they are or why they're doing this. I won't destroy Mathias's work simply because I fear for my life. I'm better off dead anyway."

Before I could react, Mathias stood up and pulled her into his arms, her head braced against his chest. "Don't ever let me hear you say you'd be better off dead, honeybee! Do you hear me? You're my best friend, and I'm not going to let some simpletons change that.

We're going to keep you safe while we sort this out, but you will be alive at the end."

"Alive but in jail," she said, her voice muffled against his chest.

"For what?" I asked, my brows raised as we waited for her to answer.

"For what I've done here," she answered. "I know I've crossed the line many times trying to get something, anything to give them without jeopardizing the true formula."

"Were you the one to run me off the road and attack Charity?" Mathias asked, holding her gaze.

"No — no," she cried, her hand going to the back of his head automatically. "I would never do that, Mathias. I would never hurt you or Charity! I was trying to protect you. That's why I didn't tell you in the first place! You have to believe me. That was one of them. I swear to God, that was one of them!"

Mathias held her to his chest as she trembled in his arms and lifted his gaze to Gulliver. "I'm not pressing charges; are you?"

"Nope," Gulliver answered. "Being stuck between a rock and a hard place isn't a reason to go to jail. It's a reason to ask your friends for help." Gulliver slid a pad of paper over in front of him. "How many guys are there when they make contact with you in person?"

"Three," she said immediately. "They're all muscle-bound and raging on 'roids."

"Which means they could have easily broken your arm with one twist," Gulliver said.

She grasped it to her stomach in a sad display of pain and fear. "Which is what they did," she whispered.

Mathias cursed again and grasped her other hand tightly. "I'm so sorry this has been going on, and I didn't realize it. Damn it," he whispered, lowering his head. "We have to end this, even if it means the research is leaked."

"No!" Honey said emphatically. "I haven't fought tooth and nail to protect it just to give it away! No."

Gulliver held up a hand. "I think we can manage to find these guys and still protect the research."

"I don't understand what the big deal is," Honey said as she shook her head. "I know why you guys want this formula, it's for the environment, but why all the violence for something that's being created to help us?"

"Because while we want it for the environment, others want it for money," Mathias explained patiently. "If we can take a product like this to market, we're talking about billions of dollars lost from current pesticide companies and funneled down into one company."

"Butterfly Junction," Honey finished.

Gulliver tipped his head in acknowledgment. "We've always expected pushback from some of the other companies who stand to lose money on their products if ours goes to market, but we didn't expect violence against our friends. I don't find their behavior acceptable, so we're going to change it this morning. Understand?"

Honey nodded and I noticed her spine straighten at his words. "I'll do whatever I can, but they know where I live, and they'll get to me if they want to. I've made peace with it," she said, her voice breaking on the last word.

That told me she hadn't made peace with it. At least not when faced with the man she loved.

Mathias put his arm around her and let her rest her head on his shoulder. "You aren't going home, honeybee. I'll keep you safe until we can end this blackmail. Gulliver and I are going to the police."

Honey struggled to sit up. "No, no, no, no, Mathias. They told me straight up if the cops got involved, it wouldn't end well for any of us."

"They can't get to us here, sweetheart," he reminded her patiently.

Honey stomped to the door that separated us from the research lab. "What's in there, Mathias?" she yelled, pointing into the glass-encased room. "Tell me, what's the lab filled with?"

Mathias sat like a deer in headlights, so I was the one to answer. "Chemicals," I said slowly.

"Exactly," she cried, her hands up in the air. "Extremely flammable chemicals, even if they are eco-friendly. They'll still go boom, won't they?" she asked, her arms dropping to her sides.

Mathias's lips were tugged into a thin line. "They will, but first they'd have to get down here. We have to trust someone, Honey. If we don't, then we're giving them exactly what they want. I'm not willing to take all the money I've put into this, and the blood, sweat, and tears of our researchers, and hand it over without a fight. I'll fight to protect it, but I'll also fight to protect you."

Gulliver tapped the table with his fingers. "Honey, if what you're saying is true, these three guys can't be the brains behind this. When you communicate in the chat room, is it with one of them or someone else?"

Honey trudged back to the table and sat. She looked exhausted and I felt terrible for her. "I don't know, Gulliver. All I know is, none of them are Einstein. As for the chat room, my guess is whoever I'm communicating with is the person behind all of it. Whether he's one of these three guys or someone who sends them, I don't know."

Mathias rubbed his temple, confusion and frustration etched on his face. "Then the person you're giving the information to isn't a scientist or chemist. If they were, they'd know what you were feeding them was bad information."

Gulliver leaned forward on the table. "From what I read in the documents Charity decoded, they don't want to formulate their own product. They want ours. Meaning they're constantly asking her for information for two reasons. They want to make sure she hasn't told anyone what they're up to, and they're keeping tabs on our research. They may not understand the chemical compositions, but they can grasp the basics. When she sends them simple formulas like she's taking off the bottles, they take it at face value. They think it's the real thing. She tells them it's the latest one we're working on, and they file it until she contacts them with the new one." He addressed Honey with his next question. "Are you the one hacking into the server to steal the research?"

Honey glanced between Gulliver and me in confusion. "What? No, I don't know how to hack."

"The reason Gulliver hired me in June," I said, jumping in, "was to find any holes in the security of the server. What I found was fully open doors."

She held up her hands, and I noticed a tremor in her bad hand as they hung in the air. Mathias lowered her hand and absently rubbed at her fingers that were twisted against her palm. Something must have happened when she was younger because while she could use her hand with no problem, when it was at rest, her fingers curled like a claw into her palm. Whatever she'd been through in life, it hadn't been kind to her. "Trust me, what you're describing is way above my abilities. Hell, getting the formula is way above my ability to comprehend. I'm not that smart. You can ask Mathias."

"Honeybee," Mathias said, his tone pointed. "We don't expect you to understand the formula. You aren't a scientist."

She nodded her head several times. "Which is why I'm giving them the stuff from the store. It was a chance I took not knowing if they'd realize it was bogus, but after the first time I did it and they were giddy, I decided to keep going."

Gulliver frowned as he tapped the pen on the paper. "Do you think we have two different groups on our hands then?" he asked me.

"That's possible, but remember, you found the evidence of a hacker before I came into the picture. It could still be them, but since I fixed the security issues, they haven't been able to get through. Whoever is behind the hacking didn't hire a black hat, I can tell you that. If they had, all your research would have been stolen long before I got here. If their skills were limited, then it could still be the same group threatening Honey. A black hat would have gotten everything on the first try."

Mathias ran his hands through his hair. "They're not going to find anything if they hack us now, right?"

I leaned back, a confident smile on my face. "Every door has been boarded over, nailed shut, and then bricked for good measure. Your cloud is empty too. I check every day. No one has attempted anything since I arrived at Butterfly Junction."

"You're saying your reputation precedes you," Mathias said with a smile.

I shrugged once. "People hire me for one reason. Google my name sometime. I have no secrets."

He grinned for the first time all day. "Oh, I have. I know if you hadn't shown up, we'd be in much worse shape."

I winked. "It's what I do."

"And taking care of my friends is what I do," Mathias said. "We're going to the professionals to help us with this, or we'll never get out of it alive."

"We might not anyway," Honey whispered. "I've come to terms with it."

Gulliver stood and braced his hands on the table. "I won't

let anyone die because of a bunch of numbers on a piece of paper, Honey! Do you understand me?" Her nod and wide eyes said he'd made his point. "Good. Now I want all three of you to listen and listen closely. Here's what we're going to do."

Chapter Twenty

Early yesterday morning, the police chief showed up at the loading dock dressed in the same outfit as the security guards Mathias had hired. He worked with them for an hour, pretending to be a new hire, to avoid suspicion if anyone was watching. We had to take the chance the three guys hounding Honey were from out of town and didn't know who the police chief was.

When it was time for his break, he disappeared inside and had a long discussion with all of us. Honey described the three men who attacked her, but other than height and build, she couldn't tell them much. All of them wore masks whenever they showed up. She always faced down Bill Clinton, Richard Nixon, and Ronald Reagan. It was Bill who broke her arm. When Chief Flats went back to work, the police tech arrived, dressed as an air-conditioning repairman, to go over everything with Honey regarding her online contacts. She let him read the information she'd saved but refused to give him copies.

Rather than upset her, he spent extra time reading the information at Butterfly Junction and making copious notes before he left with her log-in name and password to a forum for farmers. Irony.

"The police have hackers who can get into these chat rooms and get their IP address and real names. They plan to do that tonight," Gulliver said as we sat out on the shore of Lake Superior tossing flat rocks into the water. It had been a few days since the storm and people were still cutting trees and cleaning up debris.

I made the *pfft* sound, and it ruffled the hair on my forehead. "Big deal. It would take me ten minutes to get the information. What's your point?"

Gulliver whipped me around so fast I almost tipped off the log. "I'm not going to say this more than once. Do. Not. Mess. With. This. Do you understand me?" he asked in a staccato voice.

I laid my hand on his waist to calm him. "I have no intention of doing it, Gulliver. I was just saying I could." I tossed another rock into the water. The storm had riled the Lady of the Lake, and she was tossing debris onto the shore at an unprecedented rate. I'd found clothing, a boat motor cover, a cell phone — which surprisingly still worked — and an old hockey stick. I was still trying to track down the cell phone's owner, but I was pretty sure I had a good lead. "I've been curious about something since I read Honey's letter to Mathias," I said, changing the subject.

"What about it?" he asked before taking a sip from his bottle of IPA.

"Why can't they be together? It couldn't be more obvious to everyone that they care about each other."

The next rock was tossed into the water with exasperation from Gulliver. "Your guess is as good as mine. Best I can figure out is the social class is too much for them to bridge."

I wrinkled my nose at his explanation. "I don't understand."

His lips twisted, and I could tell he was arguing with himself about telling me the truth. "I asked Mathias about Honey's parents.

It turns out she's from the wrong side of the tracks."

I snorted in disdain. "Which to Mathias means they're not loaded and don't live in a fancy house."

"No, Mathias isn't uppity like that," Gulliver insisted, shaking his head vehemently. "Yes, he grew up with money and affluence, but he doesn't flaunt it or use it for anything but good. Sure, Mathias stands to get a lifetime payout when this pesticide goes live, but he's the one who put a boatload of cash in to make sure we could research it at all. He understands he has money; therefore, he feels obligated to make sure he does right with it. If he gets a windfall from the pesticide sale, he'll invest it into something else to better our planet. It's what he does."

I braced my hand on his chest in a silent apology. "I didn't mean to offend you. I'm sorry."

He grasped my hand and lightly kissed my lips. "Don't be. I know as far as you're concerned, you grew up on the wrong side of the tracks, and truth be told, you aren't different from Honey in the way you grew up, at least according to what Mathias tells me. Her parents are both recovering drug addicts, and they raised Honey during a time when they were using. She didn't always eat, go to school, or have clothes to wear. Mathias befriended her at the park one day when she was dressed in nothing but underwear. His family made sure she got what she needed from then on, without calling the authorities or Child Protective Services on her parents. I don't know if I agree with it, but it was during a time when foster care in this area was more abusive than living with your druggie parents. Honey hasn't had it easy. Hell, even her name is ridiculous."

"Well, I have nothing to say about ridiculous names, but I don't know why two people's upbringings should matter once you're an adult. The two of us together is proof of nature versus nurture. Our life experiences shape us, but our determination and will to improve our situation in life is what makes us. I think socioeconomic status is a lame reason not to have a relationship with someone when you care about each other."

He tipped his head to the side at that. "I can't disagree, but I also know they're best friends. Maybe Mathias sees her more as a little sister than a potential mate, you know? Maybe he doesn't want to screw up their friendship by attempting to make it something more."

"I guess, maybe, but little sister and big brother were not what I witnessed this morning. Best friends, yes, but there's a layer of something more under the surface." I put up my hands when he lowered a brow at me. "All I'm saying."

"I love you, Charity Puck. I love you for loving our friends the way you do, and whether you believe it or not, you deserve all the love this world has to offer you."

With my forehead braced against his, I could stare into his eyes, and the reflection off the lake made the gold strings vibrate with truth. I blinked, waiting to see if it changed to any other emotion. Fear. Distrust. Pity. It didn't. The intensity of the hazel blazed with love, trust, and honor. He wanted me to stay in Plentiful and be part of his life forever. Most of me wanted the same thing. The rest of me, the abandoned child who hid away in the dark inside me, was the reason I wouldn't be part of his life forever. My parents didn't want me after a few years. What made me think he would?

Those eyes. Those bright, honest, open hazel eyes were what made me think he would. He would be there through it all if I could find the strength to leave my baggage behind and follow him down this new road.

"Can I ask you something?" he whispered before his lips teased mine with a short peck.

"Anything," I promised.

"Promise me that you won't leave until August first?"

"I don't plan to leave before then, Gulliver," I promised, smoothing my hand down his face, "but that's over two weeks away yet."

"I know." His head nodded against mine, and I couldn't help but smile at the feeling it filled my heart with. I was in love for the first time in my life, and the consistent touch of another human was starting to weaken my reserve to take that job and leave this man. "I'm working on something that might help you make a decision about what your future will look like. I might need every one of those fourteen days. Promise me."

"I promise," I said, "and I'll even seal it with a kiss."

I wrapped my hands in his shirt and pulled him down to me, watching his mouth descend to mine while I awaited the warmth and thrill touching them offered me. He moved his against mine in a dance we both knew by heart, but the music was different sitting here by the shore. It was as though the Lady of the Lake was playing a love song for only us and we dipped and swayed to the rhythm of the waves against the shore, our tongues taking their time with each spin and dip.

I wondered if I stayed here, would the music keep playing? Would it keep filling my head with the lyrics that this man was made only for me?

"Charity!" Gulliver yelled from the front of Butterfly Junction. "Holy hell, Charity!" he yelled again. I was out the door of his office and halfway down the hall before I realized I was running. The franticness of his tone had my heart pounding.

As he reached me, he threw his crutches to the ground and grabbed me, swinging me back and forth with my feet off the ground. "We did it! We've got it! It's done!" he yelled with his head tipped back in excitement.

"The formula?" I asked, my heart going from scared to

elated. "I didn't think it would happen this quickly."

"Yes!" he exclaimed, setting me back on my feet. His hand dived into his hair, and he took a deep breath. "I can't believe it. We did it." His voice was awe-filled and quiet now. "We did it."

I put my arm around his waist and let him lean on me until we got to his office to sit down. He lowered himself to a chair while I stood between his legs. "I had no doubt you'd do it, sweetheart. I'm so proud of you," I whispered before I kissed him. "You deserve this and so much more."

He held my face in his hands, and his expression showed me pure, unadulterated, blissful satisfaction. "We deserve this."

"No," I shook my head in disbelief. "I didn't have any part in the research."

"You're wrong. If you hadn't closed the holes in the server, we might never have seen this day. All our work would be out the window. We owe a lot of our success to your ability to close and nail those doors shut. Not to mention, if you hadn't found the information in Honey's desk, my business partner and his best friend might be dead. You deserve this as much as he and I do."

I patted his face with love and happiness. "I'll take kudos for the server work, but the rest was all you guys. Where is Mathias?"

"He's downstairs staring at the finding like a fool. We're planning to go to dinner at the Apple Orchard to celebrate. We want you and Honey there too."

I tapped my fingers on his thighs. "Is being in the public eye a good idea? I mean, it could be dangerous for them."

Gulliver kissed my forehead, his lips lingering against my skin. "Mathias's security team will come with us. They're not letting him or Honey out of their sight. Honey is working in the basement now until everything settles. Honestly, it settles now because we have the formula, and there's nothing they can do about it. It's already pending patent."

"Okay, so what do you do now?"

He took my hands and squeezed them, kissing my knuckles over and over. "We market it like you've been working on, only now we have tangible proof we can change the path of agriculture and protect ourselves from starvation!"

His enthusiasm was contagious, and I grabbed his face, guiding his lips to mine. The kiss was long, hard, and had enough tongue to tell him exactly how excited I was for him. He moaned and stroked my tongue with the fever of a man who now had everything he wanted in life. Well, almost everything. If you listened to him describe it, when I leave in a few weeks, his life will never be the same, and he'd chase me to the ends of the earth to be with me. I wanted to stay, but I couldn't. I didn't want to break his heart, but I couldn't give up the stability the job in Indiana offered me. Not without checking it out for a few months at least. Maybe I'd keep Myrtle until late October, which would give me plenty of time to know if the job was for me and if I'd be staying in one place after all.

Coward, that voice in my head said. *You already know your place, and he's holding you in his arms.*

When the kiss ended, I sighed with satisfaction. "You're about to put Butterfly Junction on the map, sweetheart. My heart is bursting out of my chest for you. I've never been this proud of someone before," I whispered. "I've never loved anyone the way I love you, so your successes are my successes."

Gulliver sighed, but it sounded like relief more than happiness. "I'm happy to hear you say that."

I cocked my head to the right. "Why? If you don't know how proud I am of you, then I'm doing a bad job of showing it."

"I do know," he promised, grasping my hands in front of him. "It reflects in your eyes every time you look at me. What I mean is, things are about to blow up at Butterfly Junction and spin out of control."

"In what respect?" I asked, concerned. "You mean the lab or what?"

"I'm not making any sense, am I? My mind is racing, and I can hardly keep up with it," he said as he rubbed my arms up and down rhythmically. "What I mean is, life is about to get crazy busy around here. I can't do this job by myself anymore. I need help. Help from someone who can run a computer in her sleep, organize, schedule, print, code, update, and tour the area with me when I go out and give speeches about the product."

"What are you saying, Gulliver?" I asked, confused. "You want me to be your assistant?"

He shook his head, which made my heart sink instantly. Working at Butterfly Junction might be the only thing that would keep me from taking the job waiting for me in Indiana.

"I want you to be my partner," he whispered, his hand cupping my cheek. "I want you to be by my side, reaping the same benefits I am. I want you to be the face of Butterfly Junction. I want you, all of you, here with me. I've been working on this for a few weeks. I wanted to find you a dream job that was closer to me than Indiana because I can't stand the thought of being away from you for a day, much less for weeks at a time."

I threw my arms around his neck, and he lifted me onto his lap. "I was just thinking how Butterfly Junction could be my dream job," I teased as he squeezed me around the waist. "And I do love it here."

"You only love Butterfly Junction?" he asked, tickling my ribs.

I giggled and wiggled against his fingers. "No, I mean, I love you, and I love working here with you." I leaned back from his embrace. "Are you serious about this? You want me to work here? What about Honey?"

Gulliver possessed my lips again and moaned when he slid

his tongue alongside mine. When I was desperate for air, he tugged my lower lip through his teeth before releasing me. "Honey will stay," he said against my lips. "She's going to be Mathias's assistant now that he's going to need more help too." He dived back in for more sexed-up kisses until we had to break apart to breathe. "I'll have to hire a new receptionist because Honey won't have time. They will focus on the financial side of the business, while we focus on the education and promotion side of things."

"Which makes me your assistant," I said, nodding. "It might just be better than the job I thought was my dream job," I said, laughter on my lips. "I get to stay here and keep loving you!" I squealed, hugging him and planting another kiss on him. "God, I love you so much."

"I love you too," he whispered, planting kisses down the side of my cheek. "But you won't be my assistant. You'll be my partner. I won't have it any other way. Your salary will reflect the title, and you will have a partner's share in the business. Do you understand?"

I loosened my hands on his neck and leaned back to hold his gaze. "I don't know, Gulliver. Making me a partner when I've put nothing into it of monetary value doesn't make a lot of sense."

"You're wrong," a voice said from the doorway.

Surprised, I spun around to see Mathias standing there with Gulliver's crutches in hand. He sat on the chair opposite us and folded his hands, but the smile on his face was not easily hidden.

"Can you believe this? I can't stop my heart from pounding," he said, his head and hands shaking. "We've spent years of our life on this, and suddenly we have it," he said. "Why do we have it? Because Gulliver was smart enough to call someone in with the skills to protect our files and make sure no one stole all the research. The reason you're wrong about being a partner in this business is for the reason I just mentioned. Money is one thing, but your creative talent is immeasurable to a business like this. I've seen the documents you've prepared for the site visits and the beautiful books you've produced for education. You can't put a price on creative talent because not everyone has it. What your mind does boggles mine when it comes to writing code, organizing him," he said, pointing at Gulliver, "and being able to predict what we'll need to do before we take the next step. It wasn't on our radar about the education aspect because we were too focused on getting the research done. We need someone like you as part of this business. We've already agreed to make you a partner if you want in. You've more than earned it. Not to mention, I've never seen Gulliver happier than I have the last two months. I didn't even know he could smile until you strolled through those doors," he said, pointing out front.

I laughed and laid my head on Gulliver's shoulder. "Okay, okay, you've convinced me. I'm in!"

Gulliver wrapped me in his arms and laughed, his chest rumbling against mine. "Thank God," he whispered, his lips brushing mine in a kiss that promised a lifetime of love.

Chapter Twenty-One

I settled back against the seat of Mathias's SUV while Simon drove me toward the Apple Orchard to meet the rest of the team for dinner. He had taken me back to Myrtle to change my clothes and grab some dog food for Mojo, so Gulliver could finish up a few things at the office.

Since Mojo was happy staying at Gulliver's apartment, I left him to sleep for the evening while we celebrated. It was nice not to have to worry about finding someone to keep him when I couldn't take him with me. I guess, in hindsight, Butterfly Junction was what we'd both needed. I didn't mean the building either. I meant the comfort, understanding, and acceptance of the people who surrounded us here. They were my tribe, and the moment I knew I didn't have to let them go, my heart settled inside my chest for the first time in my life. Wrapped in Gulliver's arms, there was no more doubt, fear, or indecision. He wanted me to be part of his life forever. If he didn't, he would have asked me to be his assistant and not insisted that I become his partner.

Tomorrow I would have to talk to Laverne about Myrtle. I

would have to sell her by the end of August, since Gulliver said apartments would start coming open for rent in the fall. I didn't want to pay to store it over the winter, but more than that, selling her symbolized the end of that life for me.

"It's kind of creepy out here tonight," I said from the passenger seat while Simon drove down the road shrouded in dark shadows.

"I agree," he said. "I think a storm is rolling in. At least it won't be severe this time."

A car in the opposite lane flipped its high beams on, and Simon flashed his lights at them. We couldn't see a thing with the headlights in our eyes, and it was several more seconds before we realized the car wasn't in the opposite lane. It was barreling toward us in our lane!

"What the hell?" Simon asked, honking the horn. The car didn't budge. It just continued plowing through the night without hesitation. "What are you doing?" Simon yelled as he swung into the opposite lane without knowing if anyone was coming. The car made the same maneuver, and fear bloomed brightly in my chest. This wasn't going to end well.

"Damn it!" Simon yelled and then yanked the wheel to the right. I prayed as hard as I ever had when the tires left the road and entered the ditch. The SUV missed several large trees, and he stomped on the brake. I pretended that smacking my head on the window didn't hurt like hell as the car skidded and slid through the grass until it lodged itself on a large tree stump, wheels still spinning. Shaking my head to clear it, I struggled to get free of my belt when a thud hit the back of the car. Voices ran toward us, and bullets thudded against the SUV.

Simon was out cold in the seat next to me.

"Simon!" I yelled, shaking him, but his head lolled from side to side. I didn't want to leave him here, but if I stayed, we were both going to die.

I knew I had to get help. I was the only chance Simon had right now. I pushed the door open, crying out with joy when I tumbled into the grass.

I darted into the dark forest, a sudden pain in my ankle making itself known with every step. I had no idea what was wrong with it, but my self-preservation told it to be quiet while I ran for my life. It was more a hobble and hop, but I had to put distance between me and the car before I tried to call someone. Those guys could come after me next.

A thought struck me then. They didn't want me. We were driving Mathias's car. They wanted Mathias.

I ran in a bobbing, limping state but frequently fell from the pain in my leg. *Were they following me?* I couldn't hear anyone, but the section of forest I was in was padded with soft pine needles instead of crunchy, dead leaves. My breath came in short puffs from my mouth, and tears streamed down my face silently. *What do I do?* I whimpered to myself. My brain told my feet to keep running toward the Apple Orchard.

I plowed headlong into the darkness with no idea of where I was or how I was going to get there. There was a tree coming up on the left, and it was larger than any I had passed so far. I darted behind it, forcing my chest to stop heaving so I could listen for voices. I couldn't hear them yelling any longer, but that didn't mean they weren't there. I peeked my head around the tree, but no flashlights filled the forest. *Do I go, or do I stay?*

I patted my pants pocket, relief flooding me that I still had my phone. "Thank God," I whispered, kneeling and hiding the light of the phone in my shirt. "Please let there be bars, please," I begged. There was only one, but I decided to send a text and keep moving.

Gulliver, we need help. Someone ran us off the road and was firing at the car. You'll find Mathias's SUV three or four miles outside of Plentiful on the highway in a ditch. Send the police and an ambulance. Simon is hurt! They're after Mathias. I have to keep moving. I don't know where they are or where I am. I'll text again if I find a road. I love you. HELP SIMON! I typed frantically and hit the send button.

I didn't check to see if it was sent before I took off running again headlong into the night, praying I survived long enough to tell him I loved him in person.

I had my phone open, the brightness as low as it would go, but the dim light was enough to keep me from falling on the uneven terrain. I had been running for fifteen minutes, but I had to keep going. I had to get to safety or Simon was a dead man. If he wasn't already. I bit back a sob, refusing to even consider the idea that he wouldn't be alive at the end of the night.

There hadn't been any voices or shots in the last fifteen minutes, but thunder rumbled in the distance. My steps quickened as another low growl shook the earth. If a storm blew up and I was in the woods, I risked getting struck by lightning or having a tree fall on me. The idea propelled me forward faster and harder than I'd ever moved before. The bike riding and walking I'd done all summer had helped me more than I realized. They strengthened my arms and legs, allowing me to push on when I otherwise might have had to stop and rest. I plastered myself against a tree and noticed the forest was thinning out. The road was just beyond the trees, but which way did I go? I closed my eyes and focused my mind on being in the truck with Gulliver on the way to the Apple Orchard. An overpowering wave of love hit me, and I gasped. He was searching for me. He was trying to find me.

Which way? I hummed, waiting for the answer from the voice in the trees. It had gotten me this far, and my heart told me it was Gulliver helping me to safety. I ran to the right and paused at the edge of the tree line. I rechecked my phone, praying for service, but there was still nothing and the text hadn't sent. I scanned the gravel road, left then right then left again. I watched and waited for the perfect time to cross the road. That would leave me out in the open and vulnerable to anyone who wanted me dead, but I didn't have a choice. Chances were good that they'd already figured out Mathias wasn't in the SUV, but I suspected they'd kill me anyway, just for fun. I could be a murder of opportunity to hurt the Butterfly Junction team.

I whimpered and bit my lip, my eyes wide, but my feet were stuck to the ground. I had no idea how far I had to run down the road before it would come out at the Apple Orchard. Maybe I should just hunker down and wait for a car to come along. If I waited long enough, eventually a cop car or Gulliver would drive by, right?

The first drops of rain hit my face, and I sighed. Great. Just great. Finding shelter and waiting it out was suddenly more attractive. If I kept running and got lost in the storm, I could end up dead. Frustration bubbled up inside me. I was only a mile, maybe two, from safety, and I couldn't get there. My ankle ached to the point that every step made me cry. *You have to go, Charity,* the voice said. *Push through it and find me.*

The voice spurred me on, and I limped forward through the rain. I checked my phone one last time, but nothing. I couldn't even make an emergency call. I edged along the side of the road, watching for it to curve to the left. My steps slowed at the curve, and I rechecked the phone. The text had finally sent!

Okay, I still couldn't make a call, but the text was sent! I listened closely between the rumbles of thunder overhead, and I heard the most wonderful sound. Police radios and people talking excitedly! That meant one thing, the Apple Orchard was only a few feet up the road. I was on the wrong side of the road to approach from the front, but if I stayed in the tree line, I'd come out in the orchard. It would take more time, but there would be less of a chance of being captured along the road.

The orchard also afforded me coverage to stop and assess what was going on before I dived headlong into another dangerous situation. The decision made to stay in the woods, I dragged my right leg along behind me as I struggled toward the only person who could keep me safe.

The idea of Gulliver holding me again spurred me forward, and I crashed through the trees toward the only man I'd ever loved. I forced my feet forward until I could see the lights shining inside the barn; then I scanned the patio for anyone who could help me, but it was empty in the driving rain. I didn't let it stop me. I limped along, my leg ready to give out, but the voice in my head was still yelling its mantra to me. *Safety is only a few hundred yards away. You can do this. Come to me.*

My gaze trained on my refuge, I stumbled and ran my head into the trunk of an apple tree. I shook it, tears falling as I forced my legs under me and stood upright again. I couldn't stop. If I gave up, they'd find me dead in these trees just a few feet from salvation. I was within shouting distance of the patio when a familiar figure stepped out, his hands in his hair and his entire body racked with agony.

"Gulliver!" I screamed, my voice weak and weepy. "Gulliver, I'm here!"

"Charity!" he yelled before his head swiveled backward, and he yelled something behind him. In seconds, the lights flickered on across the patio as people poured out onto it. I fell to the ground in the middle of the trees, unable to get up even one more time — the orchard filled with cops and medics who assessed me for injuries. I swatted at them, yelling for Gulliver until a cop held me down gently.

An EMT swam into my line of vision. "Charity, we'll get you

to him once we check you out. Does anything hurt?"

I took a deep breath, shaking the fog from my brain so I could answer. "My right ankle."

"Did you hurt your neck or hit your head in the SUV?" a medic asked.

"I hit my head, yeah. My neck, no, just got jostled around when we left the road. Take me to Gulliver," I begged, grabbing his coat.

He chuckled. "I think you're in your right mind. You're little, so is it okay if I carry you alone? I'll have Officer Cassidy hold your ankle steady."

I noticed them do some kind of communication with their eyes over my head. The EMT picked me up, and the officer grabbed my ankle while everyone else made way for us. When they got me back to the patio, a stretcher was waiting, which they lowered me onto carefully. "We have to take you to the hospital now," Officer Cassidy said. "Your ankle needs attention."

"It can wait. Where's Gulliver?" I asked, searching the crowd. I caught a glimpse of a distraught Laverne being comforted by several of the regulars, but Gulliver was nowhere to be found.

"Charity," he whispered from the side of the stretcher after they buckled me in and lifted me. "I'm here. You're going to be okay," he promised, his hand brushing the leaves and sticks from my hair. "I love you."

I put my arms out for him, and he leaned down, kissing my lips tenderly with a million emotions in his eyes. "I love you too. I wanted to tell you in person." I gasped. "Simon!" I yelled. "You have to help Simon!"

He held my face upside down and hushed me with his lips to my forehead. "Shh, he's okay. He's okay and you will be too. You can tell me as many times as you want how much you love me for the rest of your life. I'm going to follow you to the hospital. Don't give the EMTs any trouble," he ordered. He wore a brave smile, but his eyes were filled with pain and guilt.

I grabbed his shirt in a desperate attempt to keep him from leaving. "What about Mathias and Honey?"

He put his finger to my lips. "Shh, they're safe. I'll explain later. First, we have to get your leg taken care of," he said.

He addressed the EMT. "Take her, and I'll be right behind you."

"We're rolling," the EMT said, nudging the stretcher forward through the crowd of people. They parted and allowed us to pass, most of them offering me a shoulder pat in solidarity. Laverne held the door open for the stretcher, and I saw that the ambulance sat with its lights spinning in the parking lot next to three cop cars from two different counties. I was safe again, and my brain let the adrenaline drain from my system.

Laverne grasped the edge of the stretcher before they maneuvered me through the door. "I was petrified. I'm so glad you're okay. Don't ever do that to me again."

I laughed with her because I understood she was just relieved that I was okay and not truly mad. "I'll try not to, believe me."

She patted my shoulder and gave me a weak smile. "I'll go check on Mojo. Don't worry about him."

I squeezed her hand for a moment in gratitude. "Thanks, Laverne. See you soon."

I dropped her hand and waved from waist level while they loaded me into the back of the ambulance. The sirens roared to life, and the heavy metal beast rocked back and forth as it rocketed down the gravel road. The EMTs worked around me, and I closed my eyes after taking the first breath of the rest of my life.

Chapter Twenty-Two

No one said modern medical care was fast, but after too many hours and a small procedure on my ankle, I was finally in Gulliver's bed. I had an ice pack over my ankle while the butterflies on the wall kept me calm. Gulliver strode through the door of the bathroom, his hair wet from the shower.

"I love you so much," I whispered when he climbed into bed with me.

"Ask anyone at the barn tonight how much I love you," he said, stroking my hair tenderly. "I think I lost my mind when I got that text."

"How did you know something had happened?" I asked, confused. "The drugs they gave me at the hospital are making everything fuzzy."

He kissed my forehead, which was starting to bruise from smacking the tree in the orchard, and my right temple had a ridiculously large goose egg on it from hitting the window in the SUV, but the doctors didn't think I had a concussion. They agreed that I was fortunate tonight.

"You texted me and said you'd be there in ten minutes. When you didn't show up in twenty, we sent the cops out to find you. Mathias's team hustled him and Honey out to safety while they searched. The police found Simon injured in the SUV and radioed it in. When they reported bullet holes in the car, I lost my mind." His eyes closed in a motion of pain and anguish. "When they told me there was blood, I'm pretty sure I would have collapsed if Laverne hadn't been there with a chair."

I stroked his cheek to calm him. "I didn't know I'd been shot. It was dark, and I couldn't see my ankle. It made sense to me that I hurt it in the crash, so I didn't worry about stopping to check it out. I'm sorry."

He lifted his head and captured my hand. "No, you can't apologize for something that's my fault. I should never have let you out there in Mathias's car. It didn't even cross my mind. It didn't cross Mathias's either. Simon said he came to as two burly guys approached him with guns. He fired back but doesn't think he hit either of them. When they realized he wasn't Mathias and he had a gun, they took off."

I lifted my other hand and ran it through his hair. "Baby, it never crossed mine either, so no one gets to carry the blame. I'll heal. You were there when the doctor told us I'd be fine. They removed the piece of the bullet, and now we just have to give it time to heal."

He stroked my cheek, seemingly needing to touch me constantly to prove I was safe, which I didn't mind. "He also said the bullet was the only thing protecting your leg. He said if you'd lost the piece along the way, you would have slowly bled out, or at the very least lost your leg."

"Shh," I whispered, my finger to his lips. "I'm okay. I'm here. It's been sutured, and it will heal. It doesn't even hurt. I'm far more worried about Mathias and Honey than my leg. If anything, the leg is a hindrance we don't need right now. Are you sure we're safe here?"

This time a smile tipped his lips up before he kissed mine gently. "Yes, we're safe and so are Mathias and Honey. There are too many guys patrolling the perimeter of the business right now for anyone to try anything. Other than this apartment, the entire complex is ablaze with lights, cars, and guys with guns."

"I just want this to be over," I whispered. "It's a pesticide, for God's sake. I'm struggling to wrap my head around attempted murder over pesticide."

"It's about money; don't lose sight of the real reason. The pesticide means nothing to them. They don't care if our pollinators continue to thrive. They care about the piles of cash they can get from selling the formula—end of story. I talked to Chief Flats, and he reported their guy is still working on getting information from the forum."

I rested my hand on my head. "I'm tired. I also lied when I said my leg didn't hurt."

He chuckled softly and shook his head. "Like I didn't already know your leg hurts. Wipe your mind of everything and sleep. You're safe here with me. I'll do nothing but lie here and watch you sleep. Hopefully, my heart will finally stop pounding."

I rubbed his face as I drifted into a drugged stupor. "You were the voice pushing me forward, Gulliver. You were the voice urging me to take the next step when I didn't think I could. I know it was you. You saved me."

He lifted me onto his chest and rubbed my arm slowly and calmly. "If I was, it's because our hearts are connected forever. When we're apart, I'll always cry out for you to come to me. You're my life now, Charity, my whole life. I'm never going to take our love for granted after living through tonight and seeing firsthand how quickly it can be taken away. Will you move in with me? I know the apartment is small, but so are you," he teased.

I grasped his shirt in my fist and gripped it tightly. "Live here?

With you?" He nodded, his finger stroking my temple gently. "I want to," I agreed, my eyes heavy. "I love you, Gulliver Winsome," I whispered, my voice soft and far away.

He squeezed me to him, letting me snuggle into his arms. "And I love you, Charity Puck, with my whole soul."

A familiar sound lifted me toward consciousness, and I struggled to wake up. When I opened my eyes, the room was dark, and I noticed the door to the bedroom was closed, but there was a light shining under the door. Gulliver was missing from the bed, and I sat up and swung my leg to the floor, unsure how it would feel once the anesthetic wore off. They'd insisted I take crutches, but I couldn't figure out how to use them, so I tucked one under the arm of my left side and tested out my ankle. I took a tentative step toward the door. The leg held my weight, which was good news, even if it was tight and sore. Mojo followed me to the door and waited expectantly for me to open it.

When I did, I found myself face-to-face with Gulliver, Mathias, and Honey. Gulliver jumped up when he noticed me, but Mathias motioned for him to wait. Mathias loaned me an arm and helped me get to the couch where Gulliver sat.

"Did we wake you?" he asked as Mojo lumbered over and plopped his head on my leg. I rubbed the dog's chin for a moment, and he shifted his eyes at me several times. I patted his head once, and he turned, walked over to Honey, and rested his head on her thigh. He knew who needed him tonight, and while it should be me, it wasn't. Honey was so sad it was impossible to miss the hunch of her shoulders and pinched face. She was struggling, and Mojo would keep her calm. She stroked the big dog's head, and his low whine of contentment brought a smile to her lips. Score one for Mojo.

"A noise woke me, and I noticed you weren't in the room. What's going on?" I asked, checking the clock. "We haven't been asleep long. Why are you guys here?"

Gulliver rubbed my back, and I struggled to wake up and make sense of the world again. "They caught the two guys responsible for running you off the road."

Honey leaned toward me. "I was able to identify both of them, and they turned in the third guy. It was the same threesome who broke my arm."

My gaze tracked between all of them. "Which is good, right? We're one step closer to getting the person behind it?"

Mathias spoke next. "Right. The two guys they picked up tonight said the guy wearing the Bill Clinton mask was the ringleader. They don't have him yet."

"Three sets of hands in the fire is never good," I said, confused. "It feels like a last-man-standing-wins-the-pot kind of situation."

"True, but it doesn't matter if all three of them stayed in the game," Gulliver said. "Even splitting the pot evenly, they'd all be billionaires."

Mathias pointed at Gulliver. "Without a doubt. The police are looking for the third man now. He's the one behind communicating on the forum with Honey and the one responsible for the hacking, at least according to the two guys they picked up earlier tonight. Are you ready for his name?"

I nodded rather than speak.

"Vincent Butterfly. His name is Vincent Butterfly."

I couldn't stop the choked laughter from escaping. "What the hell? Some people shouldn't exist in this world." All three nodded in agreement. "So who are these guys? How did they find out about the formula?"

Gulliver lifted my leg onto his lap to elevate it. "All we know right now is they are low-level management for a large pesticide company. How they came to find out about it is anyone's guess. Though, I do remember giving a speech at a consortium last year for lepidopterists and I mentioned it. It should have been a safe audience, but that doesn't mean it was. I could kick myself for it, but it never crossed my mind that something like this would happen." He shook his head with frustration. "Anyway, the police asked Honey and Mathias to stay here since the building is already under guard. They didn't want to split resources while they were trying to find Vincent."

Honey trudged to the kitchen and rummaged in Gulliver's freezer until she returned with an ice pack. I accepted it and offered her a smile. "Thanks," I said, fixing it on my ankle.

"It's the least I can do considering this happened because I wasn't strong enough or smart enough to stop it immediately."

"Honeybee," Mathias warned. She held up her hand and lowered herself to the chair, completely dejected. Her head fell into her hand, and I noticed her finger was spasming up in the air again, but she didn't seem to notice it.

I made eye contact with Mathias. *Is she all right?* I mouthed, and he shook his head no, his lips in a grim line. He rested her head on his shoulder and carefully massaged her hand again until the finger stopped tweaking and rested against the palm with the rest of them.

"I'm having a hard time grasping this," I said, shaking my head. "I know people will do anything for money, including murder, but what did they think would happen when they released the formula and you had proof it was yours? Did they think this out?"

Gulliver shook his head slowly, and his eyes rolled to the top of his head. "I don't think any of them have a lot of brain cells to rub together. The dollar signs blinded them, and they jumped in.

That or Vincent had plans to make sure none of us were alive long enough for it to matter. If we were all dead, the research was theirs. Their downfall was this four-foot-tall blonde beauty who, even in the face of a threat to her own life, stood taller than any of us and fixed the problem," Gulliver said, kissing me tenderly. "If you hadn't followed your moral compass and decided to walk away after they knocked you down the first time, I don't know where we'd be. The entire planet will never know it, but they owe their futures to you, sweetheart." He stroked my hair like a lifeline, and while what he'd said was fierce and dramatic, I understood what he was really trying to say just by looking in his eyes. They were the color of copper, but clear and open to the truth. He had found his forever love in that four-foot-tall beauty, and he was never letting her go.

Honey's shoulders started to shake, and I flicked my eyes to Mathias, who was rubbing her shoulder. "She's having a hard time dealing with the idea they attempted to kill you and Simon while thinking it was me again."

"Oh God," she cried, holding her head in her hands. "What have I done? Why wasn't I stronger? So many people got hurt," she said, the fingers on her right hand spasming as she held her head. There was nothing but tears and emptiness in her eyes when Mathias lifted her and sat in her chair, cradling her on his lap.

"Honeybee, you're okay," he promised, hushing her with his lips to her temple. "Please, stop crying, sweetheart," he begged, his right hand massaging hers in a way that said he'd done it many times.

I leaned into Gulliver and whispered into his ear, "I can't imagine what she's going through."

"I can," he whispered, running a finger over the knotted bruise on my forehead. "It's a horrible, horrible feeling," he whispered.

A tear fell from my eye at his words, and he wiped it away. "I'm sorry," I said lamely. "I'm okay."

"I love you," he whispered, his fingers twining into mine.

"I love you too. Promise me something?"

"Absolutely anything," he said, offering me a genuine Gulliver Winsome smile.

"When this is over and we're free of the danger and uncertainty, will you take me to see the butterflies? I mean, really see them, the way you do."

He lowered his head to mine, and I stared into the oceans of golden hazel in his eyes. "Baby, I'd love nothing more. That's not even a hard promise to make."

His lips feathered across mine, and then I rested against his chest, wrapped in a cocoon of forever love.

Epilogue

Two Months Later

"Where are we going anyway?" I asked Gulliver after several hours in the car. We'd left Mojo with Honey and headed south, but he refused to tell me where we were going other than to hunt butterflies. He was keeping the promise he made to me that once we were safe, he'd take me butterfly hunting.

"I told you, a friend of mine turned me on to a new garden that I haven't even seen yet. We're not too far away," he promised.

Gulliver and I had spent the last two months working nonstop preparing the educational material, giving speeches to local farmers, and planning for lectures over the winter in faraway places. I was looking forward to concentrating on him and only him for the next four days.

Mathias and Honey were knee-deep in getting the patent for the pesticide approved now that the formula was complete. Honey came back to work two weeks after the night of my accident. Mathias made sure she got plenty of help from a counselor, and when she returned, she was better, but she was nowhere near fine. She was broken inside, and every single one of us could see it. Honey's load to carry was heavy. She was still rehabbing her arm and she had to deal with her mother's heart attack and subsequent recovery. Piled on top of that was the stress of knowing people got hurt because she couldn't speak the truth.

The heaviest load, though, was her love for Mathias. It was out in the open now, and there was no pretending she didn't profess her undying love to him for everyone to read. It was for that reason I suspected she wouldn't stay much longer at Butterfly Junction. Unrequited love takes a toll on your heart and your soul, and there would come a time in her life when she would have to give both a break from the constant torture of working with Mathias every day.

As for the three guys who tried to steal the formula, they were going to prison. They were each charged with multiple counts of aggravated assault and attempted murder. After realizing there was no way out of the situation, they all took plea deals rather than go through a trial. The evidence was overwhelming, and they knew it. They'd all be old men when they got out of prison. If they got out of prison.

There were times when I didn't understand humans at all. At least not humans that I didn't know well. The humans I'd found in Plentiful were a different caliber, though. They were kind, generous, loving, and always there to help. Once word got around about my accident, we had more food and offers of help than we could ever accept. Laverne insisted on having a celebration dinner at the Apple Orchard once I was feeling better and invited the entire town. She even insisted I park Myrtle next to the front door with a "for sale" sign on it.

As luck would have it, a single guy happened by the party and was interested in her. He was young and reminded me a lot of myself when I bought Myrtle all those years ago. After an extremely short tour, he was smitten with her and asked me to hold her for him until the next day when he could get money from a bank. I refused, which made him sad until I handed him the keys and told him to take good care of her. Sure, I could have gotten a thousand bucks for her, but witnessing his shock, happiness, and joy when taking the keys was worth twice the thrill of having a little bit of money in my pocket. With Myrtle gone, a new place to live, a new job, and a new man, I was never happier. Even Mojo was happy to stay behind with Honey at Butterfly Junction and live the good life.

"What are we going to do when we get there?"

"We're going to take pictures of the butterflies. We'll see monarchs, queens, pipevine swallowtails, and hopefully, the question mark."

"Uh, the question mark?"

"Some people call them angel wings because of the way their wings are irregular on the edges. Their nickname comes from a tattoo-type question mark on the lower part of the wing. The butterfly is bright orange and brown."

"Bright orange and brown with a question mark on the bottom," I repeated. "I got it. Are they rare?"

He did the so-so hand. "Not necessarily if there's a food supply nearby. They aren't big fans of flowers. They love mud, rotten fruit, and animal droppings."

I grimaced at the thought. "Ew, maybe I'll pass."

He turned into a parking lot and pulled the truck up next to a berm. I glanced around. "This is it? There's nothing and no one here."

He motioned in front of the windshield. "Patience, my dear Charity," he scolded, climbing out and grabbing his crutches from the back, along with the high-end digital camera he used for photographing butterflies and bugs. He opened my door and helped me out, watching as I adjusted my legs after riding for so long. "Are you going to be okay on your feet in the field?"

"Asks the man using crutches," I joked. "I'll be okay. It doesn't hurt." I had to wear a brace on the ankle still, but it was improving every day and I didn't have pain anymore. The biggest problem was it would give out if I didn't wear the brace. Since I was dying to see where we were going, I'd made sure to wear it today. "Lead the way."

He struck off with his camera around his neck and his crutches crunching against the crushed pea rock. We stepped foot onto a worn dirt path, and in a few minutes, we broke over a small hill. What spread out before us took my breath away.

"This is incredible," I sighed, the field of pink and green flowers swaying in the breeze. "I've never seen so many butterflies," I gushed.

He strolled back to me, and the emotion swirling in his eyes was pure bliss. He loved me, and he loved introducing me to the only other thing he loved in this world. "This is a human-planted and -cultivated butterfly field. The master gardeners from this area run it. We're alone and can take as much time as we want."

I spun around in a half-circle, watching the flowers undulating under the butterflies' wings. "I've never seen anything like this."

Gulliver's kiss was tender when he took ownership of my lips, and I leaned into him, my body resting on his in the warm afternoon sunshine. "I've seen a thousand fields of butterflies, but none of them were as beautiful as you standing here witnessing this for the first time."

My heart melted in my chest to hear how much he loved me. "I love you, Gulliver Winsome."

"I love you, too, Miss Puck. Are you ready to start this grand adventure?"

I jumped up and down once. "Lead on. I don't know where to start!"

For the next hour we strolled, photographed, cataloged, and collected specimens, which we put in small jars. We were nearing the end of the field when I frowned. "I haven't seen any of those question mark ones, have you?" I asked, stepping into the shade of a tree to block out the warm fall sunshine.

He set his camera down and wiped his forehead. "I haven't seen any, but they usually prefer a more wooded area. I was just hoping to get lucky." He paused with a chuckle in his chest. "Then again, some would say I already got lucky, and I should count my blessings."

"What do you say?" I asked teasingly.

"That they're right," he said with a wink of one lid over an exquisite hazel orb.

I put my finger to my lips. "Don't move. There's a butterfly on your shoulder," I said, bending slowly to pick up the camera. Without standing, I shot the images from the ground of the butterfly resting majestically on his shoulder. The camera whirred, and he gingerly swiveled his head to gaze at the creature on his shirt. I noticed his eyes go wide, so I kept shooting pictures, carefully moving to the right of him to get them from different angles. I was still shooting when the butterfly fluttered away into a flowering bush.

"I've never seen a butterfly as big as she was," I said, holding the camera at my side.

Gulliver was giddy when he motioned for the camera. I handed it over and waited while he flipped through the pictures. "That was," he finally said, teeming with excitement, "a giant swallowtail butterfly. They are a rare sighting in the north where we live, but in the southern part of the state where we are, they're more common. When my eyes landed on it—"

"They got this big," I said, my fingers opening into wide circles. "It's why I kept taking pictures. I could tell that butterfly was extra special."

He palmed my cheek with one hand and directed my lips to his. "I'm so in love with you right now I want to yell something ridiculous into the air, but I won't. We're always in sync when we work together. You always know when something is important and grab the chance to document it without me having to tell you. On the way back to the car, let's watch for any specimens of giant swallowtails. They're one of the shortest living butterflies, so we might find one. In their adult form, they only live six to fourteen days."

My lips pointed down in a frown. "How sad. The only word I could think of as it sat there was 'majestic.' I've seen so much beauty today, but she was more than beautiful. She was a majestic queen."

Gulliver grinned with satisfaction. "You're right. It was a female. I'll show you how I know," he said, pointing the viewfinder at me. "See the color blend here on the hind wing?" he asked, and I nodded. "That means it was a female. You got to see something today not a lot of novice butterfly hunters get to see. You should be proud."

"I am," I promised. "I love being out here with you. I love watching you come alive when you're doing something you love. I may not know a lot about butterflies, but I know you, and your body language tells me when something is important. You know I'm nothing if not observant."

He took my hand in his. "It's more than being observant, sweetheart. You're supporting me, and I've never had anyone in my life do that before. It matters to me here," he said, patting his chest.

I bounced up on my toes and brushed his lips with mine. "We support each other because it's what partners do. I'm always going to be here to support you. Always." A butterfly caught my eye, and I followed it around the tree. "I wanted to see the question mark butterfly, but I have to say, the giant swallowtail did not disappoint."

"Charity?" he asked, clearing his throat. "Would you take the camera?"

I swung around and took it from his hand. "Sure," I agreed, slinging it over my shoulder and turning my attention back to the tree where various butterflies still flitted around us. "Maybe we should head back if you want to search for the giant swallowtails on the way to the car," I suggested, completing the circle back to him. He was sitting on the road, and I ran to him, grasping his arm. "I didn't hear you fall. Are you okay?" I asked frantically.

"I'm fine. I didn't fall. I'm here on purpose," he assured me, taking my hand. "I wanted to kneel, but you know I can't do that, so please pretend that I am. We didn't get to see the question mark butterfly, but I do have a question for you."

I took a step back when the whole picture finally materialized. "Gulliver?" I asked, my voice shaking. "What are you doing?"

"I'm trying to ask you a question," he teased, even though his lips shook with nervous energy.

He dug around in his pocket, and when he pulled out a black box, I took another step back.

"I've had this ring since the day before your accident," he explained, cracking the box open. "I didn't want to jump the gun and ask too soon, but the ring was a physical reminder to me that the possibility existed. When your accident happened, I carried it around to calm my fears about losing you. The ring reminded me you were still with me and we'd be okay. Maybe we've only known each other for a few months, but I don't need more time to know you're the woman I want to share my forever with, Charity. I didn't need more than one night with you to know you were the woman I've been searching for all these years. Your selfless love and encouragement of my dreams are more than I thought possible when I prayed for a soul mate. I got more than a soul mate, though.

I got an angel on earth. Last month I got a taste of what life would be like without you, and I didn't like it. I made a vow then and there to never take you for granted or forget for one moment how you're the most important person in my life. You're my everything, Charity Puck, and I love you. The question I ask now is with my whole heart and soul. Will you marry me and take my name? Will you be my wife, Charity?"

Tears cascaded down my face, but I wasn't conscious of them as I set the camera down and lowered myself to the ground. I grasped his face in my hands, both of us shaking with raw, unfiltered love. "Yes, I'll marry you, Gulliver," I whispered. "I love you with everything I have, and I want nothing more than to be your wife."

His smile was brighter than the entire field of flowers and butterflies. Those relieved hazel eyes gleamed with love when he tugged the ring from the box and slid it onto my finger. It fit me perfectly, and I gasped when I saw it up close. "It's a butterfly for my beautiful butterfly," he whispered.

I gazed at the ring in wonder. Four teardrop diamonds formed the wings of the butterfly. "It's stunning, Mr. Winsome," I whispered, leaning in for a tender kiss of love and promise. We fell to our butts in the dirt of a warm Wisconsin day, where he gathered me into his arms for a kiss of affirmation, joy, and peace. I couldn't help but cling to him. My little body wrapped almost entirely inside his was a symbol that he would take care of me always.

I couldn't help but ponder the randomness of life, and after spending the summer in Plentiful, Wisconsin, I had learned one very important lesson. You win some and you lose some, but this time I won the greatest prize of all.

🦋 A Letter From Katie 🦋

Let me take a moment to say thank you for reading *Butterflies and Hazel Eyes*. I hope you enjoyed Plentiful, Wisconsin, where time moves at a slower pace, love isn't easy but is always worth it, and where occasionally people get caught up in dangerous situations doing what they love. I am grateful for every single one of you who picked up this book and helped make it a success! If you enjoyed the book and want to keep up to date with all my latest releases, just sign up at the following link. Your email address will never be shared, and you can unsubscribe at any time.

Sign up here: **eepurl.com/hmY2xT**

As *Butterflies and Hazel Eyes* is a work of fiction, I have taken some creative liberties with this series. The town of Plentiful may be fictional, but the towns that surround it like Bayfield, Superior, and Duluth are as wonderful as Plentiful is. The Lady of the Lake is real and exactly as described; beautiful, plentiful, cold, and unforgiving. Any mistakes or tweaks regarding the regional landscape or information about pesticides are for fictional purposes and are entirely my own.

While Butterfly Junction is a fictional business, its purpose is not. Our pollinators are in danger and the time is now to save them! Did you know there are over 200,000 different species of pollinators? We must protect them all if we want to continue to call this planet home. Whenever possible, please use eco-friendly pesticide on your gardens and flowers so the butterflies and bees can continue to pollinate the crops we need to survive.

I love hearing from readers, so please, reach out and tell me what you thought of the book! You can get in touch with me through any of the social media outlets below, including my website. If you enjoyed the book, I'd appreciate it if you'd leave a review on Amazon or Goodreads and perhaps recommend *Butterflies and Hazel Eyes* to other readers who enjoy quality romance. Reviews and word-of-mouth recommendations go a long way in helping readers discover my books for the first time. Once again, thank you so much for all your support of this series and the ones to come.

Stay Well,

Katie Mettner

🦋 About the Author 🦋

Katie Mettner writes small-town romantic tales filled with epic love stories and happily-ever-afters. She proudly wears the title of, 'the only person to lose her leg after falling down the bunny hill,' and loves decorating her prosthetic with the latest fashion trends. She lives in Northern Wisconsin with her own happily-ever-after and three mini-mes. Katie has a massive addiction to coffee and Twitter, and a lessening aversion to Pinterest—now that she's quit trying to make the things she pins.

a author.to/katieMettner

BB bookbub.com/profile/katie-mettner

🐦 twitter.com/katiemettner

f facebook.com/wisconsinwriter

𝓟 pinterest.com/sugarsballroom

📷 instagram.com/sugarlipswi

g goodreads.com/katiemettner

Scan this code with your phone or tablet to visit my website: **katiemettner.com**

🦋 Other Books by Katie 🦋

Standalones

Finding Susan

After Summer Ends

Someone in the Water

The Secrets Between Us

White Sheets & Rosy Cheeks

The Sugar Series

Sugar's Dance

Sugar's Song

Sugar's Night

Sugar's Faith

Trusting Trey

The Kupid's Cove Series

Calling Kupid

Me and Mr. IT

The Forgotten Lei

Hiding Rose

The Snowberry Series

Snow Daze

December Kiss

Noel's Hart

The Snowberry Series (Continued)

April Melody

Liberty Belle

Wicked Winifred

Nick S. Klaus

The Northern Lights Series

Granted Redemption

Autumn Reflections

Winter's Rain

Forever Phoenix

The Dalton Sibling Series

Inherited Love

Inherited Light

Inherited Life

The Bells Pass Series

Meatloaf & Mistletoe

Hotcakes & Holly

Jam & Jingle Bells

Apples & Angel Wings

The Raven Ranch Series

October Winds

Ruby Sky

The Magnificent Series

Magnificent Love

Magnificent Destiny

The Kontakt Series

The German's Guilty Pleasure

The German's Desperate Vow

The Fluffy Cupcake Series

Cupcake

Tart

The Butterfly Junction Series

Butterflies and Hazel Eyes

Honey Bees and Sexy Tees

Learn more: katiemettner.com/books

🦋 People-first Language 🦋

People with disabilities are just that — people. We are not 'differently abled' because of our disability. We all have different abilities and interests, and the fact that we may or may not have a physical or intellectual disability doesn't change that. The disabled community may have different needs, but we are productive members of society who also happen to be husbands, wives, moms, dads, sons, daughters, sisters, brothers, friends, and coworkers. People with disabilities are often disrespected and portrayed two different ways; as helpless or as heroically inspirational for doing simple, basic activities.

As a disabled author who writes disabled characters, my focus is to help people without disabilities understand the real-life disability issues we face like discrimination, limited accessibility, housing, employment opportunities, and lack of people first language. I want to change the way others see our community by writing strong characters who go after their dreams, and find their true love, without shying away from what it is like to be a person with a disability. Another way I can educate people without disabilities is to help them understand our terminology. We, as the disabled community, have worked to establish what we call People First Language. This isn't a case of being politically correct. Rather, it is a way to acknowledge and communicate with a person with a disability in a respectful way by eliminating generalizations, assumptions, and stereotypes.

As a person with disabilities, I appreciate when readers take the time to ask me what my preferred language is. Since so many have asked, I thought I would include a small sample of the people-first language we use in the disabled community. This language also applies when leaving reviews and talking about books that feature characters with disabilities. The most important thing to remember when you're talking to people with disabilities is that we are people first! If you ask us what our preferred terminology is regarding our disability, we will not only tell you, but be glad you asked! If you would like more information about people first language, you will find a disability resource guide on my website:

katiemettner.com/disabilities

Instead of	Use
He is handicapped.	He is a person with a disability.
She is differently abled.	She is a person with a disability.
He is mentally retarded.	He has a developmental or intellectual disability.
She is wheelchair-bound.	She uses a wheelchair.
He is a cripple.	He has a physical disability.
She is a midget or dwarf.	She is a person of short stature or a little person.
He is deaf and mute.	He is deaf or he has a hearing disability.
She is a normal or healthy person.	She is a person without a disability.
That is handicapped parking.	That is accessible parking.
He has overcome his disability.	He is successful and productive.
She is suffering from vision loss.	She is a person who is blind or visually disabled.
He is brain damaged.	He is a person with a traumatic brain injury.

🦋 Acknowledgements 🦋

To my incredible and dedicated readers who have stuck with me for the last ten years by reading my books, hanging out on social media with me, and encouraging my dreams, THANK YOU! It is your passion and desire for romantic fiction about real people finding real love when the deck is often stacked against them that keeps me going. I never get tired of your suggestions for characters, hearing about how much you love reading about the Great Lakes, or your demands for 'just one more' for your favorite series. To my readers who long to see themselves represented in romantic fiction in an accurate, honest, loving way; I hope I did you justice. We are in this together, and I see your hopes and dreams in my own. You are the reason I write.

Thank you to my husband, Dwayne. I was lucky enough to find my soul mate in a singles ad, and we never looked back. You have stood by my side through all the ups and downs of the last twenty-one years, and it is only because of you that I have the courage to put myself out there day after day.

Thank you to my three E's, who aren't so little anymore, but always will be in my heart. Thank you for your love, patience, and encouragement, even when my choice of careers caused you some major embarrassment!

Thank you to my parents—Bonnie and Jim—for instilling the love of reading in me early and often. Your support means the world to me. I love you!

To Tom, Linda, Andrew, and Kisber—thank you. One thousand times over. Thank you.

Thank you to my girl gang for always having my back with my books but mostly in life. Carrie, Dana, Lisa, Maureen, Nancy, and Tobi. You are the best and the brightest in my world and I wouldn't be able to do this without you. I would have given up on my dreams years ago if it hadn't been for all your support right when I needed it the most.

Thank you to Carrie Butler for always knowing my vision for every cover without having to ask. For understanding that sometimes (okay, all the time) I write books that make it difficult to design covers, but for always digging in and finding a way to make it work. Also, thanks for randomly dressing up your dog like a bumblebee for Halloween. Together we can SAVE THE POLLINATORS!

To the bloggers who jumped in and read The Butterfly Junction Series, thank you! I appreciate your enthusiastic and dedicated recommendations of my books to your readers!

To Lisa Prodorutti for understanding my vision for these books. For supporting my dream of bringing romance to our readers in a way that is people-centeric, honest, and trustworthy. Your willingness to be part of this adventure leaves me without words. Anyone who knows me, now knows just how incredible you are! I'm never without words.

To the team at Breaking Night Press who keep showing up to make these books the best they can be. To the editing team for fixing all my "Midwest" lingo, the marketing team for putting the time in to learn and embrace the people-first language I use as a person with disabilities, and to the creative design team for making us look pretty while doing it. Your understanding and willingness to learn about the complexities of what I write has restored my faith in humanity.

Breaking Night Press

Breaking Night Press is an independent American book publisher, specializing in #ownvoices and niche genres. We publish books that don't fit neatly into just one genre. Most importantly, our titles will keep you turning pages well into the night.

f **facebook.com/BreakingNightPress**

🐦 **twitter.com/breakingnightp**

📷 **instagram.com/breakingnightpress**

We want our content to be valuable and relevant to you. That's why we've divided our newsletters by interest:

- **Readers** will get notified about new releases, sales, giveaways, etc.
- **Writers** will get notified about what we're acquiring and when we're next open to submissions.
- **Reviewers** will get notified about fun promotional opportunities.

Sign up here: **eepurl.com/hmY2xT**

Scan this code with your phone or tablet to visit our website: **breakingnightpress.com**

CPSIA information can be obtained
at www.ICGtesting.com
Printed in the USA
JSHW020201270321
12966JS00005B/13